SHADOWS ON A WALL

SHADOWS ON A WALL

RAY CONNOLLY

St. Martin's Press
New York

Library of Congress Cataloging-in-Publication Data

Connolly, Ray
Shadows on a wall / Ray Connolly.
p.   cm.
ISBN 0-312-11887-2
I. Title.
PR6053.O487S53   1995
823'.914—dc20   94-44291   CIP

First published in Great Britain by Bantam Press

First U.S. Edition: July 1995
10 9 8 7 6 5 4 3 2 1

For Kieron

Acknowledgements

Many friends helped with advice and information in the writing of this book, not least producers Sandy Lieberson and Chris Burt, directors Michael Apted and Ian Toynton, former studio executive Philip Collins, film editor Peter Hollywood, theatre director David Gilmore, actress Fiona Mollison, banker turned publisher Cameron Brown and photographer Graham Wood of *The Times*. But the greatest help came from my children, Louise and Dominic Connolly, who threw in ideas and criticisms and then tirelessly prepared the manuscript for publication, and my younger son Kieron Connolly, who, with his encyclopedic movie knowledge and dogged enthusiasm for film, has kept our whole family interested in those shadows on the wall.

RAY CONNOLLY
January, 1994

'Hey, come on, you guys, cheer up, will you? Nobody's dead, for Christ's sake. Nobody's dying. Nobody's even ill. It's only a movie we're trying to make here . . . only shadows on a wall . . .'

Sandy Lieberson, film producer,
Rome, December, 1975

Author's Note

When Napoleon set up his headquarters in Warsaw in January 1807 he was the most powerful man in the world. Emperor of the French, he was, at the age of thirty-eight, handsome, dynamic and intellectually gifted, and the Poles, who had seen their country partitioned into non-existence by Austria, Prussia and Russia, greeted his arrival as that of a liberator. Welcoming parties were convened and balls were thrown: at the very first ball he met the very pretty Countess Marie Walewska. They became lovers two days later.

Just twenty and unhappily married to a vain, though evidently compliant, man of seventy-one, Marie Walewska was regarded in Warsaw as a Polish patriot, and seen, not least by Talleyrand, the architect of French foreign policy, as a useful pawn in endearing Poland to Napoleon. It was in many interests that the affair should succeed.

Napoleon had had several mistresses before but Marie Walewska was to prove more devoted than any of the others, quickly becoming known as 'Napoleon's Polish wife' and following him to Paris where she became a fashionable figure. In 1810 she bore him a son, Alexander, and continued to see him until 1814 when she visited him secretly on Elba, offering to share that first exile. Her offer was not accepted.

The truth was, it did not matter how fond Napoleon and Marie Walewska became of each other, she never realistically stood a chance. Napoleon's primary ambition lay in the founding of a Napoleonic dynasty by marriage, and when he divorced the Empress Josephine in 1808 because she could not bear him an heir, it was not to Marie Walewska that he turned for a new wife but the Archduchess Marie-Louise, daughter of the Hapsburg Emperor Francis II of Austria.

In 1817 Marie Walewska died in Paris at the age of thirty-one, having married one of Napoleon's former generals, Phillipe Antoine Ornano, the previous year. Napoleon, by then in his second exile and over four thousand miles away on the South Atlantic island of St Helena, never knew of her death.

That is fact.

This is fiction.

Waiting with Marie Walewska to greet Napoleon on his arrival in Warsaw was her best friend, Camille de Malignon, a nineteen-year-old French aristocrat who had lost her entire family during the Reign of Terror.

The rest is movies . . .

PART ONE

Good Friday, 1993

Chapter One

He thought at first that it was a trick of the light, a reflection perhaps, or a large rock below the surface of the water. The river was flatter there, a horseshoe-curved pool in the shadow of the mountain. He did not say anything: his father was preoccupied with fishing, and never spoke much in the morning, anyway. Instead the boy sat and waited, watching as the sun rose, and the submerged mass became gradually more distinct. For a while he teased himself: perhaps it was a whale or a submarine. But he was ten years old and knew better. There were no whales or submarines in the mountains of Slovakia.

Next to him his father cast, wound and recast his rod. The boy had begged to be brought along on this expedition and the father had reluctantly agreed. It had rained so much that week, and they had spent too much time inside: the boy wanted something to remember when they went home to the city. But they had been off early, and it had been a long walk down through the pine woods into the valley after leaving the car. Now the boy was bored, and he glanced at his father, guilty at such disloyal thoughts.

At last, too restless to sit longer, the boy got up and began to wander around the wide corner of the river. Upstream, his father had told him, the water was fast flowing and treacherous where floods raced through narrow gorges, but here the flow had eased and was now beginning to form ripples around the submerged object. It could, of course, be a lost, sunken spaceship.

15

Out of sight of his father the boy felt brave enough to paddle, and, stepping into the water, he edged closer: it was something strange and out of place, long and smooth and still. For some moments he stood in his gum boots and stared. Then, treading carefully, he began to make his way further around the curve of the river. With the sun behind him the object soon began to look quite different.

Suddenly he knew. The outline was that of a car, but of a size the boy had never seen before: a strange, wide vehicle, perhaps eight metres in length, lying at a sharp angle and tilted up towards the bank.

A car? It did not seem possible. The nearest track was several kilometres away, up the mountain and through dense forest. How could anyone have put a car here?

Very carefully, and using a dead branch to prod the river bed as he went, the boy waded deeper into the water. The vehicle was lying on a bank of sand; with the fine day, the level of the water had been falling, its sediment clearing, all morning.

Putting his face close to the surface he stared hard at the car. It was indeed like a spaceship, with a flat, wedged nose and banks of broken headlights. Edging sideways he looked again. Now he could see a tyre, further on a windscreen. Another two steps took him close to one of the side windows. This time he was not at first sure what he was seeing. Objects were floating in the goldfish bowl which was the interior, a cigarette packet, the wrapping for a chocolate bar, a wine glass, a plastic folder, a man's shoe, a wad of paper. But there was something else, shimmering and moving like a sea plant caught in the current.

For a moment he raised his eyes and rested them from the glare of the water. Then, very carefully, he looked again. Now he could see: it was hair, long and trailing like a bridal veil; a woman, floating under water, one arm up as though in some vain swimming motion, her cheeks sunken, her mouth open, her eyes staring directly into his.

In panic the boy stepped back to balance himself: water splashed over the tops of his gum boots. 'Father!' he called quietly, almost secretly, his voice catching, breathless. Then he snatched his head back. *'Father! Father!'*

The boy's scream lifted off the surface of the river and echoed around the little wooded valley.

Chapter Two

(i)

Charlie Holyoake stared at the patterns in the cornice above him, listening hard. The sounds were unmistakable. Two people were making love in a nearby room, and he wondered if one of them was Belinda. Unhappily, his eyes traced the corner of the ceiling where the elaborate floral plasterwork abruptly ended. That was the trouble when once stately rooms in once stately homes were subdivided on the cheap: the sound-proofing was always hopeless.

With an oath and a muffled mew, which was not, he decided, in any way familiar, the storm of passion abated in an exhaust of moans. He was relieved. To have heard Belinda making love would have been too much to bear.

But should it? He turned his head. Next to him a pretty girl lay sleeping. Her name was Agnieszka. She was Polish and had once wanted to be an actress. Now she worked as a stand-in for the most spoilt woman in the world. He wondered if he was in love with her. He didn't know. And he thought again about Belinda, picturing her smiling at him as she had done on those sleepy mornings. She had always had the prettiest smile. He closed his eyes. It seemed so long ago. How did he feel about her now? He wasn't even sure about that any more.

He was thirty and these days uncertain of everything, a thin, fair, short-sighted Englishman who had had an idea, just a small idea, and then watched as it had grown and mutated and won control of all their lives. That was when he and Belinda had

17

begun to fall apart. Silently he sighed. Love and movies: a one-handed, blindfolded juggling act. Too difficult even for Belinda.

He looked at his watch. It was nearly twelve. They had slept through the morning; but then, virtually the entire cast and crew would be having a lie-in, too. A mass lie-in or a mass lay-in? He played with the words, pondering whether this eighteenth-century Polish mansion, the Kapolska Palace, had ever before been host to such batteries of well-organized adultery.

Sex was important to everyone, but to movie people it was an occupational obsession. Movie people knew about sex. They were diviners for it, scholars of it, gluttons at it. The first day of location shooting on any movie was virtually the declaration of an open season when it came to sex; Steven Spielberg had once said something like that, and *Shadows on a Wall* was hardly any movie. Perhaps nervous exhaustion had had something to do with it, or boredom, or simply the many months of crazy extravagance, but, as the budget, and the way-over budget, had risen to ever-more startling heights, so had the sexual energy of almost the entire company. Without doubt, *Shadows on a Wall* was an extraordinarily tumescent production, and he tried to calculate just how many couplings would already have taken place in the Kapolska Palace that morning. At least, he told himself, it took his mind off Belinda, off the movie . . .

He stopped there. No, it didn't. Nothing took his mind off the movie.

He considered the girl next to him. She was breathing softly, curled up, her arms crossed over palely freckled breasts, her face almost perfectly triangular in shape, her light hair spreading across the pillow. Such a pretty girl, Agnieszka. Agnes. It sounded better in Polish. And he wondered if she loved him.

He hoped not, but how could he tell? How could she tell? How could any of them tell anything any more? They were in the middle of a gigantic fiasco, a grand folly of unprecedented, imperial proportions. 'SHADOWS ON A WALL: SHOOTING JUST GOES ON AND ON AND ON AND . . .', a headline had run without exaggeration in the *Hollywood Reporter* the previous week. In a disastrous campaign like this how could anyone have any judgement left? *Shadows on a Wall* was a blindfolded rhinoceros of a movie, a runaway trotting wilfully across Europe, a hundred-million-dollar production caught up and entangled on a giant tusk of ego.

And yet . . . ? He knew it was madness, but he couldn't stop

18

hoping. *Shadows on a Wall* was the best idea he had ever had.

'You know your trouble, you think too much,' he imagined Belinda teasing the way she used to. 'That's all you do, just lie around in beds and baths all day, thinking and hoping.'

His pride fought back. 'Of course, I do. What else am I supposed to do? That's what writers do. They think and they hope.'

Putting Belinda from his mind he climbed out of bed and made his way to the tall window. There had been so much rain recently, soaking days of mud and confusion as they had tried, with the help of the Polish army, to re-enact Napoleon's march on Moscow. If things had gone according to schedule it would have been shot the previous autumn, but nothing had gone to schedule on *Shadows on a Wall*. And now the Polish army had been called away on Easter manoeuvres, against what enemy he couldn't imagine.

Pulling back the heavy, red curtains he looked out on the day. He was surprised. It was sunny, suddenly spring, and he allowed himself the luxury of believing that things might begin to get better. *A hundred million dollars better?* a voice inside him mocked.

Below him on the gravel driveway was a scattering of activity: electricians rolling cables, a couple of grips examining a damaged length of track, two costume assistants carrying a rail of gold trimmed cavalry officers' uniforms to the former stables where they had set up their ironing boards, and tall, thatch-haired Billy Yeo and his documentary makers, busy as ever, shooting the crew relaxing for his television series, *The Making of Shadows on a Wall*. Nearby Gully Pepper, the unit publicist, was chatting with the German second assistant director, Markus Muller, pretending not to watch Billy filming as she had been pretending for the past six months. It was her job to make sure he filmed only what the studio considered the positive side to *Shadows on a Wall*, but Billy saw things differently: theirs had been a long and unrelenting duel. Poor Billy, Charlie thought. After everything he did for me, I let him down.

Looking away he gazed across the lawn to where a young girl with straight, black, shoulder-length hair and large glasses was sitting on a kitchen chair, a writing pad in her hands, her pretty face shaded by the three-cornered Napoleonic hat she had been given by the costume department. She would never have been his choice, but she had made the perfect Camille de Malignon.

19

He stepped back from the window. Now with the crew on the point of mutiny, shooting had been suspended for the Easter weekend. They had been filming off and on for nearly six months, often extended fourteen hour days. But the more they shot the more the director wanted, and still they were nowhere near finished. Over two million feet of film exposed and no end in sight; it didn't seem possible.

'Bruno Messenger, you're a megalomaniacal bastard,' Charlie said out loud, as he ritually said every morning, and, stepping over an untidy barricade of discarded, rewritten pink pages of script, he went into the small bathroom and ran the bath water.

This was the second visit of the *Shadows on a Wall* unit to Poland, the entire production being housed in the Kapolska Palace, a mansion in the mountains in the south-east of the country where it bordered on Slovakia. Only Sam Jordan, perhaps an eccentric choice for Napoleon, but undeniably handsome, and the matchingly beautiful, if nudgingly certifiable, Yale Meredith, who was playing Marie Walewska, were not living in the palace. Being stars they had each been allocated houses of their own, two specially renovated white pavilions at opposite ends of the Kapolska estate, where they could live untroubled by anything approaching reality. In her house, Yale was surrounded by her shift-working retinue of companion, bodyguards, driver, secretary, voice coach, trainer, dresser and personal make-up artist; in his, Jordan, although he had just as many minions to call upon, lived in the vain isolation that some called mystery. No-one, other than the women selected for sex, got close to Sam Jordan.

Bruno Messenger, as director, could have demanded a house, too, but had taken instead a large suite of rooms on the first floor of the Kapolska, where he lived with his court, the cinematographer, the art director and, most importantly, his chief minister, the man doing the day-to-day running of the movie, Al Mutton.

Al Mutton was not the producer of *Shadows on a Wall*, although he behaved as if he were: Al Mutton was the associate producer, and friend of the director. The producer, and man with overall responsibility, was Harvey Bamberg. But while Harvey Bamberg fretted about the desperate calls and faxes from the studio in California, about what attitude Familia Gallego, the co-financiers, might be about to take, about the global marketing strategy the movie would need to compensate for the albatross factor which had dogged every moment of shooting, and, most of all, about the estimated final cost of production, Al Mutton took his orders from Bruno Messenger and carried on spending. And seemingly no-one could stop him: not the studio, and definitely not Harvey Bamberg. With his pot belly, baby face, shiny scalp and vague smell of talcum powder, Harvey Bamberg was no match for these fellows.

From the bedroom came the loud jangling of the telephone. Turning off the bath taps Charlie went to answer it. Agnieszka smiled sleepily as she handed him the phone. She had a perfectly guileless expression, but then she hadn't been in movies very long.

The caller was Nathalie Seillans. She was phoning from Paris. Nathalie Seillans was the wife of Harvey Bamberg, amazing though that might seem. In her day men would have done many things to please Nathalie Seillans, and Nathalie Seillans had pleased many men. This was no longer her day but, despite himself, Charlie always felt a slight blush of excitement when he found himself talking to her. 'I'm sorry to disturb you, Charlie, but do you know where Harvey is? I've been calling his room, but . . .'

Charlie couldn't help. 'I haven't seen him since we wrapped last night. Maybe he's just so tired he's sleeping right through the phone.' That seemed possible. In recent weeks Harvey, beleaguered and desperate, had been wracked with exhaustion.

'Harvey would never sleep through a ringing telephone,' Nathalie sighed. 'He might miss a deal.'

'Well, perhaps he's somewhere *doing* a deal, or out driving . . . it's a nice day here . . .'

'Well, yes. All right, Charlie. Perhaps if you see him you could ask him to call me.'

'Yes, of course,' said Charlie. Things had been difficult for Harvey with Nathalie recently. When she called he always ran.

'Thank you, Charlie,' she said quietly.

They hung up.

Charlie turned to Agnieszka. 'If you bump into Harvey will you tell him to call Nathalie. She can't find him.'

Agnieszka nodded. 'Perhaps he's with Bruno.'

'No, he hates Bruno.'

'Yes, but he was with him last night after the shoot.'

'Are you sure?'

21

'I'm sure. In Harvey's car. Penn Stadtler, too, I think.'

'Penn Stadtler?' That was more than surprising. With thousands of Polish extras waiting in the rain, Bruno Messenger had stopped shooting for two hours to talk to Penn Stadtler about the movie's music. No ordinary film composer would have turned up in the most remote corner of Europe to discuss music which could better be talked about in London or Los Angeles. But Penn Stadtler wasn't just a composer: he was a rock-star composer.

'Rock stars and movies,' Harvey Bamberg had bitched for months, nervous of anything concerning Stadtler. 'Give them a sniff and they become addicted. Who wants electric guitars and synthesizers in a movie about Napoleon, anyway?'

Charlie hadn't answered: they had both known that Bruno Messenger did. Now he shrugged. 'Oh, well, maybe that's where he is . . . with Bruno. You never know, perhaps Harvey will even start liking the bastard again.'

Agnieszka pulled a doubtful face and slipped back under the sheets.

Charlie looked at her. She was a lovely girl. For a moment he hesitated, then, giving in, he climbed into the shelter of his bed, and put Harvey Bamberg and Bruno Messenger from his mind. It was not difficult. It was a rest day, and Agnieszka was very restful. This was what movie people did on the mornings of rest days in the distant corners of Poland.

(ii)

'This actor gets home from the gym one day to find his front door smashed in, his home ransacked and his wife naked in the bedroom, beaten and bleeding.'

Simone Estoril, plump and these days piebald where the peroxide was growing out, although neat in her dungarees and *Shadows on a Wall* sweatshirt, her tinted glasses as always balanced just above her hairline, looked at her watch as she listened to the joke. Even by Bruno Messenger's standards an hour and a half late for a meeting on a rest day was pushing it. As special assistant to the producer she didn't mind for herself. She had joined *Shadows on a Wall* to learn the job of making movies, and if being kept waiting by the director was part of

22

her education so be it. But it was unfair on the others, and she would complain again to Harvey Bamberg when he showed up. She wondered where he was. It was unlike Harvey not to be around and interfering.

Greg, the storyboard artist, was still telling his joke. ' "Oh my God, what happened?" the actor asked his wife. "It was terrible," the wife sobbed. "He came here, and broke down the door and rampaged around the house, smashing everything. I tried to stop him, but . . ." '

Simone fiddled absently with the on/off switch of her walkie-talkie. She had heard this one at least three times already.

' ". . . he found me, followed me upstairs, broke down the bedroom door, ripped off my clothes, beat me and raped me savagely over and over." ' Greg was enjoying this. ' "Oh God!" the husband said, "who could do such a terrible thing?" "Didn't I tell you?" the wife said. "It was your agent." ' Greg paused. ' "My agent did these things?" the actor said. "My agent? Was there any message?" '

Simone and Shelly, the design assistant, laughed generously. Having endured six months as one of the favourite butts of Bruno Messenger's tongue Greg deserved some support as a comedian.

The wait resumed. It was some minutes since they had pre-vailed upon Judy Goldberg, the director's personal assistant, to go upstairs and, as Simone had put it, 'drag that bastard out of bed and get him down here.' Judy had not wanted to go. There had been a succession of girls in the director's bed, and she had been unsure of what she might find. Al Mutton ought really to be the man to wake the director, she had argued as she went. 'He's the only one he ever listens to.' She had been right, of course, but Al Mutton was known to be away from the Kapolska that day.

'Something's going on,' the design assistant said suddenly. She was standing by the windows looking out across the grounds. A group of English electricians who had been taking on their Polish counterparts in a game of soccer were surrounding an orange anoraked, turtle-shaped woman with a short bob of black hair and heavy tortoiseshell glasses. She was Alice Bauccio, Yale Meredith's companion and a strong candidate for the second most unpopular woman in Poland. Behind them Billy Yeo's documentary camera crew were recording everything.

'He isn't there. There's no sign of him. His bed hasn't been slept

23

in.' Judy Goldberg charged back into the room, then stopped as she saw the group by the window. 'What's happening?'

Nobody answered. At that moment Simone's walkie-talkie crackled into life. It was the voice of second assistant director Markus Muller below them in the drive. 'We appear to have lost Yale Meredith,' he breezed laconically in the flight deck style of movie functionaries, 'and Alice is very worried. If anyone knows where Yale might be, information to Alice, please . . .'

The assistant to the producer, the design assistant, the story-board artist and the director's personal assistant looked at each other.

(iii)

Belinda Johnson was puzzled. There was a crowd gathered around the front of the palace which was unusual for a rest day. Her first thought was that the movie had finally been cancelled, and she was aware of a sudden flush of relief, followed immediately by the draught of reality. *Shadows on a Wall* had cost too much. The studio couldn't afford to cancel it.

They had been out riding for nearly three hours, just Belinda and Jack Dragoman, exploring the Kapolska estate, a journey several miles in length, through the forests, around the ornamental lakes and past the white columned pavilion where Sam Jordan would be sleeping. Jack Dragoman had hurried his horse into a sharp trot at that point. He didn't like Sam Jordan. That had been no surprise. Actors, even successful television stars like Jack Dragoman, were often jealous of each other, altogether as bad as actresses. And Sam Jordan was one of the most famously handsome men in the world, while Jack Dragoman had been hired because he was not.

Relieved to be away from the tittle-tattle of the unit Belinda had spent the ride in private debate. The truth was that after all these weeks together, all those nights . . . let's face it, all that *sex*, she still felt like a stranger in Dragoman's company. But then, who was Jack Dragoman? At the moment at least half of him was the part he was playing, Will Yorke, Napoleon's American friend and confidant. Belinda had never known an actor identify so closely with his role as Jack Dragoman. He was obsessional. Charlie had invented Will Yorke while working in their flat in London. Now Dragoman had *become* that character. It was unnerving. In the States Dragoman was famous as a neighbourly, tough-talking television cop with a penchant for the lyrics of Eagles' records; but the actor with whom Belinda was sleeping was an early nineteenth-century rights of man zealot.

Now there were decisions to be made. What, she had been wondering all morning, would happen when the movie was finished? Should she accept Dragoman's invitation to go to California? Did she really want to live in Hollywood? And once there, would he be the same man? As an American adventurer in Napoleonic Europe Dragoman could be charming. But what would he be like if he was cast as Ivan the Terrible next time around?

'Well, well . . . !' Dragoman said slowly, breaking into her thoughts and keeping a tight rein as his horse tried to break into a canter on the open ground in front of the palace. 'Looks to me like a lynching party we have here?' Even his speech sounded archaic.

Belinda smiled wryly as she gazed at the crowd. 'Well, if they need any help tying the knots . . .'

Dragoman nodded as they trotted across the grass. This movie hadn't been easy for him, either.

'What's going on?' Belinda asked, as, reaching the crowd, one of the wranglers took her pony's head and she slipped out of the saddle.

Simone Estoril batted distemper-brush eyelashes. 'God knows. It's rumour upon rumour. Harvey, Yale and Bruno have all gone missing, and there's a headless chickens contest going on until they turn up.'

'Well, they're all adult,' Belinda replied. 'Can't they take care of themselves?' When it came to panicking movie people had no equals.

Simone nodded. 'Sure. But it *is* puzzling. No-one seems to have seen any of them since last night. Harvey was giving them both a lift back in his car, but the car isn't here and—'

'What about the driver?'

'Harvey was driving himself. His driver went back in one of the other cars. Yale's car came back empty, too. Apparently she said Harvey wanted to talk, although he didn't tell me that.'

'Maybe they got up early and went off on a recce without telling anyone.'

Simone pulled her pretty, plump, Shelley Winters face. 'It's possible. But they do all hate the sight of each other, don't they? And Yale's never been on a recce before. It's very odd. Alice Bauccio is worried sick.'

'So, it isn't all bad news then,' Belinda smiled, and moved on towards Charlie, who, in the midst of the crowd, was looking both faintly bewildered and very young.

'So, what is all this, Charlie?' she joked. 'No-one can go missing in Kapolska. Even I couldn't conjure that. There's nowhere to go missing to.'

(iv)

Coincidence, thought Charlie. That was what it was. But he was aware of a first shiver of panic. He put the thought aside. He was being silly. He just wished Harvey would turn up and explain what was going on. He looked at Belinda, and then across at Jack Dragoman, still sitting on his horse. Could Belinda really fancy this dope who didn't know where acting ended and real life began?

Agnieszka stepped to his side and passed him a plastic cup of coffee, at the same time offering one to Belinda, who smiled her thanks. It was all so civilized.

A shout sent a breeze of excitement through the waiting crowd. A green BMW was racing across the park towards the palace. That was better, Charlie thought, recognizing Bruno Messenger's car. Bruno should at least know where Harvey and Yale were hiding. Then he frowned. The only occupant of the car was a Polish driver, already shaking his head. He hadn't found them. Charlie looked at his watch. It really was very odd.

(v)

No-one went to check on the bedroom of Sam Jordan in his white pavilion in the far corner of the estate. Why should they?

It was a rest day. Jordan had left no request for a wake-up call, therefore no-one would wake him up. Voted the man 53 per cent of American women would most like to sleep with (*Cosmopolitan*, March 1992), he was one of the small handful of actors in the world reckoned to be worth twelve million dollars a movie. And because he was the twelve-million-dollar man his staff remembered their place and generally kept as far from him as possible, only the bodyguard insisted upon by the insurers being allowed to sleep in his pavilion, albeit in the annexe. On a rest day, on any day, Sam Jordan's pavilion, at the end of a wide green lawn and scattered now with rain-battered daffodils, was a haven of tranquillity. And if Sam Jordan wasn't in his haven with his beta carotene, and wheatgerm and Gerovital H-3, no-one was going to find out. Not yet, anyway.

Chapter Three

(i)

The team of horses strained and began to pull. A forester's whip came down on the rump of the foremost, a mud-splattered chestnut, and it stumbled, splashing in the river. The car, its roof now level with the surface of the water, groaned slightly, but did not move. Again the whip bit, this time across the backs of the second pair, and, with a shudder, the car began to emerge, sliding and scraping up and out of the river. A wall of water curtained down dented flanks: rivulets streamed from the slits between the doors. Inside, the vehicle's cargo still floated.

The boy's father shook his head and turned the child away. This was not the best way to do it, he said.

The boy was not listening. Twisting his face back he watched as the great, shining, silver fish was dragged up the bank, its bonnet and one wing caved in, one of the side mirrors snapped and dangling, a front wheel buckled and tyre burst, all four hub caps missing.

For a moment the goldfish-bowl effect maintained. But then a policeman stepped forward and wrenched open a rear door. Immediately a torrent of water flooded from the car, carrying with it the long, bare legs of the woman, her skirt up around her waist, her tiny, white pants loose at her thighs and skewed to one side revealing a dark patch of pubic hair.

There was a moment's silence. The boy leant forward to get a better view. He had only ever seen his sisters without their pants, and, one day when her mother was out, the little girl who lived in the upstairs apartment. This was different, like the naked women in the foreign magazines the older boys bought. He knew his father was staring there, too.

'You'll have nightmares,' the father said, embarrassed that the boy was still present, 'and your mother will blame me.' He had wanted the boy to remain at the forest warden's house while the car was retrieved, but the child had insisted upon staying at his side. After all, the boy had said, he had found the car, and there was, he knew, much more to see.

Now the boy stared past the police and foresters into the open door of the car. The body of the woman had come to rest outside the vehicle with her head propped against the seat, her legs wide apart as though sitting on the bank, her feet in electric-blue jogging shoes. Beyond her on the back seat lay the body of a man wearing what looked like fancy dress, a green cloak wrapped around him.

With another heave the buckled front passenger door was pulled open and the head and shoulders of another man, a massive, wide-headed fellow, his long, dark hair matted around his neck, fell outwards, a bound wad of papers falling with him on to the bank. Beyond him was another body.

Once again the father tried to cover the boy's eyes, but again the child pulled free. He was not afraid. He wanted to see everything.

(ii)

The police sergeant lifted his gaze from the pants and up to the woman's face. A tangle of wet, fair hair fell around it. The mouth was open, the tip of the tongue protruding, pensive almost, at the corner of the lips, as though trying in eternity to solve some left-over earthly mental problem.

Had it not been for the dead eyes the woman would have been beautiful. She had a small, straight nose, her mouth was wide and her lips very full. She looked vaguely familiar. Judging by what she was wearing he decided she was probably a prostitute who had been out on a drive with three men in this American car. Perhaps he had once booked her or seen her at court, he thought, and then he wondered whether any of the men, or all of them, had had her before they died. These things happened. Was that how she had got the bruise on the inside of her thigh, from the guy in the funny clothes? He looked familiar, too, although from outside the car it was difficult to get a decent look at him.

But how had they died, and come to this impossible place? And what kind of accident did this suggest? He wanted to search them, but had just received instructions not to touch any of the bodies until more senior officers arrived from Trencin. He would probably get into trouble. It had been at his suggestion that the local foresters had rounded up their horses to drag the car from the river. He had been afraid that more rain would have carried it further downstream. But he knew that whatever he did would be wrong. It was always the same when foreigners were involved. Who were these men? he wondered. Gangsters? Who else would have a car like this?

There was movement on the mountain above them, lights flashing in the trees, sirens wailing and horns blowing as more police arrived. They would soon begin to cordon off the area for the investigation.

The sergeant considered the situation. He would rather he had not become involved, but an American car with four bodies in an impossible place in the Slovakian mountains had to be worth something. He knew who to call.

(iii)

'Stuffed with corpses,' Tomas Lendak repeated. The phrase sent a thrill through him. It was his lucky day. Normally he would have been in Prague, where he made an uncertain living as a freelance photographer, and dreamt about the new Mercedes he would one day own. But, because his girlfriend had left him and he was even more broke than usual, he had gone home to his village to stay with his mother for the Easter weekend. Had he remembered that Good Friday was a fast day he would have waited until the Saturday. And if he had he would have missed it all.

'*Stuffed*,' his brother-in-law stressed. 'An American car. And I want twenty US dollars for every corpse if you sell anything abroad.'

Lendak didn't argue. He *ran* to his car, a seventeen-year-old Skoda.

A small boy stood with his father, bewildered by events. Raising his camera Lendak caught him.

'Any idea who they are yet?' he asked his sister's husband, staring at the car.

The police sergeant shook his head. 'The computer in Bratislava is down and there's no-one to mend it over Easter.'

Lendak moved on, trying to peer through the wall of police to get a closer look. Only the body of the woman was clearly visible. Through his 200mm lens he examined her. Sitting there, propped against the car, she might have been resting after a long walk in the forest. He crouched down in the mud. He wanted to get her crotch in the shot. The shutter opened and closed. He was only just in time. Suddenly a sheet was thrown across her head.

Something caught his eye. It was a sodden wedge of paper and must have fallen out of the car when the doors had been opened because it was now lying in the mud behind the hastily erected cordon. Making sure he wasn't being watched he reached out and peeled back the pages. He knew instantly what it was. He had once worked as a stills photographer at the Barrendov Studios in Prague. '*Shadows on a Wall*,' he read. 'Copyright, Buffalo Pictures Corporation.'

Tomas Lendak's dream of a Mercedes had suddenly become considerably more substantial.

Chapter Four

(i)

Billy Yeo pressed his one eye into the rubber cushion surrounding the viewfinder and squeezed the start button of his 16mm Arriflex camera. This was a shot he wanted to operate himself. Framing the contents of the top shelf he rested his weight against the kitchen wall, bent his knees and, slowly lowering himself, panned down the ranks of massed jars of pills stacked in the large refrigerator. He had already shot the hundreds of jars in the conservatory which, with its rowing machine and weights served as a personal gymnasium, the dozens in the bathroom and the unopened cartons in the hall. He worked quickly. The unit publicist and the security team the studio employed to protect their stars and director were momentarily confused. At any moment they might come to their senses, realize their jobs, possibly their careers, were in jeopardy and come storming across to throw him out of this pavilion which Sam Jordan had been using as home, apothecary and seduction headquarters. Switching off the camera he indicated the door to his three colleagues. 'That's enough. Let's go.'

The first police car, a salt-coroded blue Moskva, had arrived outside the palace at just after one-thirty. By then Sam Jordan had also been posted as missing. That made four unaccounted for: one producer, Harvey Bamberg, one director, Bruno Messenger, and the leading actor and actress, Sam Jordan and Yale

32

Meredith, who also happened to be two of the most famous people in the world. The police inspector, a stout man who had turned up for the usual free and lavish unit lunch, had listened with incredulity and then radioed for assistance.

It had been at Alice Bauccio's insistence, as she searched the palace and grounds for Yale Meredith, that Jordan's pavilion had eventually been checked, although Jordan's bodyguard had insisted that the star was still sleeping. He had been wrong. Jordan's bed was empty. The bodyguard, a former policeman, who had been known to use his position to lay the unit's leftovers, had looked foolish and began to bluster, suggesting that Jordan was probably in bed with one of the actresses, 'maybe that little English one', or possibly the make-up girl in the high-heeled cowboy boots, or perhaps even one of the extras. 'Or maybe two of them, know what I mean, because he has a hell of an appetite, prodigious, if you want to know, or what about the Italian girl with the cock-eyed tits, did you ask her? Sam screws her now and again. Or maybe he even spent the night in his trailer . . . Who knows? Don't tell him I said but he can be a sneaky kind of guy. No kidding! You know what he does with scripts he doesn't like . . . ?' As he had huffed and puffed he had become steadily redder in his cabbage face.

Later no-one at the studio would know how Billy had managed to film so much on that day without someone putting a hand over the lens, but those at the Kapolska knew. After so many months the presence of a documentary camera team had virtually ceased to be noticed. And everyone liked Billy.

(ii)

It was just after two-thirty when the first call came from California. It was Julie Wyatt, the executive in charge of production at the studio. She was mad, she told Simone Estoril who had been unlucky enough to pick up the phone in the production office. 'Can you believe it? Some radio reporter creep right here in LA drags me out of bed at half-past five in the morning saying they've had some crazy report from Bratislava about an American limousine being found in a lake. I said, "Jesus, Eastern Europe's a pretty big place, you know, fella, and, anyway, if it's Czechoslovakia or Slovakia or whatever it calls itself these days, it has nothing to do with *Shadows on a Wall*. We're in Poland, OK!" and hung up.'

'A limousine . . . ?' Simone began.

The executive in charge of production was not yet ready to be interrupted. 'It isn't fair. Every time anything happens anywhere in Europe I get these crazy calls, just because *Shadows on a Wall* seems to have some kind of jinx.'

'Julie—' Simone tried again.

'So, tell me, what's going on with you guys? And put Harvey Bamberg on, will you?'

(iii)

The girl who played Camille de Malignon shifted her position, shuffling forward on to her elbows so that she could watch more closely, her Napoleon hat tipped over one eye. She was lying on a rug on the lawn in front of the palace, her letter writing interrupted.

'. . . *all I can say is that when they give out the prize for the most peculiar day of all time they need look no further than this one,*' she had written. '*It's been a crazy six months, and, although it seems impossible, I do believe it's getting crazier. Honestly. Do you remember how I told you at first that being part of a film unit on location was a bit like being a member of an extended family? Well, put that on hold, for a minute, will you? I'm rethinking. I mean, if the* Shadows on a Wall *unit is a family I think there must have been some pretty enthusiastic cross-breeding between Lucretia Borgia, Caligula, his horse, the Marx Brothers, Vlad the Impaler, Joan of Arc, Ethelred the Unready, Lady Macbeth and Herman Munster somewhere down the line.*'

At that point she had stopped writing as two more police cars had swept through the estate, their sirens wailing.

Thoughtfully now she sucked on the end of her pen. It was a perfect setting. A beautiful, eighteenth-century Polish palace, a posse of police cars, their short-wave radios chattering, Charlie Holyoake head-to-head with an interpreter, a police inspector waiting, and 190 cast and crew watching and wondering what would happen next: the film-makers had become the audience.

'An accident? In a river? *In Slovakia?*' Charlie realized that he was trembling, but all he could think was, Is this a Polish version of Chinese whispers?

Los Angeles had had the story first but now the Polish police inspector was standing by his car repeating a crackling radio report while a production interpreter translated into English. 'Not too far over the border. A few kilometres down the river from where we were shooting yesterday. The river crosses the border near there and flows southwards towards the Danube. It is very unusual. Most Polish rivers flow north towards the Baltic.'

Once more Charlie's mind took a detour. At a time like this I'm getting a geography lesson? he thought.

The police officer spoke rapidly again. Charlie turned to the interpreter.

'He says that communications with the Slovakian police are not always as good as they should be, which accounts for the delay in his being informed . . .'

Charlie nodded, realizing that for the first time in years he was praying. A river, an American car found in a river . . . It sounded uncannily familiar.

The inspector now began a rapid conversation with his short-wave radio, which he struck from time to time as the message faded and popped. At last he turned to the interpreter, a young man, not long out of university in Wroclaw.

'He says that he is sorry to tell you but according to the Slovakian police the registration number on the car appears to correspond with that on the car driven by Mr Harvey Bamberg . . .'

Charlie swallowed. At the window of the production office Belinda stood watching.

'And he would like to ask if you would mind helping his colleagues in Slovakia?'

'Helping?'

'There are bodies . . . they need someone to—'

'Oh yes. Of course.' He did not move. He was thinking how silly they would look when everything was explained and they got back to making the movie. But at the same time he was also thinking that this was the worst day of his life.

The interpreter tried again. 'Perhaps you would like someone to accompany you?'

'What? Oh yes.'

Without being asked, first assistant director Tony Delmonte stepped forward. An olive-skinned man from New Jersey, Delmonte had the room next to Charlie in the Kapolska Palace.

As Delmonte climbed into the police car one of the make-up assistants pushed forward and pulling off her large *Prague, Czech it out* yellow sweatshirt offered it to him. Giving Charlie a little smile Delmonte pulled it over his T-shirt.

'Well then—' the interpreter said, indicating the car.

Obediently Charlie climbed in alongside Delmonte.

'It's a mistake, isn't it?' Delmonte said as the cars began to pull away across the estate. 'I mean it has to be. Right? One great Eastern European goof-up.'

Charlie didn't answer.

In the front seats the Polish driver and inspector were speaking quietly to each other, while the police radio spat its intermittent messages. Polish was such a difficult language.

For some reason Charlie thought about Agnieszka, and the untranslated things she sometimes murmured in the night. Then he thought about Belinda, and wondered how it was when she made love with Jack Dragoman. Closing his eyes he tried to turn off the pictures.

Next to him Tony Delmonte shifted, lifted the round collar of the sweatshirt up over his nose and began breathing in its scents. 'Sorry if we woke you this morning,' he murmured smugly. 'She couldn't leave it alone.'

Ignoring him Charlie looked out across the wooded mountains which divided southern Poland from Slovakia, the High Tatras, dark again now, as new rain clouds swept down from the north. Looking back he could see two cars following, the first, another police Moskva, the second, a hired Golf from Avis in Warsaw. Billy Yeo would be at the wheel, and next to him, Freddie, his operator, would already be reloading the Arriflex. For once not even Billy could offer any comfort.

He closed his eyes and found Belinda looking at him: a bright, intelligent close-up. 'What's happening, Charlie?' she was saying. 'What's going on?'

He shook his head. He couldn't tell her, not even in his imagination. He daren't even think it. The tumbril rolled on towards the Slovakian border.

The place was like a circus, with a canvas roof stretched three feet above the vehicle to keep out the rain. There were lights, police, forensic experts, detectives, a pathologist, mechanics, a photographer, foresters, four horses harnessed together and a helicopter chattering above. At the centre of it all a ringmaster of a police superintendent was directing operations; on the edge of the ring stood a small boy.

The rain had returned as the cars had stopped in the forest and Charlie and Delmonte had been led into the valley, the Polish unit interpreter beginning to fret that, although he knew some Slovak, he could not promise to translate with total accuracy. Delmonte had grumbled all the way down. 'What is there to translate? Goof-up is the same in Slovak as in Polish as in Swahili. Right?'

But it had not been a goof-up. Charlie's prayers had not been answered. Lying, still leaking, on the bank was Harvey Bamberg's silver car.

'It must have fallen from a great height before it sank under the water,' translated the interpreter, as the ringmaster spat out a crumb of loose tobacco.

'Jesus!' Delmonte said.

'And now he would like the identification, please. Is it possible?'

Charlie braced himself.

The interior of the car smelt of dank water and he almost retched, closing his eyes for a second. He opened them on the face of Bruno Messenger. An hour earlier he had hated Bruno Messenger: perhaps he had also envied him; now he wondered why. The massive head of the director lay flopped over the back of the passenger seat, his neck broken. The eyes were half closed and glazed, trickles of congealed blood ran from one nostril and one ear, and the mouth was partly open to reveal small, sharp, uneven teeth. There was a cold sore at the right-hand corner of his bottom lip. Below the head the huge body lay stretched across almost the entire front of the car, one swollen hand caught in the steering wheel.

Charlie swallowed. 'Bruno Messenger. Film director. An American citizen,' he said.

Behind him he heard the interpreter repeating the information in what could have been either Slovak or Polish. It was then repeated again. He waited. Bruno Messenger had been a young man, not yet thirty, but, perhaps because he had been so big, he had seemed older. A slight trace of adolescent acne dappled one cheek.

Another man's body lay folded in the back of the car. He was wearing a green coat with a scarlet collar and edgings to the lapels, a white linen blouse, a red-and-blue cravat, white trousers and stockings and black shoes with gilt buckles. A cloak was around his shoulders. It was the uniform of an emperor, but this man's empire had been on the world's screens, in the dreams of women. He was still handsome, even in death, his face composed, almost in a smile, as though he had momentarily fallen asleep, his thick copper hair glistening in the lights.

'Yes?' asked the interpreter.

'Sam . . .' began Charlie, but then stopped. Because of the way the corpse's right leg was folded under the body he had almost missed something. He leant forward. The buttons down the front of the white cavalry trousers were undone. Peeping out were two pink inches of the most desired penis in the world.

'Yes?' repeated the interpreter.

Charlie pulled his head back. 'Sam Jordan, film actor. He was playing Napoleon.'

The ripple of the name 'Sam Jordan' ran around the ring of spectators. *'Sam Jordan, Sam Jordan, Sam Jordan.'* Sam Jordan, the most handsome man in movies; Sam Jordan was dead.

Sam Jordan died with his flies open, Charlie was thinking. It had to be appropriate. The man 53 per cent of American women would most like to go to bed with, had died in the back seat of a car with his pecker out.

The woman was next. She must have been sitting alongside Jordan, now she was half-in, half-out of the car. Charlie ran his eyes up her body, starting at the running shoes and then the legs. No-one had tried to make her look decent, not from the waist down, and her pants, still loose between the slim thighs, were attracting every prying eye. The sheet was lifted from the face.

'Yale Meredith,' he said. 'Actress.'

There was another murmur.

He stared at the woman's face but felt nothing. Certainly she had been very beautiful. She had once enchanted him.

He remembered noticing her the previous day as the clapperboard had gone down, when the usual querulous sulk had suddenly given way to the most brilliant smile. When Yale Meredith could smile like that movie-goers would never believe what a pain she could be to work with: to know. She had died alongside Sam Jordan: Jordan with his willie out; Yale with her pants coming down.

There was one more body. He stepped around to the other side of the car. This was the one he was dreading most. He hesitated, and then looked inside the car again. The body was folded in the gap between the two front seats, facing downwards, an overcoat having ridden up over the shoulders and head. He would have to pull the coat away to see properly. Everyone waited.

The ringmaster barked a command. A lesser rank stepped forward and carefully began folding back the coat.

Charlie thought about the time he had first met Harvey Bamberg in the restaurant with Nathalie Seillans, little, bald, beaming Harvey, full of talk, agreeing with everything anyone said.

'Please?' The interpreter was asking.

Charlie looked down. The head was lying on one side, thick fair hair falling in waves around the face.

'Jesus! It's Penn Stadtler,' said Delmonte.

Charlie literally *felt* the blow of surprise. He had to look again.

The ringmaster said something. He wanted Charlie to make the identification.

'Penn Stadtler,' Charlie said.

He stepped away from the car. Now the crowd of spectators and police seemed to take a stride closer, as though he had broken some kind of spell. Until he had named the victims, the bodies had been four people found dead in extraordinary circumstances. But they were not just four people. Three of them were among the dozen or so most desired people in the world. Now their corpses were public property, and these policemen, foresters, wardens and spectators would all want a part of them. And he remembered reading how when the Porsche James Dean had died in had been put on display in a Los Angeles showroom it had been virtually ripped to pieces by fans. Would this car become a shrine, too?

It might, but before that the news had to be broken, and, even as Charlie stood there, he became aware of a rustling in the trees and bushes as new, inquisitive faces began to appear, scrambling down the mountain carrying cameras and microphones, the forward, foraging party in a media army which would inform the world.

Turning away he found himself staring into the one green and one imitation blue eye of Billy Yeo, the Arriflex focused on him.

He stepped back, pushing away a microphone. He felt unable to breathe. He found a fallen tree and sat on it, his head in his hands. He didn't know what to do. A sensation of being quite alone and wrong in the world was suffocating him.

Around him the excitement grew: the snapping of camera shutters as photographers pushed past confused foresters to get shots of the bodies, a ribald joke from someone which caused some guffaws, angry orders from police which were ignored. The circus was out of control and the clowns were taking over. Looking through his fingers Charlie could see the ringmaster impotently shouting orders, a traffic conductor in a gold rush. Everyone here would make money out of today, not least the small boy whose father was already posing him by the silver car.

'What about Harvey?'

'What?'

Delmonte had recovered quickly. 'What about Harvey Bamberg? This is Harvey's car? So, where's Harvey? Why isn't he in there, too? Last time they were all seen he was driving, wasn't he? And why the hell isn't Penn Stadtler five hundred miles away in Kiev? That's where he was going. He said he was going to drive all through the night.'

Charlie didn't answer. This wasn't how he had written it.

(v)

Taking care not to draw too much attention to themselves Billy Yeo and his team shot everything. The months of watching and waiting were being rewarded. Gazing through the open door of the car he stared at the body of Bruno Messenger. At least Bruno would never become obese as his hero had done. He ought to have felt pity for the man, for Yale Meredith and Sam Jordan. But it was difficult to feel anything. In their own ways they had all been monsters.

With the slightest touch of his hands on the elbows of Freddie, his camera operator, he indicated that they should not over-look Sam Jordan's open flies.

Freddie nodded. Of course he wouldn't miss the pecker shot.

A police sergeant, suddenly aware of what was being filmed began to shout, his arms in the air. Without a word Billy slid his hand into his pocket and pulled out a waiting fifty Deutschmark bill. The shouting stopped.

Above him on the mountain Charlie and Tony Delmonte, surrounded by police, were beginning their climb back to their car.

Billy watched them go, then looked back northwards along the curve of the river. That was the only way the car could have come, down the river, dragged by the flood. Bruno Messenger's neck had been broken, but, apart from the bruise on Yale Meredith's thigh, there were no obvious marks on the others. And he wondered how long it had taken them to drown.

(vi)

In the end the brother-in-law fixed it with his superiors. Tomas Lendak had his shots from outside the car, but so did others. He wanted more, individual close-ups, portraits, death masks. For a percentage of any foreign sales it was agreed that he would travel in the ambulance.

As everyone knew, handled properly, death could be very big business: especially Hollywood death.

(vii)

The boy and his father were driven back to their cabin by a police car. It was very late. The boy's mother and sisters and some of the other holiday-makers from adjacent cabins were waiting in the lane. The boy noticed that his mother was wearing more lipstick than usual and his sisters were in their best shorts and T-shirts. Another television crew and several photographers were waiting with them.

Again he was asked to describe what he had seen. He was

becoming quite used to answering questions now. He noticed that as he spoke his mother and sisters stood close to him, that his father patted his shoulders occasionally. He was a hero.

Later, as he lay in his bunk bed, too excited to sleep, listening through the thin wooden walls, he heard his father whispering rude things to his mother about the American actor's little penis. 'Tiny, no good at all for a woman like you,' he heard him say, and then smiled to himself as he heard him tell her again how their son had been the star of the day.

When he fell asleep he was remembering the bare, open legs of the woman, the patch of dark hair and the expressions on the faces of everyone staring.

(viii)

There was a delay over the police papers at the border crossing back into Poland, and while forms were filled in Charlie and Delmonte sat in the police car and waited. Delmonte had not spoken since the valley. Charlie could now feel his skin cold and damp with shock. A bleak, thin light glared over the barrier in the road.

Pushing his hands into the pockets of his jacket his fingers found a heavy, smooth disc, a Queen Victoria old penny.

'What's going on, Charlie?' he heard Belinda ask again. 'What have you and Harvey been getting up to?'

He clutched his lucky penny and thought about Edinburgh. It had started so well for them; for Belinda, for Billy, for him. They had been so happy together. Why had they ever wanted more?

PART TWO

August, 1991

The play

Chapter Five

(i)

He caught her earning their lunch. She had slipped away at the end of rehearsals and was standing on the Mound doing her juggling act, four white balls and three yellow hoops bobbing and spinning above the heads of the crowd, an open parasol balanced upright on the end of her toe. In black leotard and tights, her cream hair tumbling in ribbons and ringlets around her shoulders, early nineteenth-century style, she was dazzling, and for some minutes he watched, seeing her from among the audience as a stranger might, thrilled at her prettiness.

'Isn't she magic?' a quiet voice said at his side.

He didn't need to turn. 'I think so.'

It was Billy Yeo, big and generous. 'Let's hope we get as good a house tonight.'

Charlie did a quick calculation of the crowd. There were probably a hundred people watching. 'I don't know where we'd put them if we did,' he said. 'The hall only holds fifty.' And, breaking into applause as Belinda ended her act, he set an example by pushing through the audience to drop a couple of coins into her upturned top hat lying on the cobblestones.

'Thank you, sir,' Belinda grinned. 'God bless you.'

'Stick with me and I'll get you off the streets yet, little girl,' he teased as other coins followed.

'Why do I always believe you?'

'Beats me! See you in the The Last Drop in ten minutes.'

And, as Belinda began to collect her equipment, he rejoined Billy, who was forcing publicity sheets into the hands of the dispersing crowd.

'*Shadows on a Wall*. First night tonight in James' Court Hall, that's just up the road,' shouted Billy. 'Book now to avoid disappointment. *Shadows on a Wall*, the hit of this year's festival. *Shadows on a Wall*, written by Charles Holyoake and starring, direct from Philadelphia, Belinda Johnson. Tonight at seven, the world première. *Shadows on a Wall* . . .'

Nearby a human statue sneezed and gave up.

'I'm not sure you should say it's a hit when we haven't even had the first performance,' Charlie worried, as the two made their way across the Lawnmarket towards the pub. 'And Belinda's been over here for years.'

Billy smiled. 'So? Time is relative. Don't be so diffident. Of course we're going to be the hit of the festival. How can we fail?'

Charlie liked to hear this. Enthusiasm was part of what made Billy such a good director, and, in this instance, lighting, set and publicity designer. Charlie, in his producer role, was positive, too: with this director and this cast, particularly Belinda, success had to be assured. Only in his other role, that of the writer of the play, was he less certain.

Charlie and Billy had become friends two years earlier while working together on a television film. Older, at thirty-five, Billy was one of those directors able to turn his hand to anything: films, theatre, documentaries, although his determination to do only what interested him had not always made things easy. Doing commercials he could have made a fortune; in Hollywood he might have been a star director; in Edinburgh he was opening the pub door.

There were three members of the company already in The Last Drop when they arrived, Neil Burgess, who was playing Napoleon, having grabbed his usual table by the door. He was a theatrically handsome man, vain as an otter and as precious as a priest. 'If one sits by the door one ensures that anyone entering or leaving must pass one, and therefore must notice one,' he was in the habit of intoning. 'And for an actor to be noticed, albeit in a pub, but in a pub in Edinburgh during the Edinburgh Festival, cannot be altogether bad. One never knows.'

Charlie thought he probably did know in the case of Neil, but the old pro would give as good as he could, and had been very helpful to Belinda during rehearsals. For Neil, to be playing in the fringe was not what he might once have hoped to be doing as he neared fifty, but for Belinda, Marie Walewska was the biggest part she had ever had.

At the bar Billy Yeo was getting the drinks. He was always first with his hand in his pocket despite three children, a fourth on the way and a perpetual state of impoverishment. Just coming to Edinburgh had meant taking time off from a documentary he was working on at the BBC and giving up a proper salary. He was more than a good friend.

Pushing through, Charlie slid a production fund five pound note on to the bar. 'This one's on the play,' he insisted. 'The least it can do is buy us a drink.'

Billy stuck out a dimpled chin. 'It'll do more than that, I promise you, or my name's not Kirk Douglas.'

Amused, Charlie made his way through the crush to their table. Not being noticed with Neil Burgess today was a stage manager called Amanda, a pale, willing girl with a puffball of fine red hair who was also playing both the Empress Josephine and Countess Monika Wyszynska, and a young chemistry teacher called Allan, who had four small parts and had helped drive Billy's van north with the props and costumes. The rest of the company consisted of the Two Soldiers, as two of the other actors were known, in that they had to play a host of military roles from Marshall Ney to Napoleon's groom, and who at that moment were wandering through the town fly-sticking posters for that night's performance, and the second leads, the couple playing Camille de Malignon and the American Will Yorke, who had dashed back to bed as soon as the morning's rehearsal had broken.

As they drank their beer and waited for Belinda, Charlie reflected on Billy's poster for *Shadows on a Wall* stuck on the pub door. It was a copy of a portrait of Marie Walewska by the artist Davide with a photograph of Belinda's face superimposed over the original, and it was, he thought, an improvement. Marie Walewska had been pretty in a nineteenth-century style, but Belinda was beautiful. He was proud of her and pleased with the poster. *Shadows on a Wall* was his first production, mounted with five thousand pounds of his own savings and a ten-thousand-pound loan from his bank when he had found that no established theatre company would put it on. That had been no surprise. Getting a new play by a relatively new writer performed these days was practically impossible, and absolutely no-one was going to compound the risk by giving the leading role to the author's girlfriend. Being a writer could be difficult, but being an actress, no matter how talented and pretty, was far trickier. And Belinda was also American.

'Perhaps I should go back to the States,' she had sometimes mused as the parts had refused to come her way. 'They're used to American accents there.' But she had stayed. They were in love. Then one day Charlie had remembered Marie Walewska and Napoleon.

'Napoleon?' his agent, Larry Horner, strong of jaw but weak of concentration, a poor reader of manuscripts but deadly with a percentage point, had asked incredulously. It had been their once-a-year lunch. 'Don't tell me it's another of those dreadful two handers about him rewriting history while playing chess with his jailers on St Helena? He used to cheat like mad, you know.'

Charlie had known. 'No, nothing like that. It's about two women who try to change the shape of history, and how love and romance get in their way.'

'This isn't more hairy-backed feminist stuff, is it?' Larry had sniffed suspiciously, holding up his hand for the menu. 'The sole's usually very good, by the way.' He was a smart man, with a wide, turned-up nose, who, as well as *being* an agent, liked to *play the part* of an agent, a bright green handkerchief exploding out of the breast pocket of his navy-blue suit.

Charlie had shaken his head. 'It's a double love story, Napoleon and a Polish girl called Marie Walewska, who is supposed to have started out by taking her knickers off for Poland—'

'I didn't think they wore knickers in those days,' Larry had interrupted again, vaguely triumphant, as though he had just discovered a tear in the gusset of the plot.

'I was speaking metaphorically,' Charlie had persisted. 'She was a young married woman – her husband was a hundred or something who had agreed to settle all her family's debts if she married him – but then she met Napoleon and took her metaphorical pants off for the sake of her country, fell in love, had his baby and spent the next eight years following him around Europe. That bit's based on fact. Then there's a sub-plot about an American called Will Yorke who has an affair with a girl who wants to kill him – kill Napoleon, I mean. That's fictional, Yorke and the girl. I'm calling her Camille de Malignon, and she's the daughter of French aristocrats, who saw her parents guillotined during the Reign of Terror when she was five. In the play she's grown up and slightly mad, obsessed with revenge on the new regime . . . which means Napoleon, because he's the figurehead of the new system . . .'

By this time Larry had looked thoroughly bored. 'Yes, well—' he had started, as the menu had arrived. Then, unable to think of anything encouraging to add, he had begun to murmur something about 'the shortage of decent television commissions these days . . . all anyone wants is tits and bonk since Thatcher screwed everything up,' as though that were the reason his client had been driven to writing for the theatre.

'You're missing the point,' Charlie had persisted. '*Shadows on a Wall* is the most exciting thing I've ever thought of. Ever since I was at school Marie Walewska's fascinated me.'

'Really?' Larry had been looking wistfully at the wine list. In the end he would, as always when buying a client lunch, settle for a bottle of Soave.

'Yes. Really. It's such a romantic story. She followed him from Warsaw to Paris and then to Elba when he was first exiled. They were having it off in a monk's cell so no-one would know. He used to tell her they could only meet in secret, like shadows on a wall. That's where the title comes from.'

'Ah!' said Larry, and tried a diversion. 'What about Belinda? How's she getting on? Didn't I see her in a commercial for a double bed with zig-zag springs the other night? Quite sexy, really. Well, very sexy.'

Charlie had nodded. As it happened Belinda hated the advertisement for the double bed with the zig-zag springs, but hardly having worked that year she couldn't afford to turn down the money. 'I'm writing it for her,' he had said. 'The part. Marie Walewska. She'll be perfect.'

'Ah!' Larry had said again.

'She shouldn't have to do commercials. She's a good actress who's being wasted.'

'. . . and very pretty . . .'

'Pretty and *good*,' Charlie had insisted. Now in Edinburgh, after four weeks of rehearsals, he was sure that whatever happened at that night's opening he had been right. Belinda *was* perfect as Marie Walewska, balancing uncertain ambition against the vulnerability of the girl who has always been clever and pretty, but lacks confidence. Belinda knew that part of herself well.

'I don't want to raise expectations too much, but . . .' standing just inside the door Belinda was leaning over Charlie, shaking the coins from her top hat on to the table, 'according to Oona McDonald we're getting the *Scotsman* and the *Guardian* in tonight.'

'What . . . ?' Neil Burgess's black eyebrows vaulted.

'Come on, it's a joke,' Billy smiled.

'No joke. I bumped into her on the way over here. That play at the Bedlam has cancelled. The lead's gone down with alcoholic poisoning. They're coming to see us instead.'

Charlie didn't speak as around him the other members of the company volleyed a crossfire of questions. It was more than he had dared hope for.

'Didn't I say I'd get you off the streets one day?' Belinda murmured to him, pushing her hands down the front of his shirt and kissing his ear.

Charlie swivelled his head around to look at her, simultaneously rubbing the back of his head against her neck. She was still in her juggler's tights. 'No wonder those guys are coming if they've seen you tarting around Edinburgh like that,' he scolded, pretending to frown at the tease of bottom showing under the hem of her sweater. 'I hope they know it's a *serious* play we have here. Some people will do *anything* to get a review.'

'Just about, Charlie, just about,' Belinda mocked back.

'Some people would do anything to be noticed,' chimed Neil Burgess, and everyone laughed.

Suddenly Belinda leant forward and picked up one of the coins from the table. It was large and almost black. 'What's this?' she asked.

'An old penny,' said Billy.

Taking the coin Charlie peered closely at it. 'A *very* old penny. Queen Victoria old, one of the young Victoria ones, with her hair tied back. It's a collector's item really.'

He passed it back to Belinda. 'It's so heavy,' she said. 'Maybe it's a lucky penny. A *Shadows on a Wall* lucky penny.' She slipped it into his pocket. 'You keep it, Charlie. Keep it for luck. Things must be getting better. When I first started juggling I was paid in bottle tops.'

'But you were happy, weren't you?' teased Charlie.

She hesitated. 'Tonight,' she said. 'I'll be happy after tonight.' Then she paused again. 'I think.'

(ii)

The truth was she was terrified. That was why she had been juggling. It helped calm her nerves. The nicest thing Charlie could
do had been to write this play for her. She knew it was good,
possibly very good, but, if she was bad, might she not drag
the play down with her, and with it all the money Charlie had
borrowed? It would take years for him to repay the bank. That
was where the juggling came in: she was confident at that.

They didn't stay long in the pub before Billy was hurrying
Charlie back to the hall for a last-minute lighting session and
Belinda was setting off for the students' flat where she and
Charlie were staying during the festival. There was much still
to do. As well as playing joint lead she was also the company
wardrobe mistress and had costume repairs to finish before the
performance. She hurried down the steps towards Princes Street.
It was her first visit to Edinburgh and she was excited by the hec-
tic froth of the festival set against the granite of the city. Reaching
the bottom of the hill she paused momentarily to look back up
at the castle, towers, spires and old houses strung like a cut-out
backdrop against the windy skyline. 'If that doesn't inspire you,
girl, nothing will,' she said to herself, and then pushed on in
search of a bookshop. It was Charlie's twenty-ninth birthday
the following day and she had already decided on her gift.

They had met by chance four years earlier, two strangers
hiding from the afternoon in an otherwise empty cinema, and
Charlie laughing so loudly she had turned around to ask him
to be quiet. She had been twenty-one and just out of drama
school. He had apologized and then struggled to keep quiet
throughout the rest of the film, which was, in fact, funny
only by accident. In the end she'd seen the joke and joined
in. They'd had a drink together after the performance, when
she had told him she'd only gone to the cinema because she'd
thought they were showing *Day for Night* and wanted to see it
on a big screen. 'It came off last night,' he had said, and invited
her to another film that evening. After that they'd had dinner
at a Thai restaurant around the corner and then gone back to
his flat where she'd looked through his film encyclopedias and
he'd won a bet. Daphne had been the name chosen when the
Jack Lemmon character goes in drag in *Some Like It Hot*. She
had been sure it was Geraldine.

'Geraldine was the name he was supposed to choose,' Charlie had said. 'And Tony Curtis was Josephine. Gerry and Jo, you see. But at the last minute the Jack Lemmon character changed it to Daphne.' Charlie remembered these things.

She had stayed that night and, in the end, they had gone to bed, playing a movie quiz for some of the time . . . not much before, some after, but mostly in between.

She had half expected to say goodbye for ever the following morning: it had happened before. But Charlie had wanted her to stay. So she had shown him some conjuring tricks with three eggs, four spoons and an empty syrup tin.

'Where did you learn all that?' he had asked.

'In my wicked past,' she had said, and they had slipped back into bed. After that she had never really gone home to the old flat again.

She had been teasing about her past. There wasn't that much of it, the usual boyfriends, some sex, nothing serious. She had learnt the conjuring and the juggling tricks from her father, who had picked them up from an old vaudeville entertainer he had once known. Her parents were actors, too, Bob Johnson and Cherry Gilbert; at least they had been until the work ran out. They'd had their moment in television comedy in New York in the early Sixties when friends had told them that they would soon be the next Dick Van Dyke and Mary Tyler Moore. Now they taught speech and drama in Philadelphia, Cherry from home, Bob in school. Sometimes when she had been growing up Belinda had watched reruns of their one short-lived television series *Stagger Lee and Hannah* on cable in the early hours of the morning and wondered what had gone wrong with their careers. Perhaps she had always known. Cherry had been vivacious and pretty, but not particularly good. Bob could act, but the desire wasn't there. She could sense it. Teaching suited him better.

Most girls from Philadelphia with Belinda's looks and abilities would have gone to New York, but London had been her magnet. In London she wouldn't risk disappointing anybody other than herself. So much seemed to be expected. Bob and Cherry had had three daughters but only Belinda had shown any aptitude for the business. So, while her elder sisters had been out riding their bikes or dating or going to college, Belinda's life had been a regime of ballet, singing and drama lessons. She had never complained. It made her happy to make her parents happy. Cherry had protested bitterly when Belinda had decided to study in London, but her father had been a rock. 'You go, Belinda,' he had said. 'I'll settle it with your mother.'

At the time she met him, Charlie had been a film and book critic and would-be screenwriter, eventually getting a low-budget screenplay made which won some good reviews, especially in New York where the critics thought that anything small, underlit and English was probably art. Belinda's career had been slower. She was too American, too pretty and too young to be taken seriously in London.

'Sorry about that,' Charlie would joke, 'we Brits are suspicious of good looks, especially American good looks. I suppose it's because we're an ugly nation and we get jealous. We associate prettiness with flippancy and lack of character – all right if you want to play cute waitresses all your life, but if you want a *serious* career you need an interesting face, a big mouth perhaps, or Easter Island forehead, and perhaps a couple of warts and buck teeth thrown in to be absolutely certain. But don't worry, I love you, pretty as you are.' Then he had written *Shadows on a Wall*.

She found his present in Waterstone's bookshop on Princes Street. It was a new book of movie trivia, a compendium of ten thousand pieces of more or less useless information. She knew he would like it. He liked anything about film. Tonight might see his first production in the theatre, but movies were Charlie's real love.

(iii)

Billy telephoned home from a call box just before the performance. Whenever he was away he telephoned every day, just to reassure himself. Now that Ilse was pregnant again there was even more reason. She hadn't much to tell him: the bank had phoned again wondering when they might expect some 'new funds', there seemed to be some problem with the wistaria growing around the top of the drainpipe which was causing damp down one bathroom wall, and Benedict had found a frog in the garden. He told her how they were all excited about the first night, but he didn't tell her about the hole in the exhaust on the van: it would be expensive to repair and would only worry her. He spoke to each of the three children in turn, as he always did, just a few seconds each, asking them what they had been doing, told Ilse not to bother about the bank, and, as he heard her orchestrating a noisy 'good luck for tonight, Daddy', he hung up.

He was a lucky man, he thought as he headed back up the hill towards James' Court Hall, even if he was broke.

Chapter Six

(i)

'A crocodile. That's what we were, a crocodile. All the way up the Golden Mile . . .'
    'The Royal Mile.'
'All right, the Royal Mile. Everyone looking at us, Americans taking photographs to show in Iowa, Japanese giggling into their video cameras, Germans wondering why we weren't all goose-stepping . . . God, I could have died of shame.' The speaker was a square-faced, sixteen-year-old schoolgirl with a butterfly clip in a side parting, a brace on her front teeth and a stalwart chest.

Alongside her Sadie Corchoran, also sixteen, but slighter, almost boyish in figure, dark haired and pretty, was staring through the thick lenses of her black-rimmed glasses at a photocopied programme, patiently weathering the gales of indignation while trying to read. Claire was her best friend and they had been inseparable for years, Claire usually exaggerating and pretending to moan, Sadie listening and correcting. At this moment, however, Sadie was also half-reading a potted biography of Marie Walewska in the dim interval lights of James' Court Hall while waiting for the players to re-appear, and wishing that Claire would shut up for just one minute. All right, so they had been marched through the centre of Edinburgh like a bunch of Brownies, but what did it matter? There was something going on here which was absolutely special.

'If I'd known I was going to be treated like a . . .'

'. . . schoolgirl, which is what you are, what I am,' said Sadie without looking up.

'. . . I'd never have let you talk me into coming up here.'

Sadie raised the programme to the light. Claire was a wonderful girl, and as loyal as a leech, but every once in a while she managed to completely miss the point. And the point tonight was sex. The raging hormones which were swelling that brimming bust must clearly be exhausted by the time they reached her brain.

It was the last night of the Queen's Yard School cultural trip to the Edinburgh Festival. It hadn't been compulsory and, coming in the middle of the summer holidays, several girls had claimed prior engagements with families in Tuscany and the Var. Sadie Corchoran, however, had *wanted* to come; and despite the four to a room in a Dundonald Street boarding house administered by 'a sour-faced Scottish virgin of sixty' (as Claire, this week a sour-faced English virgin of sixteen, had described the landlady), despite the petty restrictions imposed by the Misses Tomlinson and Candlin, in whose care the Queen's Yard girls had been placed, despite the queues for the bathroom and jokes about synchronized periods, and the general cultural over-kill of the itinerary, Sadie was having a terrific time.

This play, *Shadows on a Wall*, for instance, was just astonishing. They had been brought to the first night in Miss Candlin's belief that it might be instructive to those taking history. 'As though there isn't enough bloody history in Edinburgh,' Claire had grumbled as they had descended the narrow alley towards the tiny, eighteenth-century James' Court Hall. But if Claire would only concentrate and stop playing with the silver foil on her packet of Polos, she would realize, as Sadie had realized an hour ago, that history hardly came into it. *Shadows on a Wall* was about sex. And few subjects were of greater interest to girls of sixteen.

'Well yes, girls . . . er, of course, the writer has obviously had to resort to trivial, titillating invention to make his dramatic points . . .' Miss Candlin had hissed during the interval as her charges, with the exception of Claire who had gone in search of a Ladies, had stood outside in the courtyard, sucking ice-creams. Miss Candlin liked her history clingfilm wrapped for authenticity, but the image of Napoleon casting aside his green frock-coat and unbuttoning his white, touch-where-they-fitted breeches as he lifted the skirts of the protesting, but not exactly resisting, Marie Walewska, would, everyone knew, stay in the memories of these Queen's Yard girls far longer than the date and terms of his concordat with the Pope.

A spotlight cut through the darkness for the beginning of the second act, hushing the murmurs. Sadie pushed an elbow into Claire's ribs and the noise from the Polo wrapper ceased. It was a tiny space, a theatre in the round, with enough proximity to the actors to be able to see them shake. Camille de Malignon was on stage, waiting for a secret meeting in the rooms of Will Yorke, her American lover, playing nervously with the bright red, thin silk band she wore around her neck. In the first act the band had been unobtrusive, hidden by a cloak and then a high collar. Now, as her conflict of purpose deepened, attention was being deliberately directed towards it. A red collar? The symbol of the guillotine, a metaphor for the scar in Camille de Malignon's personality, Sadie told herself earnestly. She was at an earnest age.

The blood red on white flesh was now strangely exciting to her. The collar, and probably much else, would surely be unpeeled during the next hour, and Sadie found herself shifting forward in her seat in expectation. Transfixed, she stared hard at the pretty girl playing Camille de Malignon. The programme had named her as Emma Powers. She was probably the weakest performer in the play, but the part was carrying her through. How lucky she was, Sadie thought, as a few feet from her Camille de Malignon knelt before Will Yorke, her blouse undone, her hair unpinned, and, speaking very quietly, began to recount in detail the events of the day on which her entire family had been guillotined. The audience in the tiny theatre went still in horror. Even Claire stopped fidgeting.

Sadie nodded in the darkness and sucked on the end of a loose strand of hair. She had just realized something she must have known subconsciously all her life. She was going to be an actress. Camille de Malignon should have been her part.

(ii)

Charlie's throat was dry, his tongue felt heavy and even shallow breathing seemed an effort. He had never known tension like it. It was one of the smallest productions in Edinburgh, but his nerves were shaved bare. The reaction during the interval had been muted, as though no-one wanted to betray how they were feeling. Oona McDonald from the festival office had been there with the chap from the *Scotsman*. He had looked bored. No-one else looked much like a drama critic: but then, what did critics look like? They couldn't all have horns and tails. Charlie had not been thrilled to see Larry, his agent, there, drinking the free wine with a pretty girl, and murmuring good luck with the expression of a defence lawyer to the condemned on the morning of execution. Larry had never liked *Shadows on a Wall*.

A few feet from him Belinda was waiting to go on. The play was drawing towards its climax. Charlie thought she had never looked so beautiful, poised as he had never before seen her. The theatre went black. Amanda, the stage manager, pressed a button on a tape recorder. A rumble of distant thunder suddenly exploded into close cannon fire; the beginning of the end for Napoleon. Belinda walked on to the stage.

By his side Billy grinned as the audience reacted to the roar of battle. Charlie and he had spent days selecting and recording their sound effects. 'Will you take a wee dram?' he whispered in a stage Scottish accent, pulling a hip-flask from his pocket.

Charlie put the bottle to his lips and tasted the malt. Billy had never cared much about drink. The tension must have been getting to him, too.

Then suddenly it was over. The first act had seemed interminable, the second had raced by. The audience was applauding, the cast were taking their curtain-calls, which, in the absence of a curtain meant they were making several trips back and forth to the small open area, and Billy was thumping him on the back.

Now Charlie swallowed a real mouthful of whisky.

'Lie to me, Charlie,' Belinda said, throwing her arms around him.

He kissed her. She was still shaking. 'No need. You were wonderful. Better than wonderful,' he said. He meant it.

Belinda was dizzy with relief. Even Neil Burgess looked pleased. 'Well, Neil, what do you think?' she asked.

The actor smiled. 'Not what I think, dear girl, although of course I think you were as brilliant as I knew you would be. What the critics think is all that matters. Has one, I wonder, been noticed?'

They were congregated in the courtyard outside the hall, reluctant to leave, Billy thanking the festival organizers, Emma Powers being cool and sexy towards an agent who was telling her how good she had been, and everyone else relishing the praise from friends and members of the public who had stayed behind. It doesn't matter what the critics say, Belinda was thinking, we have our success. This moment is perfect. These people liked it, or they wouldn't still be here. Bob and Cherry would have been proud of her.

Close by Charlie was drinking more quickly and talking more loudly than usual to a young man who had asked for a quote for the festival newspaper. 'The tricky thing is conveying great moments of history in such a tiny hall,' he was pronouncing. 'But, in a way, it helps, because although history is always on a massive scale, it's the characters that we're really interested in, and if we were able to afford a vast theatre and a revolving set and a computerized light system, the sort of spectacular things they do in West End musicals, we'd almost certainly lose sight of what the play is really about. Which is you, me and her, if you like. I don't think you need to see the armies of Europe in conflict to understand *Shadows on a Wall*. Napoleon the lover was a different man from Napoleon the conqueror. If we tried to do *Shadows on a Wall* big we'd ruin it.'

'You should hear Charlie justifying the smallness of the production,' Belinda laughed, as she handed Billy a glass of wine. 'We'll never get a transfer to anywhere, never mind the West End, if he carries on like this.'

'He isn't necessarily right, either,' said Billy. '*Shadows on a Wall* can be as big or as small as we choose to make it. That's the beauty of it.'

They stood and watched, dawdling in the courtyard, Sadie
Corchoran and a still-complaining Claire, who was certain that
the Misses Tomlinson and Candlin would make haggis of their
livers when they noticed they were missing. Sadie was having
none of it. Nothing mattered but to get close to the rag and
tag of scruffy players, in their old coats with collars turned up
against the Edinburgh night.

'They look paler and dirtier out here, and he looks older,'
Claire murmured as Napoleon and the two young men who
had mostly played soldiers strode off into the Lawnmarket in
search of a pub.

'Sshh,' Sadie hissed. The American girl, who only a few
minutes earlier had been Napoleon's mistress, was going around
filling wine glasses. Picking up one which had been abandoned
she waited her turn.

'I'm afraid there isn't much left . . .' the actress said and
poured the last of a bottle of Bulgarian burgundy into Sadie's
glass. She was, Sadie realized, even fairer than she had appeared
in the play: a beautiful, creamy blonde who, now wearing an
old black coat, carried that casual demeanour of intellectual style.
That's how I would like to look, Sadie thought.

'We loved the play,' she blushed. 'You were terrific. I think
it's brilliant.' She had enthused more than she intended and
instantly regretted it. Professional actors probably heard this
sort of flattery all the time.

But instead of looking bored the leading lady shone with
pleasure. 'Really? You really think that? That's so nice of you.
You've no idea.'

At her side Sadie felt Claire move from one heavy foot to the
other.

A fair, clean-looking man wearing glasses was hovering.

'Have you met Charlie?' The actress offered. 'Charles Holyoake . . . I'm sorry, I don't know your . . . ?'

'Sadie Corchoran and . . .' But Claire had wandered away to
get a better view of Will Yorke. *God, the writer!* thought Sadie,
words fleeing her.

Charles Holyoake looked awkward, as though anxious to
follow Belinda Johnson who was being summoned away to
say good night to someone's mother.

'I was wondering . . .' Sadie said, searching for something to say.

'Yes?'

Nothing came. '. . . if you'd sign my programme,' she bleated weakly. It was so feeble she blushed. She hadn't asked for an autograph since she was twelve. She'd been hoping to give such a grown-up impression.

But Charles Holyoake looked pleased. 'I'd love to,' he said, and, taking a pen from his pocket, he scribbled his name. 'To tell you the truth, Sadie, this is the first time anybody asked me for my autograph. It's exciting.'

'Really?'

'Really.'

That opened the floodgates. Where had the idea for the play come from? she asked. And Camille de Malignon, was she fact, fiction or somewhere in the middle? Had she been right about the red band around her neck? What was the symbolism in the ending and was there anywhere she could buy a copy of the text? Lastly came the real question. 'I wonder . . . I live in London, too. Could I perhaps come and see you, and join your company? I'm always in school plays and I want to be an actress . . . well, I'm going to be an actress.'

'Sadie!' Miss Tomlinson's voice scythed across the courtyard. Claire was already under arrest.

'Oh crikey! I'm sorry, I must go. Thank you. It was wonderful.' And with that she hurried away to join her teacher. 'Sorry,' she said. 'I was just coming.'

'God, there we were risking rape, loot and pillage at the very least in that back alleyway. I mean everyone knows what a randy lot actors are, and then in comes Skull Tomlinson looking more like the Grim Reaper with every breath . . .' They were lying in bed with the lights out and Claire was re-living their evening, over-dramatizing as usual. 'I mean, you might at least have chosen one with a bulge in his trousers, Sadie. The one you were talking to wasn't even in it . . .'

Sadie wasn't listening. She was picturing herself kneeling in a spotlight, a long dress spreading about her, as slowly and delicately she unfastened a thin red ribbon from around her neck.

Chapter Seven

(i)

It was the best twenty-ninth birthday present he could have wished himself, and he reread the final paragraph, slowly and out loud, looking for the hidden poison. There wasn't any. '*Shadows on a Wall is an almost perfect piece and Charles Holyoake a rare find among modern playwrights in that he can actually tell a story: a story which moves, amuses, engages the brain and startles, a small story set across a momentous tide of history, a story of human strengths, passions and frailties, of revolution, murder, assassination and betrayal; but, not least,* Shadows on a Wall *is a story which gives Belinda Johnson as Napoleon's ill-starred Polish mistress, Marie Walewska, the part of a lifetime. Quite simply Miss Johnson is superb. If you see nothing else this year see* Shadows on a Wall.'

Belinda's head emerged slowly from under the duvet. Her face was smudged with mascara, her eyes still closed. It had been a very late night. 'If this is some kind of joke, Charlie . . .'

Charlie shook his head. 'No joke. It's the same in the *Guardian*. I think the buggers liked it.'

'Come on . . .' Suspiciously Belinda lifted herself gently up the pillows, felt for her glasses among the books on the floor, and took the newspaper from him. As the print came into focus her jaw visibly loosened. *Shadows on a Wall* was the lead festival review in both the *Scotsman* and the *Guardian*. Under the *Scotsman* headline, 'SHADOWS OF BRILLIANCE', was

62

a two-column photograph of Belinda as Marie Walewska alongside Neil Burgess as Napoleon.

Charlie watched as she read. He had been awake early, slipping out to buy the papers from the newsagent at the end of the road, taking care not to disturb her. It might have been bad news, and no-one wants to be woken to bad news.

She read slowly, as though afraid to believe it, too. First one paper, then the other. Finally she stared in a long silence at the photograph of herself. 'They don't just *like* it, Charlie,' she said. 'The buggers don't just *like* it, the buggers absolutely *love* it. Oh, my God!' And flopping back in the narrow bed she gave a little high-pitched squeal of excitement.

Charlie smiled fondly. The *bugger* word didn't quite fit on her lips; she always sounded so much more American first thing in the morning.

'Take off your clothes, Charlie, and come back to bed,' she said at last, pushing the newspapers aside. 'I want to be ravished by a successful playwright.'

'Supposing I'm only a five-minute wonder,' Charlie replied, as he quickly undressed again and took the phone off its cradle.

'Five minutes!' Belinda's blue actress's eyes widened. 'As long as that! Things really are looking up. It must be my birthday, too.'

Making love on a Friday morning in the middle of the Edinburgh Festival in a borrowed students' flat with a corner of floral wallpaper beginning to peel off one wall, a skylight with iron bars, and a battered, hollowed single bed which creaked with every movement: this was the moment Charlie would later remember as the best of times, a stolen, extra, loving hour with the ghost of the perfume he had bought Belinda as a first-night present mingling now with the scents of their bodies and that of the freshly ironed duvet cover. Billy had been right: they did have a hit. The *Guardian* had said it, the *Scotsman* had confirmed it; and, best of all, it was a shared success.

Afterwards they lay silently for a while, Charlie gazing upwards through the skylight, watching the wind whipping clouds past the chimney stack, Belinda, her face on his chest, her breath on his skin, her body folded against his.

When conversation returned it was of a kind of future. 'Perhaps now someone will take us into the West End . . .' Charlie mused. 'Or the National Theatre. No, on second thoughts, not the National. There's more money in the West End.'

'Would that mean Jo Allen's and Café Pelican for dinner twice a week . . . ?'

'And hobnobbing at awards ceremonies.'

'Then a television version. BBC2, I think.'

'And a Broadway production . . .'

'Bob and Cherry would love that,' Belinda said. 'Can you imagine? Then, perhaps later, a shack in a valley in Provence, I think, if it hasn't been overrun, somewhere for us to do up and invite Billy and Ilse and the children to come and stay . . . or what about Jamaica in January, a year next January, of course? Then later on, more plays for you, more parts for me, leading parts . . . television roles . . . maybe even movie offers—'

Charlie stopped her there. 'Not movies. The British don't make movies: not proper movies, anyway,' he reasoned. 'Well, not often, and when we do we nearly always screw it up. You'd have to go to Hollywood to be in movies, and I hope you don't.'

Belinda wrinkled her nose. 'Shh, Charlie, you're spoiling things. Let me chase my rainbows for a while,' she scolded. 'This is my dream, too, you know.'

So they lay happily for a little longer, an hour when the world stopped on Charlie Holyoake's twenty-ninth birthday, he looked through his new book on movie trivia, and they basked in their morning-after glory.

(ii)

Belinda bought the cake, the cast paid for the champagne and Billy took the pictures: lunchtime in the Jolly Judge celebrating Charlie's birthday. By then the *Edinburgh Evening News* was on the streets with more praise. Everyone was happy: everyone had a mention; no-one had been hurt. That was important.

Billy had been having breakfast in his Leith digs when the landlady had interrupted to say there was a call from London. It was Ilse. She had read the review in the *Guardian* to the children over breakfast, although at seven, five and two she thought it unlikely they would have gathered its full significance.

It was, Billy knew, only a little victory in a career of little victories, some prestige but numerous financial set-backs. If he didn't find some decent paying work soon he would be in serious trouble. No, that wasn't true. He was already in serious trouble. For a moment he wondered if he should call his agent and see if she could get him a corporate video to direct. But even as the thought came he dismissed it. He wouldn't be any good at it. And now Charlie had spoiled him with *Shadows on a Wall*.

He sipped the champagne. So long as Ilse and the children were healthy and the work was worthwhile he would keep hoping. 'Happy birthday, Charlie,' he said, raising his glass.

A new voice boomed like a cannon across the bar. 'Yes, happy birthday, Charlie. Is it your birthday? I didn't know!' It was Larry, Charlie's agent, trailing behind him an esoteric-looking chap with a little beard, a tweed jacket and a navy-blue shirt. Billy knew him vaguely from alternative pantomime. He ran the Jupiter Theatre in London.

October, 1991

The screenplay

Chapter Eight

C harlie heard the answering machine take the call. He
was lying in his bath, the bathroom door slightly ajar.
He liked ignoring calls in this way: it built up a sense
of expectation for when he played back the messages. He picked
up his watch off the side panel. It was nearly midday. Belinda
would be home from the gym soon. He always looked forward
to her coming back from anywhere.

Stretching out his leg he wrapped his toes around the hot tap
and refreshed the water. He had been there for some time and
the temperature was down to tepid. He couldn't think in tepid
water.

When Belinda had first come to live with him it had been
to his rented squalor in North Kensington, the only tidy area
of his life being the space on his desk in front of his word
processor and the shelves bearing the hundreds of movies he had
recorded from television. For three years it had been cosy, and
extremely cheap, but in the end a decision had been demanded:
either the films would have to go or they would. Consequently
the previous winter they had moved into something bigger
and better, a flat over two floors just off the Fulham Road,
Charlie keeping his North Kensington basement as a store for
his videos and books: it was *that* cheap. 'One day I'll turn it into
a proper office so that I have somewhere to go when I want
to get away from your nagging,' he had teased. But Belinda
hadn't nagged and Charlie had rarely gone back, lending or

sub-letting his old place to poorer friends. And it had been to their new home that they had returned after Edinburgh, merry with optimism and with *Shadows on a Wall* booked into the Jupiter Theatre until December.

The Jupiter wasn't the West End, but it was next door. Once a flower wholesalers, it had a reputation for small, vogueish productions, which suited *Shadows on a Wall* perfectly. There was even a chance Charlie might begin to recoup some of the money he had laid out on the production, although he was in no hurry. He had put on *Shadows on a Wall* to prove a point and give Belinda a platform, and he had achieved both. They weren't exactly front-page news, but they had been noticed. Now in London, with more good reviews, although not so extravagant as those in Edinburgh, they were finding their audience.

The move had inevitably brought changes to the play. Some scenes had been rewritten, the first act shortened and some of the cast had left. Neil Burgess had stayed as Napoleon, but Emma Powers had gone off to do a television series in Hong Kong, not before a messy break-up with the actor who played Will Yorke, who had promptly returned to his wife and was now pursuing the sloe-eyed twenty-three year old brought in as Emma's replacement.

What was it about Camille de Malignon? Charlie wondered. They had scarcely opened at the Jupiter before Sadie Corchoran, the schoolgirl with the big eyes who had turned up in Edinburgh, had started coming around two or three times a week.

'She's obsessed with her,' Belinda had said after one visit. 'She hasn't said it, but she desperately wants to play the part.'

'Are you sure it isn't the Two Soldiers or Will Yorke she's obsessed with?' Charlie had asked.

'No. It's Camille de Malignon, all right. She's a weird girl.'

Sadie was, in fact, strange rather than weird. She was intense, yet funny. Everyone liked her. She wasn't a nuisance, but it was a relief that she was still at school. Camille de Malignon was a craze; and like all crazes it would surely pass.

In the mean time everyone's friends had been in to see the play and Charlie's parents had come up from Dorset, pretended not to be embarrassed by the sex – the latest Camille de Malignon was even sexier than the last – and returned carrying photostats of the reviews for Charlie's mother to stick in an album. They were both teachers, reserved, sensible and intelligent. Charlie was their only child. The success of *Shadows on a Wall* was no more than they expected.

These were good times all right, and now Charlie was back in his bath daydreaming about what next to do with his life.

Downstairs he heard the front door open and close, followed by the quick steps of Belinda on the stairs.

'I should have known . . .' Her face came around the door. She was smiling, her plum-coloured track suit damp from the morning's drizzle, her cream hair curling at the ends where it was wet. 'Do you mind if I take a shower now?'

'No.' Charlie didn't move.

'Are you going to get out then?'

'Do I have to?'

'You still like the show, after all this time?'

'It gets better. You're a star now. I like a show with a star.'

'Perhaps a momentary back-street twinkle,' she said, pulling off her clothes. 'Hardly a star.' And stepping into the bath she reached up and turned on the shower.

It was a kind of ritual in their lives. Charlie took so many baths, Belinda would joke, that only by getting in with him could she keep clean.

In his study the telephone rang again; once more the answering machine took the message.

'Hadn't you better answer that?' Belinda asked, her eyes closed, shampoo running in soapy rivulets down her back.

'Why?'

'Well, for one, it might be important . . .'

'And . . . ?'

'Sometimes it would be nice to take a shower and not feel your eyes burning into secret bits that even I can't properly see.'

'Believe me, your secret bits are just sensational.'

'Charlie!!' She grabbed a towel and wiped her eyes.

'Oh, well, all right, all right,' he pretended to grumble, climbing out of the water. 'You'll be sorry one day when I don't want to spend the rest of my life staring at your bottom.'

'Maybe,' she said. 'But I'll be very clean.'

There were four messages waiting. The first two were from friends of Belinda's and the third was a query from Larry, wondering if 'having got Napoleon out of his system' Charlie would like to be put up for a Home Box Office co-production on Stalin. The fourth was the surprise.

71

'Hello, this is Nathalie Seillans,' came a soft growl. 'I was hoping to speak to Charles (pronounced, *Sharle*, the French way) Holyoake (with the H dropped). Is it possible that you could call me, please, Mr Holyoake?' A number followed and then a murmured, 'Thank you and congratulations.'

Nathalie Seillans! Charlie gasped with disbelief. Oh yes! *Love in a Strange Place, Lisa and Louise, The Italian Man's Woman.* A host of vaguely erotic, subtitled, Cameo-Moulin performances mugged him. *Nathalie Seillans!* She'd been such a star. Notorious, really. *Nathalie Seillans!* More than notorious. Infamous! He paused. But that had been some time ago. You didn't hear very much about Nathalie Seillans these days. He played the message again, two, then three times, thrilled. Imagine, Nathalie Seillans on *his* answering machine.

'You know, you've got a really silly expression on your face . . .' Belinda was standing behind him, swathed in towels, looking like an Ottoman prince. He hadn't heard her come down. '. . . like a fourteen year old who's just discovered *Penthouse*. It's only Nathalie Seillans!'

Charlie grinned. 'Didn't she marry somebody?'

'Lots of people, all men, usually other women's husbands.'

'Yes. But someone new. Recently. Someone unlikely.'

Belinda shrugged and rubbed her hair with a towel. 'Well, she isn't marrying you,' she teased. 'I found you first.' And, mock seductively, she loosened the larger of the two towels and let it slide to her mid-thighs, giving him a Nathalie Seillans-type, French, long-exposure flash, this way, that way, every way, before curtsying and hurrying off upstairs to dress, giggling all the way. Belinda's magic came in many manifestations.

Resisting the temptation to follow Charlie sat down at his desk. Nathalie Seillans! Just the thought of her was daunting. At last, nervously, he dialled the number she had left. The phone rang just once.

'Hello, Harvey Bamberg!' It was a slightly nasal, New York intonation, a manufactured accent, an almost successful cover-up of what must once have been Harvey *Bamboig.*

Oh no! Now Charlie remembered. Nathalie Seillans' unlikely new husband was Harvey Bamberg. Not unlikely. Unbelievable.

'Hello! Hello?' Harvey Bamberg was demanding again.

Charlie cleared his throat. 'Er, yes, hello, this is Charles Holyoake . . .' he began. 'I had a message to call—'

The receiver seemed to pop with energy. '*Charlie*, how *are* you? How *are* you? We *loved* the play. Did I say we *loved* it? I'm telling lies. Much more than that. We *adored* it. It's so *real*, so *moving*. But you know that. Of *course* you do. You wrote it, for God's sake. It's terrific. When can we get together?'

To the best of his memory Charlie had never actually met the now very friendly Harvey Bamberg, although he had seen him a few times, usually under the arm of some statuesque, anonymous blonde. 'Well, er—' he began, thrown.

Bamberg was ready. 'I know. You want Nathalie. She's right here. Wait while I get her . . .' Then, slightly more distantly: 'Here you go, Nathalie. The guy's a genius. More than a genius.'

Charlie knew this was intended for him to hear, but he enjoyed it, anyway.

Suddenly Nathalie Seillans was on the line. 'Hello, Mr Holyoake, thank you for calling back so soon. Can I ask you one question?' Her mouth was so near the speaker it sounded as though she were whispering something dirty under the sheets.

'Well yes, of course . . .' Charlie could feel the silly expression creeping across his face again.

'Will you have lunch with me, please? It would be my pleasure.' Pause. 'Just you and me.'

He knew he was being set up. He didn't know why: he didn't care. He thought about the scene with the bidet in *The Italian Man's Woman* and booked a table for two at the Chelsea Arts Club for just one hour's time.

'Pathetic,' Belinda laughed as he wondered what to wear.

'Yes,' he agreed, but Nathalie Seillans was Nathalie Seillans and was probably used to men being pathetic.

When he arrived she was already there, sitting at a table under a large painting of a voluptuous nude which he believed to be Pharaoh's wife trying to seduce Joseph in his many coloured coat. For a moment he watched her from the doorway, plucking up the courage to approach. She was no longer the twenty-two-year old sexual waif of *La Chambre*, but, at forty-five plus, according to the film encyclopedia he had consulted before leaving home (fifty plus by his own reckoning), with her bracelets, necklaces and rings, silver streaks among the highlights and plumper across the chest and rump, she was scarcely less devastating. The table was set for three, although he had only booked for two. Obviously his request had been countermanded. Harvey Bamberg would be joining them later. He had half-expected that.

'I will come straight to the point, Charles,' she was murmuring almost before he had sat down. 'Harvey and I, we think your play is a masterpiece. Something that is perfect, almost too perfect. Do you know, I cried last night, Charles, I was so moved. Oh yes. I saw you at the theatre at the end, coming to meet your girlfriend. Am I right? I had hoped to talk to you, but I was too emotional, too in love with what I had just been a part of . . . Do you understand what I am saying, Charles?'

I wonder if she did do the three-in-a bed scene for real in *The Italian Man's Woman*, Charlie was asking himself. At the time there had been a minor scandal in France when the director had appeared to admit on a television chat show that things had got out of control during shooting. But directors always said that when they wanted to hype a movie.

The waitress came, took their order and left. Nathalie Seillans hardly paused for breath. 'Naturally, the story of Marie Walewska is better known in France than it is in England or America, and in Poland, of course, everyone knows it. But what makes your story so . . . how shall I say? . . . so universal, is the sub-plot, Camille de Malignon and the American . . . How do you call him?'

She really had the most extraordinary bosom, Charlie was thinking, almost hydraulically suspended, like an old Citroën DS, seemingly capable of going up and down independently of the rest of her body. 'Er, Will Yorke,' he said, becoming aware that she was watching him studying her breasts.

With difficulty he raised his eyes and tried to concentrate upon what she was saying, but immediately her mouth got in the way of her words. What was it about French women: why the continual pout, the bee-stung swollen lips? The language helped, of course, but he didn't remember being mesmerized by de Gaulle's lips or Mitterrand's the way he now was by those of Nathalie Seillans. And he was reminded of a scene in *Chloe Est Morte* which had consisted of nothing more than three minutes of her eating strawberries, large, juicy, pudenda-shaped ones, so ripe that she had had to lick her fingers continually as she ate. He had never seen anyone lick her fingers like Nathalie Seillans.

74

'So, Harvey says, "Darling you must meet him. Charles Holyoake is an artist. If a movie is to be made from *Shadows on a Wall* he will want only the best people to work with him . . ." '

Reality peered up at Charlie from out of his watercress soup. 'A movie?'

'But, of course. Harvey and I, we want to take an option on *Shadows on a Wall* and for you to write a screenplay. We want to make a wonderful movie, not something big with Hollywood stars. Something small and perfect. Like the play. A bijou. Do you understand, Charles?'

Charlie was confused. 'A movie for you to appear in?' He realized at once his mistake.

Nathalie Seillans gave him the longest, saddest stare. 'Charles, we have mirrors in France, too, you know.'

'I meant . . .' he began, but she was shaking her head.

'Twenty years ago I would have kidnapped you, I would have seduced you, I would have kept you in my bed until you promised me I could have the part . . .'

Charlie swallowed.

'. . . but now, I am a realist. I want to produce *Shadows on a Wall* with Harvey. I want to make a movie we can all be proud of. Something worthwhile.'

At around this point Charlie began to wonder why she had come straight to him instead of going the formal route through his agent. But before he could enquire further, a short, pink, bald, round man in his late fifties, wearing a grotesquely expensive, green, epauletted leather jacket, appeared at his side.

Harvey Bamberg, one of the most consistently unsuccessful movie producers in the world, pushed out a hand. 'What *about* this? The *man* of the *moment!*' He glowed. 'Harvey Bamberg! Thrilled to meet you at last. How are you two getting along?'

Charlie called in at the Chelsea Cinema on his way home. He needed to collect his thoughts. They were showing a new Japanese film which had received brilliant reviews. He left after the second reel.

Harvey Bamberg took the long way home because Nathalie had seen a painting in Cork Street on which she wanted his opinion. He knew that what she really meant was, 'Darling, will you buy it for me?', but she was never so crude, not when it came to money, anyway. Naturally he did buy it for her, although it cost £17,900. He even quite liked it, a harlequin with an arrow through his eye, standing on a globe in the form of an apple and blowing gently on the body of a naked girl which he was holding cupped in the palms of his hands. The man in the gallery talked a lot about surrealism, but Harvey refrained from making a joke about the surrealistic prices of one-eyed harlequins these days. Nathalie didn't always get his jokes; but she had a great ass, and she drove a hell of a bargain when it came to scriptwriters.

Chapter Nine

(i)

'**A** movie? You're kidding. They want to option *Shadows on a Wall* for a movie and you're hesitating?' Belinda had been sitting at the kitchen table writing a letter home to Philadelphia when Charlie had arrived back.

'There's a catch. They're broke apparently. They want a cheap option and a first draft screenplay for hardly any money.'

'Oh, I see.' Belinda suddenly giggled. 'No wonder Harvey Bamberg sent his wife along. Imagine, Nathalie Seillans going bust! Sorry, bad pun. What's she like these days, anyway. Gruesome?'

'Not exactly,' Charlie said.

Belinda raised one eyebrow. It was her new trick. 'Oh really? I hope you told them which way the river was they had to jump into.'

Charlie shook his head. 'Not exactly,' he said again.

' "Not exactly, not exactly"? What is this? You don't mean you're thinking about it. You're crazy.'

'Well—'

'You must see they're just trying to con you, Charlie. Wow, Nathalie Seillans must still really be some girl.'

'There's something else,' Charlie said.

'I'll bet.'

'They want Billy to direct and you to play the lead.'

*　　*　　*

77

Belinda needed a cup of tea to recover. It was impossible not to be excited. 'A movie. A real movie?' she kept repeating. 'And me the *star*? Oh my God!'

Charlie nodded. 'That's what they said. A *small* movie. A sort of art-house thing. Low budget. Tiny probably. But a movie, all right.'

'I don't know what to say. Garbo Lives!' Suddenly Belinda broke into a fit of giggles. 'Or maybe Doris Day? Wait till they hear this in Philadelphia! My mother will tell the whole neighbourhood.' She paused. 'What's he like, by the way?'

'Harvey Bamberg?' Charlie scratched his head. 'I don't know, really. A duplicitous little hustler? A smiling, fork-tongued con-man? A cuddly monster? Actually it's difficult not to like him because he's so transparently on the make, and such a hopeless liar. Maybe we should admire him, because he's been doing the impossible for years. I mean, he *does* get movies made.'

Belinda worried about that for a moment and then said: 'Yes, I know but . . . well, I mean, such as . . . ?'

'Such as? Well . . . something about dogs a couple of years ago, a sort of politically correct *Lassie*, and another about a drugs syndicate and crooked cops. And wasn't there one about mercenaries which they shot in some botanical garden in Sussex because they couldn't afford to go to Asia? That sort of thing.'

'Oh . . .' Belinda still looked vague.

'The way he tells it everybody is his friend, although I think one or two might question that. He's a good talker. He knows which shoulders to squeeze, which wives to flatter, which tax shelters to plunder and which studio executives to cut in. All that stuff.'

'But he's a rogue?'

'Oh yes, and cinematically illiterate.' Charlie pondered for a moment, then he said: 'But maybe it isn't such a surprise that he ended up with Nathalie Seillans.'

'I thought you said she still looked good?'

'Better than good. Great. But any man who has survived as long as Harvey Bamberg turning other people's money into movies by way of his own bank account must have something going for him.'

Belinda laughed. 'She probably loves him because he's a wonderful, passionate, romantic lover.'

Charlie shrugged. 'I don't know about that. But he loves her. I could see that. It's sort of touching, he's so proud of her.'

'Is that so? Well, I think you'd better call Billy and Larry before she starts touching you.'

With a couple of hours to fill before she had to be at the theatre, Belinda decided to go for a walk. The world was turning cartwheels around her and she needed to collect her thoughts. She didn't intend it, but somehow she ended up in a video shop on the Fulham Road. Shop? Suddenly it was a grotto. There were just so *many* movies. Maybe next year, she imagined, 'Belinda Johnson in *Shadows on a Wall*'.

A familiar voice cut through her reverie. 'Hey, how are you?' It was Sally Parsons, the tortured English rose from her year at drama school who had never stopped working, and without whom no television serial now seemed complete.

Belinda's heart sank. 'Oh, yes . . . hello!' Sally always made her feel inadequate. If she had seen her coming she would have hidden behind the counter.

'I see it's congratulations time. Well done at Edinburgh. I do love the fringe, it's so . . . *well, wonderfully* naïve and optimistic.'

What she really means is *amateur*, Belinda was thinking. The bitch! Still, she looked better now that her teeth had been straightened. 'Yes, it was wonderful,' she said.

'And now at the Jupiter. Marvellous. *So* cosy.'

Small, the subtitles would have read. 'It's perfect for us,' she batted back, noting that Sally's hair was still thin.

'I'm sure, I'm sure. I've been longing to come in and see you. I've heard such good things. Terrific reviews . . . the one I read, anyway. But this is my only free day in . . . God, I don't know. It seems like forever. I'm doing the new Stefan Turner film. He's so brilliant.'

And, as Charlie would say, as boring as buggery, Belinda thought, wondering if Sally was sleeping with him, and then wondered why she was wondering. She always did. 'Really,' she said.

'I do love filming. It can be *tedious*! But such fun and so fascinating, you've no idea . . .'

Belinda never knew where the words came from. It wasn't like her. She just said it. 'That would be a *television* film? Yes?'

'Well, obviously. Who gets to make real movies around here these days?' Sally laughed at the idea.

'Well . . . actually . . . we're going to be filming *Shadows on a Wall* early next year. Nothing massive, just a small, well-made English movie . . . for the cinema. We're all very pleased. I'll be playing Marie Walewska again, of course . . .'

Sally Parsons's expression quietly froze.

God forgive me, Belinda thought, as she hurried towards the Underground station, I'm going mad: two feet off the ground, balloons in my hair and floating.

(ii)

'If they haven't got the money to pay for the screenplay where are they going to find the money to make the film?' agent Larry mused lugubriously. It was nearly eight. Larry was still in his office: one of the drawbacks to being a literary agent in London was the need to stay late in order to do business with California. (On the plus side was the Indian rug, the well-stocked refrigerator and Emma, the wide-bottomed secretary with brown legs in summer, loose skirts in winter and a very gullible husband.)

'Right,' said Charlie, trying not to sound disappointed.

'It's the same everywhere these days, everyone wanting something for nothing.'

Ah well . . . Since Belinda had left Charlie had been trying unsuccessfully to get hold of Billy. Now Larry was calling back to burst all the afternoon's bubbles.

Then Larry hesitated. 'Although I suppose we might . . .' He went silent.

'We might what?'

'Well, I was just thinking. I mean, if you *wanted* to write the screenplay, I mean *really* wanted to write it, doing it like this, without a decent fee, although I'm sure I can get you something . . . well, it puts you in a hell of a strong position . . .'

'Like?'

'Well . . . look at it from the other side, the weak side where you get bundles of money up front. Supposing, just supposing, Columbia or Paramount or Fox or whoever come along and see the play and love it, and they might, they just might, stranger things have happened. And they take an option for a mountain of money and commission a screenplay for a lot more . . . And it's possible, it's not likely, but it's possible. So you set to work, and your work is brilliant, as we know it will be. And you think everything is wonderful. Terrific!'

He paused for effect. Charlie waited for the down-side. Larry had majored in pessimism.

'Unfortunately, as we all know, all it takes is for some ambitious, seventeen-year-old studio executive right out of the creative department at Burbank or Century City or wherever they grow them, some *magna cum laude* kid trying to make a name for herself, to start talking you down, saying your screenplay needs this and it needs that and a new angle if it's going to appeal to anyone under forty, and maybe a car chase or two and the occasional gang rape, no major surgery, you understand, but maybe this Marie Walewska shouldn't be Polish, Polacks don't sell movies, that maybe she should be, I don't know, *Moroccan* say, a real, foxy lady, maybe a part for Whitney Houston there or Robin Givens, a sort of reversal of Othello and Desdemona, and maybe they could even come up with a title song for her if it is Whitney Houston . . .' Larry paused again. He was on good form.

'Like I say, stranger things have happened. Or maybe it'll be the director who decides he's at that stage in his career when he wants to become known as a hyphenate, a director-*hyphen*-writer, and decides the best way of doing it is by rewriting your screenplay and taking half your points with him. And suddenly, before you know it, there you are with your upfront dollars, back on the plane out of LA, wondering what happened to all the promises and bowls of fruit they left in your suite in the Sunset Marquis.'

Charlie laughed. This was the paranoid way writers saw themselves in Hollywood: first in and first out. But perhaps there were just a lot of bad writers in Hollywood. Whatever, they were always first to cash the cheque.

Now Larry became abrupt. 'Anyway, I can't sit here gossiping with you all night, I have a wife to cheat on.'

Charlie persisted. 'What about, you know, the other situation, the strong position where I write the screenplay for hardly any money?'

By now Larry sounded almost bored. Obvious non-starters

like *Shadows on a Wall* always bored him. 'Well, I suppose you name your own terms really. A whacking great percentage, a large fee on the first day of shooting . . . a co-producer credit, if you want it, director approval, maybe even cast approval, I suppose, leading players, anyway, to make sure no-one tries to out Belinda. Everything would be open to negotiation, but as you own the thing, and they say they can't afford to buy it, which frankly I don't believe for one minute, you could insist on quite a lot. I mean you could always say "no", which has to be the ultimate control. What's Nathalie Seillans like these days, anyway?'

'Tidal.'

'What?'

'Her bosoms are tidal, rising and falling in regular cycles. It's something to see.'

'You don't say! Look, why don't I talk to Harvey Bamberg and tell him if he can't afford to pay you're not interested and to stop wasting our time . . . ?'

Charlie hesitated. At the Jupiter Theatre they would be well into the first act and he imagined Belinda, her cream hair falling in braids, her white, neo-classical gown, simple like a night-dress, square and low across the chest. Belinda was so good in the part. Could she really be a film star? Obviously Nathalie Seillans and Harvey Bamberg thought so. At last he said: 'I don't know, Larry . . . maybe it wouldn't do any harm to think about it . . .'

From the other end of the phone he was almost certain he heard an alligator smile.

(iii)

It was after eleven when Belinda arrived home, noisy, happy, and almost running up the stairs. 'Charlie, you should have been there tonight. It was a full house. They *loved* us.'

'What? Oh yes, good.' Charlie was sitting hunched over his word processor.

Going around behind him she pushed her face into his hair. 'What are you doing?'

'Oh, you know . . .'

Belinda peered at the words on the screen. ' "*Exterior. Estate of Polish Country House. Day*".' She stopped. 'This is a movie script.'

Charlie looked embarrassed. 'Not really. Nothing's decided. I was just, you know, playing with the pictures in my mind . . . seeing if perhaps it might just make a little movie.' He smiled and took off his glasses. 'Just looking at the shadows on the wall, I suppose . . .'

Belinda frowned. 'But not for me, all right. Don't just do it for me, will you? Promise.'

'Hey, come on, what do you think I am, some kind of dummy?'

'Honest answer?'

'Honest answer.'

'Yes,' she said.

Chapter Ten

(i)

Harvey Bamberg pulled his green plastic visor down and waited for the ball to be served. It was a fine day for October, but the sun was low and getting in his eyes. On court next to him Nathalie waited. She was wearing a baby-blue track suit, with a matching headband, and she was putting Edward Lampton, the fellow serving, off his stroke. This was unusual. Not much put Edward Lampton off his stroke. He was a funeral director, the best in Britain, they said: the richest, certainly, and rightly so. Lampton Funerals, the budget chain of value for money mourning, were renowned throughout the country. No-one could undercut Lamptons, with their Chiltern beech coffins and crushed cream satin upholstery, their fleets of custom-built German hearses, and specially sprung, low-geared for grief-in-comfort, ten-seated for grief-in-numbers, limousines. All this interested Harvey. Edward Lampton interested him.

The ball was in the air. A moment's tension. Edward Lampton arched. His racquet went back. There was the slightest peripheral movement from Nathalie at the net. Thud. With a spring the ball jetted towards Harvey, caught the ribbon, spun high into the air, and fell limply to the ground on the server's side. Double fault. Love-Forty. Edward grimaced. Nathalie moved gracefully to the back of the court to receive: Harvey stepped forward, a slight smile at the corners of his lips. Gamesmanship: Nathalie knew everything there was to know about gamesmanship.

Harvey liked to play tennis in the afternoons, not because he enjoyed running about, his legs were too short for that, but because tennis was a useful social skill in the movie industry: on one occasion, while staying in Beverly Hills, he had almost found himself partnering Robert Wagner. So, a couple of afternoons a week, he would spend an hour or two at the courts practising his cunning and compensating for his lack of speed with a top spin deceptively quick in one so flabby. Usually he went alone and met up with Edward or perhaps the Italians who owned restaurants in the Notting Hill Gate area, fellows like himself, fiftyish, with their afternoons free, who would take time out once in a while to watch the young housewives' class on the adjacent courts; but sometimes he would take Nathalie along, to show her off, so to speak. The Italians liked that and Nathalie didn't complain, either.

Edward was now smiling at Nathalie. She smiled back and ran the back of her free hand across her lips. Edward served, a gentleman's shot, high and bouncy and smack in the centre of the court. Nathalie stepped forward and lashed it into the far corner past Edward's partner, the sporting wife of a German banker they'd found loitering in the clubhouse.

'Our game,' said Harvey.

'And our set,' said Nathalie and smiled at Edward.

'One set all,' said Edward and smiled at Nathalie.

Renata, the wife of the German banker, who was no mean player and had seen Edward trounce men half his age on other days, wondered what on earth was going on.

'You want to play a decider?' Harvey asked.

'Well, yes, why not?'

Nathalie interrupted. 'Harvey, why don't we change partners? You play with Renata, and I will play with Edward. Would you like that, Edward?'

Edward loved it. Nobody bothered to ask Renata, but, seeing that the switch was so popular, she agreed anyway.

It was a short set. Six-two to Edward and Nathalie, Harvey missing shots he would normally put away without effort.

'Good game, good game,' Edward laughed as he escorted Nathalie off the court, his racquet, almost, but not quite, stroking her still neat, though now plump, French bottom. Since his wife died the previous year Edward had not found much to laugh about.

'Yes. Thank you,' said Renata, more confused than ever, and hurried away to meet her children out of school.

At the clubhouse Nathalie went off to shower while Harvey bought the drinks.

'So how's business?' Edward asked as the two men sat on the terrace.

'Touch wood, never more terrific!' Harvey picked up Edward's racquet, and measured its weight admiringly. 'You know, that forehand of yours . . . wow! Is that some shot! Is that the coach here? Did he put in some time on that?'

Edward was flattered. 'Well, no, not really. When Susan was alive we played a lot. She was an excellent player . . .'

Harvey nodded gently, and left the space open for Edward to fill. He had, he knew, been well primed.

It took a little time, but after a couple of false starts and dead ends Edward eventually stumbled on the right subject. 'Nathalie was telling me about a play you went to see. I don't go to the theatre very often these days.'

'You don't? Edward, do yourself a favour. Break a bad habit. See *Shadows on a Wall*. You'll love it. Did you see the reviews? Sensational! If we weren't so stretched . . .' Harvey shook his head in exasperation. 'Isn't it always the same? All of a sudden we have too much in development. That's the way it goes. Feast or famine. I hate to miss a good thing, though . . .'

'Yes,' Edward said sympathetically. 'I don't know much about theatre.'

'No, of course not.'

Harvey liked Edward. He was a tall man in his sixties, with wavy white hair and muscular arms and shoulders, the reward, he would joke, for carrying so many coffins into Golders Green Crematorium in his younger days. With his tanned, Stewart Granger looks, Edward would also joke that he gave death a healthier image. 'What we have is a growth industry,' he had recently confided between sets. 'Have you noticed how much space is devoted to obituaries in the newspapers these days? Columns and columns on people you've never even heard of. And they all want a good send-off, believe me. Death is big business now, very big, particularly international death.'

'International death?' Harvey had been intrigued.

'Absolutely. With so many people travelling abroad we were finding that more and more of our trade was coming from those succumbing away from home. And that can provoke all kinds of problems for next of kin at a very difficult moment.'

'I can see that.'

'So we started our international service, Lampton Funerals International. Now we have affiliations all over the world.'

'No kidding!'

'Absolutely not. You know, Harvey, when Susan died we were doing China, the two of us, a very interesting holiday, right out there at Badalong Pass. One minute she was taking my picture on the Great Wall; the next, well . . . Would you believe it, Lampton Funerals International had her back here before I got home myself. If ever you need us, God forbid, but if you do, we guarantee world-wide delivery within seventy-two hours of receiving the death certificate and clearance papers, perhaps a little longer at weekends and public holidays, all paper work taken care of, unless, of course, there's a police investigation, everything tasteful and dignified, and a welcoming delegate at the receiving end of the journey. Now, whose service is it?'

Harvey had been impressed. Here was a successful entrepreneur who gave a good service, who had a good service, and who was a hell of a partner when the two of them took on the Italians. He was also, Harvey had not failed to notice, slightly smitten with Nathalie, and, as the two men sipped their drinks and chatted, he noticed that Edward's eyes strayed constantly to the clubhouse door. It was just like Nathalie that when she did reappear the poor man was distracted, watching an opera in a minor key as two Italians debated a line dispute.

'So what are you two conspiring?' she breathed as she came up behind them.

'I was just telling Edward he shouldn't miss *Shadows on a Wall* . . .' said Harvey.

Nathalie, showered and sweet smelling, a fresh pink track suit and matching ribbon having replaced the baby blue, sat down at the wooden table. Edward half-stood and then sat down again. Harvey liked politeness in a man.

'Oh yes. I must see it again,' Nathalie murmured. 'It's so wonderful. It would make the most perfect movie.'

Harvey looked irritated. 'Yes, well, we've been through that, Nathalie. Any other time . . .' He turned to Edward. 'Sorry, Edward, you know how it is. Business. I just wish I'd seen *Shadows on a Wall* three months earlier.' He sighed, then instantly recovered. 'Hey, what about another drink? It's hot work playing against you guys.' And without waiting for a reply he scooped up Edward's empty glass and went off to the bar. At the clubhouse he looked back. Nathalie was smiling at Edward, speaking quietly, forcing him to lean close to hear what she was saying. He nodded happily to himself. He would take his time with the drinks, maybe take a leak, give them a few minutes alone together. It would give Edward a buzz just to be sitting so close to Nathalie. Harvey had never had a Susan, a partner for forty years, but he had seen Edward those first six months after Susan's death when the man had been reduced to bewildered silence. It couldn't be such a bad thing if they brought a little joy back into his life.

On his way to the lavatory Harvey contemplated his good fortune. Nathalie was good at bringing joy – not, perhaps, the way she'd done in the movies or the pirate videos, the fabled out-takes which he hadn't believed until she'd sat and watched them with him, giving a running commentary which would have embarrassed Nero – but joy just the same. She was a wonderful, feminine woman and now a terrific partner in business. And, unless he was way off course, at that very moment Edward Lampton would be suggesting that he accompany her to see *Shadows on a Wall*, if she was sure Harvey wouldn't mind, and she would be accepting.

By the time he rejoined them it was already decided. That coming Friday Edward Lampton was going to the theatre with Nathalie. He looked so thrilled that Harvey was thrilled for him. Once upon a time it had been German and Canadian dentists who provided the seed money for independent movie productions. Now it looked as though it might be funeral directors. Well, why not? Someone had to do it. Edward wouldn't be difficult. He was lonely. Movies meant glamour and fun. Everyone wanted to get into the movies.

'Of course I don't mind,' Harvey beamed. 'Are you kidding? Like I don't trust my friend with my wife? You go. Have a good time. I'll take care of the tickets. I'm telling you, Edward, you'll *love* it. Did I say love it? More than that; you'll be *crazy* about it. It's, how can I say, a work of genius . . . and *so* commercial. Oh yes. What a movie it would make!'

'But can we trust him, Charlie?' Billy Yeo was sitting at a Steenbeck editing machine in a Soho cutting room working on the documentary about the young Chopin he had interrupted for Edinburgh. It had always seemed to him a lucky omen that Chopin's father had taught Marie Walewska to play the piano.

'You don't, obviously,' Charlie said.

Billy rubbed the scar beneath his artificial eye, and stared at the image on the screen. 'The word is he's slippier than a baby in a bath,' he said. 'People who've been in Harvey Bamberg films tell terrible stories about having to go hammering on his door begging for their pay and being left stranded in the middle of nowhere with no plane tickets home.'

'But the films got made. Right?'

Billy nodded. He had to admit that. A producer could be forgiven much if he got his films made. 'What's she like, by the way?' he asked.

'That's what everyone wants to know. Naughty, I think. She looks naughty to me.'

'Really!' Billy smiled as he considered that.

Charlie nodded. 'Obviously if we did go with Harvey we'd watch him carefully. I'm sure he's a bit fly, but I don't think he's bad. Just cute. And he wants you and me and Belinda. So . . .'

Billy shrugged. 'What could be cuter than that? OK, I'm with you. Let's give them a shot.' He smiled. 'Now, do you want to see something wonderful?' And pressing the forward lever of the Steenbeck he watched as his Chopin film began to unroll across the spools; he had always been an enthusiast.

The lights were out when Billy arrived at his home on the lower slopes of Hampstead, although it was not yet eleven. Seven months of pregnancy were making Ilse tired these days and she often went to bed as soon as the children were asleep.

He parked his van in the road outside, manoeuvring as quietly as possible in view of the hole in the exhaust, and let himself into the large, run-down house. After Charlie had left he had worked on alone at his documentary, running the footage through the Steenbeck, making notes to himself, wondering about different ways of structuring the material. That was what he loved so much about film: the limitless choices which could be made in the cutting room.

He had not come straight home. They were showing *Closely Observed Trains* again at the National Film Theatre and, feeling like a little celebration, he had gone to see it. Now in the kitchen he had never quite finished refitting, he pushed aside a playpen and, unwrapping a take-away pizza, considered what the budget of a film like *Shadows on a Wall* might be. It would be difficult to do it properly for less than three million pounds, he was sure. What was that in dollars? Getting on for five million. That was very cheap, he knew; you couldn't get a Hollywood star for five million dollars these days. But it didn't seem very cheap to him, and he tried to imagine what Mr Witherspoon, the bank manager whose phone calls regularly brought such gloom, would say when he told him he was going to make a movie.

Ilse was awake when he went up to bed. She had heard him opening the children's doors, looking in on them, as he did every night. He loved Ilse and his children to obsession. Sometimes at odd moments of the day he would feel himself smiling inanely with his pleasure in them, Ilse, thirty-eight now, three years older than he was, and the children, Benedict at seven, Sioban at five and two-year-old Harry. His family governed his life. After a day of listening to the whinging of performers he could always come home to the honesty of the children. They enjoyed each moment.

He slid into bed alongside Ilse. She murmured a welcome. He kissed her on the side of her forehead and snuggled close. He loved the sight and touch of her when she was pregnant. To him it made her more beautiful than ever, her face fuller, her back straighter. He was looking forward to the new baby. It would probably be their last. They would all enjoy it.

They had been introduced at a television Christmas party, Ilse, tall, heavy bosomed and German, working for the BBC World Service, and Billy, a young director with a master's degree in modern history. She had been researching a programme about eyes and had been fascinated by his, the blue and the green. Girls usually hadn't wanted to ask him why he had a glass eye.

'An accident,' he had told her. 'On my father's farm during harvesting. The combine threw up a stone and it caught me. I was twelve. The blue was a mistake at first. But then I got used to the idea. And when I had to have a replacement I asked for another blue one. One blue, one green.'

They had been married within the year. Ilse had already been pregnant. She had enjoyed radio work but liked motherhood more. Now as well as looking after the children she ran a playgroup in a hut on Hampstead Heath. They were, Billy knew, an eccentric couple: Ilse, the German earth mother and environmentalist in the sandles and the smock, Billy, the ever-broke, one-eyed optimist.

They had bought their house when they first began to live together, a lofty, Victorian semi-detached villa, on some money Ilse had inherited and a very large mortgage. The plan had been to fill it with children and gradually renovate. The children had arrived but there had never been enough money for improvements; Billy's one mistake had been his assumption that if he was good the money would follow. He *was* good, a careful director, who brought the cool eye of the documentary observer to his drama. That was why there had been so many prizes and nominations. But so far no-one had ever wanted to pay very much for the care he took. The world was full of directors, slicker, more calculating fellows than him. Relentlessly the debts had risen.

He closed his eyes to dream: when *Shadows on a Wall* became a movie . . . that was when it would all come right.

(iii)

The deal was agreed two weeks later in Larry Horner's office. Charlie was there as were Harvey, Nathalie and Edward Lampton. Emma, the wide-bottomed secretary, poured the China tea. As she left the room Charlie found himself looking at the Indian rug which lay in the centre of the weathered, block floor, glancing quickly away as he felt Larry's eyes diverting away from Nathalie Seillans' bosom to glare at him.

True to his profession Larry had shifted Harvey and Nathalie some way since their original approach. Now Charlie was to be paid a thousand pounds for a one-year option on the play, as well as the Writers Guild minimum of £9,600 for writing the screenplay, rising to £23,000 on the first day of shooting. In movie terms it was, in Larry's phrase, 'smaller than peanuts', but Charlie wasn't complaining. As co-producer as well as writer he would have equal rights with Harvey and Nathalie in choice of director, which everyone agreed should be Billy Yeo, in casting, again Belinda was everyone's first choice for Marie Walewska, and in music. There was also a promise of 25 per cent of the producer's net profits, which had made Larry smile like an open piano.

'Charlie, let me warn you,' Larry had guffawed earlier, 'of all the uncertainties in life the one thing which is absolutely certain is that there will never be a net profit on any film produced by Harvey Bamberg.'

Charlie didn't mind. Getting it made was what really counted.

'I've got to say this is an unusual deal in the extreme where we have the writer calling the shots,' had been Harvey's main complaint as the details had been argued. But he had agreed, too, and now as he drank his tea and babbled about the wonderful movie they were going to make, Charlie considered his new partners. He could manage Harvey, he was sure. Harvey could always be relied upon to do the most expedient thing. Nathalie, however, would be more cunning. He watched her. She looked wonderful, sitting on the sofa, closer than necessary to Edward Lampton, her skirt slit to mid-thigh. She must already have used some cunning there.

It was the first time Charlie had met Lampton, but he recognized the situation. Harvey and Nathalie would be stinging the poor man for all kinds of development costs, including Charlie's own fee, in return for a small share of the profits and an on-screen credit as an associate producer. It was an old trick. Movie glamour was very seductive.

'So there we go then,' Harvey said as he signed the deal memorandum and handed it back to Larry. 'We're in business. When can we see a first draft?'

'I'm never sure, what exactly does a co-producer do?' Belinda asked the following morning. They were labelling the latest batch of movies Charlie had recorded from the television.

'Well, that depends. Basically in my situation it gives me a seat at the table when everything is being discussed.'

'But what happens if Harvey Bamberg doesn't listen to your advice, or brings in other writers to rewrite the script?'

'That can't happen,' Charlie said. 'Not with my deal. Besides with Billy directing it's hardly likely, is it? The co-producer thing just formalizes it. Gives us double, double protection.'

'Double, double protection,' repeated Belinda. 'That's all right then.'

Chapter Eleven

(i)

She guessed who it was before turning around. She had heard the scampering school shoes striking the flagstones in the alleyway behind her. 'Hi, Sadie. Are you going to be in tonight?' They were approaching the back entrance to the Jupiter.

Drawing level Sadie Corchoran shook her head. 'Sorry. I'd love to, but I have too much homework.'

'Well, I guess you know what happens in the end.' The girl must have seen the play at least ten times.

Sadie walked on in silence. At last she said, 'Can I talk to you? I mean, *really* talk.'

They had reached the stage door. 'Of course. If you'll make the tea while I get ready you can talk all you want,' Belinda said.

'It's about the film,' Sadie said, as she plugged in the kettle in Belinda's tiny dressing room. 'Billy doesn't take me seriously. How can I convince him that I'd be perfect as Camille de Malignon?'

At her dressing table Belinda, an old chiffon scarf protecting her hair, was squeezing foundation cream on to her face. Carefully she began to spread it across her skin, grateful that this gave her time to think of a reply. Every actor in the play had been talking about the film, wondering if any of them would be cast, and making jokey hints whenever Billy and Charlie were around, but it had never occurred to her that Sadie might imagine herself in the movie, too. Cautiously, she glanced through her dressing-table mirror. Behind those thick glasses, inside that navy-blue school coat, she could see a sensitive, intelligent, pretty girl: but a *young* girl and completely untrained. No-one had even seen her act. For all they knew Sadie might be completely without talent. It happened all the time with pretty girls. 'I thought you still had two years to do at school,' Belinda said delicately at last. 'And then what about college?'

'That was before I knew about the film. I can go to university any time. But there'll only ever be one film of *Shadows on a Wall*. That's why I have to convince Billy before he casts someone totally unsuitable.'

Belinda smiled. Sadie had never disguised her view that neither of the two Camille de Malignons had been up to the part. 'I'm sure Billy's a good judge of ability,' she said.

'But he's *pre*-judging my ability by thinking I'm just a child.'

Belinda finished the foundation. How could she let her down lightly? 'The trouble is, Sadie, and this might sound cruel, you're not a child but you are young. You might be the most brilliant actress in the world, but you're sixteen. Camille de Malignon is a very difficult part . . . grown up, if you know what I mean.'

'In the play she's supposed to be nineteen. I could look nineteen.'

Belinda moved on to the powder. 'I don't think you could. You're terrific as you are. You don't want to grow up too quickly. Besides it's a role for a mature . . .' She paused. 'Well, I mean, it's a very sexy part. And that's difficult enough to do even when you're quite experienced . . .' she finished awkwardly. For a few moments she concentrated on powdering her cheeks. She knew, because she had told her herself, that Sadie had never even had a boyfriend.

Now Sadie was watching her intently. Usually she was jolly to the point of comic, but tonight she was pinched with concentration.

Belinda hated sounding so negative. When she had been Sadie's age Bob and Cherry had given her nothing but encouragement. 'As you're so keen maybe you should consider drama school instead of university . . .'

'Yes, well, perhaps, later. But couldn't you just talk to Billy, ask him if he'll at least give me an audition? Please, Belinda.'

The kettle was boiling, pumping wet steam into the room.

Belinda capitulated. 'Yes. I could and I will. I'll ask him. But if I have to wait any longer for the tea I'll either die of thirst or be drowned in the steam.'

'Oh gosh, sorry,' said Sadie, quickly putting two tea bags into the pot and looking around for the milk. 'And thank you. You'll see. I won't let you down.'

Belinda returned to her make-up. She had been a coward. Now Billy would be faced with putting Sadie off, and she prayed that this blessed, likeable, pest of a girl would soon find a new obsession. She had never known determination like it.

(ii)

Sadie was just in time for dinner, dashing down the road from Gloucester Road Underground Station, wiping shaving cream off her coat. It was still three weeks to Hallowe'en but on the corner of Bina Gardens a group of children dressed as witches had tried to waylay her, only to flee when she had done her witch's cackle. It was, she knew, blood-chilling, a party piece from her second year at Queen's Yard when she had appeared in the senior school's production of *Macbeth*. She'd known then that she was special, the only junior to get near a senior play.

'You're late,' her mother said as she bounced down the stairs into the basement dining room. Her mother, a knife-thin woman in her usual grey suit, was opening a packet of instant mixed salad. Her father was uncorking a bottle of red wine. He was an economist: her mother was a lawyer. Neither of them would have been in long themselves. Sadie couldn't imagine how families had survived before microwaves had been invented.

'Trick or treat,' Sadie said, changing the subject, as she quickly began to set the table. 'Is it legal to beg on the streets with menaces and spray shaving-foam at people?'

'You weren't mugged, were you?' her father asked, not really expecting an answer. He was a silver-haired man with a large forehead and an academic's slight stoop.

She shook her head as her mother answered the question. 'No dear, I don't think so, although I suppose if the foam stained there could be a charge of criminal damage, assault if they laid a hand on you, or perhaps even one of demanding money with menaces.'

'But you'd have to prove that the saying of "trick or treat" and wearing a mask was intended as a threat, wouldn't you?' Sadie's father came back. 'And surely at this time of the year that kind of behaviour comes under custom and tradition . . .'

They're off, thought Sadie, satisfied with her diversion. An admission that she was late because she had been hanging around the *Shadows on a Wall* people again would have put a frost over dinner. Now, shutting her ears to the conversation, she scooped herself some lasagne from the foil dish and left them to it.

She was the youngest of three and the only one still at home, and had always known that she was the cuckoo in the nest. Born nine years after the younger of her brothers she had once calculated that she was probably the fruit of too much sun and wine one summer night in Minorca, which is where the Corchorans had gone for their holidays in those days. Her mother, renowned for blunt talking, had even on one occasion let slip that an abortion had been briefly considered, which probably went some way towards explaining Sadie's feeling that her foothold on life was at best precarious. You're on your own, Sadie, she would tell herself, when she considered how close she had been to not being. It made things simpler.

For as long as she could remember her mother had worked and she had returned home from school to an empty house, a neglected, if well-off, latch-key child. Not that she had ever minded particularly. It had given her more freedom than the other girls, the only things asked being that she excelled at school and was punctual for her mother's instant meals. To Sadie, who had never had difficulty excelling at most things, that seemed like a fair deal. Her parents had their lives and she had hers, and if they rarely met other than for dinner, they didn't cross each other either.

'What do you think, Sadie? Tunnel or ferry?' Her father was looking up from his grapes. The conversation had somehow gone from trick or treating to the Channel Tunnel.

'Tunnel as far as Dover,' Sadie said, 'and then the ferry.'

Her main homework was an essay on the events leading up to the American War of Independence and as soon as she had finished feeding the dishwasher she hurried upstairs. Her parents by this

97

time had moved their conversation on to the economic miracle in China.

They lived in a large, five-storey Victorian house in a South Kensington boulevard, a grand place from the outside, but which, since her brothers had left, stood three-quarters empty for most of the time. Sadie's room was in the eaves, an attic which looked out over the gardens and mews houses at the back.

Normally she found no trouble getting down to work but on this night she was distracted. Was she really too young to play Camille de Malignon? Or was she just not pretty enough? Had Belinda been trying to be kind? She really ought to become more aware of her looks, she thought. Perhaps she was ugly and no-one would tell her, or had a humpback like Richard the Third?

She had a small mirror which she used when combing her hair, but it was in the gloom behind her bedroom door and at night she couldn't see herself properly in it. Her only other mirror was a large rectangular one, bought from a stall in Camden Market and carried home with a complaining Claire one Sunday morning, but which, because her walls were covered in posters, she had never hung. Pulling it out from its place in the spare room she looked around for somewhere to put it. For a moment she contemplated taking down the poster for *Blade Runner* or possibly even that for *A Room with a View*. But she had measured out her life collecting and Blu-tacking these images: she wasn't quite ready to graduate from them yet. At her desk she leant back in her chair and stared upwards. Above her, halfway into her dormer window was a high, narrow ledge.

Slipping downstairs to the washroom where her father kept his few tools (through the dining-room door she could hear her parents now discussing the new hang at the Tate), she found a bag of screws and a screwdriver. Back in her room she set to work lifting and levering the mirror on to the ledge. Half an hour and four screws later, the mirror was in place.

Dropping down to her desk she took off her glasses, shone her desk lamp into her face and looked up at her reflection. She gazed for some moments in critical analysis at her nose, her mouth, her hairline. Not too bad, she thought, apart from the eyes. Surely they were too big. Disproportionate. They were massive. She'd never before realized quite how big. Was that ugliness, or was it beauty? She really wasn't sure. She continued to stare. Now she noticed that the mirror was almost post-box shape in its dimensions, like a cinema screen. Cinemascope. She turned her face this way and that, pouting, frowning, smiling. Was this how she would look on the big screen?

The American War of Independence had a long wait.

It wasn't until the following morning that she discovered the other advantage of having the mirror in the eaves, and then it was by accident. Packing her essay into her school bag she happened to step back towards the window, when, glancing upwards, she found herself staring into the bedroom window of the mews house at the end of the Corchorans' short garden. A woman in a black bra and pants was doing exercises, unaware that she could be seen. Puzzled, Sadie turned around and looked directly through the window, but from this lower angle the small brick balcony at the mews window blocked everything. Only in reflection could she see the woman.

For a long moment Sadie stared up into the mirror, wondering who the woman was. She had never seen her before, but that wasn't unusual: like most Londoners the Corchorans knew very few of their neighbours. For a second Sadie contemplated taking the mirror down again: but she didn't.

Then, picking up her bag, she hurried off to school.

(iii)

The first showing of any movie is on the writer's word processor, Charlie reminded himself, as he peered vacantly into his empty screen. So where were the pictures?

He asked himself this question most afternoons. It was almost five. Belinda would be going to the theatre soon. Perhaps he would sneak out for a coffee then, or take a bath? That was where his best thoughts came: he didn't know why, but a mind which was empty when confronted by a word processor would suddenly discover whole continents of ideas when floating free in hot water. But he had already spent over an hour in the bath that morning. Was it becoming an addiction, an excuse, a fetish even? He gazed at the wall. He knew his mind was wandering. It usually was.

The telephone on the desk beside him rang, interrupting his train of distraction. 'So how's it coming?' It was Harvey Bamberg. Harvey rang every day; sometimes twice a day. He was a very friendly man, but he had no idea of how the creative process worked. 'You want I should come over and talk things through?'

'No,' said Charlie. 'No need. I'm tearing along.' That was a lie.

'Terrific! Did I tell you Channel 4 are *very excited*, and I mean *very*. If we get them on board the rest will be a breeze. Believe me. Maybe Canal Plus in France, they're nibbling, maybe even RZO, but I think we can do better than them. A lot of people are *very* interested. Did I mention the Poles? We must get something there.'

'The Poles are broke. They're starving,' Charlie said. 'Well, more or less. They've no money, anyway.'

'Maybe no hard cash, but, come on, they have the country, a film industry, expertise, studios, maybe tax advantages. Some kind of deal has to be possible. Isn't she Polish, your heroine, Marie . . . you know . . . what's-her-name?'

'Marie Walewska. She was a Polish patriot.'

'Right! There you are. A Polish *patriot*. What about that! They've got to come up with *something* for a *patriot*, for Christ's sake!'

'If you say so.'

'That's what I say. So, how soon can I see pages?'

'When they're ready.'

'Right. Make it quick, OK! We're all waiting for you to deliver—'

'Harvey, I'm trying to work.'

'Of course, of course,' Harvey chirruped. 'Sorry to disturb you. Talk to you tomorrow. May the Muse be with you,' and, sending his love to Belinda, he rang off.

Charlie put the telephone down. The man was a menace. Going into the kitchen he made himself some lemon tea. Outside a freak early winter snow shower was blowing against the window. In the street some workmen were huddled together, sheltering. He shivered. It was cold, even in the flat. What had Harvey said? They were all waiting for him. Charlie frowned. He hated pressure. There was always someone waiting for something. *Waiting*.

100

Back at his word processor he gazed again into the blue of the empty screen. Where had he been up to? Ah yes. The snow, the street in the little town, the people waiting, sheltering. Everybody waiting for the emperor. *Waiting for him.* The pictures began to form. The closed sleigh and patrol of Polish lancers, the peasant on his dungpile (borrowed from de Maupassant), the blacksmith with his horse, the grenadiers and the welcoming party awaiting the arrival in Poland of Napoleon; and there, hidden among them, faces down against the snow, Belinda as Marie Walewska with her friend Camille de Malignon. Quickly now he began to type, rapidly and easily, copying out the pictures he saw on the screen in front of him. Pictures only. No dialogue. Dialogue belonged in stage plays; he was writing a movie.

This was the part of movie-making he enjoyed most of all, when it was all in his mind and he had complete control. After the screenplay everything was compromise: budget, style, cast, music. But at this moment it was perfect as image followed image through his mind to his fingers, into the word processor and up on to the screen, flawless performances, camera moves and cuts sweet and sharp. If Harvey Bamberg would just leave him alone he would get the pages all right; 'everyone waiting' indeed.

(iv)

Harvey Bamberg was waiting at the window of his apartment overlooking Holland Park, watching as the snow turned into sleet and then back to rain. Nathalie had gone to lunch with one of her French girlfriends after which she had planned a shopping expedition. Nathalie loved to shop and, because the clothes she bought never failed to make her look beautiful, he encouraged her. It didn't matter how much she spent. She was worth it. She made him very happy.

He had called Charlie because, as on most afternoons, he was bored. Now that he had made all the calls he could to whip up expectations in *Shadows on a Wall* there wasn't much he could do until the script was delivered.

Waiting. Making movies was always about waiting. Waiting for the script, for the money, the studio, the director, the light, the weather, the editor, the release, the reviews. He understood that. But why were they always waiting for the writer? He could never figure that out. Why did writers take so long when all they had to do was copy down what was in their heads? That shouldn't take so long. It had always seemed to him there was too much mystique and not enough hard sweat involved in writing. Perhaps if he had more time himself . . .

Wondering what to do, he wandered through his home. It was a large and opulent place on the top floor of a mansion block, half a dozen large, high, Thirties rooms decorated in a *mélange* of French antique and high tech, with low sofas, paintings, rugs, shiny wooden floors, art history books and African wood carvings. He was pleased with it: it had been especially created by a film designer with instructions that it should look like a set for the home of a successful movie producer and his film-star wife. Fashioned to impress, it impressed, Edward Lampton gazing long and hard at the painting of the harlequin with the arrow in his eye, and even longer, when he hadn't known he was being watched, at the collection of nude black-and-white photographs of Nathalie which hung in the hall. Lampton had realized by then that there had been no other projects demanding Harvey's time and money, but he hadn't tried to back out of their deal, although he was risking the best part of a hundred thousand pounds, a lot of funerals in anybody's money.

Reaching the bathroom Harvey repolished the blue of his chin with his shaver, running it up the side of his head, around his ears and down the back of his neck. He liked to have a smooth skin for Nathalie. She would joke that he reminded her of Erich Von Stroheim as he was in *Sunset Boulevard*, which, as it was many years since Harvey had seen *Sunset Boulevard*, he thought might be some kind of compliment.

He watched himself as he shaved. He was, he knew, a bumptious, plain, little man with a heavy growth, a large nose, curling, pointed ears, and a shiny head, and that his voice was overloud and unblessed by a smart accent. But when he was with Nathalie all that changed: with Nathalie he was tall and handsome, clever and elegant. With Nathalie he was Harrison Ford.

Turning he contemplated the life-sized nude colour photograph of her which he had had set behind glass as part of the shower door. Not many secrets there, he thought; nothing private about those parts. It was a picture taken for *Oui* magazine, Nathalie at twenty and perfect. Had it been in monochrome it might have been, just about, a life study, but in real-life flesh colour, this picture was about something other than tint and shade. The builder who had put it in had been embarrassed when confronted by the real thing in her bathrobe one morning, but Harvey was very pleased with it. And whenever guests called at the apartment Harvey would encourage them to visit the bathroom before they left. He wanted all his friends to know what they were missing, what he was enjoying. Everything he did, he did for Nathalie; not least *Shadows on a Wall*.

The moment she had seen it, sitting hunched up in the Jupiter, she had wanted it. Once known as having one of France's most famous bodies Nathalie now craved intellectual status, to be recognized as the producer of the sort of arty movie her cineast friends discussed at film festivals. She and Harvey had looked all year for the right project, read all the new books, seen all the new plays, but everything worth doing had gone to bigger fish. Then they had spotted a review of *Shadows on a Wall*.

Harvey had loved Nathalie for years, at first as a fan, when he had been a lowly Press agent for American stars visiting Paris and been mesmerized by her screen sensuality; later, when he became a producer, as an admirer and a colleague; and eventually as a friend. A friend but not a lover. Only at last in middle age and with her options dwindling had Nathalie seen a sort of future with him. For her it was a marriage of security, Harvey knew that. That was all he had to offer.

With her previous husbands and lovers she had been famously unfaithful, her adventures a regular source of amusement for the European scandal magazines. And now because she enjoyed sex as a regular recreation they made love frequently, when sometimes she would tell him of other lovers and enjoy her memories. In his way, Harvey would be aroused by the idea of Nathalie with other men; excited, yet ripped with pain.

He splashed some after-shave lotion against his skin. She would be home soon. Perhaps she would want to make love. He stared at the shower door, then, stepping towards it, rested his forehead against the glass outline of her body.

All his life he had been a joke among his friends, mocked behind his back. Did they think he didn't know? Then he had married Nathalie. Did they still laugh at him?

A thought gnawed at him. What would happen if he failed to get *Shadows on a Wall* made? What would Nathalie do then?

He closed his mind to it. He dare not consider the possibility of failure.

Chapter Twelve

(i)

As October turned into November the *Shadows on a Wall* stage play turned into the *Shadows on a Wall* screenplay, Charlie working fourteen hour days until, hollow-eyed, he would greet Belinda when she arrived home from the theatre with the night's news.

On one night she reported that Neil Burgess had developed a hopelessly, unrequited crush on one of the Two Soldiers: and on another that Billy had had a row with the new girl playing Camille de Malignon and would be replacing her. Charlie already knew about that.

'That part is trouble,' Belinda mused over her cocoa. 'It gets to people, gets under their skin. Look at poor Sadie.'

Charlie nodded. 'Billy's promised he'll test her when we get the money for the movie. I hope she isn't going to be too disappointed—'

'We *will* get the money, won't we?' Belinda interrupted. 'I mean, Harvey will find it. That's what he's good at, right?'

'That's the *only* thing he's good at. Of course he will. If Harvey can't, nobody can. He's *got* to.' No pessimist ever got a movie off the ground.

Sometimes Belinda went out after the show to meet other actors working around the corner in the West End; and sometimes Billy called on Charlie to see how the script was progressing and to discuss ideas for actors. Now and again Charlie and Billy would even meet Harvey in the afternoons to mull over the casting of Napoleon, because, good as Neil Burgess was, even a small movie would need someone younger, with a bigger name. (They hadn't had to tell Neil: he had told them.) But mainly Charlie worked alone, with Belinda hurrying home from the theatre to be with him.

Naturally, because she knew almost as much about *Shadows on a Wall* as he did, Belinda read every page as it came off the word processor. He valued her opinion and they would sit up late into the night as she wound down from the performance talking movies; or, if he was busy, she would work her way through his ever-growing library of books on Napoleon. She was discovering that she loved history.

'Are you ready for this, Charlie?' she exclaimed one night, looking up from reading. 'The Duke of Wellington had a tail.'

'A what?'

'A tail. "A small vestigial tail", it says here. "A short extension of his vertebrae" which meant he had to have a special saddle made with a hole in the back to tuck his tail into, so to speak. Can you imagine? Like a back-to-front unicorn.'

On another night it was another book and Marie Walewska's heart. 'Oh no! Did you know that when she was dying in Paris she left instructions that after her death her heart was to be cut out and taken back to Poland for separate burial? What about that!'

'Heartless, I'd say!' said Charlie, before adding: 'Maybe I should be writing the first Napoleonic vampire movie.'

What most fascinated Belinda, however, were the statistics. 'It says here that Napoleon's army took twenty-eight million bottles of wine with them when they marched on Moscow, two million bottles of brandy and a hundred and fifty thousand horses. And what about this? Each division was followed by a six-mile column of provisions, herds of cattle for slaughtering, masons to build ovens, and bakers to bake bread. And then there were the whores . . . carriages and carriages overflowing with them, hookers who flocked from all over Europe, following along in the baggage train.'

Charlie smiled: 'It sounds a bit like a movie on location, doesn't it?'

In *Shadows on a Wall*'s last week at the Jupiter, towards the end of November, Belinda's parents came over from Philadalephia and stayed at a hotel in Lancaster Gate. It was a touchy time. Thrilled as she was to see them, and a round trip of seven thousand miles is a long way to go to the theatre, Belinda was shredded with nerves, bursting into tears in her dressing room when she knew her mother was in the audience.

'Now I remember why I came to London rather than become an actress in New York,' she told Charlie on the telephone as he tried to calm her down. 'She expects so much. I couldn't have kept afloat with the flood of my mother's unfulfilled ambitions surging my way.'

'Parents do that to children,' Charlie comforted. 'It's what makes us do things. We should be grateful really.'

'You think so? You should have grown up in our house. Whenever the phone rang she was disappointed that it wasn't Francis Ford Coppola.'

'I didn't know your mother knew Francis Ford Coppola.'

'She didn't. That was why she was disappointed.'

After the show they all had dinner together at Café Pelican, Charlie arriving straight from home. He had handed the first draft of the finished script over to Billy for his comments that afternoon and, although tired, was demob-happy and silly. He had already had a couple of glasses of wine.

'Imagine how Napoleon felt, he couldn't unfasten her chastity belt,' he sang quietly to himself as Belinda's parents discussed the play and the menu and Belinda giggled and kneed him under the table. He had only met Bob and Cherry on one other occasion, a nervy week two years earlier when Belinda had taken him home to Philadelphia and, during which anxious to please, they had gone into a zany old *Stagger Lee and Hannah* routine.

'I have to say I was pleasantly surprised at the complexities of the themes discussed . . .' Bob Johnson began earnestly once the order had been made. While in London he was in his drama-teacher mode. Cherry looked scornful.

'Jeez, will you listen to him?' she mocked. ' "Pleasantly surprised"! It was *brilliant*! Brilliantly written and brilliantly acted.' And leaning across she kissed her daughter for the fifth time since the curtain had come down. 'Now tell us about the movie. My God, I can't *wait* for the movie!'

Charlie shrugged a smile. He couldn't wait either. In his mind the play had receded to being little more than a preparation for the film. Carefully he explained how Harvey Bamberg would now be going out to raise the money.

'And will there be stars . . . I mean in the other parts?' Cherry asked. Like Belinda she was an attractive woman, although she was now in her fifties and her once-golden hair had turned platinum.

'Not Hollywood stars. Little stars. Proper actors who don't mind not being paid a fortune. We've been making all kinds of lists.'

'So no Michael Douglas or Bruce Willis . . . ?' Cherry sounded disappointed. She had once worked with Telly Savalas before he became famous.

'No Sharon Stone, either,' Belinda laughed.

'Because you got the part, right,' her father beamed. 'Enjoy it, OK?'

By now Cherry was crooning. 'Can you imagine when the movie comes to Philadelphia, Bob. It'll make such a wonderful movie. *Wonderful!* I always knew you'd be up there one day, Belinda, just like—' She stopped.

Bob frowned, and looked at his programme again.

Charlie watched but said nothing. Every family had its tensions. No wonder Belinda was sometimes unsure of herself.

In the taxi on their way home Belinda said: 'You know, I think Dad's relieved. He always thought I was "too good" to be living with some guy who wrote for television. Theatre's OK, it's legit.'

'Maybe he'd have preferred you to have taken up with a dead writer, someone who'd already made his reputation.'

'Probably. I'd have been cold in bed at night, but he'd have been happy.' She kissed him. 'I'm glad you're alive.'

'Thank you.'

For a few moments she was thoughtful as the taxi rattled through Hyde Park. 'Sometimes I wonder if I'd ever have been an actress if my mother hadn't encouraged me,' she said. 'It was all decided by the time I was ten.'

'It would have been a waste if you hadn't been.'

She shook her head. 'I don't think so. I don't think so at all.' She went quiet.

As they paused at the traffic-lights near the Albert Memorial, Charlie caught her expression. It was wistful.

Chapter Thirteen

(i)

There were two ways to raise money for a movie, Harvey Bamberg liked to boast: the pussyfoot way and the Harvey Bamberg way. Pussyfooting involved sending out batches of three or four screenplays to the most likely potential investors and a couple of admired name actors, waiting for them to respond, and, if negatively, and more than 99 per cent of all submissions inevitably were, trying second favourites, followed by third favourites and so on. The pussyfoot way could take months; usually it took years.

The Harvey Bamberg method was more direct: a mass mailout of three hundred scripts to everybody Harvey knew in the business, preceded and followed by a blitzkrieg of phone calls, personal letters, reminders of old friendships, chance meetings, mutual acquaintances and favours owed. He had been waiting for the screenplay for two months, now burgundy-covered *Shadows on a Wall* scripts were being scattered like seed by mail, courier and Federal Express from Hollywood to Warsaw. With two temporary secretaries on successive eight-hour shifts he worked without a break. By night he talked on the telephone to friends, agents, lawyers and acquaintances in Los Angeles and anyone he could get to at Paramount, Warners, Buffalo, Fox, Amblin, Columbia, Disney and Universal, and by day he laid siege to the BBC, Canal Plus and all the other British and European television companies rumoured to have more than a couple of production dollars to rub together; then there were the

109

pension funds, offshore tax shelters, record companies, casinos, local governments, private banks and even trade unions. There were so many ways of raising money and pre-selling a movie, cinema distribution here, home video there, television, terrestrial, cable and satellite, everywhere. It was like putting together the parts of a jigsaw, but until they all fitted, until the money was in place, there would be no movie.

'Everyone and his dog has a script they're developing,' he would tell Nathalie in between working the phones. 'And every dog and his mother is looking for money. My job is to find it first.'

'My God, Harvey,' Nathalie purred. 'You're like an old sow rooting after truffles.'

That made Harvey smile and try all the harder. 'Whatever you say, honey.'

They had heard it before, of course, all those people with their hands on the money whose job it was to say no. They heard it every day of their working lives, they heard it in every language and they heard it in every accent. But, Harvey was certain, they rarely heard it with such conviction.

Harvey was in fact so busy, he never had time to read the screenplay, not properly, anyway. Nathalie read it. It was good, she said. It was very good.

(ii)

Ilse Yeo had her baby, a girl, three weeks before Christmas. Billy was present at the birth, while Belinda and Sadie, who refused to be left out of the celebrating, babysat the other children. The new baby was named Camille, which pleased Sadie.

Ten days later Charlie and Belinda accompanied the Yeo family to the local church to have the baby christened. Billy and Ilse believed in tradition. When they arrived back at the house Nathalie and Edward Lampton were waiting, glamorous and bountiful, with an expensive shawl, two Babygros, and Christmas presents for the other children.

Harvey would liked to have come, too, Nathalie explained, but, as they all knew, he was away truffling somewhere in Europe.

'How's he getting on?' Charlie asked, anxious for news.

'He tells me there is a lot of interest. Everywhere, a lot of *keen* interest.'

Billy, who overheard, said nothing. He had been trying to cast Napoleon, but so far none of the name actors to whom he had sent copies of the script had been prepared to commit.

(iii)

It was a light-headed, optimistic Christmas. Every time Harvey perceived some interest he would tell Charlie who would then tell Belinda: and each time their expectations grew.

'This time next year everyone will want you to direct their movie,' Belinda told Billy when he called to pick up the children's presents. It was Christmas Eve and she was hanging some late cards, including one showing a three humped camel from Sadie. 'Did you know that Canal Plus are definitely in?'

'Definitely?'

'So Harvey says,' said Charlie, who was pouring the drinks.

'What happened to British Screen?' Billy asked.

'They were in, now they're out. Some money problem.'

'I thought they were definite.'

'They were. Now they're not. Definitely in and then definitely out. These guys come in and out so quickly and so definitely it's hard to keep up. But at the moment Harvey reckons he's definitely raised three-quarters of the money.'

Billy smiled.

On Boxing Day, Harvey and Nathalie threw a party, an open house to which everybody they knew in movies was invited. Considering that only three months earlier Harvey had been pleading poverty it was a lavish affair, with the fattest, most heavily laden Christmas tree Belinda had ever seen in a home, and one of the most densely packed tables.

'Mingle, mingle,' Harvey muttered under his breath as he introduced Charlie and Belinda around. 'There's movie money here if we can pitch it right.'

There were certainly movie *people* there, everyone who had any status in the British film industry having been invited,

111

arriving trailing children and gifts with them, talking, as always, about ruinous Government policy, start dates, budgets, over-runs, re-cuts, grosses, above the lines, turnarounds and scripts. It was a film festival without any films where people who lived movies every day of the year could continue doing so at Christmas.

For Belinda and Charlie, who had driven back from spending a more bookish Christmas in Dorset with Charlie's parents, it was exciting and slightly bewildering. Film people were different from those in the theatre, with wealth, success and personal attractiveness on display everywhere. Would she become like these thin, aggressive, vain women after *Shadows on a Wall* was made? Belinda wondered, as she showed a group of children some simple conjuring tricks. She hoped not.

'Quite a gathering, eh?' Edward Lampton was standing over them, a plate of cold meats in his hands. For once his eyes had left Nathalie.

'A gathering of the clams,' quipped Charlie as he took another drink. 'We'll never prise any money out of this lot.'

'Ah well!' Lampton smiled philosophically. 'Did I ever tell you, I really admire you writers. I've sometimes dabbled a bit myself, you know, autobiographical stuff. I'm sure there's a film there somewhere.'

'In a story about an undertaker?' Belinda asked.

Lampton nodded. 'Absolutely. You'd be surprised what fun we have behind the scenes.'

'Confessions of a Grave Digger,' contemplated Charlie. 'You never know.'

'*No-one* ever knows,' came back Lampton evenly.

Because Harvey and Nathalie were flying off to Barbados the following day, the *Shadows on a Wall* team drank a New Year's toast with sobering coffee in Harvey's study before going home.

'To *Shadows on a Wall*,' smiled Harvey, raising a Mickey Mouse beaker.

Nathalie, coquettish as ever and who earlier had pressed her waterbed breasts into half the male guests, kissed him on the lips.

'To *Shadows on a Wall*,' chorused Edward Lampton, the Grave Digger.

Nathalie kissed him on the lips, too. He blushed.

Charlie cuddled Belinda. 'To Belinda and Billy,' he said, 'who are going to make it happen for us.'

Billy, who had brought his entire family, and whose children were anxious to leave, kissed two-year-old Harry whom he was holding in his arms. 'To good little boys,' he murmured.

(iv)

In her attic bedroom, Sadie, hiding from Christmas, television, Scrabble ('No, Sadie!' her mother had scolded, 'you can't have "onanism". Not on Boxing Day. It isn't nice.'), her brothers and their girlfriends, her grandparents, her parents and the stale smell of pre-cooked Christmas food which pervaded the house, sat at her desk, a bright red band of ribbon around her neck, very carefully applying a matching lipstick while gazing up at herself in her high mirror. On her dresser were a dozen Christmas cards. 'With love from Charlie and Belinda', read one; 'Thanks for all your help and good luck for 1992', said another. It was signed, 'Ilse and Billy Yeo and children'. Claire had sent her a rude one.

Pressing her lips together Sadie stood up and, stepping back, checked in her mirror on her unknowing neighbour in the mews below. Shadows moved across the window, the tiny silver Christmas tree shook, the murmur of music and talk carried across the small paved garden.

With tears which she did not understand now beginning to sting her eyes she drew the curtains. She had always felt marginal: tonight she felt lonely.

113

Chapter Fourteen

Charlie watched her from the crowd again, a beautiful creamy-haired American girl in a new imitation fur hat with flaps to cover her ears, as she juggled with the red-and-blue balls on the snow-covered square in front of the Mariacki Church; New Year's morning in Cracow, with the bells ringing, and the smoke from roasting chestnuts blowing across the flagstones.

They had decided weeks earlier to visit Poland for New Year, 185 years after Napoleon's arrival there in 1807. It seemed appropriate. Later in the week they would visit Marie Walewska's birthplace near Warsaw, but first they wanted to see the old town of Cracow. Billy had been to Cracow years earlier and spoken longingly of the chance to film there. Would that be possible on a five-million-dollar budget?

They had arrived late the previous night. It had been snowing heavily and they had missed supper. Somewhere outside in the blizzard they knew that people would be celebrating, but they had been too tired to go out and find them. Instead they had snuggled together in their bed, eaten the last of their chocolate and studied their phrase books.

New Year's Day was perfect, the old town a medieval fairyland on a day of celebration, families out enjoying the dry frosty air after Mass, children leaving footprints in the snow.

The street entertainers, fingers swollen by the cold, were

just finishing when they came upon them outside the old cloth-market hall.

'Do you mind?' Belinda asked. 'May I?'

The entertainers smiled and shrugged, not fully understanding until, pulling off her mittens, she began to juggle. At first they were surprised by her skill, but then a boy with long hair began to play a jig on a fiddle, and his girlfriend to shake a tambourine while holding out a jar for contributions.

Charlie stood back. Belinda was so pretty and confident, and so happy. A couple of German tourists took photographs and dropped coins into the jar as a crowd gathered, the balls soaring and falling, faster and faster.

Had Marie Walewska herself ever looked forward to a year with this much optimism? Had she ever had such fun? 1992 was going to be the best year of their lives.

'So what do you think, fella?' Belinda called, her breath freezing on the air as she laughed. 'Do we have a chance?'

PART THREE

May, 1992

Chapter Fifteen

(i)

It was five o'clock on a Saturday afternoon and Simone Estoril was disappointed. She had been waiting around at Jake McKenzie's place since three, but so far he had scarcely been off the phones for more than two minutes together. 'I'll be right out,' he had called at regular fifteen-minute intervals, but she no longer believed him. There was a problem with a movie once destined for Paramount and suddenly moved to Columbia and two of his clients' deals were up for urgent renegotiation. It was becoming steadily clearer that she could have chosen a better time to visit.

'Why don't you come over to the house and spend some time,' Jake had suggested. 'Maybe we could make a weekend of it.'

The house was impressive, for sure, out along Sunset Boulevard in Pacific Palisades, although not so big as she had expected. But then Jake was recently divorced. Presumably he was paying for a bigger home somewhere else for his ex-wife and two sons.

It was a fine, early summer's day and Simone was lolling on a lounger under a canopy by the pool-house. She was Californian born and bred and now stayed out of the sun. Through the open french windows she could hear Jake's soft, insistent voice. 'Five million. It has to be five million, Norman. We can talk about the points and everything else when we've established the five million . . .' Jake McKenzie was famous for his unblinking persistence on behalf of his clients.

The invitation had come as a surprise: Simone had only had dinner with him once, and that after a chance encounter at a screening. A handsome and powerful broker of movies, a muscle demonstrated recently when he had left the Hunt and Lamb Agency taking half a dozen of their biggest clients with him, Jake was known normally to go for younger women, actresses and models. As Simone had just finished being a humble agent's assistant over at Creative Artists and was already thirty-five, and on the plump side of shapely these days, his interest in her was flattering.

Finishing reading the second of the scripts she had brought with her, she sucked the slice of lemon from her Diet-Coke, then, hearing the phone go down, got up and went into the house.

In his study Jake's hand went up in apology. 'I'm sorry. Just as soon as I've made a couple more calls . . .' He was already in the middle of punching another number.

'Don't worry about it. Work is work. But do you have any scripts to read? I'm finished with mine.'

'Does a dog have fleas? Take your pick,' he replied, gesturing towards a low glass table which ran the length of one wall, and on top of which lay twenty or thirty screenplays.

Selecting half a dozen Simone returned to her lounger. Jake was already back on the phone.

She had discovered she liked reading scripts while working at a typing agency years earlier. What, to most people in the business was a necessary chore, was, to her, a hobby, which she would sometimes fancifully liken with that of a part-time prospector: there was a lot of dross to be sieved for sure, but now and then something came along which was a treat in itself, whether or not the movie ever got made.

She was a pretty, confident, self-reliant, generous woman, whose black hair had been blond since high school, who wore her jeans and shirts tight and who liked to wear her tinted glasses just above her hair-line, thus showing her eyelashes which were lush and very black, her best point, she thought. She was also a realist. She knew she had no special talents, other than being a good judge of a script and an efficient organizer, but she *loved* movies: she loved everything about them. Without a college education, married briefly a long time ago in Santa Barbara, and without children to support, she had worked her way through the agencies. Ambition had come to her late, but now she was single-minded: she wanted to get into movies proper: she wanted to be a producer.

She abandoned the first three scripts after twenty or so pages each: two were cop stories, while the third was another variation on *Fatal Attraction*. The other three had readers' reports attached, which meant that someone had already read them and submitted their opinions up the line. One was about a teenage gang, a second was a comedy so clearly aimed at Danny DeVito that his physical characteristics had been described and the third was something about Napoleon. The reader's coverage on the last intrigued her. It was so damning. Describing a double love story set in war-torn Europe in the early nineteenth-century, it ended with the comment: 'But who wants to see a movie about Napoleon?'

On another day she would probably have put it aside and gone back inside for another selection, but, not wishing to bother Jake again, she began to read.

They went to the Ivy By The Shore in Santa Monica for dinner, a restaurant much frequented by film people. All the way there in Jake's Jaguar Simone talked about the script she had just read. Jake hadn't read it. The coverage had put him off.

'I promise you, it's wonderful. I've read a lot of scripts, but this is special. Really!'

'Really?' He was teasing her.

'Really,' she said. 'This writer, Charles Holyoake, is he one of your clients?'

Jake shook his head. 'Never heard of him. You know how it is with scripts. God knows where it came from.'

Over her salmon and salad Simone outlined the plot. Normally she would have been intimidated in such a place, worried that she wasn't smart enough to be seen with Jake and that everyone would be wondering who the blonde was in the brassy clothes, but on this night she was too excited to keep quiet. 'What's wonderful is the way the two love stories dovetail, the famous lovers on the one side, and the everyday ones on the other, all put in intolerable situations by history.'

'I'm not sure there's a market for European costume pieces any more,' Jake said quietly. He was famous for never betraying his thoughts, but Simone could tell he was becoming bored.

She couldn't help herself. 'Just look at it, Jake. Just read it. Please! You'll see. And if you're involved in anything happening to it, just promise me you'll ask the producers to take me on as a secretary, or an assistant or even a runner. Will you do that for me?'

'I'll look at it,' he said at last.

They made love as soon as they got back from dinner. It had never occurred to her that they wouldn't. She had known that when she accepted his invitation, but she would have wished for a little more attention. Because Jake was exhausted he fell asleep quickly. Because she wasn't she didn't.

At two o'clock she crept downstairs and began to reread *Shadows on a Wall.*

(ii)

The message had come silently and slowly, but in the end it had been impossible to misinterpret. Even at only three million pounds, just five million dollars, none of Harvey Bamberg's many contacts had been interested in *Shadows on a Wall.*

'Let's face it, Charlie, we have a problem here,' Harvey had admitted at last. 'I'm not saying it isn't a *beautiful* script, and that Billy wouldn't do a terrific job directing it, but right now no-one has *heard* of Billy Yeo. And Napoleon, well, it ain't exactly a part for someone from Central Casting. These are the realities of film-making. I tried to tell your agent and I tried to tell you, but you didn't want to hear.'

Harvey never mentioned Belinda, but Charlie had known that every reference to the problem with Billy as a first-time cinema director had been an only slightly coded reminder of that facing Belinda as an unknown actress. First-time directors and unknown actresses did not bring money to movies.

Naturally Harvey had continued to truffle, sending out more scripts and making more calls. Possibly, Charlie would sometimes think, Harvey's methods for raising finance were not right for this movie: but it was equally possible that the script just wasn't good enough.

Whatever the reason, Charlie and Belinda had livings to earn, Charlie by writing episodes for a television detective series, and Belinda by taking a part in a BBC radio soap opera, *The Lyndons*, playing an American girl who comes to live with a London family during the Blitz. It was ironic that someone as pretty as Belinda should be heard and not seen, but it was enjoyable work and she was good at it.

There was still a chance, of course. Six months was *nothing* in movies. But somehow neither of them quite believed it. They had had their excitement. Now Charlie was thinking about writing another stage play. In their minds *Shadows on a Wall* was on the shelf.

(iii)

The call came almost out of nowhere, from Mo Rosenbaum, to be exact, which, in Harvey's experience, was practically the same. Mo Rosenbaum was Harvey Bamberg's lawyer in New York – mainly because they'd been to evening classes at New York City College together a long time ago. Mo was not one of the top entertainment lawyers in New York, not by a long hook, but his partner, Simon Aronowitz, had a friend, Philip Amram, who was, and whose clients were some of the big players. The biggest of all was Jake McKenzie.

Harvey Bamberg would never be sure quite how the accident happened, but in some way a copy of Charlie's screenplay found its way from the desk of Ruth, Mo Rosenbaum's secretary, by way of Gloria, Simon Aronowitz's secretary, to his friend Philip Amram, by way of Amram's secretary, and then on a plane to Jake McKenzie in California. Among Jake's biggest clients was a new director called Bruno Messenger whose first movie, *Digital Watch*, was the early summer hit.

So far as Harvey would ever discover, Mo Rosenbaum, like almost all the other contacts to whom he had sent the script, never read *Shadows on a Wall*; neither did Simon Aronowitz nor Philip Amram. But Ruth did and Gloria did, and, after Simone Estoril insisted, so did Jake McKenzie.

The following day Jake had five copies made for his five biggest clients. Four waited for the coverage from their readers before looking at it themselves. Bruno Messenger, because none of the scripts he had been developing was ready, read it himself.

According to Jake the phone was ringing off the wall when he reached the office the next day. It was Bruno Messenger. He had, he said, been up all night reading 'the script of the decade'. 'Jake,' Bruno was alleged to have pleaded, 'you got to get me this script. Please. I must do it. It's for me.' At that point Jake had picked up the phone to Harvey.

Harvey listened to Jake very carefully. It was five o'clock in the afternoon in London, a hot, close day and Harvey's forehead was splashed with drops of perspiration. Through the open french windows he could see Nathalie sunbathing topless on the balcony, slowly fanning herself with a copy of *Vanity Fair*. She did things like that from time to time, distracting him with her distracting parts, knowing that he was an appreciative audience. She still liked an audience, and she liked giving him these little treats. Nathalie knew more about men than any woman he had ever known. She knew how far she could go, too: which was quite a long way. In fact, it was all the way. He turned away, putting that from his mind.

Naturally, Harvey had heard of Bruno Messenger, he never overlooked the name of a success and at the moment the entertainment trade papers were full of the name of Bruno Messenger, but he had no idea what kind of film *Digital Watch* might be. 'Bruno Messenger . . .' he mused into the phone, as though mulling over the director's canon of work.

'Harvey,' Jake said, 'this guy is hot, and do I mean hot! Right now every studio in this town will back him on whatever he wants to do. And he wants to do *Shadows on a Wall*.'

'Isn't it kind of obscure for Hollywood, a little movie like this,' Harvey said. He was confused. He had had absolutely no response from any of his Californian connections. If the money for this movie lay anywhere it had to be in Europe.

'Bruno doesn't think so,' came back Jake. 'The way Bruno sees it this isn't necessarily such a tiny movie. I mean, was there ever anything small about Napoleon apart from the size of his penis?'

124

'It wasn't small. It was pickled,' Charlie said. 'The alcohol they bottled it in made it shrink. There was no contemporary evidence that he had a little willie, and lots of his troops saw it. He used to take a bath every morning in front of them. The Emperor's little shrunken member was just a snide English rumour.'

'Is that a fact?' said Harvey, and waited for Charlie to address the real point.

They were sitting in Holland Park in the empty wooden pews of the open-air theatre, listening to thunder moaning over West London. Charlie was miserable. 'What you're really saying is let's dump Billy.'

'What I'm saying is with Billy on board as director we're going nowhere quickly. Bruno Messenger would bring the money to the movie. Let's meet with him.'

Charlie sucked air through his teeth and shook his head. 'I don't think so, Harvey. We haven't given Billy a real chance. Why don't we take Billy out to Los Angeles and take him around the studios? He's a brilliant director, perfect for us.'

Harvey sighed. 'Brilliant he may be, but perfect for us, he ain't. Nobody wants him. With Billy *Shadows on a Wall* will never get made.'

'You're so certain?'

'Charlie, I've been a long time in this business. You have to know when you have a liability. Billy is a liability.'

'And this guy Bruno Messenger, he's this year's kid with the golden touch. Right?'

'His first movie . . .'

'*Digital Watch*!! What kind of film does that suggest?'

'. . . has done nearly a hundred million domestic in five weeks. He's turned down everything they've offered him. He's waiting for the right project. The guy's a genius. And he wants to do *Shadows on a Wall*.'

Charlie smiled sardonically. 'He's a *genius*? He's made *one* movie and you're calling him a *genius*?'

'Not *me*. Hollywood. The business. Look, do us both a favour. Come with me to LA. Just meet with the guy. Then if you don't like him, if things don't work out, if he doesn't share our vision . . . we'll forget all about him.'

125

what about Billy? What do we tell him?'

' him we did our best. He'll understand.'

.. shook his head. 'He might, but I won't. I think
we him another shot. Didn't you say that Channel 4
..ight change their minds? That Home Box Office might be
persuaded—'

'I told you a lot of *mights*. But for every *might* there are ten
might nots right alongside. No-one, but *no-one*, wants to tip a
toe in the water. I'm telling you, Charlie, right now, with Billy
Yeo, we've got a dead project on our hands. There's nothing
unusual about that. It happens all the time. But it's a shame.
You've written a brilliant screenplay. And I mean *brilliant*. If it
doesn't get made it'll be a tragedy.'

Charlie stared at the empty stage of the theatre. A couple of
large raindrops splashed heavily on to the boards and into his
hair. He thought about Belinda. What would she say? He shook
his head.

Harvey put a hand on his arm. 'This is the first tickle we've
had and it's a big one. Talk to your agent. Talk to Billy. Talk
it over with Belinda.'

'What about Belinda? What happens to her?'

'Who knows? She's a lovely girl, a terrific actress. Beautiful.
Bruno Messenger might love her, turn her into a Hollywood
star. We won't know until we meet him.'

'He might also want her out. Let's face it, that's the most
likely thing. He'll want a name star, and if he doesn't whoever backs him will. That's the way they think out there.
Let's not fool ourselves, Harvey.'

Harvey Bamberg wiped a trickle of rain off a scalp now fur-
rowed with frustration. 'What can I say? Maybe they will, maybe
they won't, but we won't know until we get there. Sitting here
in the park, we aren't making movies, we're just getting wet.'

(v)

Nathalie was dressed and watching the storm at the window
when Harvey arrived home. She was wearing the deep blue,
Muslim gown she had worn in *La Femme d'Algerie*. She was in
a reflective mood. The call from Jake McKenzie had awoken old

126

yearnings. Like most French actresses she had never worked in Hollywood. Hollywood was still the dream.

Although it had been a short walk back Harvey was already soaked and, taking a towel from the bathroom, he went into the bedroom to change. Nathalie followed.

'How went Charlie?' she asked.

Harvey grimaced. 'Why are writers always so difficult?'

She puffed out her lips. 'I think because they don't live in the real world. We have to. Don't worry about him. His friends will tell him what he must do. Now we must make our plans. We must go to Los Angeles.' With that she left the bedroom.

Harvey sat down on the end of the bed and looked into the dressing-table mirror. A dull, fat little man was watching him and he turned away in disappointment. The memory of a recent betrayal knotted in his stomach.

She had told him the night she had arrived home. She had been very tanned and glowing with sex. She had, as he had expected, spent more time skiing than taking part in the film festival for which she was one of the judges. He hadn't blamed her. Who wanted to be watching movies when the sky in Avoriaz was so blue?

'Darling,' she had said, 'you must not be cross with me but I have had a little adventure.' She had not looked in the slightest bit sorry.

Harvey had not answered.

'It was the situation. It was, how do you say, irresistible. We met on the slopes. We shared the T-bar. He was friendly, attentive. Afterwards we met for a drink. It was very romantic. We had dinner. He was very handsome. And then we went for a walk in the night. The air was so clear, the snow so crisp and deep. I went with him to his room. And let him kiss me. He said he wanted to touch me. I wanted him to. He undressed me, and then he touched me. And then he kissed my body. Everywhere. He made love to me all night. I was in a rage of desire. I did everything he wanted. He wanted everything.'

'Do you want I should get you a drink, honey?' Harvey had asked. He had recognized the speech. It was from *Chloe Est Morte*.

'Thank you, darling. I will just have my bath and then I want to confess everything and be forgiven, and you can tell me every-thing you have been doing while I have been away, and I will give you absolution, too. Have you been very naughty, as well?'

127

He wasn't jealous, he had told himself, but his hand had been shaking as he had added the ice to her Campari. He had always known this would happen. That had been the arrangement when they had married. Nathalie had been quite frank. There would, from time to time, be adventures. That was the way she was and she didn't want to change. He had agreed. Had he disagreed there would have been no marriage. But it hurt more than he had known possible.

He had sat with her as she soaked in her bath. That was when she had told him the real story. He would have given anything not to have heard.

They had actually met in a bar. He was handsome, the Latin type, Cuban, she had thought. He lived in Miami. He had bought her a drink and then another the next night. He had been a good skier and good at sex. They had made love three times on the last night, and twice the following morning. That morning. She had been very precise. 'Don't be angry, Harvey,' she had said.

He had stared sadly at her body, knowing that something of this man would still be with her. He had shaken his head. 'Promise,' he had said, wondering why it was that when they'd given out looks and charm he'd been in the toad department; although they screamed when you trod on them, everyone knew toads had no feelings.

Later on she had told him that the lover had been a wealthy man who had become interested when she told him she was setting up a movie. That was why he had gone to Avoriaz, to meet movie people and possibly find a movie in which to invest. 'Questions, he asked so many questions.' But he had wanted only a big movie. *Shadows on a Wall* had been too small to interest him. 'Give me a call when you have something bigger,' he had said.

In his bedroom Harvey finished changing into dry clothes. Nathalie was calling to him to go and watch the lightning. She made even that sound seductive. It had been her idea to offer the part of Marie Walewska to Belinda Johnson, and accept all the conditions Charlie's agent was insisting upon. 'That way we'll get a cheap deal for the screenplay,' she had explained.

'But what happens if we can't get the movie off with Belinda and Billy Yeo?' Harvey had asked.

Nathalie had just smiled. 'Then Charlie Holyoake will be grateful for whatever he gets. He's a writer. Once he's written the screenplay all Charlie will really care about will be getting his script made. We can promise him anything he wants at this stage, at the end of the day he'll do anything *we* want if it means seeing *Shadows on a Wall* on the screen. I know writers. I lived with one once. They always give in. That's why they've never had any power in Hollywood.'

Chapter Sixteen

(i)

Belinda heard the alarms before Charlie finished telling her. She had become reconciled to *Shadows on a Wall* being a fond dream they would all share: that it might become someone else's reality was confusing. 'You can't drop Billy just like that,' she heard herself saying.

'No,' Charlie said. 'That's what I said.'

'I mean it's flattering that these big-shot, Hollywood types think the script is so good. We always knew that. But Billy would make it into a great movie. We can do it ourselves without them.'

Charlie didn't answer. He was sitting at his desk staring at his script. She had never seen him so miserable.

'Isn't this why you wrote it for next to nothing. So that you would have some control? So that you could say "no" . . .'

'I *can* say "no" . . .' Charlie said sharply, and then went silent.

Belinda filled the void. 'But if you do you think you might never get another chance?'

He didn't answer.

'Billy's your best friend; *our* best friend. We're godparents to—'

'Don't you think I haven't thought about that?' he snapped.

She left the room. She didn't want this argument. They never usually fell out.

Harvey had been right, Billy did understand. 'Of course, you must talk to Bruno Messenger,' he insisted. 'It was always a wing and a prayer with me. I knew that. Wow, Charlie, this is terrific! With someone like him you'll find the money now all right.'

He had called on Charlie unexpectedly to borrow a book on Paris prisons during the Reign of Terror, looking for ways to dramatize Camille de Malignon's hysteria. He hadn't quite given up hope: not until that moment, anyway. It was the morning after Charlie's meeting with Harvey; he had hardly slept. When Billy had appeared he had just blurted out his dilemma.

In the end Billy left without taking the book. There didn't seem much point in becoming an expert on prison conditions during the Reign of Terror any more.

He took Ilse and the children to London Zoo in the afternoon. It seemed a good location in which to break bad news. He liked the idea of a desperate conversation going on while monkeys pulled King Kong faces and made obscene gestures in the background, and children giggled and shouted all over the soundtrack. He was always directing in his mind.

'Charlie wouldn't just drop you like that,' Ilse said. She had lost weight since the birth of the baby and looked tired. Billy wished he could tell her something positive just once. But he said: 'I think he ought to. He's spent months, years, working on *Shadows on a Wall*. He still owes thousands of pounds from doing it in Edinburgh. He wants to see it made. And so do I. He deserves it and Belinda wants to be in a movie. If I drop out she still has a chance, not much of a chance, but a chance.'

'But you're perfect for it, you know that. You were banking on it!'

'No. Lloyds Bank were banking on it. I was dreaming of it. Now I'll dream about something else.'

'Perhaps they'll come back to you if it doesn't work out with this Bruno Messenger.'

'Perhaps,' said Billy, although he knew they wouldn't.

'Poor Charlie,' said Ilse after a moment. 'Whatever he does he'll hate himself.' Then, putting her arm through his, they walked on through the zoo, the baby asleep in her pram and the children running around imitating the animals.

They stopped for an ice-cream by the bear enclosure. A mountain of a North American grizzly was rearing on his hind legs as the zoo keeper tossed it a bun. When it roared, Harry, their two year old, stepped back and hid his head in the folds of his mother's skirt. Billy roared back, and, emboldened, the two elder children joined in. It was only as they were walking away towards the reptile house that Billy noticed the name of the bear printed on a plaque in front of the enclosure. It was Bruno.

(iii)

The flight to California was like a sunny afternoon which never wanted to end: an extended day of uninterrupted sunshine in the first-class compartment of a Boeing 747.

Harvey and Nathalie sat together, Nathalie snoozing after lunch, Harvey reading a book about a Russian concert pianist which he thought would make a great vehicle for Michael Caine, while Edward Lampton, the Grave Digger, and Charlie sat separately in the single seats in the nose of the plane. It was the first time Charlie had flown first class: his first trip to Hollywood. The Grave Digger was paying all the fares.

In the end, and not helped by Harvey's hurry-up calls, it had been Belinda who had insisted Charlie go to Los Angeles. There was no harm in hearing what the man had to say, she had reasoned quietly; perhaps it would be in her interests, too. Charlie had known she was putting on a brave face, but it had made it easier. He had invited her to come too, but she couldn't leave the radio series at such short notice.

In truth he was relieved that she was not on board. Worrying about her would have been a distraction. He was being torn in two. He felt bad about Billy, but he couldn't help being excited about Hollywood. Anyone who wanted to be in movies had to go to Hollywood, and he had always wanted to be in movies.

Perhaps he had been made sentimental by the champagne served to first-class passengers, but without warning a wave of sadness engulfed him as he remembered childhood outings to the cinema with his parents, one on either side, and the thrill of recognition as he had learnt to spot the different Hollywood studio logos – the drums and searchlights of Twentieth-Century Fox, Paramount's mountain, the Warner Brothers shield. The movies had been James Bond and Sixties adventure stories in those days. He had assumed then that his parents enjoyed them, too, only later realizing that half their fun had been in watching his excitement. But it had been from them that he had inherited his love of movies. For small-town people they had always had a sophisticated interest in films, a left-over from their student days. His father was a Geography teacher at the Dorset comprehensive Charlie had attended, and had run the school film society in his spare time, Charlie being in charge of the splicer and Sellotape for when the film broke. That had been in the Seventies after the local picture-house had been turned into a Do-It-Yourself supermarket. Punctually at eight every Monday evening, one of the movie classics had been shown, Charlie always at his father's side helping to lace up the projector for *Jour de Fête*, *The Grapes Of Wrath*, *Smiles of a Summer Night*, *La Strada*, *Double Indemnity*, *The Third Man*, *Les Quatre Cent Coups* – only quality films allowed. Now Charlie was going to Hollywood. He thought of his parents. He hadn't told them about Bruno Messenger. They might have asked awkward questions about Billy, wondered about Belinda. They liked Belinda, although they didn't know her very well. Perhaps they didn't even know him very well any more.

'Do what you can for me, Charlie, but if the only way you can get *Shadows on a Wall* made is without me, don't dare screw it up,' Belinda had said that morning as she kissed him quickly goodbye at the door. 'I'd rather be rich and unknown and living with a successful screenwriter, than poor and unknown and stuck with a loser.'

They had both known she was kidding herself. As the taxi had driven away he had looked back through the rear window to wave goodbye. But she had already gone inside.

Now, as he stared down at the glassy screen of the ocean, he was imagining her as she had been that first night in Edinburgh, shaking with nerves, incandescent with talent. He would make sure this Bruno Messenger knew how good she was. He wouldn't let her down.

Chapter Seventeen

'It's absolutely typical of Queen's Yard,' Sadie said furiously. 'It's *Hamlet* again. They won't shift. *Hamlet* or nothing.' And she slammed her bag down next to the table.

Claire, who had been waiting in the café for her, pushed aside her copy of *Hello!* and exhaled a long, abandoned sigh of cigarette smoke. 'Bloody *Hamlet*. Bloody, bloody *Hamlet*. Always bloody *Hamlet*. Well I'm not playing Gertrude again. I got her last time. She's definitely unglam. I'd rather be Polonius than Gertrude. At least he gets a few laughs.'

'It's just not fair,' Sadie said, and went to get them two more cups of coffee.

They had arranged to meet in a stand-up Italian sandwich bar in South Kensington on their way home. Claire had been to extra tennis practice while Sadie had come straight from a meeting with their English teacher, Miss Rokeby, who was also the producer and director of this year's school play.

She had been confident when she had made her suggestion. She had every reason. Teachers courted Sadie. Clever, pretty, eager and hard working, she was good at sports, a witty debater and the best actress of her time at Queen's Yard. All through school she had played the leads: the Virgin Mary, Oliver, Tallulah, Pip, Puck, Portia, and had been a thirteen-year-old Juliet and a fifteen-year-old Hamlet. She didn't want to play Hamlet again, but she did want to play Camille de

Malignon. Usually when Sadie got a bee in her bonnet teachers listened. This time they didn't.

'Did she even read *Shadows on a Wall*?' Claire asked.

'God knows. She said she thought it was quite an interesting idea, but that we might have trouble convincing an audience that a seventeen-year-old schoolgirl was Napoleon.'

'Far easier to convince an audience that a seventeen-year-old schoolgirl is the ghost of Hamlet's father, I suppose.'

'I mentioned that. She pretended not to hear. She said the content was too near the knuckle for Queen's Yard.'

'She means she didn't fancy the embarrassed parental hush when Napoleon unbuttons his strides for Marie Walewska, and reveals a pair of school knickers filled out crotch-wise with a wodge of Kleenex stuffed into a hockey sock and an ubiquitous Mason and Pearson hairbrush, handle upwards. No, she wouldn't fancy that, or the clatter of seats going up and daughters being withdrawn when Camille de Malignon does her pants down for peace routine. I suppose she might have the vaguest point.' Claire stubbed out her cigarette. She loved to play the *louche* sophisticate, even with her side parting, butterfly clip and braced teeth.

'No, she doesn't.' Sadie shook her head. 'We wouldn't have done it that way. I kept telling her she was making a mistake, but she's done some deal with the Royal Shakespeare Company and all she could talk about were the wonderful costumes we'll be borrowing.'

'I'm still not playing bloody Gertrude,' said Claire. 'I don't care how nice the frock is.'

An essay lay unfinished on Sadie's desk. Through her mirror she was looking into the mews bedroom below where a couple were making love. It was like watching a film. It was a warm evening and the lovers had left the curtains undrawn and the windows open. *La Bohème* was playing in the woman's sitting room and carrying across the gardens. At least the music was romantic.

For months the view through Sadie's mirror had been unremarkable. But with summer, long evenings and undrawn curtains, Sadie had found new entertainment – the girlfriend who had called for a drink, begun to laugh hysterically and left in tears, the Friday evening dinner parties, and now, these past three weeks, sex. This was the fifth occasion she had watched.

She had never got anywhere near this herself, although several of the girls in her form had been doing it for years.

The whole thing fascinated her. The preliminaries: the kisses, the touches, the hand inside the blouse, between the thighs. Then the unbuttoning, the pace quickening, the unpeeling, the unzipping. Suddenly the nakedness, the intimate kisses. The first time the lovers had rushed to their conclusion, lain exhausted and then started again. Now everything took longer, the deliberate prolonging of the act, the contortions of the body, the unselfconscious demands for gratification.

Yet it was confusing, too. The books and magazines wrote of love as an act of giving. But what Sadie was watching was a mutual taking. Where did love come into it? She wondered who the woman was and who her lover might be. Was he about to become a permanent mews fixture or was this a fleeting tumbling of summer passion? But, most of all, she wondered what it was like. Making love. Sex.

She knew she was snooping, a fly on the wall without a camera making an amateur documentary about the life of a single, dark-haired, thirty-odd-year-old woman living in a South Kensington mews, that she was a voyeur, a peeping tom. But she was going to be an actress, and how else did actresses gain experience if it wasn't by watching and doing? And, with no-one around for the doing, her education would have to be confined to the watching.

The activity below her was finished. The woman put on a dressing gown, the man rested, lying alone on the bed. Sadie could see the tip of a cigarette glowing in the gathering gloom. Suddenly she realized why the love-making always took place so early in the evening, why it was always finished by ten o'clock. The man was married. He had to hurry home. And she wondered why sex was better with this woman than with his wife?

A light went on in the sitting room and the music was turned off. In the bedroom the man began to dress. All that was missing, Sadie thought, as she gazed up into her Cinemascope-shaped mirror, were the end titles.

Getting up she closed her curtains and, abandoning her essay for the night, undressed and slipped into bed.

She wasn't tired. She stared around her room at the posters and postcards, at the map of the Edinburgh fringe and the lithograph she had found depicting the execution of Marie Antoinette; the guillotine had been so much smaller than she had expected. She had seen simulated sex in any number of movies, but the idea of the couple making love aroused her. She was just seventeen. Kept young at an all girls school the mysteries of sex would not be long delayed in reaching her. And she thought about how Camille de Malignon seduced Will Yorke.

She closed her eyes and imagined the woman in the mews house. Her lover would have left by now. She would be sleeping alone. Was that how she wanted it? Was this man using her? Was she using him? Was that what romance became, people using each other, furtive couplings to a supermarket opera? She was young enough to hope for better.

Chapter Eighteen

(i)

'Rewrites? Who would want to rewrite what is perfect? Not me, for sure. No rewrites will be necessary.' Bruno Messenger smiled and wiped his mouth with his napkin.

Charlie was glad about that: Bruno Messenger had a slight tendency to speak with his mouth full.

'Of course that isn't to say that I don't think the visual scope couldn't be extended to the benefit of the movie.'

Charlie was suspicious. 'How do you mean?'

'Well, I think I'm right in saying that when you wrote the play and then the screenplay you were thinking about the constraints of theatre, and then the budget limitations of an art-house movie. Right? But if we can take away some of those budgetary constraints, well, just imagine what a gift that you as a writer would be getting.' Again Bruno Messenger smiled.

'That's right, Charlie,' Harvey was beaming. 'You'll be able to unshackle your imagination completely.'

Charlie didn't answer although he was itching to say, 'It already is unshackled.' He wanted to get to know Bruno Messenger better before he said too much. So he cut into his baby chicken and listened as the conversation drifted around him, and Bruno Messenger expounded on his philosophies of film and life.

'If I believe in anything it's that we have a moral imperative to use film to reflect on the value of our spiritual lives. And I think *Shadows on a Wall* could be an important movie because it does just that – it comments on relationships, on women's place in society, on the perspective of revolution, on ambition, on war, and on the eternal battle between good and evil. It's also two terrific love stories. I think it's uniquely brilliant.'

Harvey nodded solemnly. 'That's right,' he said, as though he had been thinking those things all the time. 'Uniquely brilliant.'

Charlie was sure he blushed. He wasn't used to this kind of flattery, and he had not expected to hear the term 'moral imperative' in Hollywood. He wasn't even sure what it meant. Bruno Messenger was full of surprises.

The first surprising thing had been his size. He was a giant, six foot four perhaps, but wide and deep, too. The second surprise had been his youth. He was young, well under thirty. And then there was his face, round and plump, with a nose pinched at the end and slightly pink, making it stand out against the bloodless complexion of his cheeks. He was not regularly handsome, his eyes being too close together, and his teeth too ragged, but some might have considered him attractive in the overdeveloped style of the moment. His best point was his black, wavy, shoulder-length hair. He was wearing a baggy, loosely fitting black suit and black silk shirt, and no tie, although the top buttons of his shirt were fastened. Shoved into the top of his shirt was a white napkin. He liked to eat. He was a big man, and likely to get bigger.

Next to him was another man, a slim, handsome fifty year old with sun-lightened fair hair and a pale ochre tennis tan. This was Jake McKenzie, the Hollywood agent reputed to be better looking than most of his clients, and who had spotted Bruno Messenger's potential while watching rock videos on MTV. The story was that Jake had worked a miracle pulling strings to get Bruno the chance to direct *Digital Watch*. Now Bruno could do whatever he wanted.

They were in one of those exclusive restaurants tucked back in the hills behind Sunset Boulevard, a peppermint-green pavilion overhung by trees at the end of a winding, wooded canyon of mansions and gardens, one of those places where every table sported either great beauty or great wealth and occasionally both, and where everybody appeared to be acquainted. It was nearly ninety degrees outside, but here, under the bamboo shades, in this oasis of air-conditioning, linen jackets and cotton shirts stayed crisp, make-up remained unflawed.

Charlie and Harvey had been in Los Angeles for four days waiting while Jake McKenzie had gone about arranging this meeting. Charlie knew that on a Hollywood time-scale four days to fix a meeting was almost instantaneous, but he couldn't help feeling that by coming to LA and then having to wait around nearly a working week before meeting Bruno in a restaurant of *his* agent's choosing, they had already lost the first round of any negotiation. Hollywood was all about status, deals and little battles. The way Harvey was behaving made them look like supplicants come to beg at the feet of the latest boy wonder. Charlie didn't like that, even if it were true.

Bruno Messenger's voice was suddenly raised. 'Redford's too old.'

Charlie felt his ears sharpening.

Bruno was shaking his head. 'Too many lines and liver spots. Only good for character parts these days. Besides, he's only got one good side. You can only shoot him looking right to left.'

That was right-to-left Robert Redford out of the way.

'What about De Niro?' asked Jake McKenzie.

Alongside Harvey was turning pink with excitement. He poured himself about twenty dollars' worth of Perrier water.

Bruno Messenger wagged his head again, his mouth full of pasta. 'Bobby's a wop,' he said, familiar and dismissive at once.

'Right,' said Harvey.

'Napoleon was a wop,' said Charlie.

'But a French wop,' corrected Harvey.

'Only just,' came back Charlie. 'He was Corsican. His first language was Corsican, which is a kind of Italian dialect. France only took control of Corsica in 1768 when the Genoese decided to sell it a few months before Napoleon was born. If Napoleon had been born a year earlier he'd have been born an Italian wop.'

Silence descended on the table. The discreet clink of silver on china and the hum of conversation as the other diners picked daintily at their low-calorie lunches seemed suddenly muffled. Bruno Messenger and Jake McKenzie gazed at Charlie.

Harvey looked slightly irritated as though to say, 'What is this, Charlie? A history lecture?'

'You think we should ask Robert De Niro if he wants to play Napoleon?' Bruno Messenger asked, his voice suddenly louder.

It was as though the whole of Los Angeles was listening.

'No,' Charlie said. 'I think he'd be completely wrong.'

'He's too modern looking,' said Harvey.

'Maybe he *is* a thought, though,' said Bruno.

'I could get the screenplay to him,' said Jake McKenzie.

'Maybe he isn't such a bad idea,' wavered Harvey. 'Yeah, Robert De Niro. Like unusual casting.'

Charlie looked at the baby chicken on his plate. Outside on the lawn a very large peacock was strolling and displaying. He watched the tail fan out and then fold in. Some birds had all the luck. He tried to imagine De Niro acting with Belinda, but the pictures wouldn't come. Then he thought about Belinda as they had sat together months earlier planning the movie and he felt lonely. She had been so cold when he left. 'I don't think De Niro would be a very good idea,' he said at last.

'Yes, well, maybe you're right,' said Bruno.

'I think so,' conceded Harvey.

Charlie thought, Harvey Bamberg, you're a craven fink. You'd agree with anything anybody said. Harvey's imaginary voice snarled back, I'm a producer, for Christ's sake, and I'm desperate to get this movie to the starting gate. Of course I'll agree with everyone.

The lunch meandered on, multi-million-dollar names wandering in and out of the conversation as they were suggested and considered, then mentally filed or rejected: Pacino looked 'too street-smart', Hoffman was 'too small', Bruce Willis was 'only one geared', Cruise was 'too cute', Jeremy Irons was 'Dr Death', Mel Gibson 'too wide-eyed', Harrison Ford 'too American', Jack Nicholson 'too crazy looking' and Gerard Depardieu was French.

'Being French is a disqualifier for playing Napoleon?' Charlie asked.

Harvey glowered at him. Bruno Messenger sighed silently.

'He isn't available,' murmured Jake McKenzie. No-one asked him how he knew. He probably didn't.

The conversation moved on. The situation was straightforward. Bruno Messenger wanted to direct *Shadows on a*

Wall and between them Charlie, Harvey, Nathalie and the Grave Digger, as producer, co-producers and associate producer, owned the screenplay. The next step was to *attach* Bruno Messenger to the project and, thus armed, for Harvey to go to the studios to find the money to make the film. That was how it was done.

It was Jake who first mentioned Sam Jordan. Sam Jordan was his top client, and generally reckoned to be one of the currently most desired men in movies, which meant, in the world. At first Charlie thought Jake was joking and giggled to himself. They were on to the pudding, Bruno chain-sawing his way through a dense weald of Black Forest gateau.

The deforestation stopped. 'Hey, yeah! What about that! Sam Jordan,' Bruno grinned.

'Why don't I talk to him?' said Jake. 'He's read the script. I know he likes it.'

'*Sam Jordan's read the script!!!*' Harvey burbled.

'I asked him to take a look at it,' said Jake. 'That was all right, wasn't it?'

'*Absolutely* all right.'

'Sam Jordan?' said Charlie. He was no longer giggling.

'A very talented actor,' said Jake McKenzie.

'Underrated.' This was Bruno.

'He's brilliant,' Harvey agreed.

'And I know he's available this fall.'

'*Fall?*' Harvey nearly choked on his sorbet. 'You want to shoot *this fall?*' Astonishment was caked in ice crumbs around his mouth.

'Fall into winter,' nodded Bruno. 'We can't wait a year. I'm committed to Paramount as of next May. It has to be this year, or never.' Seeing the look of consternation on Harvey's face Bruno put down his fork. 'Hey, come on, who knows what you guys will be doing this time next year? If we can raise the funding it can be this year. No problem.'

'And, as I say, I happen to know Sam Jordan is available,' Jake McKenzie repeated.

'*Jesus!* Fall. That doesn't give us a whole lot of time . . .' worried Harvey.

'Sam Jordan!' Charlie said again. But, preposterous as the idea was, he was aware of a tremor of excitement. Sam Jordan was a star.

★　　★　　★

Harvey couldn't stop talking as he drove his hired Buick back down the canyon. 'We're in a whole new arena, Charlie. You know that? A whole new arena. We're going to have to renegotiate. Sam Jordan! Jesus! They really think he might be interested. Can you believe it? Just wait till I tell Nathalie.'

'Just wait till I tell Belinda,' said Charlie.

(ii)

Belinda couldn't help but laugh. 'Sam Jordan as Napoleon?' she giggled. 'Well, I suppose they could have suggested Robin Williams.'

'Perhaps he'll be brilliant,' Charlie said.

'I've never been there, do pigs fly in California?' she asked.

It was one o'clock in the morning and she was lying in bed. She had been waiting for Charlie to call, but she didn't want him to know that. It was difficult to change an attitude when they were an ocean and a continent apart.

'Bruno says he'd like to see some of your work,' Charlie said. 'He wants you to get some tapes together and for you to courier them out here. I should really have brought them with me. I didn't think—'

'Oh, come on, Charlie,' Belinda interrupted, 'what's the point? I mean, what does he want to see? The girl with the bed with the zig-zag springs? That thing I did as a Martian go-go dancer? The only really good thing was Marie Walewska.'

'That's not true. There's all kinds of stuff,' Charlie encouraged. 'They don't have to be big parts. Bruno sounded really interested.' Then suddenly he added: 'I showed him your photograph. He said you were very pretty.'

'Which photograph?'

'You know . . . the one I keep in my wallet.'

'Oh, yes.' Charlie was speaking quickly and nervously, and Belinda conjured a picture of him trying to sell her to these tough movie-people while they made polite noises. Poor Charlie, he would do his best, she knew that. But then, as he talked on, that picture faded and was replaced by one of him having an exciting time out there in Hollywood, going to restaurants with stars like Sam Jordan, meeting glamorous people,

143

being seduced by their flattery. She didn't like the way he kept saying, 'Bruno this . . .' and, 'Bruno that . . .'

They didn't talk for long. She didn't have anything new to tell him, and he sounded embarrassed that he was there when she wasn't.

After they had hung up Belinda pondered the call. Why had he added, 'I love you' right at the end? It sounded like guilt. She put the light out.

It didn't happen straight away, but slowly little doubts and insecurities, for so long hidden in their contentment, began to emerge. She had never distrusted him before, but she had never felt left behind before.

For hours Belinda lay and listened to the rain on her London window, staring into the blackness. At three, four and five in the morning the magnifying glass of imagination can be a peculiarly cruel instrument of torture.

She went back to the video shop in the Fulham Road the next morning and took out three Sam Jordan movies, *Admissions Only*, *Terminal Case* and *Replay Mode*. In one he played a detective whose wife is murdered while he is in bed with his mistress who has recently been released from a mental institution; in another he was a doctor who stumbles upon a new brain virus while having an affair with the wife of a corrupt colleague; and in the third he was a TV sports journalist investigating drug taking among athletes while having an affair with a beautiful sprinter, whom he never suspects of taking stimulants until she suffers a heart attack at a race meeting. They were all typical Hollywood parts for a handsome star actor in his forties (playing mid-thirties), showing a modern man with a tangled love life and a problem to solve within a hundred minutes.

As an actor he was predictable, but he suited these parts well. She stared hard at him. He was handsome, all right, but it was his hair which put him beyond comparison. There was just so much of it, long, wavy and wonderfully thick, tousled and shining, not brown, nor chestnut, not red, nor fair, but almost light copper in tone. Hair was so important to movie stars. Where would James Dean have been without the hair, or Michael Douglas? Lots of men were good looking, but very few had great hair. And none like Sam Jordan.

144

She watched bits of all three movies while she did the ironing, one unusual thing striking her: she had never seen so much of a man's bottom on screen. 'Well, I guess Napoleon had a bottom like everybody else,' she mused aloud at the fifth sighting, and laughed out loud. Vanity in men always amused her, and she wished Charlie could see her laughing at that moment; how she really didn't care.

(iii)

'Hello?'

'He's sticking at half a million,' a familiar voice said down the line.

Charlie pulled himself up in his very large bed. Twenty seconds ago he had been sound asleep. 'Hello . . . ?' he repeated.

'I tried for seven hundred and fifty thousand, but he didn't think he'd be able to get a deal at that. I may be able to get a little more on the points, but half a million seems to be it for the moment.'

'Half a million what?' Charlie recognized the voice. It was Larry, calling from London, but he couldn't make sense of the conversation. He looked at his watch. It was after nine.

'Dollars, of course. Did you expect pounds? Isn't that being a little greedy?'

'I'm not with you.'

There was an irritated pause from the London end of the phone. 'Charlie, have you got a girl there with you?'

'No, of course not.'

'Well, you're sounding very dopey. I've just spent the last two hours renegotiating on your behalf. If you and Harvey can tie in Bruno Messenger and Sam Jordan we're into a completely different situation. Like real money. What do you think? How does half a million sound to you?'

Charlie looked around the gloom of his hotel room. It was split level, seemingly about half the size of a tennis court and was decorated in the dark, carved wood, nouveau-Spanish style of Los Angeles. The shutters were closed but he could see bright sunlight trying to razor in through the slats. It was cold. He remembered he had left the air-conditioning on too high the

145

previous night. He had been drunk. 'Half a million,' he repeated. He couldn't imagine so much money.

'Which is a bit more than the going rate for someone like you. But, as we said before, you hold a lot of the aces, and now's the time to call them in.'

'Aces?'

'Director approval. If anyone wants Bruno Messenger to make this movie you have to agree. Had you forgotten? That's an ace. You know, Charlie, this really could be a terrific film. Up to twenty-five million dollars, Harvey was saying. And shooting this autumn. It could change your whole career.'

Charlie could picture Larry sitting at his desk in St James's in the late London afternoon while Emma brought him a cup of tea. Nothing aroused Larry more than talking in millions. There was a good chance that the Indian rug would be employed before the evening was out. What would Emma's excuse to her husband be tonight? he wondered. 'I thought you weren't keen on *Shadows on a Wall*,' he said.

The reply sounded almost hurt. 'Whatever gave you that impression? Of course I'm keen on it.'

'That's all right then,' said Charlie, and agreed. Half a million dollars it was.

In his bathroom Charlie took a shower (he only took baths when he was writing) and two Alka Seltzers, thoroughly regretting the previous night. He had met up with a couple of English comedy writers exiled in Hollywood and it had been a long evening as they had taken him over to Marina Del Rey, complaining all the time about everything apart from the money they were earning and their sunny Californian girlfriends.

'In this town promises are cheap. Watch your back, Charlie, Bruno Messenger has only been around five minutes, but he went through seven writers on *Digital Watch*,' one had warned.

'That can't happen to me,' Charlie had grinned through his poached shark. 'I have a fool-proof contract. He told me that the script for *Digital Watch* needed a lot of work.'

'Whereas *Shadows on a Wall* doesn't?'

'Not according to Bruno. He doesn't want to change a word.'

That was when it had been the other guys' turn to smile.

In his shower now Charlie nursed his hangover. He was glad he had never been tempted to come and work in Hollywood. It made everyone so cynical. Then he thought about Larry's call and wondered whether half a million was absolutely the most they could push for.

An hour later, his headache easing, and having tried and failed to reach Belinda on the phone, he joined Harvey in his suite. Nathalie was already out sitting by the fifth-floor pool, while the Grave Digger had gone off to view a high-tech funeral parlour in Pasadena.

Harvey was working the phones, sitting on a sofa surrounded by possibly a dozen pieces of yellow writing-paper, each one containing a name, a telephone number and a different piece of information. A thirtyish blonde woman in jeans who looked a little like Shelley Winters was sitting at a word processor. She had not been there the previous day.

Harvey smiled. 'Charlie, meet Simone Estoril. Simone discovered your screenplay. You owe her.'

The girl at the typewriter batted four black brushes of mascara. 'Hi, Charlie,' she said. 'It was my pleasure. Anything I can do, just give me a call.'

'Thank you,' Charlie said.

Sorting through some sheets of paper Harvey held out a list of studios. 'So far we have Tri-Star, Fox, Columbia, Warners, Orion and maybe Paramount asking to see a script . . .'

A telephone rang. Simone answered, then turned to Harvey. 'Julie Wyatt's secretary at Buffalo is wondering if you can do a six o'clock this afternoon? Jake's already said "yes".'

Harvey beamed. '. . . and Buffalo,' he finished. 'Tell them "yes",' he said to Simone, then looked back at Charlie. 'So, what do you know! Suddenly we ain't pariahs no more, suddenly we ain't got leprosy, suddenly we ain't making nerve gas, suddenly people are picking up their phones again. Does that convince you about Bruno Messenger?'

Charlie didn't have time to answer. Another phone rang. It was Jake McKenzie.

'*Jake*, how're you doing?'

Charlie backed away towards the door. It was a sunny day. Perhaps he would go and join Nathalie by the pool and get some sun while he reread his script. It was going to be a busy time. There would be a lot of meetings. He wanted to look his best. And it would be nice to see Nathalie Seillans in a bikini.

Chapter Nineteen

(i)

Turning off Melrose Jake McKenzie's black Jaguar XJS slid past the old water tower at the entrance to the Buffalo Pictures lot: hurrying twenty yards behind in his Buick floated Harvey Bamberg. Above both cars, Bill, the life-sized continuously kicking buffalo motif, a famous trademark for a no-longer-quite-so-famous studio, glowered and stood guard.

At the gate a blue-uniformed porter nodded a friendly recognition to Jake and, passing him an identification tag, waved him through, before immediately lowering the bar again while he checked Harvey's name on his security list.

Everyone knows Jake McKenzie, Harvey thought, as he followed the Jaguar between the bougainvillaea-draped studio bungalows and cream soundstages towards the executive car-park. And mentally he made himself a promise: this time next year everyone would know the name of Harvey Bamberg, too. Nathalie would like that.

For years Harvey had been coming to Los Angeles hustling and sitting on his hotel bed waiting for calls to be returned – not from studio chiefs, they never made personal calls to producers in the Harvey Bamberg league, but from anyone who might be able to put a piece in the jigsaws which had made his movies possible. It had never been easy and many times he had crept home yellow with frustration. No-one loved a nickel-and-dime producer with a lousy project and that was all he had ever had.

Suddenly, however, everything was different: within the space of a few hours he had had meetings at both Columbia and Warners over in Burbank and was now about to sit down with Julie Wyatt, senior executive in charge of production at Buffalo. He had never managed to even get her on the phone before. This made Harvey very happy.

In fact, Harvey thought, as he padded after Jake into the Buffalo Pictures executives' building, had it not been for the haste with which Bruno Messenger wanted to start shooting everything in his life would have been just about perfect. '*This* year?' they'd said at Columbia. '*This* fall?' at Warners, brows knitting. It would be interesting now to see what Julie Wyatt at Buffalo had to say.

Julie Wyatt was keen. She had already read the script, not just the coverage. Harry had read it, too, she said. She meant Harry Weitzman, the chief executive officer of the studio. Unfortunately Harry was in New York. Jake nodded at that. He knew, he said. Harvey nodded, as well, pretending he knew, too: knowledge was everything in the movie business.

'And we like it a lot as far as it goes,' Julie Wyatt was saying. 'But our question has to be, how far do you think the writer can open it out? Right now it's a little European art-house movie. Too subtle for what we need, maybe too ironic for Americans. Have you thought about another writer?'

Jake McKenzie broke in before Harvey had chance to answer. 'Bruno feels that he knows how to put it right, that it needn't be more than two or three weeks' work. He'd like to give the writer another chance, and for them to sit down together.'

Harvey nodded. 'Charlie's looking forward to starting work with Bruno,' he said, thinking how glad he was that Charlie couldn't hear this conversation.

'Right,' said Julie Wyatt and made a note.

She was very businesslike. In her wide, darkly monochrome office of greys and silver, she had got down to basics as soon as they had been introduced. New at Buffalo, having stayed too long at Paramount, she was what Harvey called a 'semi' girl, one of those single, thin, pasty-faced, angular New Yorkers (Wyatt was, he believed, an Anglicization of something unpronounceable from Eastern Europe), who lived alone in the semi-shade, wore semi-slinky clothes to work and who, it was rumoured, occasionally went to bed with semi-name directors, which was nothing remarkable for a semi-attractive woman executive on the way up in Hollywood. Even her dog, a massive, fluffy, grey-and-white Old English sheepdog, sleeping now in a patch of slatted sunlight by the window, seemed to imply a semi-sad, lonely private life.

'What about Sam?' She was addressing Jake McKenzie. It was an open secret that she and Sam Jordan had once been semi-lovers, and that although she had, at his insistence, had an abortion, she still adored him.

'He can see the script needs work, and was wondering if it might not be better if Napoleon and the girl got together in the end, but in general, at this stage, subject to the rewrites and everything else, he's very interested.'

'The end bothered us, too. It's kind of a downer Napoleon going off to St Helena like that.'

'What do you think about Julia Roberts?' Harvey butted in, anxious to get the conversation away from the script. Charlie would explode if he heard the casual way history might be rewritten. 'For the girl, I mean, Marie Walewska. Wouldn't she be just terrific?'

'She'd be wonderful if she were available,' came back Jake evenly. 'As would Michelle Pfeiffer or Yale Meredith. But I know they're not available. Maybe this could be a part for somebody new.'

Julie Wyatt wrinkled her nose. 'Maybe,' she said.

Harvey understood that wrinkle. Star casting made a studio feel secure. The conversation moved on. This was the way it was with Hollywood meetings: introductions, mutual compliments, reactions, names and possible packaging. It usually took about fifteen minutes. Then came money.

'So what are we looking at . . . roughly, say, so that I can give Harry a figure when he calls?' she asked.

'Below the line . . . eighteen,' said Harvey, 'depending on the new script.' He waited, wondering if he should have said sixteen.

Jake nodded. 'Bruno's keen to put the love stories into their historical context, which will mean some pretty extraordinary set pieces. He has some stunning ideas.'

Julie Wyatt made a note of the figure on a pad in front of her. Eighteen million dollars. There was no sign of surprise, although a below-the-line estimate, which would only cover the nuts and bolts of making the movie, was only part of the equation. The stars, director, producers and writer were all 'above the line', as the terminology went, and, since Sam Jordan would be setting the rate at maybe seven million, would all be very expensive. She was, Harvey knew, probably looking at something over thirty million dollars, twenty-five million more than he had been unable to raise in the first place.

'Right, well, look, why don't I talk to Harry, and get back to you when I see if we have anything further to discuss,' she said standing up and ending the meeting.

'One thing. We have to go this fall or we lose Bruno,' Jake reminded. It sounded like a threat.

'On a movie of this scope that seems almost like an impossibility,' Julie said.

'But not quite.' Jake was smiling.

Julie hesitated, and then nodded. 'No. Maybe not quite.'

(ii)

It was almost twilight, magic hour, as the senior executive in charge of production and her dog walked the independent producer and the agent down to reception, past emptying offices and a staircase lined with posters from the Buffalo glory days. Although never one of the biggest names in Hollywood, Buffalo Pictures could trace a distinguished history, via a series of owners, right back to some classic two reelers. Now, held together by a consortium of banks, and, most importantly, a popcorn manufacturer turned semi-philanthropist, the once majestic Buffalo was lame. As they reached the reception a group from marketing were leaving a screening room, shaking their heads.

'They've been looking at *Looking Glass Love*,' Julie Wyatt said. 'It stinks. Practically everything made here in the last five years stinks. The knack's gone.'

'Well, I wouldn't exactly say—' Harvey began.

'I would,' she insisted. 'I really would. That was why Harry and I were brought in. What we need right now here at Buffalo is something big to put our marker on, something ambitious,

151

otherwise they might just as well close us down. New York are being very difficult.'

'So maybe we came on the right day,' Harvey ventured.

'With the right package every day is the right day,' came the unsmiling reply. 'Let me talk to Harry, OK?' She looked at Jake who was waiting by the door. 'And say hello to Sam when you speak to him, will you? Tell him he owes me a call.'

'I'll do that,' said Jake, and bidding her goodbye led Harvey out into the early evening.

Julie Wyatt was thoughtful as she made her way back to her office. Was this the project to turn Buffalo around? Was this the movie on which to gamble her career? The time factor bothered her, as it had obviously worried the other studios. Whoever did *Shadows on a Wall* would have to push absolutely everything to be in production by the fall. But Bruno Messenger was hot, and it was Bruno's involvement that had interested Sam Jordan. If this movie was ever to be made by Bruno Messenger and starring Sam Jordan, it would *have* to be this fall.

Idly she checked, as she did most days, the latest Wall Street listing for Buffalo Pictures in the *Los Angeles Times*. The price was down three cents. She had been given a two-hundred-thousand dollar golden-hello when she joined Buffalo with the proviso that she bought Buffalo stock with the money. But the shares were stuck in the doldrums at just above twenty-three dollars each. If that figure was ever to improve it was up to her and Harry. She worried about New York. The board were not movie-people. They didn't understand. The Candy Corn Corporation, who owned the largest slice of Buffalo, were uneasy at finding themselves involved in a product where the profits were so capricious; while their chairman, Reuben Wiener, now in his mid-seventies and famously and eccentrically secretive, was known to wish he'd stuck to the popcorn side of the movie-business where he had made his billions.

Dropping the newspaper into the bin, she left a message for Harry in New York, and then took her copy of *Shadows on a Wall* over to her sofa by the window. She liked the evenings when the studio was empty and the calls stopped coming. From the moment she arrived at her desk at eight-thirty every morning until she left at seven every night she was under siege. Now she could curl up and read. She could have gone out to dinner, to a screening or to a party, but she liked to work. Later she would return to her small apartment just above Santa Monica

Boulevard at Doheny and slip a packet of frozen vegetarian pasta-for-one into the microwave, but in the mean time she would go through the script once more. When Harry called back she wanted to be ready with her answers.

On the rug across the office her dog Marsha licked herself.

(iii)

Belinda made the decision at five in the morning: with Charlie away it was the perfect opportunity to redecorate the flat. Of course, if Charlie was going to earn half a million dollars for his script they would now be able to afford to have it done professionally, but that wasn't the point. She *wanted* to do it herself. It was their home. She wanted to be the one to make it better.

She was sorry now that she had been cute when he had told her about the new deal Larry was negotiating for him. It was just that the amount of money seemed so ridiculous. Not to worry, she told herself. He would be home soon and she would make it up to him.

And, having made that decision, she quickly fell asleep.

Chapter Twenty

Bruno Messenger took careful aim and pulled the trigger. Ping! He missed. The pellet ricocheted away into the pool and the lizard, which for some minutes had been frozen in mid-traverse as it ascended the side of the pool-house, darted upwards into the thatched roof.

'Jesus!' Bruno growled, and, reloading the air rifle, began to talk again. 'Where did you say that battle was that Napoleon won just before he got to Warsaw?'

'Jena,' said Charlie. 'It was against the Prussian army.'

'Right!' said the director, looking around for another target. 'You see, I think we have to set Napoleon up as a great conqueror before we see him as a great lover. Tell the audience that he was some kind of warrior hero, you know. A lot of people don't know too much about Napoleon, you know what I mean?'

Charlie didn't know that, so he said nothing.

Bruno snapped the rifle open and inserted another pellet. 'This is how I see the opening – maybe even pre-titles: a big battle, cannons, horses, blood, lots of smoke, mud, death, straight-faced Prussians like Panzer divisions, and the French army, white and black horses, lots of colour, red, white and blue tricolours, very romantic, Abel Gance stuff, you know. Subtle hints of the Marseillaise in the scoring. And right off Napoleon is knocking the sausage out of the Prussians, strutting around directing the battle like he's directing a movie. Do you get me? Then he almost gets into trouble. Maybe he gets careless, something is coming right at him, or some guy gets too close and takes a shot at him, but the American guy, Will Yorke, who I think should be young, in his late twenties, say, if we're going to cast him right and get someone like Tom Hanks – anyway, the American guy saves him, almost casual. And Napoleon just gives a little smile, because he never expects to get hit, anyway, and because if it's Sam Jordan playing him the audience just know that he isn't going to die in the opening titles. Then we end the credits and we . . .'

Ping!! He missed again.

'We cut to the *Lawrence of Arabia* shot. Suddenly it's silence and the sleigh is coming forever out of the desert of snow, like Omar Sharif on his camel, except that this is all white, and all we can see at first is a brilliant white screen and then a black spec. Then gradually we hear the sound of hissing and horses' hooves thudding as we pull focus and the sleigh gets closer until, you know, it's amplified to hell right off the console. And we wait and wait, real David Lean chutzpah, you know what I mean? And that's when the movie really begins . . .'

At that moment Bruno's poolside telephone rang. Without pausing for breath he picked it up and began talking in exactly the same tone to another writer about another project. It was the seventh interruption in the past hour.

Charlie waited. He knew exactly what Bruno meant. The *Lawrence of Arabia* shot had been his idea, and now the director had just repeated it as though he was making it up as he went along. In the script Charlie had written the scene for rain or snow, hoping there would be snow, but, realistic as to the limitations of the budget, expecting Napoleon to arrive in Warsaw in a mud-smeared coach. Now Bruno was saying there would be virgin snow as far as the eye could see. Charlie knew that virgin snow didn't come cheap, but he loved the boldness of the image.

Bruno put the phone down. Another lizard appeared over Charlie's shoulder running down the side of the canyon, sending loose red dirt scattering into the undergrowth. *Ping!* Charlie ducked, his hand up to protect his eyes, as Bruno missed again.

Charlie turned back to his writing-pad. 'I love the snow stuff, but I'm not sure about Will Yorke saving Napoleon's life,' he said. 'It could make the movie look like a buddy-buddy story, and there wasn't much buddy-buddy about Napoleon.'

155

The director's plump, boyish face fell. He muttered a quiet obscenity and lapsed into silence.

This was Charlie's first attempt at working with Bruno Messenger. It was not easy. When Charlie didn't agree with him he sulked. Now, he was staring moodily down the barrel of his rifle again. From the house came the sound of a Penn Stadtler album.

Charlie looked around the garden with its palely misted view over Los Angeles. It was another hot day. Perhaps he would be able to see Bruno's pictures better if he swam in the pool, he thought, but he did not suggest it.

The meeting had been arranged at the suggestion of Julie Wyatt. While Harvey and Jake were talking money at Buffalo, it was Charlie's job to start making friends. Later that afternoon he and Bruno would be going to meet Sam Jordan out in Malibu. He was already nervous about that.

Bruno Messenger's home was a small rented house which stood on the side of a hill up behind the Château Marmont, a famous old-time Hollywood hotel on Sunset. Bruno's secretary had asked Charlie to arrive some time in the mid-morning, and it had been at around ten forty-five when he had pulled his hired Toyota into the driveway alongside Bruno's Audi and a four-wheel-drive Cherokee. Climbing from his car Charlie had noticed a new Snickers wrapper lying untidily in a flower-bed. Picking it up, he had dropped it into the garbage bin and rung the bell.

At first there had been no answer, but he had known someone was at home because he had been able to hear rock music coming from inside the house. At last the door had been opened by a Japanese woman carrying a storyboard for a commercial. She looked as though she had been crying.

'Bruno said . . .' Charlie had begun as the woman hurried past to the Cherokee.

'Why don't you go and sit out on the deck for a while,' she had said. 'He's on the phone.' And with that she had driven away.

Entering the house Charlie had made his way through a gloomily shuttered ground-floor room, stepping, as he went, over an extensive and intricate model railway system. It was the biggest train set he had ever seen, snub-nosed locomotives from Canadian Pacific, Amtrak and SNCF hauling long lines of oil tankers, livestock and goods wagons past computerized signals and junctions, through bridges and tunnels, between carpet mountains and plastic forests.

Reaching the garden he had found a deck-chair and then waited for over an hour as a string of other people had come and gone, a couple of messengers, a girl who looked like a secretary, a man who, carrying a portfolio, might have been a designer. Everyone came to Bruno. And when Bruno had finally appeared, carrying a couple of cans of beer, but no glasses, there had been no apology for the delay.

From the start Bruno had dictated the conversation. Enthusiastic, but with a low attention span, he had jumped from subject to subject, taken calls in between shots at lizards, name-dropped one minute, talked about girls he'd had sex with the next, and referred continually to other people's movies. 'It's a pity Marlon got so old,' he said at one point. 'He played Napoleon, didn't he? *Desirée*. Not his best work, but he had the look. Charles Boyer, too. He was another. In *Conquest*, right!'

All the time, stretched across a lounger in the shade of a parasol, he ate nuts and cheese biscuits and sipped beer. Now, because Charlie had disagreed with him, he was in a mood.

At last, getting up to change the music he also changed the subject. 'So what about Mârie Walewska?' he asked. 'Demi Moore looks kind of European. She has a luminous quality, I always think.'

Charlie nodded. 'Yes,' he said, then added: 'I asked Belinda to send some tapes . . .'

'Ah yes. Belinda. I'm looking forward to meeting her. She's working in radio, right?'

Working in radio. He made it sound as though Belinda had some unpleasant kind of skin condition.

'Lots of very good people work in radio in England,' Charlie said. 'Top writers and actors. All kinds of people.'

'Really!' Bruno looked disbelieving. After a moment he said: 'Tell me, Charlie, do you really see Belinda as a movie star? I mean, can she cut it on the big screen?'

Charlie hesitated. At last he said: 'She was so good on stage, and so beautiful. I was really proud of her.' He hated himself immediately. It sounded so lame.

'But movies are different. Am I right or am I right?'

Charlie didn't answer. It would have seemed disloyal to Belinda to agree.

157

Bruno must have realized this because he didn't press for a reply. Instead he watched a lizard which was venturing along the edge of the pool. 'What do you know about Yale Meredith?' he asked as he tracked it down the poolside, the rifle to his eye.

'Only that she's beautiful, mad and not available.'

'Two out of three,' said Bruno. 'She's beautiful and she's mad, all right. But the backing for *Jim Crow* pulled out last night. She's available.' He squeezed the trigger.

Ping! The lizard's head snapped back.

'Hey! What about that?' Bruno triumphed.

Getting up Charlie crossed to the small, dead reptile. Its eye had been shattered. Bruno had found its weakest point. 'Good shot,' he said bleakly, and thought about one-eyed Billy Yeo.

Bruno wasn't listening. He was back on the phone, talking about money with someone called Al in Australia.

(ii)

The title-page to Sam Jordan's copy of *Shadows on a Wall* was missing. Sam Jordan knew where it was. It had gone down the lavatory.

It had started out as a joke economy measure when he had been young and regularly unemployed. Now it was a much-rumoured fact of the business. Sam Jordan, the most desired man in America, wiped his bottom on pages from bad scripts. In this way, he would tell himself darkly, 120 pages of paper would not be completely wasted. It wasn't always very comfortable, and he had occasionally considered writing to the Writers Guild of America (under a pseudonym, of course) to suggest that their members submitted their screenplays on soluble double-ply tissue-paper. But, as he usually read scripts while sitting on the lavatory, it made sense.

Sam Jordan sat on the lavatory a great deal when he wasn't working. There wasn't anything wrong with his bowels, in fact he was in perfect shape, but health obsessed him and he had frequently read in his library of medical books that a motion must never be hurried. It amused him to think that while he was sitting on the lavatory reading scripts and trying to conjure up mental images of how a film might look on the screen, he was making *motion pictures*.

Motion pictures! He liked that joke. It was one of his better ones, although he didn't like to tell it to too many people because sitting on the lavatory with his trousers around his ankles was not the image Sam Jordan liked to promote. After the Sam Jordan hair, the Sam Jordan backside was the item of American anatomy voted most highly in fan magazines (it had even been featured in *Vanity Fair*), but nothing devalued a product so much as ridicule. Sam Jordan had not forgotten the ribald jokes which had gone about when it had become known that Elvis Presley had succumbed while sitting on his throne.

As it happened he had made a rare mistake with *Shadows on a Wall*. It had not been a bad script. The missing title-page was the result of a misunderstanding when two scripts, both with burgundy covers, had appeared in his bathroom. One had been *Plague Zone*, a story about a scientist captured by a fictitious Middle Eastern country and forced to make a plague carrying bomb with which to destroy Los Angeles; the other was *Shadows on a Wall*.

Somehow he had suspected *Plague Zone* might be rubbish, so he had begun to read *Shadows on a Wall*. Napoleon! That was more like it. An hour later, with both scripts on the floor, and the actor into a third about a renegade cop, he had remembered an appointment with an aromatherapist, reached out to vent his disapproval of *Plague Zone* and, before realizing his mistake, despatched the top page of *Shadows on a Wall* into his Malibu Colony septic tank.

For some reason, this made Sam Jordan nervous. Here he was having to meet the writer himself, knowing that the top page of what, for all he knew, might turn out to be an Academy Award winning script, had been torn out, abused and then flushed away; as though, straightaway, this Charles Holyoake would be saying with one of those English accents that could shatter crystal, 'What do you mean you wiped your bottom on my script?'

Chewing a beta-carotene pastille Jordan checked his look in the mirror. He liked what he saw. Carefully he ran his fingers through his hair. That was even better. He was standing in his bedroom overlooking the ocean. He liked the way the late afternoon light seemed to bounce off the sea, softening his features, burnishing his hair.

Burnishing! That was the word. He had read it about himself once in a flattering feature in the *Los Angeles Times*. 'The old gold, burnished hair of Sam Jordan . . .' He smiled at the memory, catching his reflection in the mirror; a Napoleonic smile, he thought. Napoleon: he had had burnished hair, too – well, light chestnut, not black as most people imagined. He'd read that in a book: it looked like a good omen. Napoleon: this was a chance to show them what kind of an actor he really was. It would be good to be seen working with a young director. It would demonstrate that he was always open to hot new talent.

He looked around for the books he had sent out to Brentano's to buy, found his reading glasses, and, satisfied that he was suitably scholastic in appearance, made his way from his bedroom, across the landing and down the wide staircase to await his guests. He would talk to them in his library. That seemed most appropriate. He sure as hell didn't want any horn-rimmed, snooty, intellectual, son of a bitch of an English writer thinking Sam Jordan was all hair and ass.

(iii)

Sam Jordan's beach house lay at the end of a private lane leading to the ocean. From the road it didn't look particularly special, just a gate in a high white wall, but, as Charlie and Bruno parked their cars and were buzzed inside, there was a surprise. The frame of the Mexican mansion had been built around the two giant, glass-encased trunks of very old palm trees.

'From the beach, it looks as though the house is wearing a hat, or sitting under a sun shade, wouldn't you say?' a familiar voice said as they entered the main hall.

Charlie looked around. Leaning nonchalantly on a balcony directly above and behind the entrance, and holding a couple of books and a script, stood Sam Jordan, his face lit in a beam of multicoloured light which shone from a stained-glass porthole at the highest point of the westerly wall. Without moving a muscle Sam Jordan had made a terrific entrance.

Introductions and pleasantries over, Jordan led the way into a room lined with leather-covered encyclopedias, gold-embossed, bound screenplays and a scattering of the latest books on *The New York Times* bestseller lists; and where, with Mozart murmuring from inside oak panels, a Mexican maid served iced tea. It was such a pompous, formal meeting, Charlie kept thinking: Belinda would have had hysterics.

He studied Sam Jordan. Now that he could see him properly he was surprised. The man was obviously extremely handsome, and his hair was truly extraordinary, but in the flesh he looked at least a half-dozen years older than he ever did on film; older and smaller, his body dieted and exercised to boyhood slim, his jaw line just a little too tight to be true.

'Let me say right off, Charles,' Jordan began as the maid left, 'I think this script is a terrific piece of work. Brilliant, even.'

Charlie enjoyed the compliment from the most famous backside in America and waited for the 'but'. There was always a 'but'.

'But . . . for me to really get into this part, *really* get into it, I mean, do the part justice, I'd have to feel that Napoleon was a winner . . . I don't mean we'd have to alter history. I mean I *know* Napoleon lost at Waterloo, but that on a *personal* level he was a winner, heroic even. To be honest I've been reading quite a lot about him and I've had a couple of thoughts that maybe we could toss around.'

Across the room Bruno Messenger made an agreeable noise and munched on a cookie. At his own home he had been assertive, virtually swaggering. In the presence of the star he was quiet.

Charlie nodded. 'Of course. Feel free. Toss around all you want.'

The sarcasm wasn't intended. It just came. But if Sam Jordan registered it, he didn't react. Instead he referred to some notes he had made, speaking slowly and with great deliberation, as though his every thought had to be weighed and considered. Stars, Charlie had noticed before, always spoke slowly. Listening to Warren Beatty being interviewed was like waiting for speech to finish being invented.

'Well, it seemed to me,' he began, 'that maybe there's something to be gained in the idea that Napoleon sacrifices the chance of saving his empire for the love of a woman. Or that maybe Marie Wa . . . *looska*, is that how you pronounce it?, that maybe she was the only one he ever loved and the reason he escapes from Elba is to win back his empire so that he can make her his Empress.'

Charlie crossed his arms defensively. He's crackers, he thought.

Bruno Messenger nodded thoughtfully. 'That's interesting,' he murmured.

'And Napoleon,' the star persisted, 'I'd like him more if he was the strong, silent type.'

'He may have been the most garrulous man in history,' Charlie said.

Jordan agreed. 'That's right. He talked all the time, I read that. But I don't see him that way. Audiences go for guys who don't say too much. Look at what it did for Clint Eastwood's career.'

'Well . . .' began Charlie, as he tried unsuccessfully to picture Napoleon taking Clint Eastwood as a role model. But a grunt from Bruno told him to shut up. They were there to listen.

'Another thing . . . the battle sequences. I'm actually pretty useful with a sword. I had to learn to fence for *Blood Sweat* and I've made a point of keeping it up. I have a small gym here and a fencing instructor comes three times a week. He's an Olympic bronze. A Swedish guy. Anyway, ignore this if you like, but is there maybe an opportunity to show Napoleon becoming involved in some hand-to-hand fighting on the battle-field? Maybe during the retreat from Moscow or at Waterloo? You know, show him as a doer as well as a military strategist. Or what about a duel? Could he maybe fight a duel . . . the girl? Some guy maybe calls her a Polish slut and Napoleon fights a duel over her honour. What about the American guy, Will Yorke? Some misunderstanding. They fight, Napoleon wins and spares Will Yorke's life, who then becomes his devoted aide. And by the way I think Mickey Rourke would be wrong for this part. He's too modern. We need someone not quite so quirky. Maybe a little older, too. Not quite so . . .' His voice faded. His knuckles were tense.

Mickey Rourke? No-one had even mentioned Mickey Rourke. Bruno wanted someone more like Tom Hanks, anyway. Things were moving very quickly. Suddenly *Shadows on a Wall* sounded like an Errol Flynn film. 'Napoleon didn't fight duels. He was an artillery expert,' Charlie said quietly.

'We were thinking about Yale Meredith for Marie,' the director cut in.

'Is that right?' Sam Jordan forgot the script.

'You've never worked with her, have you?' Charlie dropped

in. Bruno had mentioned that earlier. It made it look as though Charlie had seen all of Jordan's films.

Jordan shook his head. 'Pretty lady,' he murmured. 'A real pretty woman.'

'Beautiful,' Bruno said. 'And good.'

Charlie began to nod, and then stopped himself, shocked. He had written the part of Marie Walewska for Belinda. How could he have forgotten so quickly?

Bruno was hurrying on. 'We thought of looking for an unknown for Camille de Malignon. Someone new to movies maybe. She's an aristocrat so maybe a French girl. Not American. Audiences have a problem with the idea that an American can be an aristocrat.'

A French girl? This was new to Charlie, but again he did not argue.

An indecent expression was now spreading across Sam Jordan's face. He was nearly as famous for his women as he was for his hair and backside.

'It seems to me we may be on to something important here,' he said, getting up and reaching for a book. 'Like possibly the key to Napoleon's whole personality. I mean, do you guys know what he said about his wife . . . ?' He put on his glasses. The book fell open at the appropriate page. 'Hear this – "I loved Josephine," Napoleon said, "although I did not respect her. But she had the prettiest little pussy imaginable." ' Jordan looked up. 'Can you believe that? Isn't that something!'

Bruno grinned; 'Napoleon said that?'

'Napoleon said that!' The star looked at Charlie. 'Maybe you could work that in somewhere. I think a lot of women would enjoy hearing me say that . . . fellas, too.'

He had been chatty before, but now that he was on to a subject he knew something about Jordan was as fulsome as the man he was considering playing, and for thirty minutes the intimate attributes of various famous film actresses dominated the conversation. It was not boring. Jordan had been to bed with most of the women on everyone's top ten, and a few hundred more besides.

'So we find the new Juliette Binoche or Isabelle Adjani,' he said finally, and wet the length of his top lip with the tip of his tongue, a gesture which might have been repulsive in anyone less celebrated.

'Exactly,' smiled Bruno.

163

The talk had begun to meander back to the script when suddenly Jordan stood up. 'Will you excuse me?' he said. 'I have something to do.' And he left the room.

At first Charlie and Bruno chatted on, throwing names and ideas back and forth, but after a while their conversation dried up. They waited in silence. Time passed. When, after an hour, Sam Jordan had not returned they had grown restless.

'I've got to get back,' Bruno complained, exploring the ground floor so that he might say goodbye to their host.

Charlie looked out towards the pool at the rear of the house and into the small gymnasium.

Bruno started up the stairs. 'Hello, er, hello . . .' he called, tentatively.

There was no answer.

Carrying on up, he opened a door and then another and another. 'Hello,' he called again.

Charlie watched from the hall. There was no-one upstairs, and the maid was no longer in the kitchen. Going to the front door he opened it and called out: 'Sam, Sam . . .' It was now dark outside.

'Can I help you, sir?' A small Mexican man appeared around the corner of the house.

'We, er, we're looking for Mr Jordan.'

'Mr Jordan went to New York, sir.'

'New York? That can't be. He was here. We were having a meeting.'

'Oh yes. About an hour ago. He'll be at the airport by now.'

Behind him Charlie heard Bruno Messenger swear softly to himself. 'Son of a bitch,' he muttered, and then chuckled.

'Is that some kind of a joke?' Charlie asked, as they made their way out to the cars.

'I don't know. I guess it's just something he does,' said Bruno.

He should have been angry, Sam Jordan had been extremely rude, but out in the road Charlie suddenly saw the funny side of it, and he looked into the sky wondering whether Sam Jordan was already airborne. In Hollywood the bigger you became the longer people would wait for you. It was all about waiting. He laughed to himself. It was silly, but he felt good. Charlie was a movie fan and Sam Jordan, vain and foolish though he was, was a movie star.

Climbing into his hired Toyota Charlie noticed for the first time the expensive wedge shape of Bruno's Audi. It was a handsome vehicle. It was all silly, but this was Hollywood. It might be fun to drive an expensive car for a few days. He would call the rental company the very next day.

(iv)

Harvey Bamberg looked around the bungalow. It was part of the old Hollywood preserved on the Buffalo lot for favourites of the new, and it thrilled him to be there. It was a mark of how far he had come. He loved the diffused light in these old places, and the patterns in shadow made by the venetian blinds. When he pulled them apart he could just see the kicking hoof of the Buffalo motif over the main gate.

Stretching back in his swivel chair he studied the framed photograph of Nathalie on his desk. She was out shopping with Edward that afternoon and for a moment he pictured them together. They made a handsome couple, and he wondered if Nathalie ever desired her walker. Maybe. Sometimes in the night when he and Nathalie were making love and talking dirty Edward's name would come up, and he would sense Nathalie smiling above him in the dark. But Edward was a gentleman: he would never take advantage of the situation.

For a second other pictures showing Nathalie making love to the man she had met in Avoriaz sidled into his mind, but he forced them away. Things were going well. He must look forward. The word was out that he had a hot property with a hot director attached and one of the world's most popular actors semi-attached. As three weeks ago no-one had been interested in *Shadows on a Wall* it had been worth giving Jake McKenzie an 'executive producer' credit and the couple of points he was angling for, and employing his old girlfriend – 'well, not a girl friend, just, you know, someone I know' – as his personal assistant. This town ran on favours. Jake wanted Simone off his back, and Simone wanted to break into production. And as she was the one person to have seen the potential in Charlie's script maybe she was a useful person to have around, anyway.

It was all up to Charlie now. If Charlie could open up the script the way Bruno and Buffalo wanted, they might soon be walking away with millions, and, better yet, none of that art-house stuff, either. Nathalie would soon see that real status was in the grosses. She would really love him then, when he made her rich and fashionable: Hollywood fashionable.

They would all love him, Buffalo Pictures most of all. That was why he had been given this bungalow. Harry Weitzman was gambling with a deal for a new script and a mountain of expenses that this might be the movie to turn Buffalo around. It would mean a mad rush to be ready to shoot in the fall, a crazy way of behaving. But when wasn't making movies crazy?

There was a buzz on the intercom. 'Do you still want me to hold your calls, Mr Bamberg? I have Julie Wyatt on the line.'

Harvey smiled, until his dimples quivered with pleasure. 'Put her through.' There was a click. 'Hello, Julie, how are you?'

Julie Wyatt's enthusiasm was in full spate. 'If there's anything you want, Harvey, you only have to ask. You know that, don't you?'

'That's very sweet of you,' said Harvey, and wondered whether people still laughed at him behind his back.

Chapter Twenty-one

(i)

'Oh, really,' Belinda said. 'When did this happen?'

There was a hesitation on the other end of the line. 'Well, today actually. Right out of nowhere. The studio decided they wanted me to write here in Los Angeles so that I could liaise with Bruno, and as they'd found this place for me it seemed mad not to move straight in and get to work.'

'Yes, it would, wouldn't it? Really mad.' Belinda groaned inwardly. What was she saying? Everything seemed to be coming out like a whinge. She tried to be positive. 'And *will* you be able to work there? I mean, is the bath the right shape and the water the right temperature and everything?'

'Well, actually there's a pool and, you know, one of those hot tub things.' There was a nervous giggle this time.

'A hot tub? Oh my God, how perfectly Seventies! Does that mean that everything you imagine will come up hot and bubbling?' There she went again, giving absolutely the wrong impression. She wished Charlie could see her face. She was smiling actually, pleased for him. It just didn't sound that way.

She looked around their living room. It was large and square, a high Victorian room, with the furniture now covered in dust sheets, and a plank suspended across the centre from the two pairs of step ladders she had hired from a do-it-yourself shop. She had been up until two the previous night rolling non-drip emulsion on to the ceiling and into her hair, hoping that Charlie might call. He hadn't. She had wanted to telephone Los Angeles, but pride had stopped her. She had nothing to tell him, other than that she was decorating the living room in mimosa and apple white, which hardly ranked with iced tea in Malibu with Sam Jordan and sitting in a hot tub with God knows who. She stopped herself. She didn't know that.

'I think the house is owned by a commercials director,' Charlie was saying.

'It certainly sounds like it.' It was nine o'clock on a Saturday morning in London, 1 a.m. Los Angeles time. Unable to sleep on she had been up at eight making an early start on the walls.

'I'm actually looking forward to doing some writing again,' Charlie said. 'There are one or two new ideas I want to try out.'

'So what have you been doing all this time if you haven't been writing?'

Charlie sounded vague. 'Oh, you know what everyone does out here. Waiting around. Going to the studio, having lots of meetings.'

In the background, behind his voice, Belinda could hear music playing. It sounded like synthesized rock. That wasn't at all like Charlie. She was sure, too, there was a jauntiness in the way he was speaking that was new. She didn't like the way he referred to the 'studio' these days. It didn't sound like him. He had been talking casually about 'millions of dollars' and 'points' and 'grosses' and 'above the line' for over a week now, and a couple of days ago he had traded in his Japanese hire car for a BMW with a sun-roof. For a man who had only been in California for two weeks he was sounding very West Coast, just like those English film directors whose Californian affectations he despised so much.

'What have *you* been doing?' he asked.

'What have *I* been doing?' Belinda repeated. 'Well, I haven't been sitting in a hot tub taking meetings . . .' Again she was too late to stop herself. She wondered whether she should tell him about the decorating, but she wanted to keep it for a surprise. She tried again. 'I mean, I've found things to do. Your mother called. She didn't know you were in Hollywood, she said your father would be pleased. What else . . . ?' She cast around for something to tell him, but finally said: 'I keep thinking about your new deal. I never heard of anyone being paid so much money for writing a script.'

'Well, I only get half if we don't make it to the first day of shooting,' Charlie answered casually. And then, sounding slightly peevish, he added: 'Actually half a million isn't massive by LA standards. I think Larry could have gone for a little more, especially if Sam Jordan is going to play Napoleon.'

Sam Jordan. He was no longer laughing at the idea of Sam Jordan. They were losing contact. Belinda tried a joke. 'Yes, Sam Jordan. The bouffant with the backside. Charlie, do they put something in the water out there?'

A pause, then: 'What?'

'Well, you know, something corrosive. The opposite of fluoride that works on brains. I mean, for heaven's sake, *Sam Jordan!* I thought you had casting approval.'

'His last movie grossed a hundred and fifty million domestic,' Charlie said quietly. 'He can open a movie like nobody else. He's quite an interesting guy actually. Well, maybe a little eccentric . . .'

Belinda was staring at the ceiling. She had noticed a bare patch by the window which she must have missed the previous night. She had tears in her eyes.

'Belinda . . . ?'

She didn't answer. She was remembering how when they had first begun living together they had rented a tiny house in France one summer which had been overrun by ants, a detail which had bothered her, but amused Charlie. One morning she had woken to find the words '*Je t'aime*, Belinda,' written in ants on the outside of their bedroom window, and Charlie giggling under the sheet alongside her. Later he had admitted he had got up early while she had been still sleeping, taken a jar of honey from the fridge and, dipping his finger in it, stood outside their ground-floor bedroom window and written backwards on the glass. A cast of thousands of ants had done the rest.

With a growing sense of desperation Belinda tried once more. 'Did Bruno Messenger say whether he received—?'

But Charlie was already answering. 'Bruno got your tapes. He hasn't had chance to look at them yet . . .'

Charlie stopped. Another silence followed.

Charlie put down the telephone and turned up the music. It was Penn Stadtler's latest album. According to Bruno, Penn Stadtler was 'bigger than God in rock music this year', and he had demanded Charlie take a listen because he had just done a half-million-dollar rock-video promo for it. Charlie had listened, but it meant nothing to him: he didn't like electronic music particularly. 'Wait till you see the visuals,' Bruno had insisted. Charlie had not said that he listened with his ears not his eyes, although he knew Belinda would have expected him to.

He made himself a cup of coffee. He was aggravated. Belinda didn't understand. Things looked different from this side. Yes, of course he still had casting approval, although he believed Buffalo were insisting on some movement on that when the new deal went through. But that was the way things were out here. With Sam's name on the ticket the movie was certain to be made and sure to open big. He would have been insane to protest.

For a moment he considered calling Belinda back to explain, but quickly cancelled the idea. Then he thought about Simone Estoril. He looked at his watch. One-fifteen. She should be home by now. They had been out to dinner together, just a friendly thing to thank her for reading his script and finding him this place to write. He had told Belinda a little white lie there. Although the studio were paying the rent, it had been Simone who had found the house for him. She was being very helpful. There was no reason why he couldn't have told Belinda. It was all perfectly innocent. He just didn't want to complicate matters. Anyway, why should he tell Belinda everything he did when all she did was mock? It wasn't particularly clever to call Sam Jordan 'the bouffant with the backside'. It was too easy. You had to be in Hollywood to appreciate the way the system worked.

Looking out at the hot tub with its underwater lights he remembered momentarily how William Holden had ended up face-down in a pool in *Sunset Boulevard*. He had been playing a Hollywood writer, too, he thought. Then he frowned. He wasn't *playing* a writer, he *was* a writer.

He made a note to himself. He would send his parents one of those Hollywood postcards showing the cut-out letters on the hill the very next day, and address it to the general secretary of the school film society. His father would like that.

Simone Estoril was pleased with finding Charlie the house. It was just off Coldwater Canyon and belonged to a friend who was away directing his first feature in Texas. It was the usual thing, lots of wood with a deck and a small pool. When she had taken Charlie to show him his eyes had widened. At that point she had shown him the word processor.

She couldn't help liking this English writer who was trying to pretend his head was not being turned by the possibility of having a big Hollywood movie made out of his script, when he was so obviously thrilled to bits. She had been glad, too, that he had not made a pass at her when she had gone back for a drink. All the other English men she had been out with had wanted to start with sex and move on to dinner later. Charlie had talked about movies.

Now driving home she considered her progress. *Shadows on a Wall* was her big chance and she wasn't going to waste it. She had found the script, alerted Jake McKenzie, and now she was personal assistant to the producer. Not bad. She had known that Jake McKenzie would want to drop her after their weekend together, but she knew what she had found and she had hung on.

And now she had been passed on, and, in her scheme of things, passed upwards. After years of doing the chores Simone Estoril's real career was just beginning.

Chapter Twenty-two

(i)

It was mainly to please Nathalie that they went to Penn
Stadtler's party. When Bruno Messenger had first conveyed
the invitation Harvey hadn't had much appetite to mix
socially with a rock musician who wore a diamond-encrusted
toothpick through his ear and a T-shirt bearing an approxi-
mation of Picasso's dove enclosed in a condom. But Nathalie
had been insistent. Bruno wanted Stadtler to write the score for
Shadows on a Wall so they ought at least to get to know him,
she had reasoned. What really attracted her, Harvey suspected,
was the scent of decadence that clings to rock stars. It frightened
him.

She dressed for the evening in a four-thousand-dollar, tight
blue shift which hung from one shoulder and revealed much of
her famous bosom. She was very tanned, and beautiful, if you
didn't look too closely at the pucker lines around those pouted
lips, and, because he had watched her getting ready, Harvey
knew she was not wearing any pants. That excited him, and,
as the chauffeur drove them up into the hills, Nathalie sitting between Edward and himself, he mischievously wondered
whether he should tell the Grave Digger, tempt his tumescence
and enjoy his embarrassment.

Naturally, he didn't. The poor man looked apprehensive enough.
Edward Lampton had taken to Hollywood, to spending his days
shopping or sitting by the pool reading scripts and his evenings
at screenings or in restaurants, far more successfully than any

sixty-year-old widowed undertaker had any right to. But the rock world intimidated him, too. They both knew that they were too old, even if Nathalie didn't.

A couple of generations ago Penn Stadtler's house, a rambling replica of an English Jacobean mansion, complete with high, ornate brick chimneys, would have been the retirement home of some fabled movie queen, a place to disappear into when the lights had begun to dim and all that was left was the money. But the new aristocrats of Hollywood played guitars and synthesizers and amassed their wealth when they were very young.

'It's a pity they don't know how to spend it,' Harvey said to himself as, stepping from the limousine, they picked their way between an avenue of Porsches and Ferraris to Penn Stadtler's open front door, through a hall, and out on to a wide terrace. Below on a lawn was this year's harvest of Hollywood's young, rich and beautiful. Music split the air. 'Jesus, if there's anyone else here over forty, he must be hiding in shame,' he shouted, looking around for someone he knew.

Neither Nathalie nor Edward Lampton replied. Nathalie looked less certain of herself now. Every beautiful twenty year old in Los Angeles seemed to have been invited. In the Hollywood restaurants they visited there was usually some European film buff to smile with recognition of other days; but in Penn Stadtler's house on this night the star of *Chloe Est Morte* was just another rich old bitch showing a lot of tit. Quickly they stepped back into the house.

'Quite a place he has here,' Edward Lampton said, looking around at the lattice windows and carved gargoyles on the uprights of banisters. 'It reminds me of one of those places you see in horror films, where Vincent Price is lurking in a coffin in the cellar.'

'Jesus, what is it with you and coffins?' Harvey guffawed. 'Are you hustling for business or something. Kids like these think they're immortal. Don't you remember?'

'I remember,' said Nathalie and, to change the subject, set off down a panelled gallery hung with framed platinum records.

'They think you're from the Beverly Hills drugs squad,' Harvey joked to Edward at one point as a lavatory flushed somewhere close by. All around the house they had attracted curious, nervous stares from people loitering around bathroom doors. 'Imagine, thousands of dollars worth of cocaine are being flushed away even as we speak. The rats in the sewers around here must have a hell of a habit.'

The Grave Digger grinned. 'Ed Lampton, narcotics,' he drawled, puffing out his chest the way Robert Mitchum used to.

Nathalie slipped an arm through his. 'You missed your vocation, Edward,' she said. 'You should have been in the movies, too.'

Edward Lampton swelled with pleasure.

Harvey smiled to himself.

They found Charlie standing on a terrace watching the other guests, and talking to Simone. 'Simone knows everyone,' Charlie smiled with what sounded like admiration. 'And *everyone's* here.'

'Right,' Harvey agreed, wondering who the 'everyones' were. These days they all looked so weird you couldn't tell the movie stars from the layabouts. Sure as hell half these girls were hookers, he could tell that much.

'I don't think you've been introduced to Penn yet, have you?' a voice said at his side. It was Bruno Messenger, stepping out of the darkness and towering over a court of young people. At his side was a handsome, athletic, tanned man of about twenty-five with a face familiar from forty-foot-wide album advertisements on Sunset Boulevard. Wearing a pair of knee-length tennis shorts, a T-shirt and a baseball cap, out of the back of which hung long fair hair, there was no sign of the diamond toothpick.

'I don't believe this,' the young man said. 'Nathalie Seillans. I had a picture of you over my bed when I was at school. I used to think you were watching what I was doing. I'm almost embarrassed to meet you now.' He had a soft, well-spoken English accent.

Nathalie ran her fingers happily through a strand of hair and tossed it back over her bare shoulder.

Harvey pushed out a hand. 'Penn, *love* your records. Did I say *love* them? Better that that. Terrific. Great party.' At last he could relax. If Nathalie was getting the attention she deserved, then all was right in his world.

'I just *love* the script. I mean . . .' she giggled, slightly manically, that Yale Meredith giggle, 'I mean, I *really* love it.'

So there we are: everybody loves everything, thought Charlie as he stared at the wide, fleshy mouth and the hunted doe's eyes. She was more angular, more awkward in reality than on the screen, her fair hair falling haphazardly in waves around her face, and so capriciously put together and dowdily dressed, with just an outsize, man's grey cardigan around her shoulders and an old purple vest tucked into black trousers, that he had not at first realized who she was; not, that is, until she had looked at him. That was when he realized what it was that made a star. When her eyes caught his there was nowhere to escape to.

'It's so rare to read a script by a man when the dialogue is right for a woman,' she said, leaning forward conspiratorially. 'They can't write it. Not usually. It doesn't sound right. You must be a very unusual man.'

'I try,' said Charlie, because he couldn't think of anything else to say. When she had come close he had smelt her scent. It was sharp and musky. Her expression was so intense he wondered what she was on.

'You *try*,' Yale gasped, and giggled. 'He *tries*.' This time she attempted to copy his English accent.

At her side Jake McKenzie, her escort, nodded, and looked around for someone else for her to meet.

The star put out a hand and caught Charlie's arm. 'Is it true you wrote *Shadows on a Wall* for your girlfriend?'

'Yes.'

'That's so romantic. You must love her very much.'

'Yes.'

'Oh my God . . . !' Suddenly she kissed him on the cheek, the impression of her body momentarily folding against his.

He smelt her scent again.

'I hope we get together,' she said. 'I hope they can find a way.' And with another laugh, this time more triumphant than nervous, she allowed Jake McKenzie to lead her away through the crowd.

For a moment Charlie remembered Belinda as she had been that New Year's Day in Cracow, the coloured balls tumbling around her in the snow. Then the picture was gone.

'Wow! Have you made an impression!' Simone said, tapping his cheek where Yale had kissed him. 'Some guys would never wash that spot again.'

Charlie laughed, embarrassed. 'She's a good reader of a script.'

'Maybe. But she's also spoilt, wilful and crazy. God knows why Jake bothers.'

'What do you mean? Bothers about what? He's her agent.'

Simone laughed. 'He likes to think that if he's seen socially with her people will think they're . . .' she made inverted commas signs with her fingers '. . . "together".'

'Perhaps they are.'

'Not Yale Meredith. She doesn't.'

'She must sometimes.'

'I don't think so. She just doesn't do it. Well, hardly ever. They say she doesn't like sex. That's the rumour. You must have met girls like that.'

'Me? Well, yes. No. I don't know, to be honest. But I suppose there are girls who don't and men who don't.'

'In this town it's rare. But then she's rare. She's crazy. She plays games with people.'

'What kind of games?'

'Who knows? Forfeit maybe.'

Charlie laughed again. He was enjoying himself. It was fun to meet Yale Meredith, to be at his first Hollywood party. It was his night off. He hadn't told Belinda he was going to a party. She might not have understood.

They had dinner early, selecting from a buffet the length of a cricket pitch, standing on the lawn, watching people dancing. He had never been to a party quite like it, never seen so many rich, young people at play before, the men confident and noisy, the girls uniformly pretty, on display. Occasionally he nodded to a face he thought he recognized, and a couple of times he was asked about the movie, as though he was someone interesting to know. He liked that, too. He was beginning to feel a part of things. It was exciting, perhaps just a skip and a jump from being decadent, and he wondered what these people would do when the public part of the evening ended, these men with their ear rings and slicked back hair, and these beautiful, hyperactive, smiling girls. He kept hoping that Yale Meredith would wander back, but she had apparently left early. As he watched Simone kept up a running commentary. She read the trade magazines and saw the movies, so she was a good guide. Over there was Emilio Sanchez, here was John Benton, and what about that . . . Jack Dragoman talking to Bruno Messenger!

'Jack Dragoman?' Charlie asked.

'He's in television. The star of *Bad Penny Blues*. He's very popular.'

'Oh yes,' said Charlie. He didn't watch television, but he'd heard of *Bad Penny Blues*.

It was after one when they decided to leave. By now the activity in the pool was becoming frantic, and a couple of young women, perhaps a little more-desperate-than-the-rest, were swimming naked with a gang of boys.

'You guys didn't see Nathalie anywhere by any chance, did you?' Harvey asked, as they wished him goodnight.

Charlie shook his head. 'Sorry.'

'I think I saw her with Penn Stadtler a little while ago,' Simone offered. 'He was showing her the house.'

There was a moment's hesitation. 'Ah, yes . . . Right,' said Harvey. 'Great! Well, anyway . . .' He looked quickly at the Grave Digger. 'So we'll speak tomorrow, OK! Drive carefully now.'

All the way back to Encino in Charlie's newly hired BMW they joked about Harvey's look of panic when he realized Nathalie was missing.

'I don't know whether I should say this,' Simone said, 'but I'm not really sure what Harvey is doing with Nathalie.'

'Or, let's be honest, vice versa,' Charlie laughed.

'And what about Edward? He's nice, but he seems kind of spooky, just standing around, hardly ever speaking, like some kind of matinée idol from a silent movie.'

'Occupational demeanour for a grave digger, I think. Movies attract some funny people.'

Simone reflected on that. 'I think so.'

'You only think so?' Charlie teased, glancing away from the road for a second.

'Well, yes, but it's more than that,' Simone puzzled. 'I mean, getting a movie made . . . everyone has his reasons, but no two reasons are ever the same.'

'How do you mean?'

'Well, take *Shadows on a Wall* for instance: Buffalo are desperate for a hit movie, *any* movie, to keep Reuben Wiener and the board in New York happy; Jake's an agent who wants to package all his stars; Bruno wants to be Orson Welles, so he has to make something quality; Harvey wants to please Nathalie; and Nathalie, well, I guess she wants to be associated with something respectable to clean up her whorey old image . . .'

'Something like that.'

'. . . and I want to produce. What about you?'

Charlie gazed at the lights of the oncoming traffic. 'I'm not sure. I suppose, after all this work, I just want to see the shadows on the wall.' He hesitated, embarrassed, then said: 'It's probably the same in any business, in a bottleworks, perhaps. Everyone involved sees it from a different point of view.'

Simone shook her head. 'Not quite. Bottles are bottles. A movie has a life of its own. All those different people with their different ambitions, their coming together makes a separate kind of life-force. Once you start it going you never know where it's going to end up. It's like . . .' She struggled for the simile.

'A blind rhinoceros?' Charlie offered, and laughed.

'Yes. Well, maybe a blindfolded rhinoceros. But that's what's exciting. If you're making bottles you design your shape and colour and that's it. But creating a movie that people will perhaps be seeing fifty years from now, telling a story and building characters which might become a part of the world we all share, like the burning of Atlanta and Rhett leading Scarlett to safety, or Dorothy and the Tin Man, or Indiana Jones saying, "Why did it have to be snakes?", or Steve McQueen bouncing his ball in the prisoner-of-war camp and riding his motorbike at the barbed-wire border–' she paused for breath – 'that's something else.'

Charlie knew what she meant. This was how he felt. It *was* something else. His father had known that in his school film society back in Dorset. There was nothing like watching and sharing moving images in the darkness. A novel was read alone, the reader providing his own pictures to fit the words; and a play changed with every performance. But, once completed, movies froze for ever sequences of images and sounds; moments of film universally seen and understood, and often remembered better than reality itself.

★   ★   ★

Simone had taken home some documents which Charlie needed to sign, so when they reached her apartment she invited him in. It was a neat and spacious place for a woman living alone, but somehow more an office than a home, the shelves crammed with a collection of some of the best film scripts of the past forty years. Among many were final drafts of *The Searchers*, *Witness*, *The Third Man*, *3.10 to Yuma*, *Some Like It Hot*; and even one in French, *La Nuit Américaine*.

Charlie was impressed. 'Where did you find all these?'

'When people get to know you have a hobby they begin to help out,' she explained as she made the coffee. 'I collect original final drafts like some people collect first editions. They're losing some of their rarity value now that everyone has a photocopier, but still actors and crew throw their scripts away as soon as they've finished the movie . . .'

'. . . or tear out the pages as the scenes are completed,' Charlie added.

'And that bothers writers?'

'You bet.'

He pulled out *La Nuit Américaine* – the original French version of François Truffaut's *Day for Night* – from the shelf. 'This is Belinda's favourite film,' he said. 'In a way it was how we met, but so far she's only ever seen it on television. She wants to see it on the big screen.'

Simone nodded. 'She's right. They shouldn't be allowed to show a movie about movies on a television screen.'

Charlie smiled his agreement. He felt comfortable with Simone. She was a good bloke. 'Hey, what's this?' he said. At the end of the row was a copy of *Shadows on a Wall*. 'This shouldn't be here. It isn't a final draft.'

'Which may be a shame.'

'Why? Don't you think I can improve it?'

'Oh sure. Nothing's perfect. But whether you will or not is something else.'

(iii)

'You *forgot* to tell me? You were invited to a party at Penn Stadtler's and you *forgot* to tell me?' Belinda couldn't believe what she was hearing.

'Well . . .'

'So, what was he like? Who was there? Who did you go with?' She was excited for him. She *was*. *Genuinely*. All right, she owned up, she was lying. She *hated* the idea.

'Oh . . . the team, Harvey and Nathalie and, you know, the Grave Digger.' He sounded very vague.

'Did you take a girl, Charlie?' It was said as a joke, but she wanted him to reassure her. God, why was she so insecure all of a sudden? 'I don't mind if you took someone, or met someone there. Did you meet someone? I mean, for heaven's sake, of course I don't mind, but I'd rather know if you did than not know and there to be some silly misunderstanding—'

'What do you mean? No. Of course not. A gang of us went. Everyone from the movie. Penn's writing the music for the movie—'

'Penn? Penn *Stadtler*'s writing the score? You're kidding, aren't you?' There she went again. She wished she could gag herself. But *Penn Stadtler*! What had happened to Charlie's taste? 'I don't understand,' she said. 'You used to like music.'

From the other end of the phone she heard a murmur of exasperation. She deserved it. She sounded like a total shrew. This was the way her mother had sometimes spoken to her father.

She tried again. 'So, anyway, you didn't say who was there? Anybody famous?'

'Well, yes, I suppose so. All kinds of people. Bruno, Jack Dragoman, Yale Meredith—'

'Yale Meredith was there?' Had she heard right? He was being impossibly casual.

'She's crazy.'

'Really?'

'So everyone says.'

'Who's everyone?'

'What do you mean, "Who's everyone?" ' He was irritable now.

'Who says she's crazy?'

'People from the studio, people in Harvey's office. Simone.'

'Simone!'

'That's right. She says she's virtually celibate.'

'Is this Yale Meredith or Simone?'

'Yale, of course.'

'Oh. Of course.'

There was a silence on the line from California. Then: 'She was dressed like a bag woman.'

'Yale Meredith? What about Simone? She wasn't. Right? Does she have a second name, this Simone?'

Now he was really mad. 'Yes, she does. It's Spanish . . . Estoril. She's Harvey's assistant. She's the one who found the script; remember? I told you. I'm very grateful to her. If it wasn't for Simone none of this would have happened. And if you want to know, no, I don't fancy her. Not at all. Not in any way. But she's a very nice girl . . . woman, who understands what it's like here in Hollywood, and who you will like very much when you meet her.'

Belinda went quiet. She had been asking for this. She had got it wrong. Of course she knew who Simone was. But she knew Charlie, too. Something must be bothering him to make him react so sharply.

At last he filled her silence. 'Anyway, how've *you* been?'

'I decorated the flat,' she said, biting her bottom lip. 'The living room. Mimosa and apple white.'

'Oh. Really! That's great,' he said.

'No, it isn't,' she blurted. 'It's streaky.'

They fell silent again.

Chapter Twenty-three

(i)

Yale Meredith called in the late afternoon. Charlie was sitting staring into his word processor waiting for the pictures to appear. For some reason the call did not come as a surprise.

'Hi. Er, look . . . I hope you don't mind, but, well, I got Jake to give me your phone number.' The voice was fluttery.

'I don't mind at all. How are you?'

'I mean, I'm not disturbing you, am I? Not interrupting the flow?' she worried on. 'Because, if I am, I'll go away. Just say and I'll hang up.'

'No, no, you don't have to do that. To tell the truth I was just daydreaming . . . trying to decide what happens next.'

'Daydreaming.' She laughed her sudden nervous explosion of high-energy laugh that audiences liked so much and ordinary girls were beginning to copy. 'You call it *daydreaming*. I call it, I don't know . . . *genius* in motion, or something.'

'Oh, come on . . .'

'No, *really*. There are so few good writers for movies around these days it would be criminal if I were to stop one writing.'

'Honestly. There's nothing that can't wait.'

'Oh. OK, then, if you're quite sure . . .' She laughed again. She sounded as though she hardly knew what to say next, and began asking inconsequential stuff about where he was staying and how he liked Los Angeles.

'I like it,' he said. 'It's fun being able to meet so many people involved in movies, who work in them every day.'

It didn't sound as though she was really listening to his reply because at that moment she said that she didn't really know why she had phoned, but thought it might be an idea if they spent some time together.

Yale Meredith wanted to spend time with him? He knew that in Hollywood anything was possible, but he hadn't expected this kind of anything. 'That would be . . . good,' he said.

'I sort of want to talk about Marie Walewska. Did you know I'm partly Polish? Well, my grandmother was, or maybe her mother.'

'I didn't know that.'

'No. Well . . . Look, if you're not writing, why don't you come over? Tonight maybe? Or what about now? Is that possible? I'd really like to talk to you. Can you come over now?'

Yale Meredith lived in a mainly wooden, white house deep in the Bel Air estate, surrounded by trees and hidden from the private road. In her drive was a collection of cars. A housekeeper's apartment was over the garage. When Charlie arrived Yale was waiting for him on the lawn holding a small dog; another trotted behind her as she came to greet him.

She liked the security of Bel Air, she said, as she led him inside, her famously haunted eyes glancing in the direction of the road. Usually she had a friend to stay, but the friend was away today so there was just the housekeeper and her husband. Then she laughed, skittish really, which was engaging even when there wasn't anything to laugh about. It made Charlie smile.

The interior of the house reminded Charlie of nothing so much as a dovecote. It was either very light or quite dark, the sun sliding in at haphazard angles through high windows, and the floors were bare and varnished, with only the occasional rug.

'Thanks for coming over,' Yale murmured. She was smiling at him, that only-for-you smile that Charlie had seen on the screen, her thick, light hair falling over her eyes as she spoke. She was wearing jeans and a pale blue T-shirt. Her feet were bare and her toe-nails were painted bright red, but she wore no make-up. She looked even thinner in the day, more vulnerable than ever.

183

Getting some beers she carried them through into a small conservatory, her eyes hardly leaving his. Then, because she asked, he told her how *Shadows on a Wall* had come into existence, about Edinburgh and Belinda. She already knew some of the story.

'Your girlfriend is *so* lucky! To have a part especially written for her by a real *playwright* . . . some girls would *kill* for that.'

'I don't think Belinda feels very lucky at the moment,' Charlie said. 'She wanted to play the part in the movie, too.'

Yale put a hand to her mouth, as though she had only just realized. Perhaps she had. Then recovering, she said: 'I don't blame her. It's a wonderful part for any actress.' There was the slightest hesitation, before a coy little enquiry: 'And what do you want? Would you like her to play the part?'

He paused. 'I shouldn't say this to you, but, yes,' he said, 'that's what I'd like. I think she'd be brilliant. But I don't know if it's possible any more.'

She sat on the edge of a cushion for a few moments, rocking backwards and forwards, hugging herself, taking this on board, and then abruptly said: 'Tell me about her.'

He told her everything he could think of. How they had met, the movie, *Day for Night*, their home together, the play.

'Do you love her?' she asked.

'Yes.'

'You must be missing her while you're out here?'

'Yes. We call each other every night, well, my nights, her mornings.'

She considered this and then she said: 'Would you ever, you know . . . have you ever had an affair . . . gone to bed with somebody else?'

'No.'

'No?' She looked disbelieving.

'Never.'

'Would you? I mean if someone really terrific came along?'

'No.'

'Never?'

'It's never entered my mind.'

'Never?'

He shook his head.

'And what about her . . . what about Belinda?'

'She wouldn't either.'

'You're sure of that?'

'Certain.'

184

She had stopped rocking. After a long moment she said: 'Well, that's nice. But, you know, when girls are on their own, it can be difficult sometimes.'

She left the thought lying and went to get some ice for her beer. He watched her move through the house, her tanned bare feet on the wooden boards, her legs supple and long inside a pair of men's Levi's that were too big and trailed on the floor.

'She's very pretty, isn't she?' she said as she returned. Then, seeing his look of surprise, added: 'Jake said you showed him and Bruno a photograph of her.'

'She's beautiful.'

'That's nice.' There was a long and thoughtful silence. Then, quite suddenly, she changed the subject. 'Tell me, do you think Sam Jordan is right for Napoleon?'

Charlie didn't know how to answer, but she didn't wait.

'I don't. He seems so . . . I don't know, *Californian*. Do you know what I mean? I never imagined Napoleon as a Californian.'

Charlie wanted to say that that was what Belinda had been saying, but once again Yale changed the subject, asking him this time if he liked dogs. She did.

He nodded, but it was beginning to occur to him that he wasn't really sure why he was there, or what she wanted. She asked a little about the French Revolution, and a few questions about Napoleon and Marie Walewska, but he knew she didn't take in much of what he told her.

Because she was so famous he had imagined a bigger, more positive woman, perhaps someone a little older, certainly more grown-up, and the thin, nervous girl biting the corner of her lip and fiddling continually with her hair seemed somehow a reduction of the legend. But it was impossible to resist staring at a face so beautifully alive with emotions and mood changes.

Suddenly, out of nowhere, she said: 'Hey, do you want to go to see a movie?' It was the first time one of the three most desired women in the world had asked him on a date.

They drove in Charlie's car to Westwood. Yale had put on an old leather jacket over her T-shirt, and, with her hair tied back, with a rubber band, she could have been almost any pretty girl off the UCLA campus there. Certainly no-one noticed them going into the cinema, which, in a way, rather disappointed him. She ate her popcorn sweet.

The movie she chose was a bloodied-up remake of a Fifties horror story about monster killer ants taking over a small town. In the frightening parts she turned her face into his shoulder. That smell again. And, yes, Yale Meredith had her head on his shoulder.

She said she was hungry after the show, and, nervous about where he suggested they go, he wondered aloud about trying to get in at Ma Maison or Mortons or one of the smart Hollywood places.

Yale shook her head and suggested instead a student tapas bar around the corner, but turned away when she saw the crowd. In the end she asked him to drive along Wilshire until they came to a burger place.

It was only while they were eating, Yale picking at the french fries with her fingers, that Charlie realized she had not once spoken about movies, not as an insider, since they had left the house. What she *had* talked about, almost non-stop, had been school in Grand Rapids, Michigan, her favourite subjects, the best way to put chains on a car's tyres in a blizzard, her ten all time favourite records, the courses she had taken in literature at college, her favourite moment in *The Catcher In The Rye* ('when he sees his sister skating on the ice, around and around, do you remember that?'), and a job she had once had as a receptionist in an insurance office where her married boss had got mad because she wouldn't make it with him.

The diner was almost empty, but when a group of young people came barracking in, she very neatly turned her head away, raised her collar and suggested they leave.

Outside in the car she suddenly kissed him, open-mouthed and sensuous, the way a forward girl might on a regular date.

'Let's go home,' she whispered. 'Your home.'

He felt like a spectator, watching himself sitting in his BMW with Yale Meredith halfway across the seat to him, one hand resting gently on his shoulder, humming softly to herself. She had a pretty voice, and the nearness of her body was arousing. He wanted to pinch himself: he was driving through Beverly Hills and Yale Meredith, *Yale Meredith*, was snuggling up to him. Occasionally he thought about Belinda, but then Yale would say something, and laugh that Yale Meredith laugh, and he would join in laughing with her.

186

As he drove he felt her fingers leave his shoulder and begin to tap a slow rhythm at the top of his thigh in time with a Tracy Chapman song playing on the radio. He knew what she was doing. He would never be able to tell himself that he didn't know.

Inside the house she made appropriate noises of praise as she gazed at the rewritten pages of script lying on his desk by the word processor. He opened a bottle of red wine and poured two glasses. They didn't say very much.

When they kissed again, her standing with her back against the wall, drawing him into her, he tasted the wine on her lips, smelt the musk at her neck. After a little while they went up the short flight of stairs.

He was nervous. He felt as though he was an imposter, as though he ought to be somebody else, someone better looking, more confident, more famous.

They lay on the wide bed in the absent director's large, panelled cabin of a bedroom which looked out over the pool and garden. He felt her breath against his cheek as she ran a hand inside his shirt. He kissed her on the side of the face just in front of her ear. She raised her head, craning her neck slightly with what seemed like an involuntary tremble, turning her ear to him and then away again as his lips brushed against her neck.

It was a moment of fantasy, he knew, a scene from *Eye Level* or *Business Lunch*, the films that had made her famous: the cascades of hair, the wide lips, the scent of her body. He thought about Belinda, and of how he was going to be unfaithful to her, but it didn't stop him. Nothing could have stopped him. No, he would never be unfaithful to Belinda, he was still saying in his head, as his fingers unfastened the buttons of Yale's jeans. Yes, he loved Belinda more than anything in the world, he thought, his face nuzzling Yale's small, wide breasts, his lips on her skin.

He kissed her as he entered her, and he felt her lips widen into a smile. He closed his eyes.

Her hand had picked up the receiver almost before the telephone had finished its first ring. Her voice was breathy, sleepy and soft. 'Hello.'

He felt shock run through him. Yale was holding the receiver in his direction. He could hear Belinda's voice, confused, asking if she had dialled the right number.

'That's right. Who do you want? Charlie? Oh yes, sure. He's right here.' Yale turned to him, purposely holding the phone between them on the pillow, inches from her mouth. 'It's for you, honey.' The intonation was close and intimate.

Charlie stared at her.

'Charlie, it's for *you*.' Now the voice was almost secretive: there was a hint of a giggle.

In the pale light Charlie could see her expression but he couldn't understand it. It was a smirk of victory.

She lay back and pulled on her pants. 'It's getting late,' she said.

He didn't answer.

She turned to retrieve her T-shirt. She was smiling to herself.

'I have an early start tomorrow.' She was now back in her jeans, already standing, zipping up her leather jacket. She was no longer looking at him. He heard her footsteps on the stairs, then the sound of her voice on the telephone calling a cab.

He pulled on his clothes and followed her down the stairs.

She was sitting on a sofa leafing through a movie magazine, waiting.

'Why . . . ?' he started to ask.

She just smiled.

'She doesn't do it. Well, hardly ever . . . In this town that's rare. But she's rare. She's crazy . . . She plays games with people,' Simone had said. *'Games of forfeit.'*

He telephoned Belinda the following afternoon, but couldn't think of anything to say. Perhaps if he had been practised at betrayals he would have had his lies ready.

'Charlie, who is that?' she had asked the previous night. She would have been virtually able to hear the bed creaking, the sheets rustling. Yale had lain there close to him, her body touching his, her breath on him.

After a few moments, as he had struggled to reply, Belinda had hung up.

Now the question came again. 'Who was she, Charlie?'

He told her.

There was a long silence. 'Oh, Charlie . . .' she said at last, not angry, or reproachful, just sad for both of them.

He couldn't explain.

Nor could he understand. In the afternoon he telephoned Yale. Simone, asking no questions, had got her number for him.

'I'm sorry, Yale is sleeping right now.' A woman's voice answered the call, clipped and efficient.

Two hours later he tried again.

'I'm sorry, Yale is out running right now.'

A third call brought. 'I'm sorry, Yale is reading.'

'Can't she be interrupted?'

'No.'

'Might I ask to whom I'm speaking?'

'My name is Alice Bauccio. And Yale asks me to tell you, please don't call again, you're beginning to annoy her. Goodbye.' And she hung up.

(ii)

Belinda came prepared, with her top hat and cane and packs of playing-cards, wearing a black tailed jacket with false pockets and long sleeves. The trousers must have once belonged to Charlie because they were far too long and too wide, but the overall effect was fetching, the tricks were clever and the children were astonished. Billy particularly liked the one she did with the ten-pound note, turning it into two and then three while they watched. Perhaps he would ask her to teach him that one. He would show it to the manager at Lloyds Bank the next time he was summoned. Things were getting very bad on the money front. He had never been in such trouble.

It was only when the children had gone to bed and the three of them were finishing off the wine that Belinda's front slipped. All evening she had been breezing on about how she was enjoying not having to talk about *Shadows on a Wall* constantly, when suddenly her face crumpled.

Ilse moved to sit by her.

189

At last she said: 'I'm sorry, it's just . . . *ambition*. It always gets in the way. This film . . . it's killing Charlie and me. I can't talk to him any more. He's behaving very . . .' She didn't finish. 'The only thing that seems to matter to him is the film and getting it made. I don't understand what he's doing . . . or what he wants . . .'

Billy watched her. It wasn't just Charlie's ambition that she was crying about. It was her own ambition for the happy life she had planned with him. Sitting there, her shining blond hair pulled back out of her eyes, it occurred to him that Charlie would have to be mad to betray a girl like Belinda. But in extraordinary situations people sometimes did extraordinary things.

July, 1992

Chapter Twenty-four

'*I am dead, Horatio. Wretched Queen, adieu,*' Sadie lisped, one leg flung out extravagantly across the stage, her head back on a convenient stool so that the audience might see the face of Hamlet as he died.

From the back of the hall came the sound of cheering from some of the younger girls.

Above her Claire was biting her lip as the speech continued. Then it was her turn. '*I am more an antique Roman than a Dane. Here's yet some liquor left.*'

Sadie grabbed for the pewter cup. '*As th'art a man, Give me the cup. Let go, by Heaven, I'll ha't. O God, Horatio, what a wounded name, Things standing thus unknown, shall I leave behind me. If thou didst ever hold me in thy heart . . .*'

Leaning forward Claire gave the dying prince of Denmark a smacker on the lips, a kiss so loud it echoed around the school hall. There was applause from the back rows.

Sadie dug her nails into the flesh of her hand to control the giggles. As Claire had leant over her they had momentarily caught each other's eyes, just long enough to set them both off. From the wings she could feel the laser glare of Miss Rokeby upon her. There would be hell to pay for this.

Rokeby had won, of course, the Queen's Yard Drama Society were performing *Hamlet* yet again for their end-of-term school play, and, although they had vowed not to appear in it, there was Sadie as Hamlet, with Claire as his best friend, Horatio.

'*Now cracks a noble heart. Good night, sweet prince, And flights of angels sing thee to thy rest!*' giggled Claire, tears running down her cheeks.

Sadie kept her eyes closed. All around her girls lay in the exaggeratedly mannered poses of death from poisoning and stabbing; each death having been an individual study in overacting. The audience was exploding with laughter.

It had been Sadie's idea. If it had to be an all-girls *Hamlet* rather than *Shadows on a Wall*, then it might as well be an all-girls camp *Hamlet*, young women playing manly parts in a mincing, girlish way.

Naturally Miss Rokeby had not been included in the joke. The rehearsals and first performances had been models of industry and effort, the camp version, rehearsed at Sadie's home at the weekends when her parents were away, being saved for the last night, when most of the players' parents, the headmistress, half the staff and several of the school governors would be present. There had never been a brace of queens like Rosencrantz and Guildenstern, a couple of muscular, first-team hockey players of sixteen, such a prissy, scolding women's hairdresser of a Polonius, or such pouting, jealous lesbians as Gertrude and her young girlfriend Ophelia. But the campest of all had been Sadie as, one hand on hip, her big eyes wide, she had petulantly waved a wooden monkey on a stick and minced: '*O, what a rogue and peasant slave am I*', and then fixed the audience with a comic look as though to say: I am, you know, I really am, a really rotten rogue and peasant slave.

To a roar from the girls in the hall and confused laughter and applause from the parents the curtain came down. Pulling herself up Sadie linked hands with the other players and, standing in a line, waited for the curtain-calls.

'We're in for it now, all right,' Claire said, wiping her eyes on the sleeve of her specially-hired-from-the-Royal-Shakespeare-Company doublet.

'Worth every second,' Sadie said, as, stepping forward, she took the customary bows.

Except that it wasn't quite customary because, still laughing, the whole audience, roared on by the schoolgirls among them, were giving the entire cast, and Sadie especially, a standing ovation. Five, six, seven times the curtain was lowered and raised, until, prompted by the gales of approval, Miss Rokeby herself loped on stage, her face gritted in a smile, and taking

Sadie's hand held it up to the audience for more applause.

'So nice to see you extending your range, Sadie,' she lashed out of the corner of her mouth.

But Sadie was hardly listening. She had just spotted Belinda and Billy and Ilse Yeo at the back of the hall, all three standing applauding wildly. She'd sent them invitations, but never expected them to come. Smiling wider than ever now, she bowed just to them.

Now it was her turn to be congratulated. They surrounded her in the school library while her parents were being served Chilean wine and the other members of the cast were grinning in embarrassment from behind their costumes and wigs, telling how Sadie had redirected the whole play. Miss Rokeby was believed to be in discussion with the headmistress.

'Now there's subversive for you,' Billy was teasing. 'Perhaps if we'd done *Shadows on a Wall* like that we'd have run for as long as *The Mousetrap*.' Then more seriously: 'I'm actually flabbergasted, Sadie. You were . . . well, extraordinary. Next time someone demands we give her a chance, I promise you I'll listen.'

Belinda leant forward and kissed her. 'Congratulations,' she said quietly. 'I'm sorry if I patronized you when you came asking for advice. I'd no idea . . . You were brilliant. Really.' She was smiling, although she looked tired.

Sadie didn't ask about the movie. If Belinda and Billy could be dumped, and that was more or less what Ilse had said when she had babysat at half-term, there wasn't much hope for her.

Sitting behind her parents in the car on her way home as they discussed homosexuality in the theatre, flying buttresses and the diminishing world panda population, and with Billy's praise still ringing in her ears, Sadie reached two important conclusions in life: the first was that no-one cares terribly what anyone does so long as they do it successfully; the second was that it pays to be brave.

Chapter Twenty-five

(i)

The Australian stared at the figures on the sheet of paper in his left hand while his right hand played in his pocket with his testicles. He was Al Mutton, Bruno Messenger's best friend and production manager, and he habitually played tournaments of pocket billiards. Harvey pretended not to notice.

'What do you think, Al? Am I right or am I right?' Bruno asked, his pale face resting on a clenched white fist.

'Right, Brune,' Al Mutton drawled. 'Either we do it properly or we don't do it at all.' He was talking about the retreat from Moscow.

Harvey Bamberg looked at his provisional budget. Somehow the figures just never came out right. At least another four millon dollars was now going to be needed. That put the total at over thirty-seven million dollars. Every time he met Bruno Messenger the movie seemed to have grown bigger. He couldn't imagine what they would say at Buffalo. He hesitated, hating these moments when Bruno went into a sulk. On this occasion the chill had come when he had questioned the size of the French Imperial army. Were an additional three thousand extras absolutely necessary? he had wanted to know. 'Kevin Costner worked wonders with matt paintings on *Dances With Wolves*,' he said. 'He made a small herd of buffaloes look like the entire state of Wyoming was full of them.'

Bruno Messenger didn't answer.

'Jesus!' said Al Mutton.

Harvey winced. Al Mutton, a solid mass of grizzle, was being deliberately unpleasant. They were sitting in the darkened interior of Bruno's Santa Monica Boulevard office late in the afternoon. Harvey would tell Charlie much later that when he first saw Al Mutton looming towards him out of the gloom, his first thought was that he had run into something brutal from the Middle Ages, which was unfortunate because by then it had already been decided that on a day-to-day level Al Mutton would be running *Shadows on a Wall*. Bruno and Al Mutton were a partnership, it being a matter of personal pride that Mutton could get Bruno anything he wanted to put on the screen. And, because they were a partnership, this Australian Jabba the Hutt had quickly become yet another co-producer. 'If you don't agree,' Bruno had said casually, 'I'll walk away from the movie.' Naturally Harvey had agreed.

Delicately now Harvey tried to lift the mood. 'I'm not being difficult. I mean, I know retreats from Moscow don't come cheap. But my worry is we'll push Buffalo too far and they'll get nervous about how much this movie is going to cost. In the script Charlie makes it clear—'

'The script is words on a piece of paper,' Bruno cut in. 'Words are cheap. What I'm going to do is paint pictures on the screen, beautiful, vibrant, exciting pictures. The story of Napoleon as you've never seen it before.'

'I'm sure you are. *Wonderful, wonderful* pictures. Believe me, I'm right with you, one hundred and fifty per cent. I only hope we can afford to pay for them.' Harvey had made his point and waited for a compromise suggestion.

He didn't get one. Bruno shrugged sullenly and looked back at his script. Al Mutton returned to examining his testicles.

They made a powerful team, all right, Harvey thought and realized why Nathalie had never attempted to flirt with Bruno. The only thing this man was interested in was himself.

Charlie lay floating alone in his pool. His head was back, his eyes open but unblinking. He was looking at the pictures in the fronds of the tall palm tree which waved to him beside the house. 'Come and play,' they seemed to say. He couldn't. Time was running out.

It was a crucial moment. Camille de Malignon had been caught by her American lover attempting to murder Napoleon. Now they were back in her rooms and she was recounting the death of her family in the Terror. On stage the horror of her description had been one of the best moments of the play. But Bruno Messenger wanted to *show* what had happened. Fair enough: this was a movie. But there was a difficulty. A single, straight flashback would be very ugly.

'It won't work in this movie, Bruno,' Charlie had said. 'It'll be a sudden change of style. It'll ruin our structure. Either a movie is composed of flashbacks all the way through, and you build the structure around the use of the flashback, or you don't use them at all. We can't just drop one in when the story gets difficult to explain and we want a couple of guillotinings to give the audience a cheap thrill. It's bad film grammar.'

'We need a flashback,' Bruno had said blankly.

'Yes, well, I can see the sense of it, but perhaps not so bald. Why don't we find a way of beginning the flashback convention when we first see Camille de Malignon, and maybe use it to show her schizophrenia. That might work.'

'I don't want flashbacks anywhere else. Just here, in this bedroom scene, when they're screwing and she's remembering the executions. And in the guillotinings I want to see those heads roll into the basket, I want the blood coming out into the straw like a fountain, I want the drummers, the crowd cheering, an entire square stuffed with people having a real good time, full of blood lust and revenge. And I want to see her as a little girl being lifted up by someone so that she can see what's going on. And the first thing she sees is her mother's head being sliced off and put on a spike in front of her. Then there's a great cheer, and the girl can't take her eyes off the head. And her eyes seem to meet those of her dead mother up there on the spike. That's when she comes. That's her moment of orgasm. That's the image I want her to see.'

Charlie had tried again. 'Well, yes, but couldn't we stretch it out? I mean, why not just show the first part of the execution, the preliminaries, when we first see her, and then a bit more and a bit more throughout the movie, always building, until in this scene we see the whole sequence in full. That would work.'

At that point Bruno had leant across to him. 'Let me give you a word of advice. Don't try to tell me what will work, and what won't work on screen. Leave the visuals to me, OK. I'm the director. You just write the scene like I tell you. I'll make it work. If I say I want one flashback sequence I want one flashback sequence, and only one.' With that he had left.

That had been two days ago. He had not been back since. Charlie had written the scene as requested. To him it stuck out like a sore thumb, a sudden change of style. He had also written in the love-making scene which intercut with the flash-back.

'Raunchy,' had been Bruno's instructions. 'Like in *Hiroshima Mon Amour*. And I want to see her come until she explodes. But don't write that. I'll explain on the day.'

Charlie had simply written: *They make love passionately*.

Now, in the pool, he was trying to find a way into the sequence which followed, a passing-out ceremony at a military academy in which Napoleon gently teases the American, Will Yorke, about his infatuation with an aristocrat. On stage it had involved just the two actors; in the movie it would call for a thousand boy extras. The trouble, as always, was, where to start? What was the first picture in the sequence? The rhythm of the film had been broken and Charlie was uncertain. He had been back to the beginning a dozen times, staring at the scenes in his mind, picture by picture, but every time he had come to a halt at the same place. He didn't believe what he was writing any more.

Hooray for Hollywood, danced the palm fronds.

His ten minutes were up. He climbed from the pool. The phone rang. It was Bruno's secretary. Bruno would be coming over at five expecting to see some more pages. Charlie went back to his word processor.

'The Duke of Wellington,' Bruno said. 'What about John Gielgud, someone classy and English like that?'

Charlie didn't follow. 'What Duke of Wellington?'

Bruno looked at him, but didn't speak.

'The Duke of Wellington doesn't appear in *Shadows on a Wall*,' Charlie said. 'He isn't exactly involved in either of the love stories. Besides John Gielgud is a hundred if he's a day, and was never exactly a warrior type even in his prime.'

'This Camille de Malignon, maybe she's an English spy. That's why she wants to assassinate Napoleon. If she was a spy she'd be working for the Duke of Wellington, right?'

'But she isn't.'

Bruno ignored that. 'What about Sean Connery? He's English.'

'He's Scottish, actually and the Duke of Wellington, who was then called Sir Arthur Wellesley, was Irish, but I never saw a place for him in *Shadows on a Wall*, English, Irish or Scottish.' Then he added: 'He had a tail, you know.'

'If we're going to show Napoleon in battle we have to show his opponent. That's the grammar of film.' The director mocked, ignoring the tail.

Charlie stared at the veins in his hands. They were standing out, blue and quivering with frustration. He was sitting in the kitchen where Bruno was eating from a box of muffins that Simone had bought to cheer him up. Until the row over the flashbacks Bruno had called around virtually every day, ostensibly so that he might see the new pages, but increasingly so that he could dictate his latest ideas. When Charlie liked the ideas, and some were very good because Bruno was clever with imagery, Bruno was happy: when he didn't, Bruno expected them to be worked into the script by the time he next called, anyway.

Frequently Charlie had given in: making movies was about making compromises, he knew that. But sometimes Bruno had gone too far. He was, Charlie knew, only insisting upon including the Duke of Wellington in order to attract a big name actor into a cameo part. Bruno was keen on big names: kudos by association was a useful short cut in a director's career. Little by little the story Charlie had written was being turned into a historical pageant.

'What about Robin Hood, Charlie?' he imagined Belinda teasing. 'Can't you guys find a place for him there, too?'

Prompted by the thought he said: 'Did you get a chance to look at Belinda's tapes yet? She was wondering.' That was a lie. She wasn't wondering. She had given up long ago. She had hardly spoken to him in three weeks.

Bruno looked to the heavens for strength. 'For Christ's sake, we're in negotiation with Yale Meredith, you know that.'

'Belinda's a brilliant actress. And she's beautiful.'

'She's an unknown radio actress. Who are you trying to kid?'

It was the brutality of the dismissal that Charlie hated most. He tried again. 'Just look at the tapes, will you? *Please?* I think you'll be surprised.'

The director finished off the last of the muffins. 'OK, OK, when I'm in Europe I'll meet with her, talk to her. Can I say fairer than that?' He stood up.

'Thank you.'

Bruno shook his head. He had already dismissed that subject. He went to the door and stopped. 'This isn't working, you know that, don't you? You and me, we can't do it together. Either you'll have to go or I will.'

'I'm sorry?' Charlie wondered if he had somehow missed a reel.

'Me, too. I really am sorry, but I'm going to have to give this to another writer. It seems to me your heart isn't in it.'

'Wh . . . ?' Charlie began to speak, but the words didn't come.

Bruno's did: 'Maybe you're written out. I don't know. You don't seem to know what kind of movie *Shadows on the Wall* is going to be. The dialogue's stilted. Too English. There's no broad sweep, no sense of history. We need a new writer, new ideas, someone who's comfortable with this kind of material.'

Charlie shook his head. 'You don't get rid of me like that. I have a contract. If it's you or me that goes, it's not going to be me.'

For a moment Charlie thought Bruno was about to laugh. But then, without speaking further, he stumped out of the house.

Harvey Bamberg called less than five minutes later. 'For Christ's sake, Charlie, what the hell do you think you're doing?'

'I'm spreading valium on a sandwich,' Charlie snapped back. 'It's the first sensible thing I've done in weeks. What do you mean, "What am I doing?" '

'You're only jeopardizing the entire movie. I don't know how you can do this, how you can be so selfish. Bruno's very upset. He called me from his car. He says you're telling him he's off the movie. You know you can't do that, Charlie. *Shadows on a Wall* isn't only you now. We're at a precarious state in negotiations.'

'He wants a new writer.'

'For a dialogue polish. They do that all the time out here. It doesn't mean anything. It just makes them feel more secure.'

'I'm the sole writer. That was agreed. The *only* writer.'

'I'll get back to you,' said Harvey, and rang off.

'Actually we agreed "sole credit",' Larry Horner echoed over the line from London, 'which may or may not have been strictly according to the rules of the Writers' Guild of America.'

'So what are you saying?'

'Don't rock the boat.'

'What?'

'If Buffalo get wind that you and Bruno are falling out they'll back out of this. It's because of him that they want to make the movie. Lose him and they'll close you down, and you'll be kissing goodbye to half a million dollars and the break of a lifetime.'

'But I had a deal . . .'

'Think about it, Charlie. Be reasonable.'

'Reasonable?'

'Reasonable. Things have changed. This isn't a little art-house movie any longer. Be difficult now and you'll be screwing it up for everybody.'

'You're supposed to be my agent.'

'That's why I'm giving you good advice. Buffalo haven't given the green light yet, Sam Jordan hasn't signed, Yale Meredith is dickering about like a nervous giraffe and we're still negotiating your revised deal. The next few days are crucial. We've got to keep Bruno Messenger sweet or there won't be any movie. That's the reality of the situation.'

'What about the ultimate control you said I had? All the aces?' Charlie suddenly felt lonely.

'You cashed them in when you agreed to the new deal. I tell you what, let me see if I can't squeeze another fifty thousand out of them.'

'Fifty thousand? For what?'

'For being reasonable. Talk to you later.'

The phone went dead. Charlie left it off the hook and walked out on to the deck. A dead moth was floating in the pool. He stared into the bright green electric water. Belinda was watching him. She didn't say anything.

It was mid-afternoon. He had tried to lose himself in a movie but it hadn't worked. He didn't know what to do, so he drove out along Sunset as far as the beach, where he parked and sat in his car and watched the ocean. It was a misty day. He wanted to go home, but he couldn't; not like this.

He had not spoken to Yale Meredith since she had driven away in the cab that night. *'They say she doesn't like sex,'* Simone had warned him.

He buzzed down the car window and smelt the salt in the air. In theory he could still bring the movie crashing down around him by digging in his feet, by *not* being reasonable. But he *was* reasonable. Now, more than ever, he wanted to see *Shadows on a Wall* made.

'I'm sorry, Belinda,' he said to himself.

For a little while he was distracted, watching a dog chase some joggers along the beach. When he looked back at himself he was surprised. For so long he had been at the very centre of *Shadows on a Wall*. Now he was out there at the edge with Belinda and Billy, just another spectator.

(iii)

Belinda hadn't picked up the magazine; the girl who had just washed her hair had popped it into her hands when she had finished asking where Belinda was going for her holiday. Now she couldn't put it down.

All of a sudden she was under siege from the image of Yale Meredith, those pleading impala eyes gazing out at her from newsagents' stands, video shops and cinema posters. She had never realized before how much a part of the public consciousness the image of a really big movie star becomes; how much of themselves stars give away.

The pictures were of Yale Meredith relaxing around her home, cuddling two small dogs, looking as caught unawares as was possible with half a pound of make-up on her face and wearing a different outfit in every shot.

All right, so she was beautiful. Belinda could see that. But did that mean that Charlie had to go to bed with her?

'So, how are you today?' the stylist, said, moving behind her and picking up the ends of her hair.

She didn't know why: she just came out with it. 'Not bad, really. If it weren't for the fact that Yale Meredith has taken my boyfriend and the part he wrote for me in the film he wrote for me, I'd probably be more or less contented.'

'Oh yes,' the hairdresser nodded peering unlistening at the pictures in the magazine. 'Yale Meredith. She's pretty, isn't she? Do you want your hair like that this time then?'

Chapter Twenty-six

(i)

It was lunchtime in the executive dining room at Buffalo Pictures and Harvey Bamberg was in celebratory mood. Piece by piece the jigsaw was falling into place: the director, the stars, the money. 'For the first time in my life I feel I know what the buzz is *really* like,' he beamed, 'what it was like for Henry Kissinger or James Baker, or maybe even that guy Charlie talks about, Talleyrand . . . the *big* players.'

Nathalie smiled and touched his arm. 'Darling, it's only a movie, not Congress in Vienna.'

She had read a little history since becoming involved in *Shadows on a Wall*, but it had only been a little. Or had she intended to say Congress *in* Vienna?

Edward Lampton laughed at her joke, if it was a joke. He always laughed at her jokes, although Nathalie did not seem to notice so much these days.

'That's true,' Harvey replied, looking around the largely empty dining room wishing that some of the top floor had chosen to eat there that day. He had purposely invited Nathalie in so that she could see how much they loved him at Buffalo now. 'It's not the Congress of Vienna but the principles remain the same – diplomacy, persuasion, a strategic overview. I had to do a real balancing act, I'll tell you. My heart stopped when Jake told me what he was asking for Sam Jordan. "Twelve million dollars!" I said. "Jake, that's just plain greedy." But he just smiled. You know Jake's smile. Like a wolf. So if it was

205

twelve million for Sam it had to be two and a half for Bruno and four for Yale. Jesus! But we did it, in the end we did it, and here we are, a forty-million-dollar movie just about off and running. Hell, even Jake looks pleased.'

Edward Lampton hesitated in the middle of stirring his decaffeinated. 'He ought to,' he said. 'He's pulled off a brilliant piece of packaging. If he's on ten per cent of his top three clients, not to mention who he might row in further down the credits, a wrap-up agency fee on top for making it all possible, and a couple of points on the side just for him, he has every reason to be pleased.' As he talked he prodded the air with his spoon. Slimmer and even more tanned since he had been in California he was beginning to look like someone out of a Douglas Fairbanks Jnr charm school.

Harvey winced with aggravation. This guy was a funeral director, or would be if he ever got his goddamn arm out from around Nathalie's waist and his nose out of *Variety*. How come he knew so much about movie deals all of a sudden? Did he advise him on embalming fluid? Snapping back, he said: 'Maybe, but it wasn't Jake who pulled the strings together with the studio, or had to cool Bruno, or got Charlie to see sense.'

'Of course not, darling,' Nathalie said soothingly, breathing so deeply her pneumatic bosom rose and fell and distracted a couple of guys from distribution at an adjacent table.

That made Harvey feel better. He resented the way agents got all the credit these days. He had been very busy, and it had worked. Yale Meredith had finally hiked her fanny off the fence, Sam Jordan was already giving interviews about how he had always wanted to play Napoleon, Bruno Messenger was even now in Europe looking at locations and trying to find Camille de Malignon, two bright, new, young writers, just out of the University of Southern California Film School, were rewriting the screenplay, Kenneth Branagh had been approached to play the Duke of Wellington, Jack Dragoman's agent was negotiating on the Will Yorke part and Charlie had begun to accept the reality of making movies. That had almost been the most difficult part.

'Bruno's insisting on the possessive credit,' Harvey had told him a few days earlier.

Charlie's expression had hardened in barely controlled anger. 'You mean he wants *Shadows on a Wall* to say "*A film by Bruno Messenger*"? No way. I'm not having it. This is the last straw.

This is where I draw the line. *I created Shadows on a Wall.*'

'Oh come on. All directors expect it these days. It doesn't mean anything,' Harvey had countered.

'It means a lot, which is why he wants it, why they all want it. It means that the director is wrongly advertised as being the author of the movie, the movie's *creator*, when, in fact, he is just one of a very large team. I'm the author of *Shadows on a Wall*, not Bruno Messenger. I'm not going to allow him to steal my credit even if every other writer in the Writers' Guild of America lets him.'

For a fellow who was hanging in by a thread this had been tough talk, and for a while there had been a stand-off, only resolved when Bruno had threatened again to walk away from the film unless he got what he wanted. That was what he always did, and it was very effective. This time, in fact, after some very tough bargaining by Jake McKenzie, he had got even more. Bruno's name would become part of the title, itself. '*Bruno Messenger's SHADOWS ON A WALL*', the credit would read. It had been the only way to keep him attached. And eventually, faced with the possibility of the film never being made, Charlie had backed down. Nathalie had been right about writers. They always gave in.

Actually Harvey was surprised Charlie had stayed around to argue. He had no job any more, not as the writer, anyway. Admittedly he was nominally also a co-producer, but, as *Shadows on a Wall* was up to its ass in co-producers, there was nothing for him to do there, either. Bruno definitely didn't want him around. Naturally his agent had made sure he would get some more money to ease the blows. Harvey was sorry it had turned out this way. He liked Charlie a lot.

In the Buffalo dining room Harvey's lunch with Nathalie and the Grave Digger was finished. 'Mr Bamberg,' the waiter, a smiling grinning fellow who walked like a dancer, slid the bill on to the table, 'there's a call from your assistant.'

Signing the lunch away to the *Shadows on a Wall* budget, Harvey made his way across to a house phone.

'Sorry to interrupt, Harvey, but they want you upstairs in Harry Weitzman's office immediately,' Simone apologized.

'Tell them I'll be right up!' Harvey said, smiling. He liked power meetings. They made him feel important. And, leaving Nathalie and the Grave Digger to select their afternoon movie, he marched smartly across to the elevator.

He knew what is was the moment he entered the office. Harry Weitzman, the head of the studio, was behind his desk. In the easy chairs sat Julie Wyatt, representatives from legal, production and business affairs, and a very thoughtful Jake McKenzie.

Weitzman stood up. He was a polite man who had once been an agent and probably one day would be again. The others, being younger, merely shuffled their feet. 'Harvey, I'll come straight to the point. We can't shoulder this alone. It's getting too expensive. Reuben Wiener won't wear it at forty million dollars. We need partners. We're going to have to close you down until you find someone willing to come in with us.'

Harvey could have counted to twenty before he answered. He was thinking, 'There's always something. Always.' His stomach muscles tightened around the lobster salad he had just eaten. 'You want partners?' he said. 'At this stage you want partners?'

'I'm sorry, Harvey.' Weitzman looked embarrassed. The previous day he had been talking as though everything was agreed. This was the way with movies.

Jake McKenzie polished his Armani glasses. He wasn't looking too pleased with himself any more, either.

(ii)

Julie Wyatt watched as Harvey deflated in front of her. He had bounced into the room, ripe and glowing: now his skin was shrivelling, his body slumping into his seat like a rapidly decaying fruit.

It was not unusual for the smaller studios to be overruled by their owners when it came to financing. Movies were being cancelled all the time as deals fell apart, were stitched together and fell apart again. In normal circumstances Harvey could have picked up the phone to half the other studios in Los Angeles, offered them Bruno Messenger, Sam Jordan and Yale Meredith and moved the production across town that afternoon. But with *Shadows on a Wall* time was against him.

Julie lit a menthol cigarette, and drew on the ice-cool smoke as Harry tried to pour balm on Harvey's wounds. She was disappointed, too. Inwardly she cursed Reuben Wiener's timidity. He was too old to control a studio. He hated taking risks. Buffalo was too small and at this rate always would be. Forty million dollars wouldn't have fazed Warners or Columbia.

Across the room Harvey was begging. 'Just do me one favour, will you, Harry? One favour.'

Weitzman didn't answer.

'Give me a week. Don't close us down. Not yet. If you close us down now we'll be dead.'

Weitzman shook his head kindly. 'Harvey, let's not fool ourselves. A *month* wouldn't be enough for you at this stage. You know that. I'm sorry.'

'Five days, make it five days. You know you love the project. Jesus, it's in your interest, if you want to get back some of the pre-production money you've already spent. Just five days. Please. Just give me a chance.' He stared at Weitzman, his eyes were wet, his bottom lip was quivering. 'Please, Harry.'

Weitzman looked away, embarrassed, and then exhaled very slowly. 'Three days. That's the best I can do.'

Harvey was back on his feet, his hand going out. 'Harry, thank you, thank you! You're a friend.' And quickly, as though afraid Weitzman might change his mind, he began backing away to the door. 'I promise you, you'll never regret this, Harry,' he said finally, and hurried out.

Jake McKenzie stared at the back of his manicured hands. 'Well, I guess that's that then.'

Julie Wyatt looked out of the window at the kicking buffalo. She wished she'd stayed at Paramount.

(iii)

To them it was just another movie: to Harvey it was his life. The irony of the situation mocked him as he hurried to his car. Charlie's original screenplay had suggested too small a movie to attract any stars or investors. Now the budget for the same story was too big. But if they were to make it smaller again they would lose Bruno Messenger and his star cast. He was trapped. He dare not disappoint Nathalie.

He drove straight back to the hotel, and set to work: back to truffling.

By the time Nathalie arrived home she had already heard the news. Charlie had called her on her car phone when the lines to the suite were continually busy. He had been talking to Simone who had heard it from Jake.

They had a room-service dinner alone, just Harvey and Nathalie, Edward Lampton sensing the tension and going off to a screening at Fox. Naturally Charlie called wanting to talk (why did writers always want to talk when the end of the world was at hand?), and Jake McKenzie came on the line offering vague contacts in a Japanese bank in one breath and, in the next, mentioning availability enquiries he'd already had for Yale Meredith and Sam Jordan. His message was clear: his voice carried no hope. Jake was an agent: he would cut his losses and move on.

All through dinner Harvey worked the phones. Nathalie watched, saying nothing. At ten she went to bed, early for her. He dared not follow. Disappointment brooded in her eyes: her bottom lip, always swollen, was puffed out bitterly, an ugly, selfish expression. He hated to see her like this, and blamed himself. It was his fault for making her unhappy.

When he finally slept, at around four, it was on the sofa.

Chapter Twenty-seven

(i)

It was humid and overcast in Miami. As promised, a limousine was waiting at the airport. It was driven by a muscular, physically confident young man with luxuriant black hair. Would it have made any difference for him with Nathalie if he had had hair? Harvey wondered. It was a foolish thought, he knew; the thought of a foolish man in fear of losing his wife.

The traffic from the airport was heavy. Soon they were staring out at queues of unmoving cars. There must have been an accident on the road ahead, the young man offered unnecessarily.

It was fitting, Harvey thought. Whichever way he looked he was stuck. For three days he had struggled, calling everyone he knew, all those smooth-skinned executives who had suddenly become friendly when he had had Bruno Messenger and Sam Jordan on the point of signature. He had pleaded with bankers from New York to London to Hong Kong, begged heads of studios, raced from meetings in Burbank to Century City, to Paramount, to Disney and all the way back out to Universal again, talking into his car phone all the time. He had hardly slept, and when he had it had been across the hotel passageway in a single room. It had all been hopeless. 'Next spring, Harvey, we might be able to do something next spring,' he heard everywhere. But he couldn't wait for spring.

At the end of the third day, as the impossibility of the situation had closed in, Nathalie had put a hand on his shoulder, her first touch in days. 'My friend in Avoriaz,' she had reminded him. 'You remember? The Cuban.'

How could he have forgotten?

'He said to give him a call when we had something bigger. I think he meant it.'

Harvey had felt sick. 'You want I should consider going into partnership with the man who made a whore of my wife?' he had wanted to scream. But he had stayed silent.

She had gone into her room, and a little while later slipped a small lemon calling card into his hand. The writing was in italic script: an address, several telephone and fax numbers and a name, Carlos Gallego, of Compania Familia Gallego. On the reverse was a scribbled private number.

Still Harvey had hesitated, his mind convulsing. But when Nathalie had gone to bed early again he had made the call. That morning he had taken the first flight to Miami.

In the limousine the driver shook his head and wiped a finger along the line of his moustache. 'It's bad,' he said, indicating the traffic. 'Carlos doesn't like it if he has to wait.'

At least Nathalie wouldn't have made him wait.

He was slighter than Harvey had imagined, although a hint of belly was swelling under his belt, and, while he stood two inches taller than Harvey, that was mainly because he was wearing boots with platform heels. He looked, Harvey thought, like an older version of the way John Travolta had appeared in *Saturday Night Fever*.

About thirty-eight, he was wearing a cream silk shirt under a dark brown, Italian-style, lightweight suit. His tie was sober, of matching striped autumn shades. When he spoke it was with a slight lisp, a ghost of a Latin-American accent and an asthmatic wheeze.

He was, Harvey supposed, attractive in a quietly wilful way, with fine features only just running to fat under his chin, and intelligent, brown, watchful eyes: the sort of man who might have looked dashing on the streets at eighteen, but who now, with his expensive clothes, finely cut black hair, and surrounded by his associates, suggested an aura of manicured boardroom power.

As Harvey shook his hand and smelt his aftershave, he thought: 'This man's penis pushed into and emptied inside my wife.' But he smiled and said: 'Nice to meet, you, Carlos. May I call

212

you, Carlos? Nathalie asked me to give you her very best regards.'

'And how is, Nathalie? I know, beautiful. You're a lucky man, Mr Bamberg, to have a wife like Nathalie.' Carlos Gallego spoke in the gracious, measured tones of a man who might have had only a formal relationship with a woman, and largely for the benefit of his companions.

Did they know? Harvey wondered. Had Gallego boasted? What man wouldn't boast if he had slept with Nathalie Seillans?

The colleagues watched carefully. Later he would not remember much about them as individuals other than that three out of the five were dark haired, smart, hard-faced men in expensive suits listening keenly to what was being said. Harvey guessed they were family. The others were a wiry man with thin fair hair who made notes to himself during the conversation and was introduced as a financial adviser, and a white-haired man in a dark blue suit, a company lawyer.

Gesturing for Harvey to sit at a white leather sofa, in front of which was a table heavily laden with books on history and political biography, Gallego ordered some coffee and sandwiches by phone. Three other sofas surrounded the table which was at the end of a wide, light room, the penthouse floor of a tall, pink hotel. On the opposite side of a glass door at the end of the room, and with the sound just audible, a television was showing an old black-and-white episode of *The Untouchables*, with Robert Stack apparently speaking in Spanish, in front of which a boy of about nine sat watching. It was an unusual domestic situation for a business meeting.

'I would like him to read more, but my son likes to watch the movies,' Gallego smiled. He had an engaging smile: Nathalie had commented upon that. 'His mother is visiting her mother in Bogotá with his sister, so I'm a babysitter. Today I brought him to the office, but already he's bored.' And he laughed to himself.

The concentrated, silent male tonnage made Harvey feel uneasy. This was a large and extremely wealthy organization. Somewhere there would be offices, pretty, sweet-smelling receptionists and cute secretaries, but when the driver had delivered him to the hotel Harvey had been met and shown up to this roof-top suite by two other young men.

Nathalie had known nothing of Gallego's business, but Harvey's New York lawyer, Mo Rosenbaum, had provided a partial picture.

'They're very big, Harvey,' Rosenbaum had reported when Harvey had called him from Miami airport. 'Who knows how big? A family company. Construction, parking lots, hotels, casinos, one of those mushroom private companies that came up overnight in the Eighties, and they're spreading like wildfire. Money's no object it seems. He's the centre of it all, Carlos Gallego. They say he's very bright, very ambitious.'

Now Gallego was watching Harvey carefully. 'So, Mr Bamberg, you have a movie to discuss,' he said quietly.

Harvey nodded. Why did this man who had so casually cuckolded him make him feel so nervous?

'I brought you a screenplay,' he said, sliding Charlie's latest script across the table.

Gallego made no attempt to pick it up. 'You say the budget is forty million dollars and Buffalo are in for twenty million.'

'That's right. But their New York owners, mainly Reuben Weiner at Candy Corn, are insisting that they put up no more than fifty per cent of the equity. I think if you read the script . . .'

Carlos Gallego smiled. 'Why would I need to read the script?' he asked. 'Would I understand it if I did? Would Buffalo Pictures be prepared to invest twenty million dollars of their stock-holders' money in a bad script? I don't know anything about movie scripts. I'm a business man. My son Anthony there . . .' He indicated the boy on the other side of the glass door, 'Anthony knows about movies. But he doesn't know about business. Maybe if he pays attention one day he will know about both. It could be a good career for a boy.' And he looked towards his son, busy watching the FBI engaged in a shoot-out with an organized crime syndicate on television.

Harvey nodded.

Gallego weighed the script in his hand. 'I don't know, maybe this movie will be an interesting investment for us here at Familia Gallego, maybe not. As always, it depends on the deal. We've been looking around for something in movies for some time, for the way in. You understand what I'm saying? But it has to be the right something. Too many producers want to take our money and keep all the profit, or they want to make some little movie that won't ever get distributed, or maybe a porno movie or something of that nature. If we want to make a porno movie we can do that ourselves. Maybe we will . . .'

He suddenly laughed. Some of his associates smiled. One glanced at Harvey and looked quickly away.

They do know, Harvey thought.

'If we want to become involved in movies, it has to be a legitimate Hollywood movie. When I met Nathalie in Avoriaz I wanted to help her, but we're not interested in little projects. This proposition, however, this Sam Jordan movie is interesting to me. Joining Buffalo Pictures on an equal footing, as equity partners, that sounds interesting to me.' He sat smiling at Harvey for a moment, then said: 'But it has to be fifty–fifty all down the line. Too many Hollywood companies take their partners for suckers, creaming commissions off distribution and foreign and video sales while the guys who put up the production money bleed.' His voice dropped to a whisper. 'We here at Familia Gallego won't bleed for anyone.'

With the curtains drawn Harvey lay on his hotel bed. Closing his eyes he felt a warm tear squeezing between his eyelids. He had had to go as a supplicant to the man who had plundered his wife. All through the meeting he had been imagining them together. Nathalie had provided the pictures so carefully: the vigour, the intimacies, the smoothness of his body, 'almost no body hair, Harvey,' she had said, 'it was like making love to a boy of twenty . . . to a girl.' Gallego could not have known that Nathalie had told him; he would hardly have expected it. He had spoken of her as someone he had scarcely known, but whom he remembered with respect. But nothing in her account of their night together had suggested respect. And now to keep her Harvey was forfeiting his right to her respect. No wonder his friends laughed at him.

Eventually, he got up and going into the bathroom washed his face. Nathalie may not be worth it but he loved her. He would do whatever it took to keep her.

Picking up the telephone he dialled Buffalo Pictures.

Weitzman had been waiting. So far, he said, the Buffalo lawyers had unearthed nothing too unpleasant about Familia Gallego, although there was some surprise at their continuing speed of development, and wonder at their diversification.

'So what do you think, will he make a suitable partner?' Harvey asked.

Weitzman was cautious. 'That'll be up to Reuben and New York. It's possible. It's going to be a hell of a deal to get through if he wants in on distribution, but nothing is impossible. Pre-production

215

costs have already become very expensive. Reuben will want to see his money back. If the money's there, and there's nothing obvious which might jump out of Miami and embarrass us too much, the lawyers might be able to hammer something out. Gallego's already got his bank talking in New York.'

'Really?' Gallego had moved quickly.

'Car-parks,' Harry Weitzman mused, 'maybe that was the business you and I should have gone into, Harvey. At least we'd be able to sleep nights.'

Harvey forced a laugh. 'That's right,' he said, though secretly he doubted that Gallego could always sleep at night. He was surprised. He was sure none of the other studio heads would have considered running with Gallego. Buffalo must be more desperate than he had realized.

His next call was to Nathalie.

'Hello, darling,' she murmured. 'I was thinking of you. How went today? Was it terrible for you?' Her voice was almost caring.

'Not at all, not at all,' he bluffed. 'Carlos is a nice guy. We got along just great. But then, I always knew he had to be something special.'

'And what about our movie? How does our movie go?'

Harvey tasted a tear on his lip. 'I think, yes, Nathalie. I think maybe our movie goes after all.'

At the other end of the line Nathalie unfolded a sigh of satisfaction.

August, 1992

Pre-production

Chapter Twenty-eight

(i)

Simone Estoril sipped her coffee and watched as the two men made their way across the Pinewood car-park towards the main production building. She wondered what they were, carpenters, set builders, crane operators . . . ? They had been coming for two weeks now, the other ranks of the film industry. Naturally the officer positions had been filled in California – Harold Armstrong, the Buffalo accountant, Giorgio Pescati, the Italian cinematographer and his team, Judy Goldberg, the director's assistant, Hal Jobete, the art director and Tim Westwood, the excitable young editor who had worked on *Digital Watch*. But it was at Pinewood that the main body of troops was being recruited for the army which would soon begin filming *Shadows on a Wall*.

They were so many, coming from all over, from other productions, other countries, other continents, from commercials, from retirement, from television, from unemployment, legions of people who all apparently knew each other, links in the international chain of film technicians – old friends and worst enemies, rivals and partners, former lovers, former spouses, seasoned location adulterers. They came singly, they came in pairs and they came in teams, each one with requests for equipment to be hired, cameras and lenses, lights, tracks, cranes, walkie-talkies, hair and make-up vans, cars and buses to transport the crew, campers, limousines and Winnibagoes for the director and the stars, portable lavatories for everyone.

To Simone everything was fascinating, and every day she would visit the production offices to sit in on meetings, gaze at the storyboards, and examine the perpetually revising schedules which hung on Al Mutton's office walls.

At the centre of everything stood Bruno Messenger. Hardly more than a boy in Simone's eyes, he was planning his campaign on epic lines, his self-belief pulverizing. Not yet present were the stars, Sam Jordan and Yale Meredith, who, everyone knew, would soon bring their own distinct problems and whose egos were already the stuff of anticipation, and the smaller names who could often be the most difficult of all. Nor were all the supporting parts filled, as Bruno and his casting directors continued to trawl Europe and America for the right names and faces. American television actor Jack Dragoman had confirmed as Will Yorke, but Kenneth Branagh was unavailable to play the Duke of Wellington, and, finding the 'new Isabelle Adjani' for Camille de Malignon was proving easier said than done. After seeing virtually every young actress in France, Bruno was now planning auditions in London. And time was running out.

'So what do you think?' It was Harvey. Simone hadn't heard him come into the room. He was holding a brochure out to her. Harvey had been very quiet since his visit to Florida, but he had got what Buffalo wanted. The money was in place. The movie was going to be made.

'I think it's a car,' she said, taking the brochure.

'But what kind of car?'

'Oh, come on, Harvey, what am I, a salesman or something? It's a big car . . . a snazzy car!'

Carefully, so that he didn't crease it, Harvey opened out the brochure. It was one of those which unfolded into three segments and which extended the car in length as it did. 'It's a . . .'

'Noblesse . . .' read Simone. 'Well, what do you know? A Noblesse American. Terrific!' To her one car was much the same as another.

Harvey smiled quietly. 'That's right, terrific. And it's on its way.'

'I don't follow.'

'I bought one. It's being shipped over from New York. It's my present to myself. Don't ask what it cost. Too much. Isn't it beautiful?'

'It's a car, Harvey. They have cars here in Europe, too, you know.'

He shook his head. 'Not 'ninety two Noblesses, they don't. Not cars like this one. Just wait till you see it! Just wait till they see it in Poland. Just wait till Nathalie sees it.'

She refolded the brochure and passed it back to him. 'If it makes you happy . . .'

Actually she was pleased for him. A lot of people in movies sneered at big American cars these days. They thought they were vulgar. Harvey Bamberg didn't mind being thought of as vulgar. She liked that. Some people probably thought she was vulgar, too.

As Harvey padded off to show somebody else Simone turned to the mountain of faxes her assistant had just delivered. It was Simone's first visit to England and already she had her own assistant. That meant she had status. She liked that, too. But more than anything she loved the job. It would be a crazy, helter-skelter rush to be ready in time, but it was all wonderful – well worth a weekend in Pacific Palisades waiting around until Jake McKenzie found a moment to take her to bed.

(ii)

Charlie arrived home early in the morning, slipping into the flat almost apologetically. Belinda was in the kitchen making some coffee. 'The plane was early,' he explained, 'pushed by a following wind. Perhaps it's a good omen.'

She couldn't think how to answer. He looked embarrassed to be there. Anticipating his return she had hardly slept. He had been away so long.

He grazed her with a kiss; she saw it coming and turned her face away. At that moment she made the decision she had been putting off for weeks. She didn't want to sleep with him any more.

'I think it would be better this way,' she said, as she carried pillows and sheets into his study. 'I don't know how I feel about things at the moment.' She was surprised at how detached she could be, how much she sounded like her mother.

Charlie watched her without question, as though wondering

221

what she was going to do next. He was tanned, but the easy optimism was gone, and with it the little grins and silly jokes.

She asked no questions about the film. She no longer cared. It wasn't the tiny *Shadows on a Wall* of which she had been part, and he was no longer the writer. She wanted to tell him to forget about it, to begin writing something else, but he wouldn't have listened. He had the look of the permanently distracted.

'The decorating . . . it looks wonderful. You must have worked very hard. I love the colours,' Charlie called after her as she collected her radio script from the bedroom. His voice sounded like an actor who doesn't believe his part.

'Thank you,' she said, and hurried off to rehearsals.

Waiting at the end of the Underground station staring into the tunnel she let three trains go before she stopped crying. Around her the film posters mocked her with their wet-lipped, glossy-thighed evocations of sex and romance. Sex and romance: that was only the half of it.

She returned in mid-afternoon. Charlie was not there. The pillows and sheets no longer covered the bunk in his study. The word processor was gone, as was the book on movie trivia she had bought him for his last birthday.

She wasn't surprised.

(iii)

Claire spotted it, a single paragraph on the show-business page of the *Daily Mail*. Sadie's parents didn't take anything as vulgar as the *Daily Mail*.

'Hear this,' Claire shouted, pulling the newspaper closer to the phone. '*After drawing a blank in Paris top US director Bruno Messenger of* Digital Watch *fame is in London auditioning unknown young actresses to play a sexy French aristocrat in the film version of the Edinburgh Festival success,* Shadows on a Wall.' It was the school holidays, and Claire was in France with her family, phoning from a call box outside the *mairie* in Quimper. 'That must be the Camille de what's-her-name part,' she trilled. 'You should go along. If you can be a gay Hamlet you can be a sexy frog any day.'

Sadie needed a couple of seconds to take this in. It was a hot day and she had been sitting in the garden reading *Anna Karenina*. August was dull. Her parents were planning a cultural package trip to Mexico in November and there would be no family holiday that year. With Claire away for three weeks and the house empty all day she had been steadily working her way through the Russians. When the telephone had interrupted, her eyes had been satisfactorily wet. 'Read it again,' she demanded, 'what else does it say?'

'I can't, I've got to go. I've no more money. I've met a *fabulous* French bloke. He looks like a cross between Penn Stadtler and Rob Lowe. I'll try to . . .'

The line went dead.

Five minutes later, Sadie was examining the newspaper herself in the corner shop. There was one obvious problem. The venue for the auditions wasn't given. At first she considered phoning Belinda and asking for Harvey Bamberg's number, but quickly dismissed the idea as tactless.

Instead she called the show-business department of the *Daily Mail*, where she was quickly put off by a secretary. She tried again, and again. On the fourth call she reached a reporter who asked her a lot of questions and who, in the end, charmed, or perhaps exhausted by her persistence, eventually gave her the address of a hotel in Knightsbridge.

'Remember, I didn't tell you, and if you get a part and become a famous film star I want an exclusive interview,' he joked.

Sadie promised gravely that she would remember him.

'You aren't on the list,' the production secretary complained irritably. She was a tough, mannish girl, with big, old-fashioned, Joan Collins style shoulder-pads in her jacket. ' "Jaspers", you say. These agencies are so disorganized. I'm sorry.' She shook her head firmly.

Sadie stood her ground. 'Are you sure? I know my agent said this afternoon. I've come all the way from Winchester.'

'I'm sorry.'

Sadie didn't move.

The girl stared at her.

Sadie waited. It was easier to brazen things out when the world

looked that little bit less distinct and she had purposely come
without her glasses.

'I'm sorry about that, but I don't think they can fit you
in . . .'

'Oh dear . . .' Sadie was sure she looked quite dismayed. Still
she waited.

The secretary gave in first. 'Well, perhaps if you could hang
around till the end, I'll see what I can do . . .'

'Oh yes. Could you? Thank you.' She would have waited all
week. Taking her place in the queue she smiled at the girl next to
her, a tall, red head with a clown's white skin and a tiny band for
a skirt. The girl had just told her she was from an agency called
Jaspers. Until that moment Sadie had never heard of Jaspers.

'What did you say your name was?' the casting director asked
two hours later. 'Did Penny send you?' She was a punky-looking
woman with spikey, henna-rinsed hair and a pointed nose which
seemed to prod at Sadie as she talked, as though trying to prick
her into admitting her lie. Another, older woman sat next to
her, saying nothing, watching closely. 'It's very difficult when
we haven't seen your c.v. Can you tell us what you've done?'

Sadie swallowed. 'Well, quite a lot, actually. *Hamlet*, I was
Hamlet. And Puck, and, er, I was Tallulah in *Bugsy Malone*. I
was Joseph in *Technicolor Dreamcoat* . . . erm, Juliet . . .'

She could see the spikey casting director's frown creasing.
'But where, Sadie?'

'Edinburgh . . .' Sadie said, adding, '. . . the Fringe. And
Oxford. And, er, the Bristol Old Vic.' That was when she
pushed it too far.

The casting director's mouth snapped. Her colleague smiled.
There were whispers. 'Well, you're a very pretty girl, Sadie,
and enterprising, but—' the casting director began. It was like
school: a lecture brewing.

'Please, wait . . . !'

'I'm sorry . . .' The spikey-haired woman was already picking
up the phone.

Sadie knew what she must do. Taking one pace back she
span around three hundred and sixty degrees, washed her face
of expression and began to speak softly but directly. She knew
the lines so well. '*It was morning. There was excitement: a crowd.
I was told to stand at the window. I heard the drum, the single regular*

beat which told of the approaching tumbril, of the day's victims on their way to the guillotine . . .'

At this point the spikey-haired woman tried to cut in. 'Yes, well, thank you, Sadie . . .'

Ignoring her Sadie turned her eyes on the other woman. She appeared to carry more authority. *'I didn't understand. The man at my side wore a black coat and hat. Below us there was shouting and cheering, and as the tumbril grew closer the roar became deafening, men and women crushing forward to get a better view.*

'My own view was perfect. My guardian had made sure of that. "Can you see all right, Camille de Malignon? I would not want you to miss anything." ' Sadie hesitated. There was no interruption this time.

'The guillotine stood across the cobbles beneath the window. A troupe of militia armed with bayonets surrounded it, facing the mob. A man in a black hat with a white-powdered wig stood on the platform, while other men in red bonnets busied themselves preparing the scaffold. I thought I was watching some new kind of circus.

'But then as the cart stopped I saw them, my father and mother, brothers and sisters, even Jean-Paul. He was just twelve. I waved and shouted. I was happy. I thought they had come to fetch me and that we could now go home. They did not see me . . .' She paused again. *'They took my father first . . .'*

The older woman put her hand up. 'Can you come back tomorrow?' she said.

'And how was your day then?' her father asked as they waited for the vegetarian lasagne to be heated.

'Well, quite unusual, I'd say,' Sadie said. 'You see I went for a sort of audition . . .'

There was a sudden crash from the other end of the kitchen. 'Blast!'

Lasagne lay splattered on the kitchen floor. Her mother tottered over it, her hands up in the air wagging helplessly inside vast oven gloves. Sadie hurried to clean up the mess. Her father passed her mother a glass of claret.

'Bad luck,' he said.

'I'll make some more when I've done this,' Sadie offered.

Her mother looked thoroughly bored. 'Couldn't we just go out?'

'Of course we could. D'you want to come, too, Sadie?'

She could have said 'yes', tagged along with them, three paces behind, while they wittered on. If he had taken it for granted that she would go with them she would have done just that. But he had asked. 'Sorry. P'raps I'll stay here, if you don't mind. I've got some reading to do.'

'Oh well, suit yourself.'

Had they even been listening? she wondered as she took some ravioli out into the garden fifteen minutes later, *Anna Karenina* back under her arm. Had they even heard her mention the audition?

She opened her book.

The following day there were more girls and Polaroid pictures were taken. 'Don't tell lies in future,' the spiky-haired casting director scolded, but, intrigued that Sadie knew the play so well, she was not angry.

At a third meeting with still more girls, Sadie was asked to read from a script for a video camera, then act out a small scene with the casting director. Before she left they double-checked her telephone number.

She did not attempt to tell her parents again about how she was spending her days. They were busy most evenings and the moment never arose. Claire phoned from France a couple of times. The Penn Stadtler-Rob Lowe lookalike she fancied obviously didn't fancy her, because by the third call she had decided he must be gay.

Sadie's account of the auditions intrigued her. 'But watch out, Sadie,' she warned. 'Remember Fatty Arbuckle!'

'Who's Fatty Arbuckle?'

'I'm not sure. But I don't think he was terribly nice.'

(iv)

'What do you mean . . . *repossession*? I don't understand.' Billy knotted his large hands and stared blankly with his one eye across the bare desk into the two button eyes of Witherspoon, the bank manager.

Witherspoon, a withdrawn, freckled man, who had let the

dread word slip while they had been distractedly watching two pigeons on the window-ledge, sighed quietly, a more-in-embarrassment-than-in-sympathy kind of sigh.

'Repossession means . . . well, repossession,' he said. 'Every month that goes by you impoverish yourself further. Year in, year out your overdraft has been going up, eating into the value of your house. You have very little collateral left. When you reach, as you will shortly, the position where there is no further collateral the bank will be forced to repossess your property. I'm sorry to have to put it so bluntly, but we have warned you many times over the years . . .'

Billy forgot the pigeons. 'I've got four children, you know. Four under eight.'

'You also have one of the biggest overdrafts I have ever come across in a private client, with a fluctuating income which in some months doesn't even cover the interest your overdraft is accumulating.'

'I'm up for an Emmy,' Billy threw in desperately, pushing his hands through his hair.

'An Emmy?'

'It's a prize they give in New York for the best television programmes. I've been nominated for my Graham Greene film.'

'Oh, well done! How much will that realize?'

'I'm sorry?'

'How much money will the prize be worth . . . should you win it?'

'Oh no. No money. The prize isn't in the form of money. An Emmy is a prestige thing . . .'

Witherspoon opened and closed his mouth and then looked sadly at a sheet of figures on the desk in front of him. 'Unfortunately, Mr Yeo, as you will appreciate, prestige doesn't pay bills.'

Outside the window one pigeon was now excitedly fluttering on top of the other. The one underneath looked bored. Billy wished he had a camera. Had Eric Rohmer been directing this scene he would have cut to the pigeons at this point. What was a director supposed to do that was new with a bank manager and client confrontation, for heaven's sake?

Across the desk Witherspoon was tapping his pen quietly on his desk, bringing Billy back to reality. This wasn't a scene. This was the repo man in a blue-striped suit giving his final warning. Suddenly he stood up and pushed out a hand. 'Well, then, I think that's about all. I do hope things work out for you, and that . . . well, you'll be able to manage your finances better in the future. If I were you I'd put your house on the market as soon as possible and start again somewhere that you can afford. Thank you for coming in.' And walking quickly to the door he held it open for his client.

Outside in the street Billy looked back at the black horse prancing on the lighted green sign of the bank. They should put a monument to me up there, he thought. With the amount of interest I pay I should be their symbol.

He had always been choosy in the work he did. Now he made himself a promise: he would do anything. Anything at all.

(v)

On most days Charlie went to the pictures. On other days he sat in Kensington Gardens and read. Sometimes he didn't bother to read.

He had returned to his old basement room in North Kensington. It had been an impulse decision. He didn't deserve Belinda, he told himself. If they had still been friends, lovers, he would have told her about his blind rhinoceros theory of film-making. But he couldn't expect her to understand, not now.

He hadn't known what to expect when he arrived back, only that suddenly he was redundant – to the film and to Belinda. He had been flattered and dazzled by Hollywood. But when he had stepped back into their home he had been struck with surprise by the freshness of her beauty. She was magical. How could he ever have forgotten? Now every day he made a point of listening in to *The Lyndons*, Monday to Friday, Radio 2 at 4.30, just to hear her voice. He had always loved the way she spoke.

On one day he wrote to Bruno Messenger, reminding him of his promise to look Belinda up when he was in Europe. There was nothing to be lost in trying.

The days passed. He ate alone in restaurants, his face in a book. Frequently he would stand in bookshops and peruse the new titles, or wait in cinema lobbies staring at the posters, reading the names of every actor and producer. He didn't know why. In the night he would edit and file his movie collection, trying to find the door into sleep. Some of the time he wondered if he was going slightly mad; and all of the time he wondered what was happening to *Shadows on a Wall*.

Chapter Twenty-nine

(i)

A deep electronic groan filled the stadium, a single, portentous, Titanic-in-the-fog moan, and the heavy summer air seemed to bend under the weight of the sound. There was a ripple of expectancy. A laser-beam cut into the evening sky, then a second and a third, swords of light fencing above the city. From beneath, the earth began to pulse, a universal reverberating heartbeat. Quietly at first, then building and insistent, came an eight-note guitar riff. Above the heads of the crowd a squadron of aircraft landing lights jetted into an eighty-foot altar constructed along one end of the ground where normally goal posts would have stood. There was a roar from the crowd. The fresh bite of dry ice hung in air exploding with sound and light and rhythm. The performance was about to begin: or was it a ritual? Belinda shook her head. Penn Stadtler wasn't exactly self-effacing.

Suddenly there he was, jogging out of the shimmering man-made clouds, the little man high on the altar, the performer turned shaman, an athletic figure, the long, fair hair swinging through the hole in the back of the baseball cap, the uniform of T-shirt, knee-length tennis shorts and ear-ring already copied by so many disciples in the audience. He waved, one hand above the crowd in recognition of the welcome. Then, as the other found a keyboard, a computer threw a meteor shower on to a screen and the concert began.

Belinda didn't like the music particularly but she could appreciate what Penn Stadtler did: writing and recording everything himself, playing each instrument, he was a one-man band of the electronic era, a high-tech theatrical wizard.

The invitation to the concert had come unexpectedly from agent Larry Horner's wife, Virginia. Larry had been given a whole row of seats, and was putting a party together. Would Belinda care to join them? At first she had refused. There had been a *putsch*. Penn Stadtler was involved in *Shadows on a Wall* and she and Charlie were not. But in the end curiosity had won. They would all be there, the new *Shadows on a Wall* team. It would at least be interesting to meet them.

But now, as she submerged her senses under the howling, roaring bombardment, she had the uneasy feeling that she had become a collaborator in the enemy encampment.

Belinda came upon Nathalie Seillans after the performance, standing with Penn Stadtler in the guests' marquee, smiling at him as he made a little private joke.

'Wasn't it just the most wonderful concert?' Nathalie breathed. 'Penn is so talented. He'll write such wonderful music for *Shadows on a Wall*.'

At her side the Electronic Sun God was signing autographs and casually accepting general adoration. Nobody is ever so fêted as a rock star after a performance, thought Belinda.

They took over a Soho restaurant for dinner. Nathalie had arranged it, the movie's budget bearing the cost because it was here that Penn Stadtler's association with *Shadows on a Wall* was to be officially announced. By now Belinda had discovered that Harvey was in Miami for further negotiations with Carlos Gallego and that, at Nathalie's suggestion, the Grave Digger had accompanied him. Now Nathalie sat alongside Penn Stadtler at the head of a long table, waiting as he flirted with the waitresses and bantered with his friends, the handsome young man of the moment and the slightly portly, middle-aged French woman.

They had reached the pudding when Bruno Messenger joined them, bringing with him Al Mutton and a couple of unspeaking glamorous girls. 'I've heard a lot about you,' Bruno smiled as Larry introduced Belinda.

'Ditto,' Belinda replied, without encouragement.

'Charlie wrote reminding me about you,' the director went

on. 'I was going to ask you to come down to Pinewood. Now I don't have to.'

Belinda had not known of Charlie's letter. It made her feel even more disloyal. 'It's growing into a bigger movie than I ever imagined,' she said.

'Isn't that the way with movies!'

A waitress came to take Bruno's order. He wanted some pasta and explained exactly how it should be cooked. He was so certain of himself and his place as the centre of attention among the movie people present. It was, Belinda thought, as though everything flowed from him and to him, a relentless two-way traffic of energy. He was the great patron: the director as a star.

He didn't stay long, just long enough to eat and be photographed with Penn Stadtler. When he left he offered Belinda a lift.

'You understand, don't you, it wasn't my fault about the Marie Walewska part?' he said as the car cut a channel through the paparazzi.

She didn't reply.

'I mean as far as the studio were concerned it *had* to be Yale Meredith.'

Belinda was actually wondering how she could ever have imagined she might have got the part in the first place.

'But there are other parts, ladies of the French and Polish courts, for instance. Nothing great, but something to get yourself noticed, and that's what it's all about.'

'Yes,' she said, without enthusiasm.

'I mean, look at Suzie Bruton.'

'Suzie Bruton?' She had never heard of her.

'She got a walk on in *Beyond the Sea* where she gets up to go for a pee in the nude in the middle of the night, and next thing she's starring in *The Girl in the Window*.'

'So you think a nude pee is a good career move?'

'Don't you?' he exclaimed, and laughed so loudly the driver jumped. Then, remembering something, he grabbed the car phone, punched a number and began to speak very quickly into it.

Belinda looked at her watch. It was after one. The recipient of the call sounded as though he had already been asleep.

'I don't care what it costs,' the director was thundering at her side. 'Al will clear it. Just get it. OK!'

He's trying to impress me by bullying someone, Belinda thought. What a dummy!

Abruptly ending the phone conversation Bruno relaxed and turned back to her. 'The trouble with location scouts over here is they're always trying to save us money, offer up second best. They've learned some bad habits. Only the best is good enough for *Shadows on a Wall*.'

'*Only the best is good enough* . . .' Belinda thought. She would tell Charlie that when they next spoke.

'What I want to make is the greatest love story ever filmed. *Shadows on a Wall* has to be the film of the decade, the film to end the century. The audience has to *feel* the frostbite of the retreat from Moscow, to *smell* the blood of the battles, experience the desires of these two couples, *real* desperate desire, that feeling that tears at the pit of your stomach.' As he spoke he stared so closely at her she could feel his breath upon her face.

Belinda remembered playing Marie Walewska in Edinburgh. No-one had spoken about *Shadows on a Wall* then as the 'greatest love story ever'. They had just wanted to get it right for those tiny audiences. This is what hype does to you, she told herself. It makes everything outsized, the *biggest*, the *greatest*, the most *beautiful*, the *richest*. But does that mean, the *best*? How do you judge *best* in movies, anyway? Her mother had liked big: her father had wanted good. No wonder they hadn't always got along.

Bruno was smiling now. 'Can I ask you something? Why does an American actress as beautiful as you live in England when they hardly make movies here any more?'

She ignored the compliment. 'I like London,' she said.

'Yes, but your career . . . ?'

Belinda shrugged. 'There's Charlie, too.'

'There is, or there was?'

She didn't rise to that.

The car sped on.

'Like I was saying,' Bruno came back, 'there are other parts. Maybe the Empress Josephine would have been interesting, but she was dark, and Buffalo wanted . . .'

'Delphine Claviers,' Belinda said.

'Right. But, for my money, Monika Wyszynska is the best. She's lively, bitchy, a gossip, promiscuous, spying a little by sleeping with both French and Russian officers . . . a sort of

233

fun lady, I think. You would make her a real honey of a girl. If you were her, people would understand the temptation those guys were facing.' He raised his eyebrows.

He was playing with her, she thought. According to the scripts she had read virtually everything Monika Wyszynska did was an off-screen joke, a cutting-room-floor part.

He read her thoughts. 'I should tell you the new writers are already fleshing her out. To be honest, I think maybe Charlie could have made more of Monika Wyszynska.'

'Really!' For a moment she imagined two young men in a white, Thirties studio screenwriters' building with a water dispenser and big portable typewriter, the way they always showed them in old movies. Then she thought about Charlie, and the way he would stare for hours into his word processor looking for the pictures.

'So, what do you think?' The car had pulled up outside her flat.

'I'm sorry?'

'Do you want to play Monika Wyszynska?'

'This is a serious offer?'

'Certainly it's a serious offer. You'd be perfect. I knew it the moment I saw you.'

She hesitated. She didn't know what she wanted any more.

'We'll speak to your agent tomorrow,' he said.

The driver had already opened the door. Leaning forward Bruno took hold of her hand. He had soft, fat fingers.

'Well, anyway, thanks for the lift.'

He squeezed her hand, a sensual, little caress.

Quickly she pulled away, and slipped from the car.

'The trick is getting noticed,' he said again, confident in his offer.

'Good night,' she called, as, going up the steps, she felt in her purse for her keys.

But the car was already pulling away, with Bruno once again punching the phone buttons, waking up somebody else.

(ii)

Simone waited as Harvey went through his address book. Finally he smiled. For a plain little man Harvey had a generous smile.

234

He had, he said, just had a brainwave, and he scribbled down a number on a piece of paper.

Returning to her desk Simone dialled the number. A man's voice on an answering machine told her that he and his family were on a bucket-and-spade holiday in Devon and could not be reached. 'First things first,' the recording ended.

Leaving a message Simone returned to her schedules. Across the office Harvey was back on the phone, talking to someone at the BBC.

(iii)

Sadie went to meet Bruno Messenger on her bicycle, which was eccentric because it was a sticky day and her hair, which she had tied in a red ribbon on top of her head, came tumbling down about her ears long before she reached Knightsbridge. She wished then she had taken the bus, but she was young and too excited to be demure.

'Yuk!!' she exclaimed as she padlocked the bike to the garden railings facing the hotel. She had smeared oil on her fingers.

Making her way to the lifts, and vainly rubbing her hands with a tissue, she realized she wasn't even nervous. The whole situation was too unreal for nerves.

The younger casting director was waiting as the lift door opened, seeing off a familiar face. It was Emma Powers, the girl who had played Camille de Malignon in Edinburgh. It seemed like decades ago. She looked cool and confident, and she was certainly pretty; but, Sadie remembered, she was hardly an actress.

'Tell me, how old are you, Sadie?' the casting director asked thoughtfully as she led her into a sitting room where four other girls were already waiting.

'Seventeen.'

The casting agent frowned. 'Seventeen. Right. Don't let him bully you,' she murmured.

It was a bit like being in a doctor's surgery, Sadie thought, as the first of the other girls was called, and, running her eye along the line of actresses, she wondered what illnesses they might have. That one's consumptive for sure, she diagnosed of a languid, black-eyed Susie who was reading a Mario Vargas Llosa novel, probably slightly anorexic, and prone to bouts of bulimia. The second, a reborn blonde was sitting sharply upright, a secretary type with too much eyeshadow and a clenched jaw: gynaecological problem, probably, wondering if she shouldn't stick to the Pill after all and risk a coronary at thirty-five. The third girl was fair, had large lemonade-coloured glasses and was feeding a little dog thin slices of salt beef from a handbag. Raving distemper, no doubt about it!

They called her next, the previous girl hurrying out with what looked like damp eyes. Oh, my God, the Committee of Public Safety, she thought, as she entered the room.

Seated at a rectangular table were three people, Bruno Messenger in the centre. She knew him from a photograph she had seen in a Sunday magazine, but she had not expected anyone quite so young, or so big. He was sucking a Malteser and the round chocolate ball was bulging rhythmically, like a movable tumour, under one cheek. Fatty Arbuckle lives! she thought. At one side of him sat a dumpy, pleasant woman with black frizzy hair, who appeared to be his assistant, and on the other was the older casting director. The two women stood to greet her, the director remained seated.

Sadie waited. For several moments Bruno Messenger examined a page of typed notes. Then he stared at her, long and carefully, taking another Malteser, but not offering her one. 'OK, Sadie, I believe you know the part, and therefore you know that really we're looking for someone a little older than you are. But maybe that's splitting hairs. Who knows when the Reign of Terror was anyway?'

On the point of saying ,'1792 to 1794', Sadie bit her tongue.

'So now I'm thinking maybe we could cast the part a little younger. We'll see. But first there are things I have to ask you, and I want you to be straight with me. Right? What I need to know right off is how would you feel about nudity, about taking your clothes off in front of say, six or seven guys? You know what I'm saying? There's no hiding place on a movie set. I'm not talking about anything dirty or pornographic, but people will be looking at whoever does this part, and looking again in the movies and on television and video all over the world. How would you feel about that?'

If I waver, I'm dead, Sadie told herself. 'I wouldn't feel anything,' she said. 'I'm used to having people look at me naked.

236

My parents are naturists. I've hardly ever worn a swimsuit in my life. Of course we can only go to certain beaches.' She was lying. That story had come from Claire who had lightened many a wet games day with her accounts of how she had once accidentally found herself in the middle of a Minorcan nudist beach.

At her side, Sadie noticed the spiky-haired casting director cross her legs in disbelief.

'Is that so? Because you wouldn't believe how touchy some girls can get when you ask them to take off their clothes and show their pussies. Really, very upset.'

Pussies! Sadie thought, and volleyed it straight back. 'Well, yes, that's girls and their pussies, I suppose. Touchy and non-touchy. I'm definitely non-touchy.'

The plump assistant laughed at that and wrote something down. Bruno Messenger looked puzzled, wondering perhaps if he was being reprimanded. Standing up, he crossed to a silver teapot and cups. 'Milk or lemon?' he asked.

Over tea they chatted on. Obviously Bruno Messenger had some idea of what he was looking for, but Sadie couldn't help feeling that in his black shirt and suit he was as much an actor as she was, trying hard to affect how he thought a confrontational Nineties film director ought to behave. She had no idea what he was thinking but she knew she was doing well with the women by the way they nodded their heads and smiled at her jokes. She didn't tell them she was friendly with Charlie and Belinda; that would have been like admitting a fondness for the *ancien régime*. When asked why she had lied about her previous experience she said she would have done anything to get an audition, and promptly proved it by saying she had finished school that summer and was completely free. Actually, she still had another year to do.

It seemed to Sadie it didn't matter what she told them because it was all just a holiday adventure. It would be September soon and her mother would be getting out her school uniform and waking her up for a new term.

She talked for probably half an hour during most of which Bruno sat staring at her. When she was told they might need her back for a screen test, she nodded happily, hardly believing them. This sort of thing didn't happen to girls who went to Queen's Yard.

Then suddenly it was over. Outside in the street she wheeled her bicycle along the pavement, trying to make sense of the meeting, remembering that night in Edinburgh when she had first seen the play. She didn't know what she should have expected of a Hollywood director, but Bruno Messenger had been a disappointment. He had hardly discussed the character of Camille de Malignon.

They made love again that night, the couple in the mews behind Sadie's bedroom, and once again she watched. One never knew when a working knowledge of sex might come in handy.

(iv)

'What would you say if I told you I want you to direct a six-hour television series about the making of *Shadows on a Wall*?'

Harvey Bamberg peered across the table at Billy, his face pink with the joy of giving.

Billy didn't say anything. An invitation to lunch at Pinewood Studios had been waiting on the answering machine when the Yeos had returned from holiday. Of course he had accepted. Who could refuse Harvey now that he was a Hollywood producer?

Harvey was rushing on. 'No, don't answer. Let me tell you. I respect your work, Billy. It would have been good if we could have worked together on the movie itself, but that wasn't to be our decision. I've been talking to Julie Wyatt at Buffalo, to the BBC and to WGBH in Boston. Every big movie these days has a television spin-off about its making, but so far as I know no-one has ever done a whole *series*.

'I want you to make a series which will show everything, something which will unfold, a true fly on the wall, a liver spots and pimples picture of the making of an epic movie.'

This is madness, thought Billy. An hour of most promotional documentaries was too long. But he said: 'What about Bruno Messenger? What does he want?' Just being there, in the panelled restaurant at Pinewood, made him feel like a trespasser on somebody else's set.

'He thinks it's a *terrific* idea. He guarantees *complete* access to *everything*. And, he wants you to know, he stressed *everything*. He's a wonderful guy. You'll love him.'

'I will? And the artists? They say Yale Meredith is barking mad.'

'Oh, come on, Yale's a pussy cat. Pussy cats don't bark, you know that,' said Harvey and laughed at his own joke.

Billy cut a new potato in half. 'I read that Buffalo are only in for half the money,' he said, playing for time while he decided how to reply.

'And have they done well! A hotel and car-park company called Familia Gallego down in Miami are picking up the rest. Terrific guys. You'd think that with twenty million dollars invested they'd be looking over our shoulders all the time. No way. It's a complete hands-off situation. There's *no-one* here from Gallego. So long as we do the job, they're just not interested.'

Billy shrugged. The financing of movies and the motives of their financiers had always puzzled him. 'Why me?' he asked.

'Can I be candid? Because I feel like a louse, because I know you need the money, and because it's the only way I can help you.'

Billy frowned. He didn't need to be patronized. Or did he?

Harvey tried again. 'I also know that you'd do a terrific job. And, OK, to be honest, it was your name that made the BBC interested.'

That was better, Billy thought. 'What about editorial control?' he asked.

'Yours, subject to fair comment and the laws of libel.'

'You mean that?'

'I'm a man of my word.'

Billy cut another potato, thinking: No, you aren't. You're a con man, but you mean well.

'What do you think?' asked Harvey. 'I know it will be difficult when it could have been your movie . . .'

Billy didn't answer.

'It will be nine months out of your life, but it might just be something special. And I can *guarantee* great money. Buffalo want to get the best man for this, and I've told them it will cost.'

The bank virtually had the repossession notices up. For once in his life Billy could be well paid. It would be humiliating, all right. Bruno Messenger would be creating a legend, his own, while filming another, Napoleon's. But what choice did he have? 'Thanks, Harvey,' he said. 'I'd love to do it.'

239

'Thank *you*,' said Harvey. 'It's going to be *wonderful*.'

Billy had heard that before.

One of the guinea pigs had died when Billy arrived home and the two elder children were in tears. He explained, as best he could, that guinea pigs were nervous creatures and prone to heart attacks, and then with due solemnity went into the garden and dug a grave in between the sand pit and the raspberry bushes, promising that a stone with the guinea pig's name, Andrew, would be erected just as soon as he had time. Then, with the children comforted and Ilse making jelly for Benedict's eighth birthday party the following day, he sat down and wrote to the bank.

'Dear Mr Witherspoon, Further to our recent conversation I have good news for you. I have today been asked to make a six-part television series. It will be extremely well paid, and should go some way to reducing the overdraft. I hope there need now be no more talk of repossession.'

The magic of movies worked in mysterious ways.

(v)

She couldn't imagine what she was doing there, but an hour in make-up, another with a hairdresser and a costume director with a rail full of dresses to try on, and Sadie Corchoran, schoolgirl, was ready for her screen test as Camille de Malignon, woman of destiny.

She hadn't told her parents that she was going for a screen test. How could she? They had no idea of how she had been spending her days, and it wasn't exactly the sort of information you dropped casually between the Corn Flakes at breakfast. At that moment, if her mother thought she was anywhere, it was in the British Museum researching Philippe de Commynes, who had been one of Louis XI's ministers.

The studio hired for the test was in a small commercials house behind Covent Garden. This time she *was* nervous.

'OK Sadie, all we want at this stage is to get some idea of how you get along with the camera pointing at you.' Bruno Messenger was standing to one side of a large Panavision camera.

Arranged around him was an arc of about a dozen people. 'If anything's bothering you, don't be afraid to ask. Understand?'

Sadie nodded. It was an uncomplicated shot of her sitting, fanning herself while she spoke bitterly about the irony that during the Reign of Terror the rights of man, in whose name the Revolution had been launched, had not been extended to aristocratic men. Bruno's instructions had been minimal: no French accent, no shouting, only the slightest movements in front of the camera. After three takes he was happy.

Next, after a two-hour break while the set was re-lit, came a more complicated scene in which she had to goad Will Yorke, played for the purposes of the screen test by a young National Theatre actor, about his betrayal of principles. She had learnt the scene in bed the previous night: the dialogue was about morality in war, the subtext was sex.

But Bruno didn't say that. 'Let's see you play it the way it seems right to you at first, Sadie, OK?'

She had thought it out carefully, she knew the moments when the gears of the scene should change, and she had stood at her mirror and watched the love-making in the mews below often enough. Now, quite simply, with the camera turning, she set about seducing the astonished young actor, sliding into his lap, her hand inside his shirt, then dropping to her knees.

'And cut!'

There was a silence on the floor. The actor's shirt was unfastened, his breeches undone. He looked embarrassed. By the camera Bruno Messenger watched thoughtfully.

A nude scene to confirm that she had no unsightly scars on her body came last. Again the instructions were minimal. 'Undress as you would in real life,' Bruno said.

In real life she would not have been wearing a slip like this, in real life she would have worn a bra. Dignity, Sadie thought. Dignity and simplicity.

Slowly she slipped out of her clothes, stood motionless and then gently swivelled around to look into the camera. It was the first time she had stood naked before anyone since childhood, but she was hardly aware of herself. In her mind the lines of Camille de Malignon were cutting a path through her memory. *'They took my father first. His hands were tied behind his back. He was in his shirt-sleeves. The collar of his shirt had been ripped off. I watched as he mounted the scaffold. At the guillotine he turned back for one last look at my mother. I thought I saw him smile to her. A fond word. Then nodding at the executioner he waited as they strapped him to the plank. It was the shortest wait. I would not have believed there could be so much blood. My mother was next. She kissed my father's blood on the plank as she lay waiting to join him.'*

'And cut! That's a print! Thanks, Sadie, that's fine.'

That was when she became embarrassed. She put her hand to her eyes and was surprised to find that they were wet.

In the dressing room she drank a glass of wine while she washed off her make-up and dressed, wondering if she had time to go to the British Museum and get in an hour on Phillipe de Commynes before dinner. Probably not, she decided. 'Never mind,' she told herself. 'Just wait until Claire hears how I spent the afternoon *sans* knickers in front of all these cameramen. It beats the turtle out of getting lost on the wrong beach in Minorca.'

There was a knock on the door. It was the younger casting director.

'Sorry about the tears. Did I look completely feeble? Ah well . . .'

'Sadie, Bruno's very pleased. Nothing's decided until he sees how you look on film, but I think it's time we talked to your parents . . .'

That was when reality struck. 'Oh crumbs!'

(vi)

Charlie read about it in the *Evening Standard*. There was a picture of Sadie on the front page with her chin resting on a pile of history text books, her eyes looking larger than ever as they peered out from behind her horn-rimmed glasses. *'London schoolgirl wins top film role,'* ran the headline.

He looked again. There was a short article. *'Sadie has the most perfect stillness in all the girls we've seen,'* Bruno Messenger was quoted as saying. *'That was what initially attracted me. She has wonderful, luminous eyes. She is also innocent in the best possible sense, raw material to be shaped into whatever the part requires. Instead of an experienced actress* playing *Camille de Malignon, Sadie Corchoran will be Camille de Malignon.'*

For a long time Charlie stood in the street, puzzling silently. Finally he smiled. 'Good old Sadie.'

PART FOUR

October, 1992

Location

Chapter Thirty

(i)

The Noblesse American bounced gently across the moss, its headlights probing a way through the murk. Now that they had left the road and its yellow lines, the fog seemed to have become denser. In the back seat Harvey fretted quietly and asked his driver to take it a little more slowly. The car had only arrived at Helsinki docks the previous day. It would be a tragedy if it were to be scratched on its very first outing. When the fog cleared he was going to enjoy showing it off to the unit.

Harvey had always liked swanky cars, and this car was *beautiful*, with its black, kid-leather seats, 'smooth as the inside of a woman's thigh', he liked to say, its television, telephones, computer and cocktail cabinet, a virtually silent, powerful, gleaming wedge of metal and glass, as comfortable inside as the most perfect bed. And it was *silver*. A silver Noblesse was the kind of car the new, successful Harvey Bamberg wished to be seen in, the only car Nathalie should ever travel in. It was a pity she had chosen not to come to Finland for this day.

Delicately the car edged between the clumps of grey, huddled together against the cold. It had taken an hour and a half to cover the thirty miles from the hotel: the unit was late assembling.

'Maybe you'd better stop here, Frank,' Harvey said to his driver as they reached the end of a row of parked vehicles.

'There's a lake somewhere around here and it would be a real shame if we drove into it.'

Frank Bennetti shrugged, mumbled something like, 'You think I never driven before or something?', and drew the car to a halt.

'So, are you ready to begin the best part of your life?' Harvey beamed to Simone, who was sitting alongside him feeding the movie schedule into the computer.

Simone switched off the computer. 'I've been ready for years, Harvey. Good luck!'

And, opening the car doors, they stepped out into the fog and the first day of shooting on *Bruno Messenger's SHADOWS ON A WALL.*

(ii)

The cold bit into Simone, heightening immediately the vague feeling of alienation which came from knowing that she was somewhere on the edge of a wilderness which she could not see. She moved forward. Members of the unit flitted past, walkie-talkies to their mouths, busy in their preparations, confused by the weather. Infantrymen in red, white and blue uniforms wandered out of the mist talking in a language she presumed to be Finnish, and muffled English and American voices called to each other against the rhythm of a chugging, unseen diesel generator. Within a few moments she had lost sight of Harvey.

Simone knew about location. She had heard the stories: she had seen what happened, how on location everything is intensified – every love affair, friendship, insult, misunderstanding, confusion, extravagance, yearning and fear. For years, from the emotional fortresses of the Los Angeles agencies, she had watched film-makers go off into the field, happy bands of gypsies, eager with expectation. The most optimistic part of any movie is always the few weeks before it is actually shot, when there is no limit to the dreams of what might be achieved. But she had seen film-makers return, too, three or four months later, exhausted, haunted, anxious to shore up careers, struggling to repair marriages.

Now she was part of it herself and she was tentative. Things happened on location: sometimes such irrational, spiteful, self-destructive things it almost seemed that a panic virus must be at large. Perhaps that was what kept the adrenalin running. That and the sex. There was always plenty of sex on location, and she remembered how a film director, with whom she had once had a brief affair while his actress wife had been away on location, had put it. 'For most of the time,' he had said, 'a film unit is a group of overpaid, artistically self-regarding people, obsessed with conspiracy, shut out from the rest of the world, working very long hours, frequently under great physical and mental strain, spending large amounts of other people's money, living in too close proximity to each other and sleeping with people they know they should not. For the rest of the time it's kind of tedious.'

Standing in the fog, her ample body lost in a quilted coat and thermal ski trousers, her pert nose, wet and poking from a gap in her scarf, ankle deep in Finnish moss still covered by the early morning rime of a sub-Arctic night, Simone Estoril did not think *Shadows on a Wall* was going to be tedious.

(iii)

Billy blew on his hands.

'They say it'll be gone by ten,' snarled Al Mutton, stumping past, his whiskery face mauve with cold, his breath freezing on the air as he exhaled.

'Good,' said Billy, carefully wrapping his long arms around himself to keep warm.

It was just after eight and the morning location smell of frying bacon was curling close by. By Christmas, all being well, Harvey would have his movie and be back in post-production at Pinewood Studios, and Billy would have his documentary series and a very much smaller overdraft. In the mean time they were standing on a grassy hill on the edge of a pine forest by a lake about two hundred kilometres north of Helsinki. This was where Bruno Messenger had decided Napoleon's battle of Jena against the Prussians should be refought, and where nearly ten thousand soldiers from the Finnish army were apparently being

247

lined up just below them in the block battle formations of the early nineteenth century. When the fog cleared it would, Bruno was telling everyone, be a spectacular sight.

But it wasn't yet. Billy peered into the swirling mist. It was eerie. The sounds of battle preparations came from all sides, but there was nothing to be seen. It had all been such a rush to be ready to start on this day, the uniforms and costumes only being delivered from the manufacturers in Bulgaria two days earlier, the canvas tents and plaster cannons arriving from Pinewood the day before. Now no-one could see them, anyway. Fog is the one true enemy of movie-making. With lights, night can be made day: with filters, day turned into night. But in thick, grey fog there is little anyone can do but wait.

For Billy it was a situation not without irony. He was there to make the film of the film, or, at least, the television series of the film he had once been asked to direct. And now looking across at Bruno Messenger, huge and commanding among the anoraked semicircle of technicians drinking coffee around the camera, he wondered for a moment how he might have shot the Battle of Jena himself. Quickly he put the thought from his mind. It was not possible to compare the film he and Charlie *might* have made for five million dollars with the one Bruno Messenger was now making for over forty million.

Bruno's film would be big; everything here was already on the giant scale: the 160 members of the cast and crew, the fleets of cars and horse boxes, the scores of military buses and trucks for the army of extras, the rows of location diners assembled from all over Northern Europe; so very big and certain to get bigger. Nothing less would do for a Bruno Messenger movie about Napoleon.

By contrast Billy's documentary series, *The Making of Shadows on a Wall*, could scarcely be smaller. That was the way Billy liked to work, just himself, a four-man crew, and a couple of 16mm Arriflex cameras and Uher tape-recorders. They had begun weeks earlier, filming interviews with Julie Wyatt and Harry Weitzman in California, followed by Carlos Gallego down in Florida. Gallego had been a surprise. Billy had expected an older, coarser businessman. This fellow with his quiff and platform heels was vain, almost effeminate, yet steely. He looked as though he had come from the streets, but his dozens of questions about documentary film-making were from neither the streets nor the boardroom. To Billy he was an enigma.

Back at Pinewood Harvey had preferred not to talk about Gallego, directing Billy and his crew to Al Mutton's production tirades, to Hal Jobete and the design team, Oscars already in their eyes, to Ruth Blumberg, the costume designer, and on to the set builders, the plaster shop, the military historians and the wig makers. After that had come Sadie and her parents: a cold experience. No wonder Sadie had spent so much time hanging around the Jupiter.

'The sooner she gets this whole silly nonsense out of her mind the better,' Mrs Corchoran had said bitterly. 'She's throwing away her education.'

Out of her mother's line of vision Sadie had pulled a funny face.

Charlie had been next, a stilted, difficult interview. 'The trouble is,' he had mused when the camera had been switched off, 'we were all too innocent when we started out. Herod had more time for innocents than the movie business.'

The crew had smiled at the joke, but the cute line had bothered Billy. It sounded flip and much used, and was, he guessed, borrowed from those in Hollywood who made a profession out of feeling sorry for themselves. That had not been the Charlie he used to know.

Now noticing that Bruno and Sam Jordan were in head-to-head discussion Billy touched the arm of Freddy, his operator. Immediately their camera was refocused. Since six o'clock that morning the documentary team had been putting together a mosaic of the events which went into the first day of shooting. Bruno Messenger wasn't filming yet: in the fog, he couldn't make his beautiful pictures. So Billy was filming him not filming; *he* wanted realism rather than beautiful pictures. 'Just follow me around,' Bruno had instructed. 'I want you to show what a director like me really *does*, not just the "action" and "cut" stuff, but the picture painting that goes into every shot. Hell, you're a director. You know what it's like.'

Billy knew exactly what it was like, but not on this scale. He hoped he never would.

A cannon roared somewhere in the woods and a flock of geese rose in squawking panic from the nearby lake, emerging out of the mist like large grey projectiles. There were said to be elk shying around these forests, and reindeer, too, not much further north. Billy would keep his good eye skinned. He had promised the children he would try to get them pictures of a real live reindeer for Christmas.

(iv)

Harvey had never seen so many horses, *herds* of them, smartly saddled and decorated, now all having nosebags clipped to their bridles.

'It's a pity we can't feed the extras in the same way,' he said out loud. No-one heard him: no-one laughed, anyway. It was lunchtime, everyone was eating, thousands of extras tucking in and still no break in the weather, still nothing being filmed. 'There sure are a lot of horses,' he said.

'This is nothing, wait till we get to the Battle of Borodino, the march on Moscow and Waterloo. Then you'll see horses,' Bruno promised, surprisingly relaxed.

'We can afford to *pay* so many horses?' Harvey joked, offering a handful of hay to an adjacent grey which was sporting a Revolutionary tricolour between its ears.

'If we're to do this thing right, we can't *not* afford them,' Bruno said carefully. 'Don't worry. It's worth doing the opening sequence big, that's the thing that grabs the public. We'll be able to make savings further into the movie.'

At the director's side his lieutenant, Al Mutton, nodded. 'Did you know we have the entire Finnish and Norwegian Olympic equestrian teams out there as our cavalry today?'

'So Simone tells me,' Harvey said. He could hardly hide a small smile of pride. The entire Finnish and Norwegian Olympic equestrian teams: not bad for a plain little guy from Jersey City.

He shivered. He had never much enjoyed the discomforts of location work. Not many producers did. He was glad they would only be staying in Finland for the three days necessary to film the opening battle and set up Napoleon and his American friend, Will Yorke. The thought of Will Yorke worried him. He hoped they had the right actor. There had been talk in the summer of getting one of the new, young, Hollywood bloods to play him, some guy the kids went for, but Sam Jordan had suddenly become very touchy about the casting.

'Sam doesn't want to influence you guys in any way,' Jake

250

McKenzie had come on the phone, 'but he thinks he might have a problem if Will Yorke is played by anyone much younger than himself. That isn't the way he sees it.'

'He doesn't have casting approval, you know,' Harvey had said.

'Absolutely not. You guys must choose whoever you want. Sam just wanted you to know how he felt. It could be a real problem for him if you cast some kid.'

That had been it. There was no point in upsetting your major asset. So all the pretty boys were out, and, at thirty-nine, American television cop Jack Dragoman, plain co-star of *Bad Penny Blues*, selected. Dragoman was popular, but, unlike Sam Jordan, he was not regularly handsome. For a moment, because it was Dragoman's big chance to graduate from television to movies, Harvey had thought he might get a bargain, but, *Shadows on a Wall* was not lucky like that. In the end it had taken five million dollars to compensate the TV series for his loss.

Money still made Harvey uneasy. With nearly six and a half million dollars spent before shooting had begun, deals agreed for a further twelve million if it were cancelled, and a dollar mountain beginning to melt away at over half a million a week now that production had begun, there had, right until the last minute, been disagreement about the feasibility of Al Mutton's budget.

'It can't be done,' wise old production heads at Buffalo had insisted, looking at the schedule. 'Not for forty million. Not in the time.'

Bruno had sulked, threatened to walk away, complained that everyone was trying to ruin his masterpiece, and won the day. The budget had been revised upwards, to forty-five million dollars, Carlos Gallego keeping to his word to match Buffalo dollar for dollar. Even at forty-five million Bruno had not been happy, the movie needing to be completed in two weeks less than he calculated necessary. This time he had raged, but, with Reuben Wiener insisting upon no movement from the studio, he had suddenly backed down. *Shadows on a Wall* would take no more than sixty-six days to shoot: it would be finished by Christmas.

'He's OK, you see,' Harvey had exulted to Nathalie that night. 'The guy's brilliant but he needs someone to protect him from himself.'

Nathalie had not had time to talk. She had been hurrying out. She was always going somewhere these days.

Standing in the fog, watching as the riggers laid the tracks, Harvey lit a small panatella, a little superstitious ritual he practised on the first day of every movie he produced. When this movie was finished, when they had their success, Nathalie would see the real Harvey Bamberg, and love him as he loved her.

'Any word on when we might go for a take?' he asked as Simone emerged out of the mist.

She shook her head. 'They're telling us now the fog might lift by mid-afternoon.'

'Mid-afternoon? Jesus!'

'Apparently fog is common in these parts in October. They say we should have checked.'

Harvey didn't answer. One of the location scouts had mentioned it, but Bruno had set his heart on Finland as the only place to suggest the forest and marsh wilderness of a Europe of two centuries earlier. Bruno was a perfectionist. He didn't mind waiting for the weather. Harvey was not. He did. He rubbed his pink bald head. The trouble with hanging around movie sets was that it gave him too much time to worry. And throwing away his panatella, he went off in search of the location scout who hadn't emphasized the likelihood of fog strongly enough.

(v)

Simone missed nothing. All morning on this first day Jack Dragoman, now the sombrely dressed American idealist Will Yorke, had sat in his trailer and fretted. In the business he was famous for his worrying, his attention to detail and his identifying with his part. By lunchtime he could take it no more. 'Do you have a minute, Bruno?' he asked. Today he was an everyday man, with an honest face and a slow delivery. Even the shape of his face was known to change with the part.

Nearby Sam Jordan, in white breeches and green cavalry greatcoat, his auburn Napoleon hair just visible under his three-cornered, beaver-skin hat, leant casually against the cartwheel of an ox wagon, chatting to a young Italian dresser, pretending not to hear.

'Sure. What's the problem?' Bruno had the look of a man who already knew the problem.

Dragoman winced. 'Well, maybe I'm not seeing something right, but when I accepted the part it was my character in the opening sequence who saves Napoleon's life after the battle, which I thought was great character-building stuff for Will Yorke. But last night when I got to the hotel I found these waiting for me . . .' He held up two rewritten pink pages of script.

The director chewed on a sausage. He looked irritated to be diverted away from discussing a sequence of shots with the storyboard artist. 'You don't like the rewrites?' he asked.

'It isn't what I agreed to do.'

'Things change,' Bruno said. 'This is a movie. Not television. We go for perfection in movies.' There was a hint of a sneer.

'I go for perfection in my work.'

'Right!'

'It isn't fair. My part has been downgraded. Devalued. I liked it the way it was.'

'It's better now.'

'I don't think so.'

'I promise you.'

Dragoman turned to Simone on whom he had already rehearsed his complaint: she looked down at her call sheet. If she were honest, she considered the rewritten pages neither better nor worse than the original ones. The changes had been made solely to keep Sam Jordan happy. 'Jesus!' Jordan had moaned back in Los Angeles, 'if Napoleon has his life saved by some side-kick it'll make him look like a wimp! Isn't it better if it's reversed? If *I* save *his* life?'

It had been the star prerogative being exercised emphatically. As Simone knew from her agency days, stars will only play heroes.

Now Bruno was staring Dragoman out.

Quickly Dragoman saw that this was a battle he couldn't win. 'Well, I guess if everyone else is happy, who am I to complain?' he said, and retreated unhappily into the fog.

By the ox cart Sam Jordan was smiling to himself, his arm almost, if not quite, draped around the Italian dresser.

The unit wrapped at four when the fog became thicker and the transportation manager began to worry about the difficulties of getting the Finnish army back to base. Not one frame of film had been exposed. The champagne Harvey had brought to celebrate the successful completion of the first set-up stayed in its refrigerated hampers.

Walking back toward his car, sadly unadmired because so few had been able to see it, Harvey pulled out his schedule. The three days set aside for this sequence were never going to be enough. At the end of the first day they were already a full day behind.

'Don't worry, we'll go quickly when we get into the movie. No problem,' Bruno called as he passed him.

'Sure we will,' Harvey murmured, slipping into the No-blesse. 'Sure we will. It's going to be wonderful. Won't it be wonderful, Simone? I just wish Nathalie could have been here today to see those horses. Did you know she's always liked horses? Just wait till I tell her.'

Simone didn't reply. There were new rumours about Nathalie Seillans.

Chapter Thirty-one

For thirty-eight years it had worked on some kind of rotary principle, and now it was gone. Julie Wyatt didn't believe in omens, but she wished it hadn't happened. Staring out of her office window she drew on her cigarette and gazed across the lot at the small crowd of sightseers surrounding the old water tower. Despite all the security, someone, probably a deranged film buff, had broken into the studio during the night, scaled the tower and made off with the mechanically pawing hoof of Bill, the Buffalo Pictures' trademark.

Objectively she could see it had been quite a feat in house-breaking terms, but it bothered her. This was not the time for Buffalo to be looking weak. Several of the Los Angeles radio and television breakfast programmes had already run stories about 'the mystery of the hoofless Buffalo . . .', and she had just had to waste useful time answering foolish questions from a creep on the *Hollywood Reporter*.

'What do you mean, "lost our kick"?' she had exploded. 'Do you call Bruno Messenger and Sam Jordan and Yale Meredith and *Shadows on a Wall* losing our kick? A forty-five-million-dollar production is some kick, believe me.'

'But only half of that is Buffalo money. I hear Familia Gallego drove a hard bargain.'

'We have a deal with Familia Gallego which will benefit both partners,' she said coolly, repeating the line the publicity department had put out. 'Is there anything else you want to know?'

'Sorry, Julie, only teasing,' the reporter had backed down. But the dart had found its target.

Now she was regretting having been so sharp. She could just imagine him gossiping away to someone at Columbia or Fox, telling them how Julie Wyatt was very tetchy this morning. But then, she was tetchy. Familia Gallego's involvement unsettled her. There were too many eyebrows raised whenever their name was mentioned.

The slow start was not unusual. That happened on lots of movies. The first days were always the most difficult. What was more important was the material finally being shot. She had seen some footage for the first time the previous night, Sam Jordan sitting on a black horse watching what looked like Armageddon Now!, and it had been stunning. No wonder Bruno Messenger was so much in demand for commercials. She had never seen Sam so still, so beautiful. She had left a message at his hotel to tell him so.

For a moment she daydreamed a memory of a motel in Cincinatti. She had been new to Paramount, going out to see how shooting was progressing and progressing quickly to Sam's bed. He had been playing a racing-car driver with a drink problem, a little unlikely perhaps, but it had grossed nearly a hundred million dollars. Now Sam was Napoleon. There was nothing like movies.

Her secretary's light winked on her telephone. The latest rewrites for *Shadows on a Wall* had just arrived. Asking for them to be brought in she slipped behind her desk.

She had her secretary telephone and invent an excuse to the friend from Paramount she had arranged to meet for lunch. With a salad from the commissary she stayed at her desk and began to go through all the various drafts and changes to the *Shadows on a Wall* script.

The slow start to shooting didn't worry her: but the latest rewrites from the new writers were something else.

Chapter Thirty-two

(i)

Belinda saw her for the first time at the airport as she slipped into Poland between her troupe of assistants, head down, slate bags under her eyes, a damson sweater falling from thin shoulders halfway down narrow, jeaned thighs. Hopelessly casual, she looked thrown together, all angles, her eyes too far apart, her mouth too wide, her hair not only unbrushed but unwashed, a cheap canvas bag slung unfastened over one shoulder, its contents in imminent danger of spilling out over the Warsaw customs hall; in short, a chaotic mess. Yet still she was mesmerizing. No wonder Charlie had been tempted.

They were to make their entries into *Shadows on a Wall* in the same scene and were arriving within an hour of each other, Belinda first, met by Gully Pepper, the red-haired unit publicist from St Louis. 'We have a car outside but would you mind waiting until Yale gets here? I want to make sure she gets through customs safely,' Gully had asked.

Belinda hadn't minded. She was curious to meet the actress who, so far as the world was concerned, would soon become Napoleon's Polish mistress instead of her; to see the woman who had seduced Charlie. She had wanted to know how she would feel. But now, as she watched the star with her caravan of companion, voice coach, personal trainer and bodyguard, with, according to Gully, a personal dietician, cook, dresser, make-up artist and hairdresser having arrived earlier, she was surprised only at herself. She hardly felt anything.

'Welcome to Poland, Yale.' The publicist, stepped forward and held out a hand, simultaneously introducing Belinda.

Yale ignored the hand. 'Hi,' she murmured in a tiny voice. She didn't look at Belinda, although she caught the name: she definitely caught the name.

At Yale's side, bossily directing several porters pushing over-burdened trollies, was a short, dark-haired woman in a bright orange anorak and emerald golfing trousers; she wore thick-lensed, rimmed glasses and had a pale, shiny face. 'I'm Alice Bauccio,' she barked. 'Yale's kind of tired. It's been a long flight. Is the car waiting?'

Yale Meredith fiddled with her hair absently, looking as though she wasn't altogether sure what was going on. Was she on something, Belinda wondered, or was she always like this?

Three unit cars were ready on the forecourt. Slipping quickly into the rear seat of the first, Yale slammed the door hard, leaving her retinue to organize the suitcases. A crowd of Polish travellers and airport workers peered in at her in undisguised fascination. One hundred and seventy-four years ago Marie Walewska had been a famous Pole who had had a love affair with the most powerful man in the world, but few people outside court circles would have recognized her. Today everyone knew Yale Meredith. Twentieth-century fame was like no other.

'One thing I should tell you,' Gully said quietly as they watched the loading. 'We've fallen further behind. You and Yale have both arrived a little early. We won't be doing your first scenes for a few days yet.'

'How far behind?'

'Quite a bit. They're rejigging the schedule now. Yale will scream blue murder when she knows. She hates being kept waiting. That's her forte.'

The journey to Kapolska took six hours along the pot-holed roads of south-eastern Poland, the unit Mercedes in which Belinda and Gully were travelling keeping a respectful distance behind the gliding Cadillac carrying Yale. Behind them came the third car bearing Yale's travelling troupe of ego boosters.

Gully had not been pleased to see Alice Bauccio. 'Apparently she's some sort of feminist barnacle who's attached herself to Yale's backside,' she complained as they travelled. 'And she's becoming a pain in everybody else's. It's always the same: the bigger the star the more determined the hangers-on. I can tell now this one's going to make my job impossible.'

Gully was, Belinda quickly realized, the unit talker, chattering non-stop about the crew and the problems with the movie. She tried to concentrate but she was surprised to find herself in this situation, and had never heard of most people Gully mentioned. Seeking comfort, her hand went to a brooch pinned to her sweater. It was of a small glass rhinoceros with the eyes Tipp-Exed out. Charlie had called around the previous day, bringing it as a good-luck present.

'He's blind, you see,' he had explained. 'It's the blind rhinoceros interpretation of film-making. Once he's off and running all you can do is hang on and hope he doesn't trample on anyone too seriously along the way.'

It had been the first time they had met since he had moved out, although they had spoken on the phone a couple of times. It had been at his insistence that she had taken the part of Monika Wyszynska. She had been uncertain.

The news about Sadie Corchoran had astonished them both.

'I don't know,' she had puzzled, 'maybe Bruno Messenger goes for schoolgirls. Errol Flynn did and Charlie Chaplin. Lots of those guys do. And she's good. Possibly she's brilliant.'

'You told me she'd never been kissed.'

'I said, never been kissed *properly*.'

'You mean there's a proper and an improper way of kissing?'

Each time they had spoken the strain had eased. When she had finally seen him she had wanted to say that it was all right, that she wasn't upset any more. But the words hadn't come. Instead she had tried to discuss arrangements for the flat. He had changed the subject. They could talk about it after the movie.

He had put on a brave face when he left, but she had known how abandoned he would be feeling, staying behind as everyone went off to make the film he had dreamt up.

'. . . it was the panoramic shot from the floating high balloon that was really difficult . . .'

With a start Belinda realized she hadn't been listening. 'I'm sorry?'

'That's why we're so far behind schedule,' Gully was explaining. 'Oh yes.'

'Bruno wanted it to start wide in the clouds and descend slowly into the midst of the battlefield. It was an afterthought, but once he'd come up with it he wouldn't let go. A helicopter could have done it more efficiently, but helicopters always blow everyone's hats off. So we had to get the balloon and balloonists over from Hamburg to Helsinki, and then, after the fog, it rained for two whole days. Then we had to get the Finnish army back and the two equestrian teams, but the Norwegians had gone on tour to Canada and not all the caterers were available.' She sighed.

In the end the opening sequence which had been scheduled for three days had taken ten days to complete, which, in turn, had meant a rescheduling of the Battle of Wagram in Austria. But that sequence had been slow, too, taking seven days too many, and putting the indoor riding school sequence back by a further week. 'But it all looks amazing,' Gully finished.

'That's all right then,' Belinda said.

It was dusk when they reached Kapolska. The drizzle had eased and patches of mist were forming as the three cars swept off the road, under a baroquely cherubed stone archway and into a park which stretched away across rolling, wooded hills. In the distance a large herd of cattle grazed across a wide meadow.

'So, what do you think of our cows?' Gully asked.

'Our cows?'

Gully nodded. 'They're all going to be movie stars, too. Like in *Rawhide*. Pity we can't get Clint Eastwood. Bruno wants them for the march on Moscow, but they got here too soon, so we're keeping them until they're needed for shooting. Apparently the amount they eat is fiercesome. They keep having to be fed extra hay and moved from field to field. They'll be too fat to walk soon.'

For a moment Belinda remembered a happy evening and a history lesson in Charlie's study. She said: 'Couldn't they have been sent back until they're needed?'

Gully shrugged. 'There must be a reason. There's always a reason.'

The cars drove on. Rounding a curve, a large, classically proportioned palace came into view.

'Oh boy!' Belinda said.

'Welcome to the Kapolska Palace,' said Gully.

'It's beautiful.'

'But draughty,' qualified Gully. 'Apparently the local baron who commissioned it was so thrilled by a visit to Versailles he had a scaled-down version built out here in the back of beyondski, which is very handy for us since the real Versailles is usually stuffed full of tourists.' She peered through the car window. 'That way is the Ukraine, and those mountains over there to the south are in Czechoslovakia. Or is it just Slovakia now?'

At that point the cars carrying Yale Meredith and her companions turned off the main carriageway and cut away through the meadows.

'Yale and Sam Jordan didn't like the idea of living in the big house with the rest of us so they've been given a lodge each on the estate,' Gully explained. 'The decorators only moved out of Yale's yesterday, so I hope the paint is dry.'

'You redecorated just for them?'

Gully laughed. 'You know how it is with the stars. If you don't pamper them they don't feel loved.'

(ii)

Harvey watched Simone carefully as she read the fax. They were in the turret room of the palace which Harvey used as a retreat. Downstairs in the production office it would be the usual chaos of Polish versus English and German babble with Al Mutton and the first assistant director Tony Delmonte bellowing louder than anyone else. Harvey liked tranquillity.

The fax was from Julie Wyatt at Buffalo. She called and faxed several times every day. Today's edition concerned the rewrites. It read: '*I'm very worried by the new pages from the new writers. It seems to me the script is now in very real danger of losing its shape, while the dialogue is becoming increasingly flip. If we shoot some of this material I think we risk the danger of getting the wrong responses from the audience. Something must be done immediately if we are not to jeopardize our very fine movie.*' Attached was a long list of what Julie Wyatt considered to be poor examples of cinema writing.

Harvey was irritated. Why was it that the people in the front office always had to interfere? He had been hoping to go across the park and invite Yale Meredith to a party that evening to welcome her to Poland. She was known to be a tricky woman and would have to be kept very sweet. Now he had this new aggravation. Every day, every hour, there was some new problem. 'What do you think?' he asked Simone.

261

Simone pursed her raspberry lips. 'It's tricky,' she said carefully. 'Charlie's original script was terrific—'

'Things have moved on,' Harvey interrupted. He didn't want to get into all that again.

'Yes. Right. Well, I suppose I agree with Julie. Bruno's blind spot, or deaf spot, I suppose, is dialogue. He doesn't care what anyone says so long as the pictures look good. Lots of directors are like that. But he's adding so many bits and pieces and getting so many old friends writing different parts for him the whole thing is becoming chaotic. What we need is a Ben Hecht to come in and sew the whole structure back together again.'

'So, let's call him.'

'Ben Hecht died in 1964.'

'Is that a fact!' Harvey was unfazed. 'So, who do you recommend?'

'As a script doctor? You could try Robert Towne, or see if William Goldman is available, or Tom Stoppard, or . . . well, there are a whole lot of good people. But the best ones are booked up months in advance, sometimes years.'

Harvey stared at a production wall chart and frowned. 'It's all too rushed. It always has been. OK! I tell you what. Make me a list of the top ten script doctors along with their agents, and send a copy of it and a copy of the Buffalo fax across to Bruno. Let's see who's available.' He sighed and shook his head. 'Why is it always the goddamn script that's wrong?'

(iii)

He had been to better parties, if a party it was. To Billy it looked more like a tournament, a power game at court being acted out in Levi's and Giorgio Armani by three despots, Bruno Messenger, Sam Jordan and Yale Meredith.

Being new to despotism Bruno had seized the initiative by insisting that the party be held in his rooms on the first floor of the palace. For a man who had dropped out of the University of Southern California Film School to make rock videos, the elegance of his quarters was impressive.

Perhaps Sam Jordan *was* impressed, and perhaps that explained why, immediately on arrival, he had fallen into deep conversation with a nimble buttocked, young journalist who was writing a profile on the director for *Premiere* magazine. For the past two days she had been cosying closer and closer to Bruno Messenger, but now Sam Jordan was cosying up to her, and she was loving it.

Bruno was not. Actors did not normally go after women being lined up by the director. But then Bruno had never worked with a star like Sam Jordan before.

Naturally Yale Meredith was very late arriving. When she did come, however, she made sure of an entrance, suddenly laughing that kooky Yale Meredith laugh, so that everyone turned to look, and giving Billy and his documentary team time to pan around and refocus the camera.

'Oh my!' she mouthed as she tottered into the room, all sweatshirt and leggings, her expression wide-eyed surprised-little-girl-at-a-grown-ups-party, before scampering across the room to kiss cinematographer Giorgio Pescati on his handsome forehead. 'Giorgio, how are you? It's so *wonderful* to see you again.'

'She knows who to kiss first,' Billy murmured. It would be Giorgio Pescati who would be making Yale look beautiful on film.

The entire room watched her, conversation ceasing instantly. Even Delphine Claviers, selected to play Empress Josephine because of her dark eyes and overwhelming self-confidence, and whose thigh had been gently kneading Jack Dragoman over by the fireplace, went silent.

Billy was beginning to understand. The truth was everyone was nervous of Yale. Perhaps that was the secret with all movie queens, those women who appeared to walk through life on the edge of razors. 'So, what do you think?' he asked Belinda.

'An unguarded flame,' Belinda replied.

He nodded. 'And who knows who and what she'll choose to burn next?'

Across the room there was a sudden flurry of consternation in Yale's camp as she noticed Belinda and Billy talking, looking at her. She stared hard at Belinda. Then her eyes went to Freddie and his camera.

'Oh dear!' Billy murmured, but it was already too late.

With a brittle crack Yale's voice cut across the party. 'Jesus! Do I have to take this? Everywhere I go there's someone filming me. For Christ's sake, aren't I allowed any privacy? Who let those guys in here? I thought this was going to be a private party . . .'

'Keep shooting,' Billy said quickly to Freddie. 'We were invited.'

'Hey guys!' Harvey was hurrying over, panic stretching across his head.

Alice Bauccio got there first, her fat hand covering the lens of the Arriflex. 'That's enough. You're upsetting Yale,' she said, pushing the camera out of the way, and knocking Freddie heavily against Belinda.

Freddie stopped filming.

'Sorry, Yale,' Billy said, putting up both hands in a gesture of surrender.

'Are you all right?' Jack Dragoman said, putting a hand out to Belinda.

'Jesus!!' Yale was still moaning to her band of retainers, who nodded sympathetically because that was what they were paid to do. 'Can there be no moment in my life when there isn't some guy peering down a camera at me?'

'I thought she knew we'd be filming,' Billy said to Harvey.

'I guess she forgot.' Harvey was embarrassed by the outburst. 'Look, maybe you guys had better go and have dinner.'

Billy looked at him, a one-eye-sees-more-than-two look. 'I don't think she forgot, Harvey,' he said.

Belinda raised an eyebrow. 'Come on, Harvey, she's being a pain in the ass, you know that!'

Sam Jordan overheard. 'Absolutely, but as asses go hers is terrific.' Sam Jordan knew all about great asses. Then, as if to prove it, he put a hand on that of the girl from *Premiere* and gently guided her from the room, talking all the time. 'What d'you say we have a quiet dinner over at my place? You haven't been there, have you? You'll love it. They tell me it was built for the girlfriend of some Polish king hundreds of years ago. She must have been a hell of a girl because it's a hell of a place . . .'

Bruno Messenger stared bitterly after them. 'Great party, Harvey,' he snapped unpleasantly at the producer. He had to snap at someone: there was absolutely nothing he could say to Sam Jordan.

It had been a short contest, Billy thought as he left, just a sparring contest really. But of one thing he was already certain: with these egos around it was going to be a long tournament, no matter what the schedule might say.

Belinda could have left with Billy, but she caught sight of the disappointed expression on Harvey's face as he watched the party disintegrate. So she stayed and together they had dinner at the end of the main dining hall reserved for the officer class of film makers. Despite everything, she had grown fond of Harvey.

'Maybe if Nathalie had been here the atmosphere would have been less competitive,' Harvey worried. 'She has a way of making everyone happy. You know what I mean?'

Belida didn't know: in fact, quite the opposite. She knew that Nathalie made Harvey very unhappy.

Yet still he loved to talk about her, as if by mentioning her name he was drawing her closer to him. 'I called her a couple of times earlier,' he said, and then hesitated. 'Once in a while she'll go out by herself to see a movie, or something like that . . .' There was another pause. 'You see, Nathalie needs people. I hate to think of her feeling neglected.'

From what she had heard, Belinda considered it unlikely that Nathalie would be suffering much neglect, but Harvey would not need her to tell him that.

'How did you meet?' she asked after a moment.

The little man's face lit up, and he opened his palms outwards, as though in a gesture of thanks. 'I met Nathalie on a wet Monday evening in a movie house in Montparnasse. That was when I fell in love with her, too. The same night. First date, so to speak. I'd just arrived in Paris and spoke hardly a word of French, so I was taking lessons and my teacher said I should go to see lots of movies as an aid to learning. And then there was Nathalie up on the screen, twenty-two years old and perfect in every detail. After that there was never a day when I didn't think about her, didn't want her. It took a little while to persuade her to marry me . . . nearly thirty years, as a matter of fact.'

It was the perfect fan story: almost perfect. Nathalie didn't deserve him. After a while, Belinda tried to change the course of the conversation, talking about her parents, movies, Poland, but somehow it always came back to Nathalie.

'You know, everything I do is for Nathalie,' Harvey reflected over the dessert. 'Marrying her was the best thing in my life, the culmination of all my ambitions. That was all I ever wanted.'

He stopped talking, then said quietly: 'I'll tell you something else. Once, years before we were married, I plucked up the courage to ask her to go to bed with me. And when she told me that she wanted me only as a friend, that she just didn't desire me, you know, physically, I went away and tried to kill myself.' He stopped talking for a moment and examined the wine in his glass. 'I couldn't even do that right. I collapsed in the car park at Nice Airport and the hospital pumped me out. It was close. I never told Nathalie. She wouldn't understand. She doesn't like weak men, you see. Actually, she despises them. But when it comes to her that's what I am, a very weak man. Can you blame me?'

It was a bleak moment of introspection. The vulgar little hustler without his coat of bombast.

Then the smile returned. 'But, you know, if it hadn't been for Nathalie you and I wouldn't be sitting here now collaborating on the greatest movie of the decade. No way, no way at all.'

He had been listening to Bruno Messenger again.

She was not tired, so when at eleven Harvey hurried off to call Nathalie again, Belinda went down to the bar hoping to meet up with Billy. Not finding him she set out to explore. The Kapolska had once been a beautiful palace, but now it had the functional, musty smell of a barracks requisitioned by yet another army.

Turning away from the sound of the photocopier in the production office she wandered down stone-flagged corridors, peering into once stately rooms, now neglected and stuffed to overflowing with lights and cables, drilled racks of uniforms heavy with gold bees and braid, standing frames of tricolour flags and battle emblems, companies of plaster statues and batteries of plastic-moulded heavy guns.

In a small ante-room a picture leaning against a wall caught her eye. It was the portrait of Marie Walewska over which Billy had superimposed her own face for the posters in Edinburgh, but which was now bearing Yale Meredith's features. For a moment a wave of envy overcame her, but it quickly passed as, looking at the low-cut dress and the swelling, exaggerated bosom, she remembered how they had cut Marie Walewska's heart from her body after her death to carry back to Poland.

They wouldn't be able to do that with Yale's heart, she told herself. They'd never find it.

She discovered the library by accident. It was at the end of the house and looked like a building site. Stepping inside she stared around at the wreckage of what, until very recently, must have been an elegant, eighteenth-century reading room. Scaffolding was holding up the delicately moulded, cracked plaster of the ceiling; wooden panels, shelves and leather-backed books were stacked against one wall. Stone rubble lay at the end of the room, brushed to one side.

'You should have been in here when we were shooting.'

She looked around. Bruno Messenger was leaning on the door frame grinning at her, a stick of grissini in his hand, the defecting journalist evidently forgotten.

'The library wasn't long enough to lay our tracks. We had to pull down a partitioning wall . . .' he explained, pointing. 'That gave us a terrific track from one end of one room and out at the other end of the next, Napoleon striding along, planning wars, dictating letters, talking about love, sex, the scent of flowers in Corsica, all kinds of stuff. It looked wonderful.'

'You mean you wrecked the library just for one scene. Are you allowed to do this?' Belinda asked incredulously.

'Well, obviously officially no. The place is some kind of Polish national monument. But Poland is a poor country. Dollars talk. Don't worry. Al says he'll have it put back more or less the way it was. No-one's ever really going to notice the difference.'

'Couldn't you have shot somewhere else?'

He shrugged. 'Here was beautiful. We were here.'

She looked again at the wreckage. 'Here *was* beautiful.'

'It'll be worth it. Believe me. When our movie is finished it will last just like this palace has lasted. That's what we're doing here. We're making beauty. We're making art.'

'Even if it means destroying art and beauty along the way,' she said, walking past him back towards the staircase.

He followed her. 'You think we did wrong?'

'Don't you?'

He scratched his head. 'What if I told you that two hundred and fifty years ago they knocked down a beautiful medieval monastery, said to be the finest ever built in Poland, to build this palace. What would you say?'

'I'd say they were vandals, too. Just like you. Did they?'

Bruno shrugged. 'I don't know. Maybe.' He almost smiled, but his lips were caught around the grissini.

She climbed the stairs ahead of him. When they reached the first floor he said: 'Do you have a minute? I want to show you something. Maybe this will convince you.' And he led the way along the landing to his suite of rooms. The traces of the party had already been cleared.

Closing the door behind her, he gestured to a sofa, then, turning on a television, he selected a video from a stack, pushed it into a cassette machine and turned down the lights.

As the video engaged a clapper went down on the screen to reveal the library they had just left. Shot from only one side the damage could not be seen.

'Now isn't that beautiful?'

It was indeed beautiful, a shimmering afternoon light stretching like curtains of mist along the length of the room as Sam Jordan walked slowly and alone, the most handsome Napoleon in history.

It was the first Belinda had seen of the movie, and she felt flattered. She knew the scene well. It had hardly changed since that first night in Edinburgh when Neil Burgess had said the lines in his toupee in James' Court Hall.

'You see what I mean about how wonderful it's all going to be, how perfect. This movie will be here when we're all gone. It will survive. When we're ashes people will be watching *Shadows on a Wall*.'

She didn't answer. She was thinking about the illusion of film: downstairs the reality of the library was a wreck, yet on this screen Giorgio Pescati's gossamer lighting was turning it into a shimmering distillation of history.

She stared at the rushes, stunned by the colours, the details of the uniform. Even Sam Jordan was almost believable. Bruno had a good eye, and Buffalo Pictures and Familia Gallego were providing the money for him to use it. She settled back. The rushes ran on. Take after take after take. It was hypnotic, Sam Jordan stolidly repeating the lines, the walk down the room, the pauses for effect, the little Sam Jordan smiles, his trade marks, in the same spot every time. When the scene was in the finished movie it would last no more than three minutes, but which version would Bruno choose? On the twenty-second take Belinda felt she wanted to giggle.

At that moment she felt Bruno's arm around her. 'What do you say we go to bed?' he said.

'What?'

His hand grabbed her breast. His fat lips slid on to her mouth. She froze, her eyes focused over his head on the television screen where Sam Jordan was still impersonating Napoleon. Bruno stood up, pulling her towards him.

'Er . . . Bruno . . .' Her hands went up to his chest. He was so big, so heavy to push off.

Now smiling in expectation he took her by the wrists and tried to kiss her again.

She pulled away from him. 'I think I'd better go.'

'What do you mean "go"? Where are you going to?' He was still grinning, still unable to read the rejection. 'You're very pretty, you know that? I'm really glad we met. You're going to be terrific in the part. You could have a great future.'

She recognized the tone, but was surprised. Did this still happen in the movie world? 'Thank you. But it's getting late,' she said.

She turned to leave, but he caught hold of her again, more determinedly this time, simultaneously pushing his hand up the front of her skirt and between her legs.

'Bruno!' She heaved him off. 'Bruno! I really want to go. Stop that! *Stop it! Stop it!*'

He did stop, his normally white face puffed in embarrassment and anger.

'I'll see you tomorrow. Good night now.' She went to the door and opened it.

His voice followed her. 'Who the hell d'you think you're playing with?'

'Look, I'm tired. I'm going to bed,' she said. The door was ajar.

He moved towards her. 'I thought we might have something going here. Why do you think I cast you? Because you were an actress in a *radio* show? *Radio?* Are you kidding? You're making a big mistake.'

'No,' she said, stepping out into the corridor. 'You made the mistake.'

He followed her to the door, his voice growing louder. 'You want to know something? You want to know why you never get a break? I'll tell you. Because you're a loser. If you run with losers you end up a loser. You hear me?' The voice was now a bellow.

Belinda heard but marched on. Doors opened to find out what

the row was about, designer Hal Jobete, gay and these days celibate, they said, looking out of his room, but then going quickly back inside again when he realized it was Bruno, and Beverly, the prettily painted English make-up artist, appearing, at another door, fastening a man's towelling dressing gown round her.

Blast! thought Belinda, but she was more upset with herself than with Bruno Messenger. He was a bully, all right, and a vandal, but she ought to have seen it coming. The signs had been there back in London when he had offered her the part. Was that really the only reason he had wanted her in the movie, so that he could go to bed with her when no-one else was available?

'Are you all right?' She was back at the staircase. Jack Dragoman was standing half a flight up looking down at her. He must have heard Bruno Messenger roaring his frustration. It was the second time that evening he had asked her if she was all right.

She shook her head. 'Not really,' she said. 'Good night.' And suddenly hurrying in embarrassment she ran past him up the steps and along the corridor to her room.

He watched her from the stairs.

Jesus, I'm such a dummy, she thought, as she locked the door behind her and sat down on her bed. How could I ever have imagined I could be a movie star? I'm a juggler: first, last and in the middle. Why didn't my parents ever tell me?

She cried for a little while, silent tears of disappointment. At last she considered the next day. There would be no escaping it. By breakfast the entire cast and crew would have a dozen different accounts of what had happened. That was the way it was on location.

She couldn't sleep. Something her mother had once said years earlier had resurfaced in her mind. 'Success in our business isn't just a matter of talent or looks or charisma. It's also about *wanting*. I wanted, your father didn't. He's a wonderful man, a better actor than I ever was, but I always knew he was never going to be Dick Van Dyke. He didn't want to be.'

At three in the morning she began a letter home. '*Everything is very exciting here in Poland and everyone is being really helpful and kind. I was so lucky to get this part because* Shadows on a Wall *is*

270

going to be a much bigger movie than Charlie and I ever imagined. I'm really looking forward to starting filming . . .'

Even if she was hurt she saw no reason to disappoint anyone else.

Chapter Thirty-three

(i)

Charlie heard the telephone as he was entering the flat. Since Belinda had been in Poland he had been living at home again.

'*Charlie*, how've you been?' The receiver popped with energy. It was Harvey.

'Fine.'

'We've missed having you around.'

'I've been around here.'

'Right.' There was a pause from the Polish end of the line. Charlie waited.

'Charlie, we have a problem. What would you say to rejoining the team? How would you like that?'

Charlie puzzled for a moment, then tried a joke. 'You want me to play the Duke of Wellington, is that it?'

'As a kind of script doctor.'

'I wouldn't like it.'

'More like a script overlord.'

'Not a duke. A lord. An *over*lord. Dukes are better . . .'

'Charlie . . .'

'Overlording who? Or is it whom?' He was inexplicably flippant.

'We need someone to take the best from wherever, maybe several different sources, and then make it all work. You were our first thought.'

'What happened to Bruno's pals from film school?'

'They're making the studio nervous. They're too smart ass. It's coming out like *Saturday Night Live*.'

'Tell me.'

'Well, what about when Marie Walewska first meets Napoleon. In their version they have her saying: "I've often wondered, sir, why do you always have your hand inside your coat?" To which he replies, "Would you rather I put it inside yours, madam?" '

Charlie laughed. It was a strange sound. He hadn't laughed in weeks. Not properly. 'That's funny,' he said. 'I like it. You should leave it in. I thought it was going to be the one about him feeling a right tit. You're joking, aren't you?'

'Would I? Bruno's trying two or three different writers, and he's writing stuff himself. But . . .'

'. . . it somehow doesn't get any better.'

'Right! So, what we need is a kind of script doctor . . . *overlord*, to rewrite the rewriters' rewrites and keep up with Bruno's ideas. Someone who knows the history so that we don't goof up.'

'You mean a historian turned secretary? Did you try a university?'

'We'll pay you, Charlie. On top of everything you've already had. We'll pay you more. How much do you want? Give me a figure, and let me see if I can get it for you.'

'This is crazy!'

'I think so, too, but what do I know? The studio wants you back. Sam Jordan wants you back. Bruno wants you back. Will you do it?'

'Bruno wants me back?'

'Well, yes . . . of course. He might be selfish and overbearing, loud and uncouth, but he isn't stupid. He doesn't want to screw up either. Let me call your agent and see what we can get for you.'

Charlie sat down. It was his turn to hesitate. 'I don't know, Harvey. I got ripped in half last time.'

'That was then. Things are different now.'

'Really! Can you honestly promise me that there'll be no more monkeying around?'

'Absolutely.'

'You're lying.'

'I'm a producer.'

'If I come back in you'll have to promise me that when I've

written, and Bruno likes what I've written, that's what will be shot. I don't want any writing by committee.'

'You have my word.'

Charlie closed his eyes. Wouldn't it be nice if he could believe him? 'How's our movie coming along?' he asked at last.

'Wonderful, wonderful. Wait till you see what he's done with the Battle of Wagram. Boy, does this guy have an eye . . .'

'And the budget?'

There was the slightest hesitation. 'Not bad, though it's looking more like a little over fifty million now. But that's OK. Bruno's assured me he'll be bringing it in for less than that.'

'*Fifty million?* Fifty million dollars?'

Harvey didn't answer.

'And the studio are happy with that?'

There was another pause. 'Well, you know. He's a wonderful director. It'll be worth every penny.'

'What about the Gallego people?'

'No complaints from them so far, either. So come on, Charlie. What do you say? Will you do it? Will you do it for me? Please. It would be a real favour. You're the only one who can get it right . . .'

'Let me call you back.'

'*You'll do it!*' Harvey triumphed.

(ii)

Coolly Simone Estoril dipped her spoon into the tub of fat-free yoghurt she had saved from lunch.

Across his turret office Harvey forced a thin grimace into a smile. 'Maybe we'd better put those faxes from William Goldman and Bob Towne through the shredder before Charlie gets here. He might not like it if he found out he was our last resort.'

Simone wasn't amused. 'You don't deserve him.'

'Maybe not,' Harvey agreed. 'But I'm sure as hell doing the best I can to make him rich. Would you believe that son-of-a-bitch agent of his just took us for another fifty thousand dollars? Jesus! Whatever happened to those schmucks with typewriters they used to tell us about?'

'They bought computers,' Simone said, getting up and throwing the yoghurt tub into the bin. 'But if you ask me they're still schmucks for taking all this from you guys. When I first read it I thought *Shadows on a Wall* was brilliant. Now I don't know what it is.' With that she left the office.

Harvey shook his head. She was probably just cross because she'd been putting on weight from too many location lunches. But then who wasn't? That was all any of them seemed to be doing – waiting, eating, getting fat, and wondering when Bruno was going to start speeding up. God, but he was slow.

Maybe writers weren't such schmucks after all! Maybe he was the schmuck for going into this uncertain business in the first place, where he never seemed to do anything but cajole, bribe, lie and pamper bruised egos. Bruno had never said he wanted Charlie back. It was Buffalo who were *insisting* he came back.

'*Someone's* got to get this script back into shape,' Julie Wyatt had screamed down the phone. 'It's going out of control, and when a script goes out of control so does a budget and so does a movie.'

Harvey hadn't told Bruno that. It would only have annoyed him and slowed him still further. There was now no chance of being completed by Christmas. Buffalo recognized this and so did Gallego. It was clear why Bruno had backed down over the schedule. He had known that once shooting began it would be difficult to stop him. Please God he meant it when he said he could bring the movie in for under fifty million dollars. *Fifty million dollars!* How could any movie cost so much?

Going to the window Harvey watched the activity outside the palace. So *much* activity; so many cars; so many people – and they all had to be housed, paid and fed. And Jesus, could they eat!

'No problem,' Harvey would lie every day when Harry Weitzman called. 'We're doing the difficult stuff first.'

'I hope so,' Weitzman would sigh. 'Reuben and Candy Corn are going crazy in New York.'

Only Carlos Gallego was not screaming. He called, of course, his voice wheezing down the phone requesting information. But what he was thinking Harvey couldn't begin to imagine.

On the gravel below two teenage Polish boys who had attached themselves to the unit were polishing Harvey's new car. He watched them, wondering what the transport scam would be on this movie. There was always a scam with the cars. From across the meadows came the lowing of 320 cows. It was always the same at this time of the afternoon. God knows why Al Mutton had insisted on the cows being housed on the Kapolska estate.

The boys were now spreading polish on to the silver flanks of the Noblesse American. From this angle Harvey could see his script lying on the back seat. To be honest he didn't understand why Julie Wyatt was complaining about the new dialogue. He liked the joke about Napoleon putting his hand inside the woman's coat. He was sure Napoleon would have liked it, too. Napoleon was a woman's man. These modern semi-women had no sense of humour.

Then he thought about Carlos Gallego's hand at Nathalie's breast and his face creased in pain.

November, 1992

The day of the albatross

Chapter Thirty-four

(i)

Sadie was awoken by the sound of cisterns flushing. She opened her eyes, then quickly closed them again. The starched sheets still held her tightly in the single bed. For the moment she was safe. In her mind she ran through the details of the call sheet she had been presented with the previous night. An exterior, scene 24, was scheduled for that day, the first day in her life as a film actress. She was seventeen. Her mouth was dry with fear.

When she opened her eyes again it was on a small, cell-like, eighteenth-century room. On a table beside her bed was a telephone and an alarm clock. The time read five minutes to six. She stared at the fingers willing them to go more slowly. She had hardly slept. Would make-up be able to disguise exhaustion, she wondered, or would Camille de Malignon make her screen appearance with bags under her eyes, as well as trembling from head to toe? The first day of examinations was nothing compared with this.

She pulled the sheets over her head, willing herself back into the cosiness of her attic room in London, but all she could see was the face of her mother, jaundiced with anger, as she tottered about in her tight, lawyer's suit shouting, 'You can't possibly be in a film. It's absolutely out of the question. You're too young. You have to go to school'. But Sadie had already accepted the part.

With a sharp drill the telephone rang. 'Good morning, Sadie.

279

It's six o'clock,' came the laconic voice of Skip Zieff, third assistant director and the young man in charge of artistes. 'There's coffee in the hall. A car will be ready at six-thirty to take you to the location.'

'Thank you,' she murmured. It had begun.

In her small, robust bathroom she stood beneath a shower which sprayed water on to the lino, and thought about Claire who, after being uncharacteristically cool, had turned up on Sadies's last night at home with a jumbo pad of stationery and an assortment of pens.

'All right so I'm as jealous as a kipper, but I want blow by blow,' she had prattled. 'So, write soon and often, with all the stickiest details. And if, by the grace of God and a bottle of best vodka, Sam Jordan insists one night in a small town in Poland, promise you'll surrender on the spot and think of me while he's ravishing you, and perhaps that way I'll get the odd telepathic tremble when I'm in the middle of an essay on Irish Home Rule.'

She would write tonight, Sadie promised herself. There was already much to tell. She hadn't met Sam Jordan yet, but she had seen Jack Dragoman. This was the man she was going to have to make love to and she had wondered what it would be like. He seemed so old: mid-thirties, at least. Would she enjoy it? Would she fall in love with him? No. She was sure about that.

She had arrived at the Kapolska late the previous evening in a race from Warsaw Airport. After kicking her heels around London for the best part of an extra month, it had suddenly been a mad dash to get her there in time. She was learning quickly: movie-making was a matter of very long waits and exceedingly short sprints.

She dressed quickly, and, grabbing her script as though it were her homework, clattered down the wide palace staircase into the marble hall. Charlie was waiting by a coffee urn.

'I wanted to wish you good luck,' he said, kissing her on the cheek. 'I know you're going to be terrific. And, although I didn't, when you're a famous actress I'll tell everyone I discovered you and made you into a star.'

She hung on to him. He had been working through the night and looked very tired and very young. When she had first met him in Edinburgh he had seemed so grown up – the only playwright she had ever met. Now he didn't seem that much older than she was.

Together they sipped their coffees, the plastic cup warming her fingers through her mittens. Then, at exactly six-thirty, Belinda appeared in the hall, gave Charlie a friendly, if slightly distant, kiss, and led the way out to the waiting car.

It was unreal, she thought as the car pulled away from the palace. She ought to have been getting the bus to school, not being driven through the Polish countryside to appear in a film. 'It's going to be a nice day,' she said, trying to force conversation.

'Mmm.'

She looked at Belinda. She was frowning, her hands gripping her bag. When she had first seen her on stage she had appeared cool and confident. Now she was just another nervous actress. Worse than nervous: she looked terrified. That made Sadie feel better. At least they could share their fear.

By the time they reached the small town chosen for shooting crash barriers were being erected to keep the sightseers back. Mud was everywhere apart from in the main square and on one of the roads leading into it. There a localized Polish mid-winter had taken over, drifts of dry chemical snow lying inches deep on the asphalt, pavements, roofs and window-sills. It looked very odd.

The unit trailers were parked in a playing field next to an old school and Sadie and Belinda were immediately hurried into make-up, where, sitting alongside each other, gowns over their bras, they were prepared for the camera. To Sadie it was all new, and she felt very pampered, like one of those stuck-up rich women she saw in the hairdresser's who always demanded a posse of attendants while everyone else had to wait their turn.

The costume trailer was a treat, a little girls' dressing-up party. Belinda was slipped into a deep lilac gown, Sadie into crimson. She had spent days at fittings in London, but now that she was wearing the costume as though it belonged to her it was a different feeling. It *changed* her. When she looked in the mirror she saw Camille de Malignon.

'You look beautiful,' Belinda told her.

Sadie blinked her big eyes.

Behind her the hairdresser and dresser stared critically at their handiwork. Then, satisfied that the dress was right, the hairdresser muttered something about having to make sure the waves lasted until shooting, and, shepherding Sadie back to the make-up trailer, quickly transformed Camille de Malignon back into Sadie Corchoran in glasses, curlers and a lady's dress.

'It's like being behind the scenes in a circus, isn't it?' Belinda said a few minutes later as, sitting together in their trailer, they ate breakfast and watched the unit preparations.

'And we're the clowns?' came back Sadie, taking a large bite of her bacon sandwich.

'Did anybody ever tell you that you have the same quality as a young Isabelle Adjani?'

Sadie froze, bacon in mouth. The soapy sincerity of the delivery was unmistakable.

Sam Jordan was looking into the trailer, smiling at her. 'I'm sorry. Did I surprise you? I just thought I'd tell you. It's an uncanny likeness. You're Sadie, aren't you? I'm Sam Jordan.'

'Oh,' said Sadie at last, swallowing the bacon, wanting to kick herself. Of course he was Sam Jordan, everybody in the world knew he was Sam Jordan.

'I just thought I'd say hello.' And, with a wink at Belinda, he bowed from the waist, presumably in what he considered Napoleonic style, and walked on, the tails of his frock-coat whisking against his breeches.

'God!' groaned Sadie.

'Not quite,' Belinda teased.

They were still sitting there at nine-thirty when a Cadillac turned into the field and Yale Meredith, already in costume and make-up, slipped into her trailer carrying a small dog. Alice Bauccio followed, carrying another.

For another hour nothing happened, but as emissaries began to hurry with increasing urgency between Yale's trailer and the set, a rumour began to circulate. There was a problem with Yale. Some thought it was her hair, others her make-up, others her dress. No-one could say for sure.

At ten-thirty Bruno, accompanied by an anxious Harvey, hurried to Yale's trailer. Further up the field, Sam Jordan stood watching.

After a few moments the group, now accompanied by Yale and Alice Bauccio, marched across to Sam Jordan, Alice indicating something in the script.

'It looks as though it isn't her dress, her make-up or her hair . . .' said Belinda. 'Which leaves . . .'

'Poor Charlie,' said Sadie.

From the other side of the field the smiles told them that the problem had been resolved.

'Sadie, do you have a minute?' Skip Zieff, a walkie-talkie

in his hand, stood at the trailer steps. He was a moustached, olive-skinned, young Californian in a black sweatshirt with the arms torn off; he smelt strongly of almonds. 'Bruno would like a word.'

Obediently Sadie followed him across the field.

'Oh hi, Sadie.' Bruno looked her over cursorily. 'Have you met Yale yet? Yale, this is Sadie Corchoran. I'm sure you're going to get along fine.'

Sadie gazed at the most beautiful woman in movies. We're meeting as equals, sort of, she told herself. But she didn't believe it.

'I was hoping to get you two together last night to run through a few things,' Bruno continued, 'but there just hasn't been time—'

'Bruno . . .' Tony Delmonte, the first assistant director, put up a hand for attention, and the director was gone, striding off to his other duties.

The half-smile on Yale's face disappeared. Turning away, she whispered something to her hairdresser, who smiled obsequiously.

Sadie wondered if she had been dismissed.

'When you're ready, Sadie, Bruno would like to do a line-up,' Skip Zieff said.

'Oh yes, of course.' Lifting her skirts Sadie followed him back across the field.

'Just to warn you. Yale doesn't like to be spoken to before a scene,' he said. 'It ruins her concentration.'

'Mine, too,' said Sadie. They had a name for girls like Yale Meredith at Queen's Yard.

(ii)

This is when the shadows on the wall come to life, Charlie thought as he made his way down the street. And what shadows. In his wildest dreams he could never have imagined the scale of the shot Bruno was planning. No wonder they were so far behind schedule. He gazed around. He had dreamt this up while staring into the empty screen of a word processor, and here it all was, hundreds of extras and crew and horses, even the peasant with the fork on the dung heap and the farrier shoeing the piebald horse, just like the picture he had painted in his mind. In fact, it was better because he was standing in the middle of it, a real–life, virtual–reality situation, all to be achieved with a brand-new monster of a crane, which could run on caterpillar tracks across the length of the square.

He had arrived in Poland a week earlier, anxious not to get in the way, keen to avoid Yale Meredith and determined to make a go of it second time around with Bruno. Harvey had virtually kissed him, shown him to a word processor and begged him to start writing and saving money. Even Julie Wyatt had called wishing him well. The script *was* in a mess. So much had been added. Always slightly long, now it read more like a mini–series. He had set to work immediately and, if Bruno had not looked thrilled to see him, neither had he complained. Perhaps he didn't have time. At least with so many battles being shot very little of the new dialogue had found its way on to film yet. All week Charlie had pruned and reshaped. It would never be the movie he had set out to write, but he would make it work.

'Charlie!' A voice called from across the street. It was Jack Dragoman. Out of costume because he wasn't needed on this day, even his everyday clothes looked earnest. 'Do you have a minute?'

'Of course.' Charlie waited in a doorway for Dragoman to join him as a troupe of cavalry trotted past on the artificial snow.

'It's about Belinda.'

'Yes.'

'What I mean is . . . I know that you and Belinda . . .'

Charlie waited.

'You were together.'

'I wrote the play for her.'

'That's right. But you're not together now.'

'No.'

'I just wondered . . .'

Charlie waited. He had noticed Dragoman watching Belinda, but then half the crew had been watching her. For a famous person Dragoman was surprisingly reserved. 'Yes?' he asked.

'Would you mind if I asked her out . . . to dinner maybe?'

Charlie nearly laughed. 'To dinner? In Kapolska?'

Dragoman didn't smile. 'I meant it metaphorically. I meant would you mind if I took more than a professional interest in her?'

'Shouldn't you ask her?'

'I wanted to clear it with you first, to make sure you didn't mind.'

Of course he would mind, Charlie was thinking, but what could he say? It was over. 'That's OK,' he said.

'I just wanted to be sure,' Dragoman said.

Charlie watched him go. Why should he mind? On a day like today when the most exciting film sequence of the Nineties was about to be shot, why should he complain if some bozo actor wanted to try his hand at getting off with Belinda? He didn't stand a chance, anyway. Anyone could see that. Belinda had never gone for actors.

And, turning back towards the main square to see how preparations were going, he slipped under the barrier and joined the extras.

Chapter Thirty-five

(i)

The old man shifted uncomfortably as he woke. All morning they had been waiting for the arrival of the Emperor. Now, as the snow blew into his face, his bones ached. His chair was carved and narrow and he wished he was brave enough to ask for a cushion. At his age even sitting could be tiring. He had needed to go to the lavatory for some time but was afraid to ask permission.

He fidgeted in his linen shirt and woollen breeches. He felt foolish to be dressed in such clothes, and the high boots they had insisted he wear were at least a size too small. Another flurry of snow stung his eyes and he wiped his brow with the sleeve of his frock-coat. He was sweating, drops of perspiration running down his forehead and out along the double crags of his famous broken nose. He had no illusions. It was because of his camel-humped nose that he was sitting there, that and his lantern jaw which curved around and upwards towards the pinched potholes of his nostrils. He had always had an extraordinary face.

From around the corner came the sound of a horse whinnying, and then the muffled drumming of hooves, before, to an ironic cheer, a troupe of Polish lancers trotted their mounts down the street in front of him, escorting an empty two-seat sleigh carriage. For the first time all morning it looked as though something might be about to happen, and the farm girls who had been placed behind him practised their waves, before breaking into giggles. They had been making eyes at the cavalry earlier.

He had seen that. Some lucky lads would be having a fine time of it before this day was through.

A sharp pain bit in his breast and he winced. He wished he had not eaten so many sausages at breakfast, but it was not easy to control an appetite when there was so much and it was free. For a moment he thought of summoning help but one look at the beanpole of a boy who was patrolling the line of spectators dissuaded him. The boy was German and noisy, and was now shouting instructions in very bad Polish. 'Don't applaud until the sleigh passes. And remember you're *cold. Very* cold. Look cold!'

The old man peered into the snow-filled sky, beyond which the sun shone through a thin autumn mist. He was not cold. He was hot and his mouth was dry.

The boy leant over him. '*You!* Old man! You don't get up. Do you understand? When the sleigh comes just sit and stare.' And pushing a length of tricolour into the old man's hand he hurried off to a group of three women in long dresses, cloaks and bonnets who were just then emerging from a hotel doorway.

Such beautiful women, the old man thought, the one in the blue more perfect than all the others, and a smile of appreciation ran in agreement along the pavement.

'She's even better in real life,' gasped one of the farm girls, craning her neck, cheeks inflamed with excitement.

The centre of all attentions, flaxen trinkets of hair escaping from under her shawl, stared ahead, seemingly oblivious to the effect she was creating, familiar and weary with the burden of being watched.

Momentarily the old man's pain eased and he relaxed, his camel-backed nose enjoying her scent.

Suddenly heads began to turn as a small party could be seen approaching on foot. Leading the group and issuing orders was a tall, heavy young man with shoulder-length, black hair. In his hand he held a banana. Through misty eyes the old man watched, relieved. At last the Emperor, he thought, and he waved his tricolour, although the exertion made him gasp.

The giant stopped, but, instead of waving back, he stared long and hard, from the old man to the beautiful woman, who responded with a slight arch of her neck. Then casually he began to unpeel his banana, speaking quietly to his attendants, some of whom nodded and broke into a shared joke. Emperors had that effect upon other men, the old man thought: when an emperor smiled the world smiled, too.

'Come on, we want you further forward.' The tall boy had broken free from the party and was shouting down at him, and before the old man could answer he and his uncomfortable chair were being carried forward across the pavement until he was alongside the beautiful woman. 'And a little higher.' Another shout and miraculously a cushion appeared from the back of the crowd.

In the street the Emperor munched his banana and watched. Then, his orders completed, he began to make his way up the steps of a scaffolding tower which had been erected across the square, as attendants hurried to obey his commands. At the old man's side the beautiful woman in blue was having her make-up reapplied by a servant in leather trousers, while behind her, a dark-haired, younger woman, no more than a girl, with eyes which seemed almost too big for her pretty face, was biting her lip anxiously. Such women! Finally from the steps of the scaffolding tower the Emperor made a sign with his arm and, just as suddenly as it had begun, the light snow turned into a blizzard. With a wave of his hand this Emperor could control even the elements.

At last all went still. There was silence, and for several minutes the old man dozed again.

A shout awoke him. There was a murmur of hooves in the snow, and peering down the street he watched as four black horses emerged through the storm, towing behind them the carriage sleigh, accompanied by a troupe of cavalry.

At the old man's side the beautiful woman raised her chin, and smoothly, as the old man watched, the coachman made a large turn in the square and drew the sleigh to a halt directly in front of the waiting crowd.

Slowly the sleigh door opened and a man wearing a three-cornered black hat stepped down into the snow.

But of course! This was the Emperor. The real Emperor. Now the old man remembered. And as the beautiful young woman and her friends stepped forward in welcome he raised his tricolour again.

The Emperor smiled, and, snatching off his hat, bowed gracefully in reply.

As if by magic the blizzard eased. What a day this was turning out to be!

Had he understood English the old man might just have heard the beautiful woman say: *'Welcome, sire, a thousand welcomes . . . all Poland is overwhelmed to feel your step upon her soil.'* He might also have heard the man reply: *'You, my child, are the most exquisite of welcomes.'* But he would not have seen the promise in the woman's eyes as the man stepped forward and kissed her hand, or heard the sudden cheer of welcome from the surrounding people. The old man's pain had returned without warning: a certain, efficient, vice-grip to the heart. There was no opportunity to cry out, nothing to cry for. For a second his lips parted in the spasm, but then the pain was gone, quickly and finally, leaving him sitting, comfortable at last, in his chair in the snow, his camel nose apparently luxuriating in the woman's perfume, the tricolour still hanging from his fingers.

(ii)

'And . . . cut! Looked pretty good to me. What do you think, Stock?' The director's voice rasped into a hundred walkie-talkies.

Perched on the furthest fingertip of the giant Eiger crane, camera operator, Stock Holden, switched off his Panavision camera and began to unclip his harness. He was trembling. It had been a difficult, dangerous, crazy shot, rehearsed for days when the streets had been empty, but terrifying with snow-making machines, spectators, crew, actors and whatever street business Bruno could devise all over the damn place.

He had done brilliantly, he knew, an elegant, soaring, one hundred and eighty degrees *Battle of a Soldier* shot, over four minutes long, through a chemical blizzard, starting, *Lawrence of Arabia* style, nearly a mile away on the end of a 600mm lens with the cantering hooves of Napoleon's cavalry bodyguard before crabbing around to observe the Emperor through the glycerine-smeared windows of his sleigh coach; then soaring up and over the roofs of the better-preserved parts of this medieval Polish town, a great, sweeping arc which had returned to street level as the sleigh had turned the corner into the main square where the serf had been forking his dung; a shot which all the time kept the sleigh in the corner of the frame as it raced past the grenadiers in their bearskins, before finally coming to rest as the sleigh door had opened and Napoleon had stepped out to see her for the first time, Marie Walewska, blond doll and Polish patriot. New Year's Day, 1807, on celluloid better than it had ever been in history.

And the amazing thing was, it had gone perfectly the very first take. It hadn't seemed possible. When Orson Welles had pulled off his *Touch of Evil* single-take *coup de cinéma*, and challenged every directorial prodigy to better him, the car had been going at a walking pace and Charlton Heston's expression was always carved in stone, anyway. But Bruno Messenger had got a racing sleigh, a blizzard, and the biggest, newest, moving crane in Europe doing all kinds of tricks it wasn't supposed to do. The matt painters back in California would fill in the rest.

Bruno Messenger didn't deserve it, but it would be the shot of the year. Everyone had got their parts right, even the genius in casting who had come up with the ugliest old man in Europe to sit alongside Yale Meredith. My God, what a nose to end on. Beauty and the Beast. For the rest of the day, maybe even half tomorrow, they would be shooting all around the scene as it progressed. But nothing would match that skimming, eagle's eye, four minutes and seven seconds of perfection. Lucky Bruno Messenger.

The operator gathered himself together. 'That was great for me, Bruno,' he said, more nonchalantly than he was feeling. 'Mike's just checking the gate . . .', and he waited while his focus puller withdrew the film cartridge and peered inside the camera for any problems. Then the nod. 'Yes. That's fine, Bruno. To be honest I didn't think it was possible, but—'

The voice of the director cut him off. 'What about you, Giorgio?'

(iii)

High above the little Polish town in the scaffolding eyrie, specially constructed so that the director and his senior crew might observe this moment, Bruno Messenger was looking at Giorgio Pescati, the director of photography.

He needn't have asked. Throughout the progress of the shot

Pescati, in his elegant, quilted yachtsman's suit and white silk scarf, had been gripping the back of the director's canvas chair, staring at the monitor. 'It's a miracle,' he exalted, relief blushing through his handsome face.

'And you, Al?' Bruno asked, biting into a Snickers bar.

The back-of-the-nostril Australian whine of Al Mutton came scything from the front of the hotel. 'Terrific, Brune. Terrific! My God what a face! Did you see it? Jeez! Ugly old bastard? A regular gargoyle.'

From the back of the eyrie came single nervous applause. It was Harvey Bamberg. 'Bravo!' he bubbled. 'My God! What a shot!'

Bruno ignored him.

Silence now fell in the eyrie as Bruno re-ran the video recording of the shot. For four minutes and seven seconds all eyes were upon the small screen. Had a miracle really happened? This collection of hard-eyed film-makers, Giorgio Pescati, Tony Delmonte, the sweating first assistant director who had hurried up to the eyrie as soon as the shot had been completed, Hal Jobete, the designer, assistants Judy Goldberg and Simone Estoril, the location scout who had found this town, the slack mouthed executive from Buffalo Pictures getting experience in the field, and Jenny Walters, the script supervisor . . . all these people wanted to be absolutely certain. Only Charlie, hidden at the back of the eyrie, did not care.

At last, after three careful viewings, Bruno Messenger was as satisfied as was possible until the film had been processed. It was official. A miracle had indeed occurred. He turned away from the video link and started on another chocolate bar.

'So, that's a print then, Bruno, right?' Jenny Walters asked as she sat on a camera case to make out her continuity sheets. A cautious girl, she liked to have everything confirmed.

'That's a print,' came the reply. And, smiling around at his admirers, the director put an arm around Giorgio Pescati and led him down the scaffolding staircase. Immediately the eyrie began to empty.

Outside the loud-hailer voice of the first assistant director filled the air. 'OK, that's lunch, everybody. Back at two o'clock. Be sure to make a note of your exact places. And will someone save that goddamn snow?' A shouted translation in Polish followed, and the flurry of snow, which had been falling from one of the cannons, eased and stopped. The miracle was complete.

'*What about* that, Charlie? Wasn't that *something*?' Harvey, his face as round and shiny as a pomegranate punched one chubby, pink fist into the other, relief oozing from him.

Charlie took off his glasses and covered his face in his hands.

'He may take his time, and, my God, does he take his time! But when he gets it . . . Wow! I can't wait to see the rushes. Buffalo are going to love this!'

'Did you hear her . . . ?' Charlie's voice was a croak. He cleared his throat and tried again. 'Did you hear what she said, Harvey?'

'What? What who said?' Harvey had stopped punching.

'*Welcome, sire, a thousand welcomes . . . all Poland is overwhelmed to feel your step upon her soil.*' Charlie mimicked Yale Meredith's delivery. 'I mean, for Christ's sake, Harvey, couldn't someone have told me?'

Harvey sniffed awkwardly.

Charlie stood up. 'You spend a week setting up one of the most expensive, complex shots ever filmed, hundreds of thousands of dollars worth of production value, rehearsing the camera moves for days, blocking off traffic in the town, hiring extras by the thousand, paying God knows how many millions to get two of the most expensive people in the world into the same place at the same time . . . and at the end of it what do we get? Stuff that Maid Marion would have been ashamed to say in a Saturday-morning cliff-hanger.'

'Oh Jesus!' Harvey's head was no longer jigging.

'Harvey, you *promised* me. That was why I came out here. Since I arrived I've worked night and day cutting out all the terrible lines Bruno and his pals had slipped in. And now, at one of the most important moments in the movie . . .'

For a moment Harvey hesitated. 'Don't take it personally, Charlie,' he said at last.

'What do you mean, "Don't take it personally"? It is personal.'

'No, it isn't. Not to you any more than to me.'

'You're not making sense. If it isn't personal, what is it?'

'It's your chromosomes.'

'What?'

'Yale thinks your chromosomes are wrong. You're a man. She insisted on having the line rewritten by a woman.'

'You're joking.'

'You think I have time to joke?'

'When did this happen?'

'She told Bruno when she arrived this morning. You weren't around. He didn't care what she said so long as she got her ass on to the set. And, to be honest, neither did I.'

Charlie shook his head. Since he had been in Poland Yale had refused even to acknowledge his existence. 'Hi, Yale,' he had said casually as he had accidentally come across her in the unused Kapolska orangery on his second morning there. Sitting with the costume director, Ruth Blumberg, she had glanced up when he spoke, and then gone on with her conversation as though he wasn't there. 'I don't get it,' he said now. 'Back in Los Angeles she told me she loved my writing. Every word of it. She said she'd never known a man who could write women's dialogue so well.'

'I guess she changed her mind.'

'She's a lunatic.'

'I think so, too. But, lunatic or not, we're stuck with her.'

'So, did she write the line herself or . . .'

'Alice Bauccio wrote it.'

'What? The Barnacle?'

'Yale loves her. She's got a Ph.D. in American literature.'

'She's a moron.'

Harvey pulled a face. 'Oh, come on. It wasn't that bad. Didn't you think it sounded OK, Jenny?'

Cradling her typewriter, script supervisor Jenny Walters slipped quietly off the end of the camera case where she had been finishing her continuity reports. 'I have to check something with the sound crew . . . I think I'll . . .' she began as she fled towards the steps leaving the two men alone.

'It was terrible,' Charlie repeated.

Harvey sighed. 'Give me a break, Charlie. This is the first day on this movie *anything* has gone right for me. Let me enjoy it for a while, will you? It really was a hell of a shot. When the guy does it he really is a genius.'

Charlie held up an arm. '*Genius?* You still think he's a genius? You're miles behind schedule, the latest projected cost of delivery is over fifty-five million dollars, fifteen million more than Buffalo said they couldn't afford in the first place, money is flowing like Niagara, and you're looking the other way because the bastard pulled off some fancy shot that will excite the critics and add not a single penny to the box-office.'

The producer's fruity face ripened, and he puffed out his chest. He didn't enjoy being criticized. 'Come on, Charlie. Maybe you do need a little help in getting the dialogue right.'

'*Help! From Alice Bauccio!*' Charlie's voice rose in indignation. A runner who had climbed the scaffolding to get the producer's order for lunch took one look into the eyrie and retreated down again. 'I need *help* from her?'

Harvey sighed. 'Charlie, we're in deep enough trouble. Don't make things worse than they are. Lots of stars demand their own personal rewriter. Look at the way Dustin Hoffman behaved on *Tootsie*. If Yale Meredith wants a woman to write her lines we've just got to go with that and try to work around it. If she wanted a Martian we'd get her a Martian. We can't afford to have her throwing a tantrum and sitting in her caravan all day holding us to ransom. Try to get on with Alice Bauccio for a couple of days. She'll get tired of it all by the end of the week. Amateurs always do.'

Charlie stared silently at a Snickers wrapper Bruno Messenger had dropped on the floor. 'It'll be too late by then,' he said. 'I should have known. Alice is a moron and Bruno's an even bigger moron. And a rat. I shouldn't have come back.'

Harvey leant over him. 'Of course you should have come back! But make it easy on yourself. Try looking at it from Yale's point of view. Maybe she has a point. Maybe your chromosomes are wrong. You are a man, you can't deny that.'

'I'm a *writer*.' The word came out almost as a scream.

Slowly the producer buttoned his green Italian leather jacket. At last he put a hand on Charlie's arm. 'Charlie, I'm your friend, all right? You hear what I'm saying?'

Charlie listened to the silence for a moment. 'You're not saying anything, Harvey.'

'I'm saying maybe Yale is a pain, possibly Bruno is a verging-on-the-disgusting human being. We have room for agreement on that. Maybe Bruno's also a vandal and a bully, a spendthrift, dishonest, a liar and a blackmailer. And maybe he is slow. Very slow. All true. But today he created an incredible shot for a movie that will do wonderful justice to your vision and your screenplay.'

'The idiot's allowing Alice Bauccio to turn my screenplay into a creamcake.'

Harvey pulled open the flap of the eyrie. 'Oh, come on, what is this? One lousy line? You're acting like a–' he searched for the appropriate simile – 'like a forty-year-old feminist who's found a fingerprint on her bra.' His eyes twinkled. 'D'you like that? I'll give it to you. You should use it some time.'

Charlie shook his head. 'I'm acting like a writer who's getting stuffed. For God's sake's, *A thousand welcomes, sire, all Poland is overwhelmed to feel your step upon her soil.* Nobody ever spoke like that, Harvey. Not even in the movies you made.'

'And your line was so much better?'

'There *was* no line in my version,' Charlie gritted. 'No dialogue. We don't need a line. One word each. *Sire* and *Madame.* Their faces should say it all.'

Harvey's lips peeled back in astonishment. 'You mean, *no-one changed anything*? Alice Bauccio didn't change your line? So what the hell are you getting so uptight about?'

Charlie groaned. He shouldn't have to explain these things. 'Harvey,' he said, 'she *added.* That's *worse*! It makes the scene melodramatic, bathetic, and . . . it makes me look like a lousy writer, which I'm not.'

'Of course you're not. But there isn't another director in the world could get the stuff Bruno's coming up with. You saw the rushes last night. I mean, Jesus, to go right through the ceiling like it wasn't there. Where does the guy get these ideas?'

'In that instance right out of *Citizen Kane.* You should know that. Every film critic in the world will.'

'OK. So the shot's an homage to Orson Welles.'

'The whole lousy film's turning out as an homage to Orson Welles.'

Harvey sighed. 'Jesus, Charlie, it isn't easy for me either, you know.' He pulled on his yellow gloves. 'Come on, give us a smile.'

'What do we have to smile about?'

'What do we have to smile about? This is a serious question?' Harvey drew himself up to his full five foot six inches. 'Come here. Look down there . . .' Putting an arm around Charlie he stood on the top step of the scaffolding and pointed down. Already several figures were at work brushing away some of the artificial snow in an area of the square which would not be required for filming. 'You see those people down there . . . ?'

Charlie gazed down at the workmen. Alongside them a dozen

or so extras were waiting in their costumes by the location lavatories. 'Is this another homage, Harvey?' he asked.

'Just look at them? Proud to be Polish, and not one of them
owns a potato in a pot. Think about it. We've got stuff to smile
about, Charlie. We really have. Come on, I'll buy you lunch.'

Charlie picked up his coat. 'We're on location, Harvey,' he
said. 'Lunch is free.'

The producer shook his head. 'And still you complain.'

(v)

In the cab of the mighty Eiger crane the driver Klaus Alberts
was shaking. Thank you, God, he thought. Thank you, God,
for the miracle of the single, perfect take. Thank you, God,
for Stock Holden's cowboy heroics out there at the end of the
arm. And thank you, God, for Bruno Messenger's luck. He lit
a cigarette to collect his nerves.

There wouldn't be any more heroics from Stock Holden, not
for the next few days, anyway. It had happened the moment
'Cut!' had been called. Alberts had heard the call down his
headphones, and immediately felt the sag. The hydraulics had
gone. There could be no question of retakes, or even getting
the vast arm up again. The capabilities of the Eiger had been
stretched too far. No crane in the world was built to do the things
Bruno Messenger wanted. A Sky-Cam or Hover-Cam should
have been used. Now the crane was busted. What had they
expected? He'd warned everybody. The Eiger wasn't designed
to do these things. There could have been a disaster. It could
have fallen on the crowd. Alberts wiped his forehead. Thank
you, Jesus, he thought again.

Buzzing down the electric window he looked around for Al
Mutton. The associate producer would have to be told. Klaus
Alberts would not want to be around when his message was
conveyed to Bruno Messenger. Absolutely not. But now he
was going to telephone his wife, and tonight he would get
very drunk and sleep with the waitress who worked in the
café on the corner whose husband was in jail. In the mean
time, thank God, they had their shot.

Chapter Thirty-six

(i)

'Don't give them anything. They're only Ukrainians on the scrounge. They'll go away if you ignore them,' Skip Zieff snapped as he led the way to the catering vans.

He doesn't like babysitting, Sadie thought. Now wearing her school coat over her crimson gown, and with a scarf covering her rollers, she stared out through the playground railings at the family of beggars gazing numbly at an awesomely laden table of cold meats, cheeses, salads, fruits and eight varieties of slimline yoghurt.

Next to her Beverly, the English make-up artist in jeans and high heeled, rhinestone-studded cowboy boots, was casually scraping a plate of turkey breast into an overflowing polythene waste bag. 'That's the trouble with location lunches,' she was muttering to her assistant, 'I put on nearly two pounds last week.'

'It isn't the Ritz, but I think you'll find something here you like,' Zieff said, woefully attempting an upper-class English accent, and, with a fey shrug, hurried away.

Sadie looked at the queues. There were five catering vehicles drawn up in the playground, and, according to the day's call sheet, just under five hundred and fifty to be fed, over four hundred extras, who would take their stews and dumplings across the street to the canteen of a former brick factory, and 142 cast and crew. Naturally, being of higher status, the cast and crew had more choice, and would eat in the school class-rooms, while, higher status still, the director, assorted producers and principal performers (which actually included Sadie, had Skip Zieff remembered to tell her), had a special restaurant trailer with a cordon-bleu cook, two waitresses, good china and silver, and a choice of wines.

Selecting a raspberry yoghurt, and putting some salmon and salad on to a paper plate, Sadie followed a trail of arrows past a line of grinning Polish grenadiers into the school. It was a brick-built, nineteenth-century place of dark browns and greens, shiny walls, glass partitions and noticeboards filled with the inevitable lists of names. Whether in the perils of Poland or the depths of South Kensington, school was school.

The first two rooms she tried were filled with bellied English electricians and bearded American camera technicians wearing baseball caps. Belinda had gone off with the wardrobe mistress for some repairs to her dress and Sadie was disappointed not to find Billy, but, seeing an empty table near a window in the third room, she sat down and, pulling out a copy of *The Rough Guide To Poland* which one of her brothers had given her, began to read as she ate.

She didn't see him approach and when he asked if he might join her she was surprised because there were empty tables available. He looked so young, not much older than she was, and his hair curled out in shock masses from his head. He was tall and broad shouldered, slightly uncoordinated, and, gazing out at her from behind large, horn-rimmed glasses, his expression flitted between mischief and that of someone slightly manic. At first she thought he must be a runner, or perhaps someone's son being given work experience, and when he told her he was an editor, *the* editor, she was unsure whether to believe him. He was American and his name, he said, was Tim Westwood.

'I didn't know editors went on location,' she said, displaying her sum knowledge of film editing.

'They don't normally, but the studio thought it might be an idea if I came out to see what's happening,' the young man returned quietly. 'They've got one or two worries. I'm actually based at Pinewood. I arrived with the rushes last night. I noticed you then, but when I looked again you'd disappeared.'

'Oh . . . yes . . . ! There was a fitting. They thought I'd lost weight since they measured me in London. I had. There's a safety pin holding me together at the back.'

'Is that nerves?'

'Terror.'

He smiled. 'Don't worry. You're going to be fine.'

'Thanks, but you don't know that.'

'Oh, I do. I was watching you all morning. You were terrific.'

Whether he meant it or not, and whether or not he knew what he was talking about, it was good to hear. 'It must be nice to be so sure of things,' she said.

'Not things. Just movies. I don't know anything about anything else.'

'And is that enough?'

'No, but it will have to do for now. Besides no-one else in movies knows about anything else either. Certainly they never talk about anything else.'

At that point, slightly unsure of where the conversation should go, they went quiet and got on with their lunches, Sadie looking out of the window towards the stars' trailers. What, she wondered, would Sam Jordan and Yale Meredith be having for lunch? Would they be eating together or did Yale really despise Sam Jordan as much as everyone said?

'How was Yale? Was she all right?' The boy was following Sadie's gaze.

'I don't know. She hardly spoke to me.'

'That will be because she's jealous of you.'

'Oh, come on,' Sadie laughed.

He looked surprised. 'I mean it.'

'You mean it! Why should Yale Meredith be jealous of me?'

'Isn't it obvious? You're younger than she is; you're more beautiful than she is; and you've got the best part in the movie.'

Sadie looked at him. Was this some kind of joke, or a terrible chatting-up technique?

'I'm not trying to flatter you,' he suddenly added, embarrassed. 'I'm describing your situation.'

'But I'm playing—'

'Camille de Malignon. I know. It's a brilliant part.'

'Well, yes, of course, *I* think so. I always did, from the moment I saw the play in Edinburgh, although it's much shorter in the film script. Yes, it's brilliant for me. I still can't believe I'm here. I don't think I should be, to be honest. I'm sure there were stacks of better girls. But, Camille de Malignon is very much the subplot. The film is about Marie Walewska, and Yale's incredibly beautiful. And good. *Very* good. I'll probably get cut out before the film's even finished.'

The boy put a hand through his hair. 'I think when this movie is finished you'll be the one they're talking about,' he said quietly.

In her mind Sadie began the first sentence of the letter she planned to write that night: *'Dear Claire, Nothing on the Sam Jordan front as yet, other than to report that he's smaller in real life. Aren't they all? But boy, oh boy, have I met a weirdo! His name is Tim Westwood and I suspect he's got kangaroos in the top paddock . . .'*

'I thought you might like some tangerines and bananas,' Sadie said, emptying the contents of her pockets into the hands of the three Ukrainian children outside the playground gates. 'They're very good for you. Vitamin C and all that, I think. Prevents scurvy, they say. Anyway, I must go now. Bye.'

(ii)

Sam Jordan watched Yale Meredith from behind the gap in his blind, kneeling in full costume at his trailer window, taking care to stay hidden. Napoleon the peeping Tom, he thought, and the association of images made him smile.

He enjoyed location lunch-breaks, although he rarely ate anything more than a lettuce sandwich of wheatgerm, anti-oxidants, L-cysteine and beta-carotene, and never spoke to anyone. It was his time for plotting, when, alone and in the darkness of his trailer, he could plan his campaigns, consider his conquests and dream up tricks to be played on his retainers. Most men in his situation, and their global total did not number more than a handful, enjoyed the company of their minders, chauffeurs, secretaries and hangers-on. But Sam Jordan had never been that kind of star. He had his retinue, of course, and there were six at the moment, because the movie paid for them and because without their presence on location his status would be irrevocably reduced. But he did not socialize with them. Retainers were servants. He was playing an emperor.

He leant closer to the window. Yale was standing at one end

of her trailer, hoisting the hem of her skirts above the mud, bending over. He liked it when she bent over. Neat! Even in a crinoline and cloak she was neat. What neat little secret was she keeping wrapped up under there? he asked himself, and wondered whether Napoleon had had such thoughts.

'You bet he did,' he murmured out loud. Hell, he ought to know. As his preparation for the part, he'd told an interviewer from *The New York Times*, he'd read everything there was to read on Napoleon, 'whole libraries, biographies, history, stuff the scriptwriter's never even seen'.

He was the expert all right and, no doubt about it, Napoleon would have just loved to get himself into Yale Meredith, leading lady, beautiful beyond comparison and as cuckoo as a clock. Mysterious? Eccentric? Mad? Sure. Who wasn't in movies?

Outside in the field the most beautiful of eccentrics was now holding one end of a tape-measure in her hand. Alice Bauccio, the crabby bitch who had just written her the worst line in the history of movies, held the other end. Yale liked Alice because Alice was plain, at best, and had pretensions to being a feminist intellectual, which made Yale feel intelligent and gave a stamp of educated legitimacy to her most outrageous demands. For all the same reasons Sam Jordan hated Alice Bauccio.

Pressing his face to the window Jordan watched, puzzled. From what he could see the two women seemed to be measuring Yale's trailer, first the length, now the width, Yale writing down the dimensions on the back of her script. Disappearing inside she returned instantly with a chair on which she climbed to measure the vehicle's height. She had to stretch to do that and her cloak fell open to reveal the laced-up bodice of her costume. Sam Jordan smiled again. He liked that, too: all wrapped up like a present at Christmas. He enjoyed a challenge, although he rarely got one.

The truth was, Sam Jordan was besieged by sex. It came at him from all sides, in all forms, all colours, all shapes, all ages and in every situation. It came at him as a full-frontal battery and it sneaked in behind his defences, stealing into his car when no-one was looking, lying waiting to ambush him as he returned to his bed at night. It was an ever-running campaign: climaxes, counterfeit or real, raging around him. If he had once experienced rejection, perhaps as a boy growing up in Oregon where his beautiful face and dark golden hair had not always been quite enough to separate a girl from her virginity, if he had once known the finality of the word 'no' when meant as something other than some opening negotiating position to be quickly surrendered, it was now a dim memory. And it was all so unfortunate, because the man the majority of American women would most like to sleep with liked nothing more than a challenge. Yale Meredith would be a challenge.

A sudden barking made him pull back from his window as two dogs bounded down the steps of the facing trailer, one of them landing face down in the mud. Yale and her dogs, a blind spaniel and a dachshund, whose legs cocked instantly at a trailer wheel, first one, then the other; then they sniffed each other's. Why did dogs do that? he asked himself. And why did actresses insist on taking dogs on location where they would be the biggest nuisance imaginable. 'Dogs should be a compulsory listing in *Spotlight* and then we could make sure we never hire actresses who own them,' an English director had once grumbled to him. Alternatively they should be drowned, Jordan had suggested. But the movies would have hired Yale Meredith if she turned up with all the monkeys in the zoo. She had whatever it was audiences paid their dollars to see. She wasn't just a beautiful actress; she, like him, was a movie star. The reality was flesh and blood, bones and hair and organs which worked better or worse depending upon which substances had most recently been pumped into them. But stars, real stars, who could open a movie in two thousand theatres on a Thanksgiving weekend, were more than real. They were mystical. The camera loved them. The camera did things when it saw Yale Meredith. It transfigured a beautiful neurotic bitch into a billion incandescent dreams. That nervous face, worried and fretting off-screen, became washed with vulnerability and tenderness when the film began to roll. Yes, she was mystical, all right, and he was mystical, forty-foot-tall icons of transferred emotions. No wonder people like them sometimes went mad.

He laughed to himself. Who cared? Mad or bad, whichever she was, he would get there before the end of the shoot. She'd invite him inside and he'd stay a while, show her his tricks, and she'd consider herself lucky. He was determined. One way or the other he'd share her secret, no matter what she might now be thinking.

Suddenly he realized that Alice Bauccio was looking his way. Had she seen him? It wouldn't do for Napoleon to be seen peeping through windows. He dropped to the floor and waited, crouching in a corner, then, very delicately, he lifted the bottom half-inch of the blind. False alarm. Bauccio had disappeared, the trailer measuring had finished, and Yale Meredith was holding the spaniel in her arms, petting it and loving it and allowing it to lick her face.

Jesus! Sam Jordan put a hand to his mouth and wiped it in distaste. Who knew what else that dog had been licking?

He looked again. They had gone. Now sitting on the floor, in the dark corner of his trailer, the actor reached for his three-cornered, beaver-skinned hat. Napoleon Bonaparte. A hand mirror told him he looked good, so much better than the real thing. He smiled. Crawling across the floor he reached his fridge and, opening it, felt inside among the stacked vitamin jars for a hypodermic needle and a bottle. Nothing serious: Sam Jordan was too vain for anything dangerous. Three injections, three times a week: Gerovital H-3. Well, hell, who wanted to get old? Now all he needed was a little pick-me-up: another needle, another prick and his face brimmed pink as his arm filled with vitamins and the malty taste of yeast reached his mouth and nostrils. That was better.

He stood up. Napoleon was ready. It might take weeks of spying, skirmishing, planning and plotting his campaign, and it might not be an easy victory, but one way or the other, he would get there in the end. Lucky, lucky Yale Meredith.

(iii)

Charlie felt as though he had climbed out of one pit only to be sliding into another. He understood Harvey's position: the rhinoceros was picking up speed and heading in his direction. He wondered what Julie Wyatt and the Buffalo people would say when they heard the line. *'Welcome, sire, a thousand welcomes . . . all Poland is overwhelmed to feel your step upon her soil.'* What kind of university could have given Alice Bauccio a Ph.D. in literature?

He wasn't particularly hungry and seeing Belinda standing by the luncheon trailer talking to Jack Dragoman destroyed any last vestiges of appetite. She saw him and smiled, but did not invite him over. There was no reason why she should. Perhaps there had been a chance of reconciliation back in London, but they had slid past that moment, like two punts going in opposite directions on a river.

Uncertain of what to do, he took an apple from the dessert table, told Harvey that he had some cyanide to crush and set off to explore the small town. In the time he had been in Poland he had been so busy rewriting he had scarcely left the Kapolska. Now passing a pile of neatly labelled television aerials, dismantled by the unit riggers in getting the look of this town back almost two centuries, he stepped across the frontier of movieland and entered the state of Poland.

Behind the square lay a characterless, grey street of slab-sided, post-war tenement flats. There had been no filming here and there was no artificial snow, although some fragments of torn-up call-sheets blew with the leaves in the gutter. A couple of teenage girls, their make-up exaggerated and their skirts too brief for their fat legs, were lolling on a corner, awkwardly smoking, their eyes cast hopefully in the direction of the set. He had noticed them the previous evening in the Kapolska bar with a couple of stuntmen, both drunk, unable to speak English, excited at being close to so much glamour.

He walked on through the backstreets, idly watching the smoke which steamed from the chimneys of the new town beyond the railway, passing a group of workmen standing in the mud by a bus-stop. They watched in silence, hostile. He didn't blame them.

On the outskirts of the town he came upon a small park with a worn patch of grass and some children's swings. Finding an unvandalized bench he sat down and bit into his apple, but it was soft and tasted of polythene packing, and before long he threw it into a flower-bed where some late dahlias struggled between the weeds. Putting his head back on the bench he closed his eyes.

He was there for some time. It was peculiarly peaceful. He was disappointed but calm now. In fact the longer he sat the more he realized he wasn't particularly upset. It was even funny. He wasn't a bad writer, after all, it was just that his chromosomes were wrong. That was funny. His father back in the school film society would have seen that joke. Suddenly he became aware that he was smiling. A few moments later a giggle escaped his lips, followed by another. No wonder he had been blighted on this project, he told himself, his hormonal balance was getting in the way. His testosterone level was too high. He had testicles and a penis. That was why he couldn't get it right. Why hadn't he thought of it himself? Well done, Yale Meredith, for spotting his problem. She knew all about his penis and testicles, of course, and obviously she hadn't thought much of them. Ah well, *c'est la guerre*, as Napoleon used to say, before they pickled his.

He was still laughing when he saw her. She was moving around the edge of the park, loitering uncertainly. For a second, seeing only a blur of military khaki out of the corner of his eye, he thought she might be a soldier come to move him on, but he quickly realized his mistake. Tentatively she approached him. She was tall, wearing a heavy, surplus Soviet army greatcoat over trousers stuffed into fleece-lined, knee-high boots and a bright red scarf. On her head was a grey, fur, Red Army officers' hat, on the upturned flaps of which were pinned badges of Nelson Mandela, Sinead O'Connor, Laurel and Hardy and John F. Kennedy.

'Hello,' he said, wondering suddenly if she was soliciting. Another look disabused him of that notion. She was stunning, in a stern, intelligent way, with light eyes and fair hair which streamed from under her hat. She was, he reckoned, in her mid-twenties.

'Why are you laughing?' she asked.

'Sorry,' he said. 'Isn't it allowed here? It was a private joke.'

She considered this for a moment and then said: 'A private joke in a public place.' Her English was good.

'Something like that.'

She looked at him. He knew she was plucking up her courage. Finally she came out with it. 'Can you tell me how I can meet the people in the movie?' she asked.

He should really have told her that there was no way; on another day he would. But now he had discovered cynicism. It made things so much easier. 'What's your name?' he asked.

'Agnieszka.'

He got up. 'Well, Agnieszka, I suppose the best way is to follow me.'

(iv)

Simone found him. Having hurried through lunch she had been first back on the set. At first she thought he was sleeping, and she

305

wondered whether anyone had bothered to bring him anything to eat, or even to tell him where to go.

'Excuse me,' she said, touching his arm. 'Excuse me.' That was when she realized.

The old man was already beginning to go stiff, his head rigid against the carved back of the chair, his fingers clutching the tricolour across his chest. In life he had been widely known for his ugliness, for the dimensions and apparently random and contradictory angles and surfaces of his nose, and his strangely curling chin. In death fate was perversely kinder, and his features had composed into a not ignoble expression.

'Oh, my God!' she gasped.

Markus Muller, the tall German second assistant director who had been vainly following her back in the hope of engaging her in banter of a sexually provocative kind, hurried over. He knew at once. *'Mein Gott!'* he shouted, louder than ever.

Chapter Thirty-seven

(i)

'I'm not reading you, Al. Are you saying there's some problem with the guy with the nose?' Bruno Messenger had stopped in front of his storyboard, a chicken leg in his hand. He had been revising the afternoon's order of shooting with cinematographer Giorgio Pescati and operator Stock Holden. An assistant hovered, ready to pass him a cup of coffee should he signal.

'The problem is the guy's dead,' Al Mutton said flatly. 'Looks like a heart attack.' Behind him Simone stood with Harvey. She was afraid she was about to become hysterical.

Bruno grinned. 'He can't die. He's in the master shot.'

'I'm telling you he's dead, Bruno.'

Simone nodded, Harvey, too. Stock Holden turned to Pescati.

The director was still confused. 'Is this some kind of joke? Because, if it is, it isn't funny.'

Al Mutton shrugged. 'Dead's dead, Bruno. The bastard died.'

'Son of a bitch! Really dead?' He took the coffee.

'Stiff as a board already. He's still sitting out there if you want to see for yourself.'

Simone winced.

'It's very sad . . .' Harvey began to say, but was silenced by a growl from the director.

'Jesus!' Bruno swore and bit hard into his chicken leg, before dumping it into an escarpment of rice on a paper plate. 'Just when it was finally going perfectly. There's always some bastard.'

'We could get around it if we—' Al Mutton began to suggest.

'There's no way around it,' Bruno cut him off. 'He's got to be there. What do you want, a hole in the middle of the screen and maybe a card up saying: "Sorry, folks, this is where the ugly old bastard with the nose sat but selfishly he died on us, so, if you wouldn't mind, just pretend you didn't see him and we'll carry on without him"? Is that what you're thinking?'

'Hey, come on, Bruno, I didn't kill him,' Al Mutton flushed.

'We'll just have to reshoot the master. It's the only thing.' Bruno was looking at Stock Holden.

The camera operator's face crumbled.

'We can't do that, Bruno,' Harvey said quietly.

'What?'

Harvey cleared his throat, but Mutton continued for him. 'We can't reshoot. Not today, anyway, or this week. The crane's broke. I was going to tell you later, didn't want to bother you with what you didn't need to worry about, but—'

'Hey. Wait a minute! No crane! Is that what you're saying?'

'Some problem with the hydraulics. We could have had a disaster. We were very lucky,' Stock Holden contributed, looking as though he believed it was his fault.

'The insurance will cover—' Harvey began to explain.

'We're not talking insurance,' the director barked. 'We're not talking lucky. We're talking movies. And I'm being jerked around. We've no crane, no back-up crane, and a goddamn stiff in the master shot. Is this what you're telling me?'

'The doctor is looking at the old man now—' Harvey tried again.

'*Now?*' Bruno exploded. 'Now's too late. He should have looked at him this morning. Who hired him? Didn't anyone check on his health? Who is it that's trying to sabotage my film.'

'It's no-one's fault, Bruno,' Harvey began, but was immediately shouted down.

'It's *always* someone's fault. Someone screwed up. And I'm the one who has to pick up the pieces.' And he glared at Harvey, making it clear where he thought the fault lay.

Simone shook her head. Working in the agencies she had known difficult directors, lazy ones, hysterical ones, first timers who were terrified, guys who were stupid, others who were drunk, all kinds of fellows: but Bruno led for sheer brutishness.

Harvey tried again. 'There must be something we can do.'
'Like . . . ?'
There was a silence. Giorgio Pescati mumbled something vulgar in Italian. Stock Holden slumped into a canvas chair, looking like a man who may have risked his life for nothing.
At last Al Mutton spoke again. 'I don't know if this will work, but in these circumstances it has to be worth a try . . .'

(ii)

If anyone could shoot it Giorgio Pescati could. Pescati was a minor artist, a genius of lighting, a two-times Academy Award winner. With his lenses and filters, barn doors and French flags, Giorgio Pescati could breath life into anything, even, it was now hoped, a corpse. Whether he should was never questioned.

Charlie was told when he returned from his giggle in the park, trailing Agnieszka at his side. At first he didn't believe it.

'We have no choice,' Harvey whispered furtively, anxious that as few people as possible should know. 'I don't like doing it either.' His forehead was shining with sweat.

Charlie shook his head. 'Another miracle. Amazing!'

'What?'

'The Lazarus act. You've got to give it to Bruno, Harvey. He's resourceful, all right. Lucky we didn't do the master shot last week.'

'What do you mean?'

'Well, imagine, if the guy had already been buried we'd have had to dig him up, Burke and Hare stuff, and get him back into his costume. It could have been tricky. Corpses swell. The costume might have been a little tight. And then there are the maggots. Maybe the Grave Digger could have helped. He knows about corpses. Why don't you call him and ask his advice? He could do us a very nice funeral here with all the trimmings.'

'Jesus, Charlie, have you been drinking or something? You're one sick bastard, do you know that?' Harvey replied. 'Don't say anything, will you? And who's that?' His eyes had fallen on Agnieszka.

'Why would I say anything? Who would I tell? No-one would listen,' Charlie said, then, nodding towards the girl, added: 'She's a Polish orphan looking for her dead grand-father. Seems to me she came on the right day.' And he led an astonished Agnieszka away behind the camera. He wanted to be sure they both had a good view.

For once the crew really did have something to gossip about. Beverly, from make-up, said the thought of it made her feel sick. 'No. Absolutely not,' she hissed. 'There's no way I'm going to make-up a corpse. It isn't hygienic. God knows what he might have died of.'

'Look at him,' snapped Al Mutton. 'He died of old age, for Christ's sake!'

'And so will I before I put a powder-puff anywhere near him. And no one's borrowing my equipment either.'

'Jesus Christ!' said Al Mutton.

'Whatever happens, Yale mustn't know,' Harvey muttered as he moved between the members of the crew. 'Just don't let on, OK?'

'She'll never notice,' Al Mutton counselled confidently. 'The bitch is as blind as a bat without her lenses, which she doesn't wear when she's filming. Anyway, the only thing she ever looks at is the mirror.'

The slack-mouthed young executive from Buffalo Pictures, in Poland to ascertain why things were going so slowly, loosened his collar. He had been applauding the four minutes seven seconds single take that morning, now he looked as though he was wondering how this would look on his curriculum vitae.

'Robert Redford didn't give seminars on how to handle a flakey lady and a corpse at the Sundance Institute, right?' This was Charlie.

Sam Jordan, because he had to look directly in the old man's direction, had to be told.

'Get out of here,' he exclaimed, cocking his Napoleon's hat askew. Then he laughed. 'Don't worry. I've worked with some of the biggest stiffs in Hollywood. Yale will never know. I'll make like the old guy's having the time of his life.' And, grinning mischievously he went up to the corpse and gazed into the old man's staring eyes. 'What d'you think, old fella? Is there anything out there? Is it like *Flatliners*, or more like

310

Heaven Can Wait? Hey, if you bump into Napoleon tell him he's going to love his close-ups.'

Leaving Agnieszka with the crew Charlie crossed the street to where a costume assistant was making some last-minute examinations of Belinda's dress.

'It's gross, Charlie, you know that, don't you?' she said.

'Yes.' He hesitated. He gazed at her. She looked beautiful, extensions to her hair falling in ringlets around her shoulders. 'Jack Dragoman, I think he likes you,' he said.

Belinda didn't reply.

'Well, anyway . . .' He was embarrassed. 'Good luck this afternoon.' And he quickly returned to the activity around the camera, where a group of riggers had formed a wall to block the views of inquisitive extras. Behind them Al Mutton knelt on the pavement rubbing rouge into the corpse's cheeks.

For a moment Charlie considered advising Harvey to call off the shot and insist that Bruno reconstruct the scene. But he knew there was no point. Harvey would never have the nerve to disagree with Bruno. If Bruno had wanted to fill the entire scene with corpses from the town morgue it was doubtful that anyone would have stood in his way. They were so far behind schedule that so long as Bruno kept shooting no-one was going to complain over a dead Polish octogenarian with a double hump-backed nose. Nobody even knew the man's name.

It was a late start after lunch, Yale Meredith being encouraged to stay in her trailer until shooting was about to begin, while the camera crew rehearsed their moves with the help of the other actors and Yale's Austrian stand-in, Helga.

Normally it would not have been a difficult scene. Napoleon would be walking Marie Walewska through the crowd of welcomers, when an attempt would be made on his life by a Cossack spy, Sirhan Sirhan-on-Bobby Kennedy style. In the mêlée, however, the Cossack would catch the hem of Camille de Malignon's cloak with his dagger. At this point Napoleon would leap to her rescue, thus setting up a conflict in her mind: could Camille de Malignon kill the man who had saved her life?

At last they were ready. Fully reassured that no-one ever looked more beautiful, Yale Meredith emerged from her trailer and took her place in front of the camera. For some reason she was in a bright, almost flirtatious, mood, clucking at Bruno, even smiling at Sadie.

From behind the camera Charlie watched suspiciously, glad that Alice Bauccio had been waylaid, asked by Gully Pepper to help select some transparencies of Yale for publicity. Alice missed nothing.

Bruno, meanwhile, was becoming nervous. 'Hey, come on, you guys,' he grumbled through a mouthful of chocolate, as the focus puller measured again the distance between Sam Jordan and the camera, before adding in a louder voice: 'We'll be shooting the rehearsal everyone. So, *concentrate*. Ready now.'

'Where the hell's the goddamn snow?' Al Mutton bellowed.

Tony Delmonte, the first assistant director, shouted a command into his walkie-talkie and the blizzard recommenced. 'OK! Sound!' he called to a man wearing headphones and sitting on an orange box at the back of the pavement.

'Sound rolling,' came the response as the boom operator stepped forward and suspended his microphone over the stars.

'Mark it.'

Nimbly, the clapper loader, dashed in front of the camera. 'Twenty-five, take . . .' he started.

'Er . . . could I have a word with you, Harvey?' Yale Meredith had suddenly noticed the producer among the arc of observers.

'Jesus!' spat the director into his chocolate.

Harvey looked nervously towards him. 'Can it wait, Yale? Couldn't we just get the shot?'

Yale Meredith's concentration washed away. She looked as if she were about to cry, like a child who has suddenly woken and found herself in strange surroundings.

'Now look what you've done,' Bruno Messenger hissed at Harvey.

Operator Stock Holden switched off the camera.

Harvey hurried forward. 'Yes, Yale . . . ?'

'It's my trailer.'

'I'm sorry?'

'My trailer.'

'Your trailer?'

'Save the snow,' bawled Tony Delmonte. The blizzard ceased.

'Yes. My trailer. It's too small.'

'Christ Almighty!' Bruno spun away, his face a pudding of frustration.

At his sleigh Sam Jordan's grin spread wide.

'Yale . . .' Harvey's bald head was bobbing nervously on its stalk. 'Do you think we could discuss this later?'

'According to my contract, the producers shall endeavour to provide me with the best and biggest trailer available in the countries in which the film is in production,' Yale Meredith quoted her contract from memory. 'The biggest and the best. Right? But I've noticed that Sam here . . .' she smiled at her co-star for the first time since she had been in Poland, 'Sam's is thirteen inches longer and six inches wider than mine.'

That made Sam Jordan smile even more. 'What about that, old fella,' he murmured towards the corpse. 'Thirteen inches longer and six inches wider. Can't be bad, eh?'

'And something else. My toilet isn't sound-proofed. It can be very embarrassing.'

But not too embarrassing to prevent her mentioning it in front of the entire cast and crew, thought Charlie, wondering how he could ever have been attracted to this mad, spoilt woman.

Harvey stared in bewilderment at the leading lady, who, to everyone's consternation, now moved and stood directly by the sitting corpse.

Glancing at the lights Charlie wondered how long it took before dead bodies began to smell.

'It's the biggest trailer we could find, Yale . . .' Harvey began weakly.

Yale stared at him. 'Harvey, if Sam has a bigger trailer than I do, then mine cannot be the *biggest* trailer you could find, it must be the *second* biggest trailer you could find. Right?'

At this point Bruno Messenger led Harvey forcibly four paces away. 'What the hell is going on?' he demanded for all to hear. 'This is deliberate, isn't it, you little bastard? Whose side are you on?' Then turning back to the leading lady he said: 'Yale, I'll sort this out, I promise. No problem. You'll get your trailer.'

Yale smiled. 'Thanks, Bruno. I knew you wouldn't let me down.'

She had played her little game for the day, Charlie thought. She had humiliated the producer and won another battle. Now perhaps they could see some of that four-million-dollar magic.

Glancing around Charlie's eyes fell on Sadie. She was giggling, a schoolgirl in silent hysterics, stuffing her sleeve into her mouth to disguise it. He dare not meet her eyes. She was probably the only sane person there. Thank God for Sadie Corchoran.

313

'OK, can we go for one now?' Bruno yelled again.

'First positions everyone,' Tony Delmonte shouted. 'And snow makers . . . now!'

As the blizzard recommenced the actors returned to their starting positions.

'Ready everybody,' this was Tony Delmonte.

'Camera rolling,' called the focus puller.

'Sound rolling,' came the sound man.

'Mark it.'

Again the clapper loader sprinted in front of the camera. 'Scene twenty-five, take one . . .' he called, and brought the clapper down hard.

'OK, lots of energy everyone in the background . . . And . . .' Bruno waited as the young man playing the Cossack spy nervously adjusted his hold on his dagger. 'Action!'

For a fraction of a moment there was stillness before Napoleon pulled off his hat, bowed low at the feet of Marie Walewska and began to walk her through the crowd, followed by Sadie and Belinda.

Slowly the dolly grip slid the camera along the tracks as the couple, their eyes never leaving each other, moved past the old man to enter the hotel together.

Well, well, it's going to work, thought Charlie. The seconds during which the camera passed the corpse would be too quick to show his lack of animation.

Suddenly, through the crowd of extras, came a bustling and pushing, more violent and earlier than in any of the rehearsals. With a roar the Cossack spy hurled himself at Napoleon, dagger in hand.

Everyone could see disaster looming, but it was already too late to stop it. The actor playing the Cossack was too soon, too nervous, and had taken the call for more energy too literally. Yale Meredith was hardly past the corpse when he attacked. The lunge meant for Napoleon and scripted to catch Camille de Malignon's cloak missed both targets and, as he lost his footing, the Cossack fell heavily against the slender, perfect body of the most beautiful woman in America.

For a moment Yale Meredith struggled to keep her balance. But then, as the Cossack's weight became too much, over she toppled, throwing out her arms to save herself towards the old man sitting in his chair.

The old man did not, could not, try to catch her; the stiff old man whose glassy stare greeted Yale's beautiful eyes as

314

her face fell against his, her momentum sending him and his carved, uncomfortable chair flying off the pavement and into the street.

There was a terrible hush. Yale Meredith, the enchanting, mystical Yale Meredith, was sprawling in the snow, her face and lips pinned under the rouged skin and frozen, cracked mouth of a ninety-year-old gargoyle of a corpse.

For a moment she lay gasping, trying to push the corpse's mouth from hers. Only, as realization struck, did she begin to scream.

'And *cut!*' said Tony Delmonte.

(iii)

Up in the otherwise deserted scaffolding eyrie Billy stared down the 200mm lens of the Arriflex at the kicking, screaming, beautiful actress.

'Oh dear,' he murmured. But he carried on filming.

If Harvey hadn't tried so hard to discourage him from being around that afternoon Billy might well have taken his team off to recce the site for the Battle of Borodino as he had originally planned. Poor Harvey. It was just one thing after another.

Chapter Thirty-eight

(i)

A s Simone left him Harvey was scratching his bald head so vigorously she thought he might be about to draw blood.

'Of course we're in control. But film-making isn't an exact science, you know, Julie. And Bruno wasn't really thrilled when the crane broke down. Jesus, how do I know if the guy had medical insurance? This is Kapolska, Poland. Even the Pope didn't have medical insurance when he lived in Poland.'

Closing the door on the turret office Simone made her way to the basement where she ordered a large vodka and tonic at the bar, took out the lemon and sucked it. She needed the drink, she told herself. She had not quite recovered from the shock of discovering the corpse, or the ensuing black comedy when the ambulance driver had requested Sam Jordan's autograph on his duty roster before he would remove the body.

'It's like there's some goddamned curse on this entire production,' Harvey had moaned as he had taken the call from California.

But Simone knew it wasn't only bad luck. She had seen megalomania on the hoof before, albeit from the sanctuary of the agencies. Things are containable in Los Angeles. Megalomania on location, in the backwoods of Eastern Europe, was different altogether. With the meter ticking on 'Bruno Messenger's movie to end the twentieth century', it was becoming ever-more evident that for him no shot or set could be too extravagant, no whim too extreme, no crowd too large or vista too wide, no delay too long.

Rumours about roaring budget flames had been circulating since filming began, but, with the studio's every request to hurry ignored, and every opinion contrary to the director's own calculated as part of a conspiracy to destroy his masterpiece, urgency had all but ceased to be a factor. Inevitably dreams of glory were spreading. While designer Hal Jobete dressed palaces and equipped armies more splendidly than Napoleon himself could ever have imagined, and costume director Ruth Blumberg dedicatedly copied by the hundred the tiniest details of uniform, Giorgio Pescati was bathing everything in celestial light. As Bruno kept repeating, it was all going to look wonderful. He had stopped saying *when*. No wonder sixty million dollars was the figure now being whispered.

Reaching the dining hall Simone watched the cast and crew settling in for another long, noisy, location dinner. Now several weeks into shooting, new friendships were breeding, new pairs forming. Over in the corner the German crane operator was entertaining the Polish woman with the permed fringe and the tight skirt who worked in the café in town; beyond him were the stuntmen and local girls; further on the whizz-kid film editor was with Sadie Corchoran; Jack Dragoman sat with Belinda Johnson, and Charlie was alongside a new Polish girl. There was something definitely romantic about being on location, everyone felt it, and as if to demonstrate, Markus Muller, the second assistant director, smiled and made room for her. Simone kept on walking. He had been trying to get her into bed since the movie began. It was vaguely flattering, but he wasn't right.

Seeing Gully Pepper with Billy at the back of the hall she joined them. They were, as usual, in full argument.

'You *denied* it?' Billy was incredulous. 'Can you believe this, Simone? Gully has been denying what happened this afternoon to the *Associated Press* man in Warsaw. Doesn't it bother you when you tell lies, Gully?'

Gully pushed the red cabbage to the side of her plate. In the Kapolska red cabbage came with everything. 'Of course not. I'm a movie publicist. If the studio says there's a news black-out, then there's a news black-out. I'm *employed* to tell lies. Can you imagine the fun *The Sun* or the *National Enquirer* would have if we owned up to using a dead man as an extra?'

'But they're bound to find out,' Billy persisted. 'Everyone saw it. Everyone *heard* it. Yale was wailing like a banshee.'

'Alice Bauccio was very upset, too,' Simone interrupted, smiling at the memory of the orange-and-green barnacle hurtling neckless on to the set, demanding to know which bastard had left a corpse lying around for Yale to trip over.

'Alice made it even funnier. Helga, the stand-in, was in hysterics,' said Billy. 'How can you deny all that?'

'Easily,' said Gully. 'It didn't happen. Not in my version. What everyone saw was a scripted scene where Marie Walewska saves Napoleon from assassination by a very old man who then dies in the attempt. It was just a typical day in making movies.' And, noticing that one of the palace staff was summoning her to the phone, she hurried off to make more denials.

'The rumour is Yale's lawyer has already been on to Buffalo demanding compensation for mental damages,' Billy said as they watched her leave.

Simone nodded. 'That's right. Within minutes. She must have called him from her tiny trailer with the noisy lavatory. Personally I think it's a lot of bluff. The doctor says she's fine. At first she was screaming that she was going straight back to Los Angeles, but that was a bluff, too. She needs this picture, and she's being paid a fortune to do it. She'll calm down. She isn't so crazy that she'll throw away a great part and put herself in breach of contract. She'll only push it so far.'

Billy shook his head. 'I can never understand why the studios put up with it all.'

Simone smiled. 'I know what you mean. I sometimes think they're just bewitched, scared of the magicians.'

'Magicians?'

'You know, those guys who've got it right a couple of times, people like Sam and Yale and Bruno. The studios think they're wizards who know some secret spell, and they're terrified of getting on the wrong side of them in case the spell stops working. That's why they always give in, to make sure the spell keeps working. Silly, isn't it?'

'And knowing this, about the spells and potions and wicked witches, you still want to be a producer?'

Simone nodded. 'More than ever. I want to be the good fairy, the person who helps the magicians get their spell right.' She looked across the room towards Charlie. 'Maybe if you and Charlie had had the right good fairy when you started you would

318

have got to make your little five-million-dollar movie with Belinda as Marie Walewska and still all have been friends.'

(ii)

Belinda wasn't spying, but she couldn't not be aware that at the other end of the long table which ran down the centre of the hall, Charlie was sitting with the extraordinary Polish girl the crew had christened Ninotchka. She was certainly a pretty girl, and, in the flickering candle-light of the dining room, rather ghostly, like one of those beautiful heroines of silent films who never appear to be quite real. Had Belinda been jealous she would have wondered who she was.

She was having dinner with Jack Dragoman, who people all over the world knew as Sergeant Harry Twomey from *Bad Penny Blues*. She had never actually watched an episode of *Bad Penny Blues*, not right through, but she knew that it was about the Los Angeles Police Department and was universally liked, and that the man purposely burning his fingers with hot candlewax at her side was one of its most popular characters. What was odd was that in person Jack Dragoman was almost totally unrecognizable from his television role. Maybe it was the slowness of his speech, or his almost priest-like demeanour, but this definitely was not the man usually seen on television beating the brains out of drug pushers and pimps and giving lip to his superiors. The part of Will Yorke called for an idealistic, serious man, and Jack Dragoman was fitting it like a glove.

She had known for weeks that he was interested in her, but surprisingly for such a famous fellow, he had been reticent in approaching, although he had asked questions about her. She had been told that by the girls in make-up.

Now, leaning his arm on the back of her chair, he was talking about acting. 'So you went east and I went west and we learnt different skills,' he said.

'Not that different, I don't suppose.'

'Pretty different. You've acted on the stage. Do you want to know something? I've never appeared professionally on a stage in my life. I don't know anything about stage technique. I envy you. The only audience I've ever known has been a camera.'

'You don't get a lot of feedback from a camera.'

'That's right. But there's no-one around in real life to applaud you all the time, either.'

She frowned, unsure of what he was saying.

'What I mean is, I was taught to become the part, to wear it like a new skin, morning until night. Even when I'm not working I try to do that.'

'You mean right now I'm really having dinner with Will Yorke?'

'Sort of . . . my version of Will Yorke.'

'What about when you play bad guys. If you'd got the part of Hannibal the Cannibal would you have gone around eating people between takes? It would have played hell with the schedule.'

He didn't really see the joke. 'If I was playing a cannibal I guess I'd have to restrict myself to visiting institutions for the criminally insane for my preparation.'

'Ah,' said Belinda, and looked across the hall for Charlie. He would have enjoyed this conversation. Method actors always amused him.

But Charlie was no longer there.

(iii)

'*Making movies, shooting's delayed . . .*'

'*Making movies, so we're getting laid!*'

'Hey, how would you like to be a stand-in?' Al Mutton leant across Charlie to the Polish girl, cutting across the karaoke warbling of a couple of drunken electricians doing their version of *Grease Polski*.

'A stand-in?' The girl mouthed her surprise.

The basement bar was full and sweating with drinkers.

'*Need a retake, hair in the gate . . .*'

'*Let's go again, the action was late.*' The response came from a spark wearing a blond, Olivia Newton-John wig.

'For Yale Meredith. We need a stand-in.'

'We already have a stand-in,' Charlie shouted above the din. 'We've got Helga.'

Al Mutton turned to him. 'No more we haven't. Yale wanted her off the picture.'

'You're kidding. Why?'

'She said she should have told her about the stiff.'

'Uh, oh, location blues . . .'

'Action cut, action cut, are we losing the light?' Other sparks and riggers around the bar were joining in, banging glasses and chairs in rhythm.

'Half the crew should have told her,' Charlie said. 'You should. I should.'

'Maybe.' Al Mutton was wearing his shiny expression.

'Yale wanted Helga out because she's popular with the crew, didn't she?' Charlie said. 'And because she laughed when Yale fell over.'

Al Mutton continued to smile, but said nothing. Charlie noticed now that a couple of specks of white powder were sticking to the hairs in his nose like pollen to the stamens of a red snapdragon. Now he understood the smile.

'Action cut, action cut, is her make-up on right?'

'Well, well . . .' Charlie shook his head. 'There's always someone gets it in the neck, always someone small . . .'

'So, what do you say?' Al Mutton turned back to the girl. 'Do you want to be a stand-in?'

The girl looked at Charlie. She had hung her Red Army coat and fur hat on a peg by the door. Without them, in a black sweater, she looked younger.

'Well?' The associate producer was in a hurry.

Charlie waited. He had been getting on well with Agnieszka, one of those mouth-to-ear conversations, which had involved leaning closely into each other's bodies to communicate. All evening he had been trying to let her down lightly, explaining how difficult it was to get into movies, and now here was the most brutal-looking associate producer in the world offering her a job.

'Extras waiting, the producer will fret . . .'

Al Mutton needed an answer. 'Do you want to give it a go? You're about the right size and build.'

'Yes. I want to do it,' she said.

Al Mutton grinned. 'Of course you do. OK, the production office will get you a room. You ask them about money in the morning. You'll soon get the hang of it. Just don't let Yale see you smiling about anything, and don't get too cosy with the crew . . .' He turned to the bar. 'So, what do you want, another vodka? Hey, Stan!' His bawl cut through the noise of the karaoke. 'Two more of the same again on my tab. See you tomorrow.' And with a wink he barged away, past the drunken figure of Klaus Alberts, the crane driver, who was now semi-smooching with his married date.

'*Uh, oh, location blues . . .*'

With a cackle of facetious applause the entertainment ended as the two sparks ran out of lyrics.

'Does he mean I've got a job?' Agnieszka asked.

Charlie nodded.

'I don't understand. Why?'

Charlie smiled. She knew why. She was very pretty. It could have happened to any other fair-haired girl of that height and size on that evening. But she had shown impeccable timing. The drinks arrived. 'Cheers,' he said.

'*Na zdrowie!*'

'*Na zdrowie!*' he repeated.

Only in movies, he thought. That morning she had caught the bus from Cracow where she wanted to work as an actress but where she usually made an uncertain living as a guide taking tourists round Auschwitz. And now she was a stand-in for one of the most famous women in the world. Only in movies.

'Did you know that I followed you today?' she said.

'No.'

'I followed you from the school. I had asked to see the director, but the man would not let me get close. Then I saw you. I thought a man who walks alone will be able to help me.'

'And then you discovered I was only the writer,' he laughed.

'Yes. The writer. Very good.' She nodded.

'Well, I used to think so. Maybe I will again. I'm surprised they turned you away.' He was actually amazed. He suspected she had made the mistake of approaching Skip Zieff.

'Me, too,' she said, with a laugh. 'I, too, was surprised.'

He looked at her. She had a jokey confidence in herself which was refreshing. She was slender, her face wide across the eyes, going to a pointed, dimpled chin.

Earlier in the evening he had noticed Belinda watching them. She had been with Jack Dragoman again, laughing and joking, having a wonderful time. Every time he saw her she seemed to be with Jack Dragoman. He couldn't think why. He was so wrong for her. Why did women have such terrible taste in men?

'*Na zdrowie!*' said Agnieszka to a couple of stand-by carpenters who were raising their glasses in her direction.

'*Na zdrowie! Na zdrowie!*' came a collective and rowdy response.

Agnieszka smiled. She was already a success.

(iv)

They went for a walk after dinner, Sadie Corchoran and Tim Westwood, she, huddled inside her coat against the surprisingly frosty night, and Tim striding along, his parka undone, his frantic dark hair billowing out in waves, talking all the time and so quickly she sometimes could scarcely tell what he was saying.

He had turned up again during dinner. She had been sitting with the English actor who was playing Marshall Ney, when Tim had suddenly appeared at her side, talking about how artificial snow was better for making movies than the real stuff, and asking her if she knew that Frank Capra used three hundred tons of plaster and three thousand tons of shaved ice in 1946 on *It's a Wonderful Life*. Frank Capra, he said, was his hero. It was over the pudding that he had suggested the walk.

'Why are we hurrying?' she asked, as she trotted after him up the lane past the long line of cars, vans and generator trucks.

He shook his head. 'I don't know. I can only think when I'm hurrying. I feel that if I don't do everything and say everything immediately my life will be over and I won't have done anything at all. Do you know what I mean?'

'I think so,' Sadie said. 'Sometimes I feel the same. That's why I never rely upon anybody else to do anything for me.'

'We're like minds. I knew that as soon as I saw you.'

Sadie smiled to herself. It was virtually a full moon and the boy's face was the palest blue in the reflected light. I'm with a madman, she thought as they hurried along, and it's so exciting.

He was talking again, not looking at her, just gazing ahead as he strode on. 'Of course, that's part of Frank Capra's philosophy of film. The importance of the individual.'

She had to own up. 'I'm sorry, but I'm not certain I know very much about Frank Capra.' Actually she didn't know anything about Frank Capra.

'Really?' He looked astonished. *'Mr Deeds Goes to Town, It Happened One Night.* You must have seen *It's a Wonderful Life.* It's on television every Christmas. James Stewart. The town's called Bedford Falls. All those Spielberg-type films always model their small towns on Bedford Falls. It's about this guy, George, he's James Stewart, who has all these ambitions to travel and see the world, but who stays behind and does the right thing, and marries his childhood sweetheart, and makes the world, or his little piece of it, a better place. But, you see, he doesn't realize it until he tries to kill himself one Christmas when things go wrong and an angel, played by this old guy Henry Travers, shows him how the place would have been if he'd never existed. It's wonderful. I'll get a copy for you on video and we'll watch it together.'

He had said all that so quickly she hadn't quite followed, so she said: 'It's a film about frustrated ambition, you mean?'

'No. Just the opposite. He thinks his ambitions have been frustrated, but they haven't really. It's about how ambition doesn't have to be setting the world on fire. Ambition can be little, too. Doing the right thing, in a small way. That's ambition.'

'Oh yes,' she agreed. But then she said: 'I want mine to be big.'

'Me, too. But there are other ways.'

'Mmm.' They walked on. 'What's your ambition?' she asked.

'Oh, to direct, of course. Like everybody. I went into editing because I want to know everything about the technical side as well, like David Lean. I reckon you learn quicker in a cutting room than anywhere else. After *Shadows on a Wall* I have to get into directing. I'll do it. In a couple of years. Some little movie, you know.'

'Yes,' she said. There was a silence. On the other side of the fence which ran along the side of the road she could hear cattle disturbing as they approached. She thought it was her turn to speak, so she said: 'Are you always like this? I mean, do you often go charging off in the middle of the night giving lectures on film?'

He stared straight ahead, slowing his pace as he concentrated on the words. 'No. Not always. In fact never before. But I'm nervous with you. You're English. You sound like you're

324

educated, and you're beautiful. And ever since I saw you last night I've been thinking about you all the time. And I don't know what to say to you. I just want to get to know you, and I'm scared that if I stop talking for just one minute you'll get bored and I'll lose your interest and I'll have thrown away my chance with you. And to be honest, and I never said this before to anyone, never even thought it before about anyone, I think I'm in love with you.'

He had stopped walking and there was a short chasm of silence. Sadie caught her breath. Then he was off again, hurrying faster than ever, avoiding looking at her.

'God, I'm so embarrassed,' he said. 'I'm glad it's night and you can't see me blushing.'

'Are you blushing?'

'I don't know. My cheeks are glowing, for sure, but it may be the frost.'

She slipped an arm through his. It seemed the least she could do after such a declaration. 'Can we go a little slower, please?'

'Why?'

'I want to remember this moment.'

He slowed. 'Really?'

'Really.'

'Why?'

Sadie thought for a moment and then said: 'It's romantic; my first romantic moment.'

He stopped.

She smiled.

They were perhaps half a mile down the road, standing looking at each other. Beyond them was the Kapolska, almost every window lit up, and beyond it the dark outline of the mountains of Slovakia. Somewhere on a bell tower a clock chimed the half-hour.

'Hey, did you hear that?' he said. 'An angel just got his wings.'

'I'm sorry?'

It's a Wonderful Life.'

'Yes, isn't it!'

He smiled, and then kissed her, warm mouths together, cold damp noses touching, his arms loosely around her, hers flapping at her sides like a penguin.

I want to see me now, she thought. I want a camera up there in the sky looking down at me, Sadie Corchoran, in the middle of the night in a Polish country estate, standing at a roadside with a herd of cows watching in the field behind, being kissed by a madman on my first night as a film actress. Then she kissed him back.

'*Dear Claire,*' she began to revise her letter in her mind, '*You're never going to believe it, but I've had a most extraordinary first day of filming . . .*'

(v)

Harvey hugged the telephone close to his face. He was lying back on his bed, his eyes glazed with frustration. 'Well, no, to be honest, things didn't go too well today, honey,' he sighed. 'But that's all right now that I can talk to you. You make all the difference. You know that. How've you been? Are you taking care of yourself? I called you a couple of times but I guess you must have been sleeping or shopping or something because I kept missing you.'

There was a slight pause from the London end of the line. Then: 'Oh yes, darling. You know that sometimes when I want an early night I will put on the answering machine. And then the following morning when I wake up and find your voice sounding so lonely I am so upset that I have missed you.'

'I figured that was what it was because I called quite late last night, you know . . .'

'Oh darling, I am so sorry. And now you sound so tired and depressed and I cannot be there to comfort you. Is that not awful? Tell me, Harvey, is the *enfant terrible* not making us a beautiful movie? A movie that will make me very proud of you?'

Harvey hesitated. How could she be proud of him? 'Oh sure, he's doing that all right. A *beautiful* movie.'

'Ah good. That is all that matters.'

Harvey didn't answer. It was by no means all that mattered.

She began to tell him how she had been shopping that day, and of all the things she had bought for herself, silly, pointless little gifts which would only interest the rich and idle. But she loved to shop. It made her happy. And he loved to see her happy.

326

He closed his eyes and listened. The sound of her voice was soothing, but the pictures in his mind were wrong. He thought of the dead old man, with his broken twisted nose and sunken cheeks as he had sat in his chair; and the obscenity of the corpse's tussle with Yale in the artificial snow.

He should have stopped it, he knew. A dead extra could only bring the movie bad luck. And this movie couldn't take any more bad luck.

He would never forget this day; the day when things began to go septic; the day of the albatross.

Christmas, 1992

Intermission

Chapter Thirty-nine

(i)

It was the first time she had met him and he frightened her: he was so quiet. She knew it as he came to greet them, flanked by his lieutenants, his lawyers and accountants, and she knew it as he pressed his left hand on top of hers. She knew it in the way he smelt, and in the confident way he smiled at her. All through the negotiations and first weeks of shooting he had stayed in Miami or New York dealing with Harry Weitzman and the Manhattan office. She had never even spoken to him on the phone. Only now that there were problems in shooting was Julie Wyatt included.

What fascinated her was the deference with which Harry Weitzman and the entire Buffalo party were treating him. Harry was the head of the studio, Reuben Wiener's own nominee, yet here he was kowtowing to this slightly fey little Cuban who had suddenly popped up out of a Florida car-park. And here *she* was on the last day of shooting before Christmas, sitting like a raisin in this over-the-top slice of Thirties' Old Spain looking out between the palm trees at the Atlantic Ocean, and feeling his eyes on her body. She didn't like that. She was picky about whose mental skin flick she starred in.

'Thank you for coming,' Gallego had said as the Buffalo entourage had entered the mansion, Harry and herself, Ted Sheh from the legal department, Bukowitz from budgeting, Ernie Sakov from finance and, naturally, Harvey Bamberg. Harry and she had already had a session with Harvey over at the hotel. It showed. Harvey was slightly coming apart. The bounce had gone. Now, in the presence of Gallego, his eyes were strangely glassy.

Gallego would not come apart so easily, she had thought, as he showed them past a silver Christmas tree into his house. He was a serpent, smooth and soft, talcum dry rather than oily, like one of those reptiles Martin Scorsese liked to make movies about.

She crossed her legs defensively. She had just spent two days in Poland trying to bully Bruno Messenger into going faster. It had not been easy. He promised more speed, but he never delivered. She had wondered if Sam Jordan might know a way of getting through to him, but Sam had been too busy to meet her on this visit, although she had sent messages to both his trailer and his lodge. She was disappointed, naturally, but no doubt they would get together later in the shoot.

Now the problem was making sure the shoot continued. They were in Florida because Gallego had issued the next best thing to a summons. If Buffalo wanted more Familia Gallego money they had some explaining to do.

The curious thing was Gallego's calm. He was absolutely still. He had seen his share in the cost of this venture rise by ten million dollars in ten weeks' shooting, but nothing in his expression conveyed that. When he had first become involved in *Shadows on a Wall* he had claimed innocence of the movie business. The skill with which he and his lawyers had negotiated the deal had partly dispelled that, but now his grasp of commissions, fees, mark-ups, foreign sales, video deals and rentals, and general budget and scheduling know-how was indicating something quite different. He was learning quickly.

She looked around the room. Like the house it was ridiculously large, but, apart from the books and a photograph of an attractive, dark-haired woman with three pretty children, it was strangely anonymous, sparse and light with peppermint carpets and glass tables and pale, comfortable sofas. The books made it: they were everywhere, all new and on a variety of topics – history, geography, zoology, finance, oceanography, anthropology. On either side of a fireplace were two paintings, colourful daubs of the pre-school variety which had been expensively framed. A child's doll with a pretty, almost impudently sexy, grown-up face and blond hair, sat on a window-sill. In the garden a bicycle lay by the pool, while on a table was a gossip magazine in Spanish carrying a photograph of Yale Meredith wrestling in the snow with the dead man. Just about every popular newspaper in the world had carried the same photograph. Some enterprising extra had done well.

'What I don't understand,' Gallego was saying, glancing at a sheet of figures which Ernie Sakov had given him, 'is why this director keeps spending our money when you tell him not to. Is he an employee or isn't he?'

'I guess he has a vision of the movie,' Harvey stammered, 'and he doesn't want to let us down.'

'Let us down or let himself down?' asked Harry Weitzman bleakly. Although he had never said it, Julie knew he would be blaming her for dragging Buffalo into this Napoleonic swamp. That was the way it went in Hollywood; in New York Reuben Wiener would be blaming him for the bad publicity and the new fall in the Buffalo share price, down now below nineteen dollars.

'And how can we tell it'll stop at sixty million?' Gallego lisped quietly.

'We have Bruno's word on that,' Harvey said awkwardly. 'The problem with Yale and the dead extra proved expensive. He lost nearly a week there. And the broken crane meant some difficult rescheduling. But now that we're getting out of Poland things will be easier.'

'But we'll be going back to Poland.'

'Well, yes, but later,' Weitzman said carefully. 'We weren't able to complete everything, so after Prague and France we'll be going back for maybe a week, ten days at the most. That seemed the most prudent way forward.'

There was a silence as Gallego considered this. Around him his counsellors and lawyers leant forward in their chairs waiting for his reaction. He was the single centre of decision.

'By the way, did any of you get the chance to see rushes of the English actress, Sadie Corchoran, yet?' Harvey suddenly erupted. 'My God, is she good! A star is born. No doubt about it. I can't wait for her scenes with Jack Dragoman! Believe me, she's sensational! Did I say sensational? Better than sensational! Just terrific . . . wonderful. And so pretty . . .'

Everyone looked at him, a foolish desperate man who never knew when to keep quiet.

At last Gallego spoke again. 'Have we considered the case for abandoning the project?'

Julie was still watching Harvey as his eyes closed involuntarily. When he opened them she noticed that a blood vessel had burst and the corner of his right eyeball was a wash of red.

Harry Weitzman nodded to Ernie Sakov from finance. They had anticipated this suggestion.

'To abandon the movie at this stage would leave us having to write off over forty-five million dollars,' Sakov said brusquely, examining his notes. 'Maybe a little more.'

'We can't afford to abandon,' Weitzman said. 'This far in we can't afford not to finish the movie.'

'At any price?' Gallego said coolly.

'I don't believe it will come to "any price".' Weitzman sounded irritated.

Gallego changed tack. 'What about the artists? They'll be out of contract soon and the movie won't be finished. They'll have us over a barrel.'

'We're talking to Jake McKenzie and the other agents all the time,' Weitzman said. 'I think everyone agrees it's in no-one's interests for them to be unreasonable.'

'What's reasonable?' came back Gallego.

Nobody answered.

At last Gallego said: 'Did you think about firing him?'

'Firing Bruno Messenger?' Weitzman shifted awkwardly.

'Replacing him. When I have an employee who screws me around I get rid of him.'

'In movies, especially a high-profile movie like this, that would be a last resort. We at Buffalo still have faith that Bruno Messenger can deliver us a very commercial movie.'

'Can we see it, the work so far, take a look and reassure ourselves that he's doing the job we think he is?'

'We see rushes every day,' said Harvey, trying again. 'They're sensational.'

'Sure, but what about some kind of assembly, whole edited sequences and scenes.' Gallego looked around the room. He *was* learning quickly.

There was an awkward silence broken finally by Weitzman. 'Bruno doesn't want anyone taking a look at the movie until he's had the opportunity to do some work with the editor, when he's finished shooting.'

Gallego smiled sardonically. 'Do we *care* what he wants? What do *we* want?'

Julie felt her fingers tightening on the file she was holding.

Weitzman let the air slowly out of his lungs. 'It was actually a contractual point we conceded to him,' he said. 'We don't take a look until he's ready to show us.' He tried to joke. 'You know what prima donnas these directors can be about their work being seen before they're ready.'

It was nothing to do with prima donnas, thought Julie. It was outrageous that Jake McKenzie had managed to get such a clause for his client. This was only Bruno's second film.

'Is this usual?' Gallego asked, looking at her.

She swallowed before she spoke. 'It's not as unusual as you might think.'

From the other side of the room Harvey began shuffling his feet, nodding vigorously. 'It seems to me that all these artists are the same. Michelangelo probably didn't want anyone taking a peek at the *Mona Lisa* until he was through. Hell, Nathalie's the same when she's putting on her make-up.'

Everyone ignored him.

Harry Weitzman coughed. 'I don't think there'll be any objection if we ask to see a reel or so of cut material, just to get some idea. Let me talk to Bruno.'

Gallego nodded. He was staring at Julie. She caught him looking and he smiled. She looked away quickly.

Weitzman pushed on. 'At the moment we're less than a third of the way through shooting, and, as Harvey says, the difficult set pieces have been shot first. So after Christmas the pressure will be on Bruno to start making savings. Maybe we won't be looking at such a disastrous overspend as we fear.'

Gallego stared at the sheet of figures. His slightly pretty features had hardened.

Julie watched him. She knew he had already made up his mind. He just had to play the scene. He was enjoying himself. This man likes power, she thought, and she wondered where his wife was and what she was like. Something told her she would always be invisible.

'So we go on,' Gallego said simply. 'You can tell Reuben I'll keep backing him, dollar for dollar.'

Across the room Harvey closed his bloodshot eye in silent thanks.

Julie Wyatt looked at the books scattered across the tables, stuffed into the shelves and piled high on the carpet. For a man who was making his millions from car-parks, hotels and casinos, and who knew what else, Carlos Gallego had an unusual spread of interests. He still frightened her.

(ii)

Belinda would never know for sure why she agreed to spend the weekend with Jack Dragoman. It wasn't because she was in love with him: she wasn't; or that she was particularly attracted to him sexually; that wasn't it, either. But in his Will Yorke incarnation, and she knew no other, he was an upright, serious man who liked her and he hadn't been afraid to ask. Women had been known to marry with less reason.

And then, of course, there was Charlie and Agnieszka, the new stand-in. Were they having an affair? Not quite, she thought, but it wouldn't be long. She didn't mind, she told herself. Why should she mind?

'I should warn you I will want to sleep with you,' Dragoman had said with Will Yorke honesty as she had considered his invitation. That had been the previous day. They had been standing at the back of a ballroom, waiting as the camera rehearsed a long track towards Marie Walewska, who, for the purposes of the rehearsal, had been in the shape of Agnieszka.

'Yes,' Belinda had said.

Not needed for filming they flew to Berlin on the Friday afternoon, the last day before the Christmas break. Belinda was not sorry that she would miss that night's unit Christmas party, but, all the same, she was aware of a slight thrill of truancy as the plane took off. Or was it the shiver of new sex?

Berlin was Dragoman's idea. He had once appeared in a television movie made there, *Berlin Pimpernel*, in which he had played a double agent con-man who smuggled scientists across the Wall. 'It was an exciting and dangerous time,' he said.

'The filming or the smuggling?' she teased.

'Both,' he replied quite seriously.

They took adjacent suites in the Hotel Kempinski and the porter unlocked the adjoining door. When he left them, smug at having met an American television star, she felt awkward. It was so formal. She wondered how they would ever make the

336

jump from colleagues to lovers. They had never even kissed.

'Perhaps we should have some dinner before it gets too late,' he suggested.

She was relieved.

A taxi took them to a small restaurant in the Scheuneviertel where, because they were away from the rest of the unit, they talked not of the film as they usually did, but of their families. His parents were farmers in Indiana and slightly embarrassed by his profession and celebrity. She told him about *Stagger Lee and Hannah*, her mother's ambition and her father's talent. When he touched briefly on the two failed marriages he had had before becoming a television star it was as though they had happened to an altogether different person. Was that how she would one day think of her life with Charlie? she wondered.

After dinner they made their way down Unter den Linden to the Brandenburg Gate and then on to Potsdamerplatz, where he had been filmed smuggling brains from Communism through Checkpoint Charlie. As they walked through the old East Berlin and Dragoman explained the plot and the character he had played his accent changed, his speech and actions becoming more urgent; and for a moment Belinda forgot that this man was usually Will Yorke from 1807.

It was a frosty night as they waited for a cab back to the hotel, his arm politely, if not over-affectionately, through hers. Soon she would be in bed with him, she told herself, and she wondered why. But more than *why* she wondered *who*. Who would make love to her tonight? Would it be Will Yorke or Jack Dragoman, Sergeant Harry Twomey of *Bad Penny Blues* or the Berlin Pimpernel?

For a tiny, panicky moment, she contemplated changing her mind and closing the interconnecting door, but she knew she wouldn't.

It took a little time. They were both nervous. At first he fixed them both a drink and they watched the news on CNN. Then he found a movie channel with Jack Nicholson apparently speaking in German. When he finally kissed her he was tentative as though half-expecting a rebuff, but she encouraged him with her mouth and body, and, emboldened, he put his hand on her breast. Will Yorke's hand or the Berlin Pimpernel's?

At that point haste took over. They were both excited. He undressed her. She helped, slipping out of her pants and unbuttoning him at the same time, his lips searching her body, hers finding him.

Lying on his bed, her head lolling off the end, she opened her eyes and saw the room upside down. It was dark. The light had been switched off, but she could see through the open door to the sitting room that the television was still turned on, with the sound off. It was the scene from *Chinatown* where Jack Nicholson slaps Faye Dunaway's face.

She closed her eyes again as Dragoman pulled her towards him. It wasn't love, not in any sense, hardly even affection. It was sex, and she was glad. And it was then as they made love in the dark that she realized that she could not remember, not properly, not exactly, what Jack Dragoman looked like.

It didn't seem to matter.

He slept afterwards, his head down in the pillow as though hiding it from her. She gazed into the darkness, wide awake. She was remembering her first appearance in a school Christmas play. She had been playing the Tin Man in a junior-high production of *The Wizard of Oz*. Her mother had stayed up an entire night to finish the costume made from aluminium kitchen foil in time for the first performance. The whole family had been there, proud of her. And she had dried. Not once. That might have been understandable. But over and over. She knew those lines as well as she knew her name, but on that night she wouldn't have known her name. Everyone had been kind to her. 'It could happen to anyone,' they had all said. But it had happened to her.

(iii)

In his room in the Kapolska Charlie stared into the amber screen of the word processor Harvey had given him to use. In London his screen was blue. He wondered if these changes could affect what a writer wrote, whether *Apocalypse Now* was written on an amber screen and *Jean de Florette* on blue. He should have been restructuring the middle of *Shadows on a Wall* so that they might shorten it by fifteen minutes and save several million dollars, but, for no good reason, he began to make lists of what he thought might be blue-screen and amber-screen movies. *Broken Arrow* would have been on blue had they had computers in the forties, *The Searchers* would have been on amber, *Kes* and *A Place In The Sun* blue, *On The Waterfront* and *Lawrence of Arabia* amber. Or was it orange?

He was, of course, wasting his time. He did a lot of that. He was a film writer.

For a moment he imagined Belinda and Dragoman in Berlin for the weekend. New pictures filled the screen. Belinda and Dragoman. Orange seemed appropriate. He and Belinda, they had been on a blue screen. Blue had been the colour of the titles in *Day for Night*. Blue on black. They had never seen it together, after all.

From the basement bar came the sounds of the unit party. He would join it shortly and make sure that no-one made off with Agnieszka. Half the crew wanted to go to bed with her; Sam Jordan preened whenever he went near her, Giorgio Pescati charmed, and Bruno frequently put his arms around her, accidentally-on-purpose copping a feel. Even camera operator Stock Holden cast envious glances. For her part Agnieszka waited for Charlie to make up his mind.

He turned off his word processor. The amber faded to black. He just had.

Chapter Forty

(i)

Sadie saw Claire as soon as she got back on Christmas Eve, telling her everything she could think of while trying not to sound as though she was showing off. 'The trouble is it's difficult not to drop names when the people you've been cheek by jowl with, as it were, have some of the most famous names in the world,' she apologized.

'I don't mind. Drop anything you want. Cheeks, jowls, the lot. Have you? Will you?'

As it happened she hadn't. After the kisses among the cows in the Polish lane, Sadie had half-expected to be carried off to a secret editing room in one of the Kapolska turrets. Instead Tim Westwood had politely said good night at the door of her room, and the following day been ordered back to Pinewood. Of course he had telephoned, but by the time she had arrived back in England he had been in California.

'He's had to take a reel of cut material to Los Angeles to show the studio,' Sadie explained, and then blushed as she registered Claire's blank expression. 'A reel of cut material' made him sound like a tailor or butcher. She and Claire had been together for so long, and now, for the first time, they were beginning to speak different languages. Was that a sign of growing up? 'He left me a present,' she added feebly. 'It's a video. *It's a Wonderful Life*. James Stewart's in it. We could watch it together, if you like.'

'*James Stewart?* Oh . . . yes . . .' Claire, with a jazzy new haircut, long at the sides and front, and short at the back, and who no longer wore her slide, looked less than enthusiastic. She had grown up a lot in two months. There was some boy nibbling at the outer fabric of her life.

In the end Sadie watched it by herself on Boxing Day morning. Claire was packing to go skiing with the school, while Sadie's parents always went racing with friends on Boxing Day. Even the woman who lived in the mews seemed to be away for Christmas. With her lover? Probably not. He would be in the bosom of his family. Sadie sometimes wished her family had more of a bosom.

She enjoyed the film, well-meaning ghosts were fashionable again, but she was sorry she was seeing it alone. With the unit she lived as part of a group, spoilt and teased in equal proportions, and now she was missing the camaraderie. She wondered if things would ever be the same again with Claire, and what Tim Westwood's Christmas would be like in California. She didn't know him well enough to miss him, but she missed the idea of having a madman tell her he was crazy about her.

After three days at home she was desperate to get back to work.

(ii)

It was Billy's idea to shoot Penn Stadtler over Christmas. Penn had a house in Chelsea and would be using the break to work on the movie's main theme in his private studio. What could be better than for the documentary to chart the creation of the music right from the beginning?

'Sure,' agreed Stadtler. 'Sounds fine to me.' He was a rock star. He could never get enough publicity.

Billy was enthusiastic. He had done documentaries on rock musicians before and enjoyed the casual, but deceptively thorough way they worked. The day after Boxing Day he and his team – just Freddie, Andy the sound man and an assistant called Debbie – carried their equipment up the path of Stadtler's London home. Benedict carried the clapperboard. He had just begun taking piano lessons and Billy had asked Stadtler if he might bring him along as a treat.

341

A Filipino maid let them into the house, explaining, as she showed them down to the basement studio, that Mr Stadtler was not yet up. Billy hadn't seriously expected that he would be.

'What are you thinking?' he asked Benedict as the boy helped them set up the camera and lights in the studio.

Benedict looked around at the numerous keyboards, instruments, microphones, speakers and the mixing console. 'I was wondering what Penn Stadtler got for Christmas,' he whispered.

There had been little entertaining at the Yeos that Christmas. Billy had had no appetite for it. Still, the bank had stopped complaining about the overdraft, the children had their photographs of reindeer, and Ilse was Ilse. Thank God for Ilse, Billy had thought as she organized their Christmas. Ilse and the children kept him sane. For weeks on location he had lived on the cusp of conflicting whims of vanity, impatience, greed and cussedness. *'Turn that camera off,'* Sam Jordan would rasp for no apparent reason. *'Jesus Christ, no more filming!'* Yale would spit. And even Bruno Messenger, the man who earlier had delayed scenes so that he might be filmed directing them, was increasingly snarling, *'Get that camera out of here!'* It was all piling up, of course, hours and hours of evidence of extravagance, temperament, spite and pettiness. And talent, too. There was a lot of talent around. Billy could see that. But at what price? Ilse liked his old friends better. A Christmas card had come from Charlie in Switzerland. He was with Agnieszka rewriting the big love scenes to be shot in Prague. Charlie didn't complain any more. He just got on with whatever was demanded. Neither did he say much to Belinda. She was spending Christmas with Jack Dragoman. James' Court Hall in Edinburgh might never have happened.

Penn Stadlter arrived just over two hours late, but friendly enough, his baseball cap already in place for filming, the diamond toothpick pushed through his ear-lobe. There was a girl with him, a very young, startling-looking, red-haired Australian model, in a tiny black skirt and vivid cloak, fully six inches taller than he was. He introduced her, then she left, kissing him on the forehead, promising to call him later. Benedict watched without a word, bemused by such glamorous people.

Understanding instinctively what Billy wanted, Stadtler immediately set to work on a melody line. It was difficult not to be impressed. One moment he would be joking with the crew, suggesting to Freddie that he try to disguise the bags under his eyes, and the next be rapt in concentration as he worked at the basic melodic structure, explaining in laymen's terms as he went. After a while, amused by Benedict's open-mouthed expression, he asked him to stand in front of the camera and play a single note at a regular beat while he improvised around it.

'You see, Benedict,' he teased, 'anyone can be a rock star. All you need is one good finger, a toothpick through your ear and about fifteen years' practice.' He knew how to charm television audiences.

They were just finishing when Nathalie Seillans arrived, bounding plumply down the steps, her skirt perhaps even shorter than the model's, her bust projecting out of her half-open coat.

'Ah darling . . . I am not interrupting, no?'

'Just waiting for you,' breezed Stadtler. He had an easy, flirty way with all women.

With not much more than a nod of recognition towards Billy, and completely ignoring Benedict, she squeezed past Freddie to be at Stadtler's side. 'It went well?' she asked.

Stadtler shrugged, and put an arm inside her coat and around her waist. She leant forward and kissed him, more or less in the same place the model had kissed him a few hours earlier. Then taking him by the hand she led him from the studio.

Quickly the crew packed their equipment and made their way back up the stairs. In the hall Billy hesitated. He didn't like to leave the house without thanking Stadtler. It seemed rude. He could hear murmurings coming from a room at the back. Benedict was closest. 'Is Penn in there, Benedict?' he asked.

The little boy peered carefully around a door into the room. Then stopped, and pulled his head back quickly, shocked. He stared at his father, confused.

Billy was already kicking himself. 'Come on then, let's go,' he whispered, shouting in a louder voice as the child hurried to his side. 'Bye, thank you.'

From the inner room came a gurgle of a reply, a giggle and then a soft groan.

Benedict was subdued on the way home as he sat clutching the clapperboard Freddie had given him for a Christmas present. Finally he said quietly: 'Daddy, that lady, she's rude . . .'

Billy nodded sadly. 'I think so, too, treasure. But, if you don't tell anyone, I won't either.'

He wasn't really watching, but the television was on, and he wasn't doing anything else. It was four in the morning, the heating had gone off long ago, and he was cold. Still he made no move to go to bed. Why would he go to bed? He wouldn't be able to sleep, not until Nathalie came in, anyway. He had no idea where she was. When she returned she would tell him she had been out with her girlfriends, and he would pretend to believe her.

He shivered and pulled the new red cashmere cardigan she had bought him for Christmas more closely around his shoulders. He had a glass of Jack Daniels on the table in front of him, but it didn't help. Drink had never helped Harvey Bamberg.

Christmas had passed. It had been desolate. Everyone in the industry was talking about *Shadows on a Wall* as a runaway disaster of a movie, making jokes about the final cost of delivery. He couldn't face them. For the first time in years Boxing Day had passed without a Harvey Bamberg Christmas party.

Nathalie had been acting very coolly. She didn't want sex. Not with him. He could stand that. Just. But what if she didn't want to be *with* him any more? What would there be to live for then?

He wondered who the new man was. It wasn't the Grave Digger. He had seen Edward Lampton himself earlier that evening. He was writing a film script. That had almost made Harvey want to laugh. At any time half of everyone involved in movies was writing a script.

He tried to concentrate on the movie on television. It was in black and white, one of those old classics. Some little guy who looked like Edward G. Robinson was lighting a cigarette which was tucked into Fred MacMurray's mouth. Fred MacMurray was lying in a doorway bleeding. He'd been shot. The picture suddenly faded to black and the end title and Paramount logo popped up on to the screen in a final blare of brass.

Harvey switched off the television. From outside in the street came the sound of a diesel engine as a taxi idled, then the trill of Nathalie as she laughed. The cab driver must have made some joke. Nathalie always flirted with taxi drivers.

Getting up he went into the bedroom and began to undress.

He heard the sound of the elevator. He would not confront her. There was still a chance that *Shadows on a Wall* would confound all the rumours, that they would get it right in the end. Nathalie would love him then.

(iv)

Charlie stared out at the snow. It was falling heavily and the gaily dressed figures on the mountain had suddenly become grey and indistinct. He tried to spot Agnieszka but she could have been any one of them.

It had been his idea to come to Switzerland. Agnieszka had been thrilled. She had never been out of Poland before. The apartment they were staying in belonged to Charlie's agent. They were lucky: it had snowed early this year.

Charlie turned back to his script. Bruno had called late the previous night from Canada where some of the unit had already resumed shooting. He had had some new ideas. Charlie had stayed silent. For every saving he managed to make, Bruno immediately dreamt up two even more expensive shots. They no longer argued very much. Charlie knew his place now, and the arrangement must have suited Bruno. They had, Bruno told him, an extra week to get the script right before the main unit moved to Prague, because somehow they had already fallen behind schedule in Canada. They were starting a new year, but it was the same old story.

Below in the street Charlie could now see Agnieszka treading her way back through the snow, her skis at her shoulder. Even from here she looked dazzling in her new, pale blue ski suit. What was it about these Polish women? When Marie Walewska had latched on to Napoleon she had charmed his entire court. Now Agnieszka, the stand-in for the woman playing Marie Walewska, was the belle of the unit. If she had been really ambitious, as Marie Walewska had been ambitious, she would have teamed up with Bruno Messenger, he had told her. She would never become an empress by hanging about with a writer. But she had just smiled. He knew about the whispers, the spiteful suggestions. She was using him, they said, anyone could see that. Maybe. But, more than that, he was using

345

her. Wasn't that how the world went? He frowned. But it was true. Agnieszka had wanted to become involved in the movie: he had wanted a companion. They liked each other. They were lovers. This was movies. Who could ask for anything more?

PART FIVE

January, 1993

Chapter Forty-one

(i)

Sometimes, it seemed to Simone Estoril, there was a fine line between being a film director and being a lunatic: and on days such as this Bruno Messenger overstepped that line. For, while Sam Jordan was *playing* Napoleon, Bruno Messenger was *becoming* Napoleon.

She was standing with the camera crew on a low hill watching the remnants of the movie's *Grande Armée* struggle through the snow from one horizon of Quebec to the next. It was the fifth such procession of the day, each one almost exactly the same as the last, yet still Bruno was not satisfied. This was New Year's Day in the Canadian wilderness, but if there hadn't been such dazzling snow-whiteness it might also, from this distance, have been the Israelites following Moses into the desert, the way Cecil B. De Mille had seen it. All that was missing was the child who had lost his parents.

She snuggled inside her coat; a fur hat she had bought in Poland covered her hair, now with a racoon streak at the parting where her roots were showing since she had given up dyeing it, while a pair of snow goggles blocked the glare. For once it had stopped snowing. Earlier a helicopter had flown low overhead blowing a storm of fine snow over most of the unit and she could feel sharp crystals freezing to her cheeks.

The scene being shot was a re-creation of the retreat from Moscow, and she would never know how the Canadian casting agency had come up with so many extras prepared to suffer these conditions over a New Year holiday. The magic of movies! Little wonder, though, that as soon as the establishing shots of Sam Jordan, a solemn Napoleon in retreat inside his berliner, had been completed, the star had returned quickly to his hotel, leaving Jack Dragoman trudging with the troops to continue the story. Dragoman was like that. He had to *feel* the pain to get the character right. Sometimes she thought that, in his own way, he was as mad as Bruno.

For Simone it was all rather dreamlike. She had forgotten, if she had ever known, how little daylight there was in mid-winter in Canada. Plans had been well advanced when the unit had arrived and the accommodation was adequate for so far north; but the nineteenth-century replica sleighs which were being shipped from Europe were late, and so were the uniforms. And, when they had appeared, there had been a problem with the snow. Bruno was fussy about his snow. It was the wrong type of snow. In the end he had decided to change the location: and then to change a crane. Titan cranes and cherry pickers are not common in the Canadian backwoods but the Royal Canadian Air Force had obliged as best they could, ferrying them in by helicopter from Toronto. Four days late, the unit had begun to shoot. On the scale of delays for this movie four days wasn't bad.

Now Bruno was sitting on a Ski-doo swathed in a quilted, thermal suit, an outsized toad spilling over the sides of the pillion, observing the retreat through massive army binoculars, his long hair hanging outside his sheepskin hat. It was, Simone thought, like being in one of those war movies with a crazy general who is blind to everything but eventual victory.

At her side Edward Lampton, wrapped from top to toe in an expensive red ski suit, stared at the retreating column. He had given location in Poland a miss while he walked the producer's wife, but now that she was rumoured to be increasingly distracted by Penn Stadtler, he had joined the filming, only to find himself fascinated. He was a strange fellow, this Grave Digger, not really the sober old matinée idol Simone had first thought. They had danced together the previous night at what had passed for the unit's New Year's Eve party and he had told her about the script he was writing. She hadn't laughed at the idea of him writing a movie. She had an open mind and had promised to read it. She liked his manners. He was a gracious man.

'And cut,' Tony Delmonte shouted through a loud hailer. Next to him a worried Canadian second assistant director was speaking in French into a walkie-talkie. There was a new problem. They would have to go again. One of the three cameras had frozen up.

Across the wide, white plain the ragged army came to a halt. It was snowing again.

Later when Simone would try to remember the weeks in Canada she would not find it easy. Sure, they trekked through the snow, this way and that as the whim took the director, they bivouacked, they smashed the ice in a river so that the *Grande Armée* could cross the Niemen, and they were attacked by tame wolves brought from Montreal and Cossacks on horses who came from a Mountie exhibition troupe in Winnipeg. But what else? Well, several of the extras were treated for frostbite and were flown out, and Al Mutton drank too much and had to dry out. That was the trouble with the long nights: there wasn't enough to do. Harvey spent too much time trying to reach Nathalie on the phone, ('I never knew her be out so much. It's good to see she's having a good time,'), Billy filmed Sam Jordan winning a small fortune off some extras in a poker school and Edward Lampton flew back to England to take personal charge of the funeral of an earl. She missed him when he left. Then there were the representatives from Buffalo who came and went, Julie Wyatt shouting abuse at Bruno and Bruno affecting not to hear, and Sam Jordan staying in his room the whole time she was in the hotel. One week Charlie flew in, discussed more rewrites with Bruno and then flew out to write them, and in another Jack Dragoman had to spend two nights in hospital suffering from hypothermia after insisting upon doing one take too many.

Harvey suggested several times that Simone should go on ahead to Prague, where half the crew were already preparing the next stage of the movie, but she stayed. She felt she owed it to the little man. He needed a friend; now more than ever.

Towards the middle of January Carlos Gallego visited the studio. As usual he came with a retinue: two well built young men and two lawyers. Harry Weitzman, under daily siege from Reuben Wiener in New York, was visibly nervous before his arrival; Julie Wyatt stayed in her office, ready to be summoned. Gallego surprised her. He came to her.

'I was thinking that maybe if you're not too busy you might like to show me around a little,' Gallego said, standing at the door, his face creased in smiles, as Cathy, the secretary, backed away. This man had an aura of steel.

'Show you around?' Julie was already rising nervously to her feet. She had been examining the latest processing reports from the laboratory in England: already nearly one million feet of film had been exposed. It was terrifying.

'If you don't mind. Believe it or not, I've never been to a film studio before. This is my first time. Here I am investing all this money in a movie . . . and I've never even been around a studio. I thought it might be nice to take a look while I'm here.'

She gave him the full tour, just the two of them, with Marsha, her dog, trotting along behind, through the soundstages, the workshops, the editing rooms, the dubbing suites. It didn't take very long. Buffalo wasn't like Universal, it didn't have giant sharks and rock falls to thrill visitors. It was just a small, old-fashioned, under-financed studio from more modest days of movie making. All the time the Familia Gallego lawyers sat in their car waiting and the two young men watched a low-budget television comedy being rehearsed.

Gallego hardly spoke as they walked, but he listened intently. He had very quickly grasped film finance: now he was concentrating upon production. 'You studied movies at college, right?' he asked, standing in the gloom of the dubbing theatre as Julie explained how sound was heightened and re-recorded.

'Not really. Maybe a couple of courses. The classic age of the American cinema. That sort of stuff. I majored in psychology.'

He nodded, interested. 'I didn't go to college,' he said simply after a moment. 'But I like to learn things.'

Outside in the pale winter sunlight she was aware that he was watching her again. She refused to catch his eye.

The young men were waiting for him by the cars. She wondered skittishly if they would have bulges under their jackets, but she did not dare look too closely.

'So, thank you for your time,' Gallego said, turning to her. 'I hope I didn't waste too much of it.'

'Not at all.'

There was the slightest pause and then he said: 'My son, he likes the movies . . .' Then he stopped, as though he might have betrayed a weakness.

Then suddenly they were gone, the two cars slipping quickly into the late afternoon.

Julie sighed with relief as she walked back to the executives building. She didn't understand. She wasn't Gallego's type at all.

February, 1993

Chapter Forty-two

(i)

Absently Sam Jordan stroked the rump of the girl lying beside him. She was sleeping stretched on her stomach. Her breath hissed as she exhaled. He measured the shape of her buttocks with his hand and kneaded the flesh, but she did not respond. He stopped. He was exhausted. Perhaps it was better that way. She had been pretty enough, and spoke quite good English, but had irritated him by giggling too much. 'I know old American songs,' she had said during the night, perhaps wanting to please. 'We learn them in school. Shall I sing you my favourite old American song?' He had not replied but she had begun to sing, anyway, a low, smoker's warble: '*Que sera, sera, whatever will be, will be* . . . Do you know this song?' she had asked. 'No,' he had lied. She was a hairdresser, she had then told him, and only did this with very special people. What she had been about to do had been quite special.

'Like special people who can afford five hundred dollars a throw?' he had asked.

'Dollars, yes. Many dollars,' she had agreed. She had had a friend at first, another hairdresser, who also only did it with special people who had many dollars. The friend had gone home at four in the morning, many dollars happier.

Now something was playing at the back of Jordan's mind, trying to be remembered, something this girl had giggled about. She had been amused when he had told her he was playing Napoleon in a movie, and had said something in Czech. When

357

he had asked her to translate she had talked about making up a game to play in bed with him, and that they could call it *Waterloo*. They had learnt about Waterloo at school. That had made her laugh some more. What kind of game? he had pursued. She had shrugged. 'I don't know. Maybe a battle kind of game would be good,' and she had moved on to something she did know about.

He put the thought from his mind, wondering if this Czech Doris Day was ever going to haul ass and let him get a few minutes in front of the mirror before he had to go to work. It promised to be quite a day. Napoleon had to seduce Marie Walewska in a couple of hours and so far on this campaign Yale Meredith was still putting up a solid resistance. He admired her for that. He really did. She was like the lines of Torres Vedras. He had learnt some history, too.

Looking at the girl he wondered if condoms were a certain safeguard against HIV infection, and whether Napoleon had worried about syphilis when he sent his officers out to select prostitutes for him. At least he had that over Napoleon. He could pick up his own girls. He had spotted this one the previous night in the lobby of this Prague hotel, loitering with her friend by the boutique, looking through a German movie magazine. She had recognized him instantly which had been both flattering and disappointing because it had not stopped her driving a hard bargain. In the States Sam Jordan got hookers for free.

He climbed from the bed, and, pulling on a silk kimono he had inherited from a movie about a renegade Vietnam War pilot who goes native in Bangkok, he went into his sitting room and felt in his jacket pocket for his wallet. He was now regretting having promised to pay so much. He had been showing how little he cared about money, but that wasn't strictly true. He liked a bargain even when he was earning twelve million dollars a movie. The other girl had been paid when he had been too drained to think straight. But she had been the cuter of the two: better value. Carefully he pulled out four one-hundred-dollar bills and a single ten-dollar bill. Then very neatly he paper-clipped them tightly together, the ten-dollar bill fourth down. It was the oldest of tricks, but she wouldn't know.

Picking up the phone he roused his bodyguard who slept in the next room. 'Get this tub of lard outta here, OK!' he said, and put the phone down. He liked that expression. *'Tub of lard.'* He had first heard it said in *Carnal Knowledge* about the Ann-Margret character. He often used lines from movies.

Returning to the bedroom he turned on the lights and pulled back the sheets. 'OK, honey! Time to go home.'

The girl turned over and curled into the foetal position. She was a jug-breasted, plump little thing, and now in the strong light he could see that she was even younger than he had believed, perhaps no more than seventeen. He should have guessed from the firmness of her flesh and her eagerness to please: it was her repertoire which had misled him.

'Come on, baby.' This time his voice carried more of a snap. 'I have to go to work.'

She opened her eyes as the bodyguard entered the room. His name was Stanton and he had once been a cop in Chicago. He smiled when he saw her. She made no attempt to cover herself.

'I want dollars,' she said, and yawned. Her back teeth could have done with a little work.

Sam Jordan passed the bodyguard the money. 'Give her this when you get her down to the lobby,' he said. 'Not before.' And quickly he retired to his bathroom, vitamin pills and mirror to prepare himself for Yale Meredith.

(ii)

'No. No way. No tits. No nudity. No any damn thing. I don't want that man's penis anywhere near me. God knows where it's been.' Yale Meredith in full costume dunked her cigarette in a paper cup of cold coffee. At her side Alice Bauccio nodded her shiny, white face.

Bruno Messenger had stopped in the middle of consuming a chocolate éclair, a ribbon of clotted cream forming around his lips. Dressed as Napoleon Sam Jordan stood in front of the fireplace warming the most celebrated backside in America, trying to appear unruffled by the leading lady's outburst.

Harvey stared at the floor, pressing his foot on a bubble in the vinyl which had been laid over the seventeenth-century marble. The marble was beautiful and authentic but the pattern was three centuries worn and had less shimmer than vinyl,

359

and Bruno had wanted shimmer. Now, shimmer they were getting: filming they were not.

It was a stand-off. Giorgio Pescati's camera crew was ready; the bedchamber, a perfect, classical, octagonal room in Prague Castle had been pre-lit the previous day and was divine; and the bed waited, lace drapes billowing gently. It was a room made for elegant, romantic love-making, and Yale Meredith, in her Marie Walewska semi-virginal gown with its tiny, pink, embroidered flowers, was the most exquisite subject for seduction. Except that even before the first rehearsal was finished, she was busy dismantling, questioning everything, taking the sex out of the sex scene.

'What do you mean, no nudity?' said Bruno Messenger, his mouth full of pastry. 'What kind of a screw do you have in mind? Back seat of the car stuff, so no-one can see anything?'

Yale shook her beautiful colt's head. 'Who says they screw at all? How do we know they did? Maybe they did it some other time?'

'What other time?' Bruno looked mystified. 'The script says they screw here, in this scene, so that's when they screw. Here, in this scene. That was why Napoleon sent for her, so he could screw her.'

'I don't think so.' Yale's wide mouth snapped in a grimace.

'You don't think so?'

'She wouldn't do it. Marie Walewska wouldn't screw on a first date. I know her. I know what she feels like. The script is wrong.' With every word Yale's voice grew louder.

Alice Bauccio grinned fervently, her head bouncing up and down again in agreement. It had been a relief for everyone when she had grown bored of rewriting Yale's dialogue, but now she was questioning both the story and history. 'What does a man know about what a woman would do on a first date?' she rasped.

Bruno Messenger groaned. 'Jesus wept!'

Yale's stare was expressionless.

Sam Jordan made a move. 'When you guys have sorted out whether, when or how Napoleon gets laid I'll be at the hotel,' he said, and stalked out of the room with as much dignity as he could muster. Harvey could almost sympathize. It was, after all, his penis which was being questioned.

Bruno swore again.

Harvey looked at his watch. It was already nearly midday.

Another morning had come and gone with nothing to show. They could have had this row back in December in the Kapolska. They *should* have had it last summer in Los Angeles when Yale had agreed to play the part. No nudity! What was this? Every film Yale had appeared in had had her in the nude. Christ, she'd done more nude scenes than Kim Basinger! And what about the *Vanity Fair* cover showing her back *and* front naked in the dressing-room mirror! Or the *Playboy* spread, a laughing, giddy Venus arising, a bare Yale Meredith unashamed on every magazine stand in America. It just wasn't fair. Now when it was their turn to take a peek she was coming on coy. 'You agreed to do this, Yale,' he said quietly. 'It's stipulated in your contract.'

'What's that?' The leading lady's voice macheted into him.

'It was agreed that there would be some nudity.'

Yale shot a glance at Alice Bauccio. 'Look, I've nothing against nudity as such, not when it's artistic and essential to the plot. But not in this scene. I mean, what is this, a porno movie? Is that what we're making here? Because if it is you've got the wrong girl.' Her voice spiralled towards hysteria.

Bruno Messenger tried this time. 'No way, Yale. Believe me, it'll be tasteful. It'll be beautiful . . . artistic.'

'Oh yeah! How many times have I heard that?' Yale's face twitched involuntarily. 'Every time they say that "it'll be beautiful, Yale, it's an integral part of the plot", and every time it comes across like I'm showing my pussy to give all you guys a thrill.'

'But Napoleon and Marie Walewska are *making love* in this scene. People take their clothes off when they make love. How much more integral to the story can you get than that?' This was Harvey.

'Who says they do? Who says they screw? The lousy writer. What does he know? Was he there? Did he watch them?'

Alice Bauccio nodded. 'We're talking exploitation here, Yale. Don't let them use you.'

'Will you just back off,' Harvey snapped. 'No-one asked for your opinion. What the hell are you doing here, anyway? I don't remember hiring you.'

That did it.

'Jesus! You don't have to take that, Alice.' Yale was already walking. 'Maybe when we get some apologies . . .'

Alice smirked. The door slammed after them.

361

Harvey sank into a chair. His eyes closed. Bruno Messenger peeled the paper off a lollipop.

(iii)

The castle was under siege, but, as in most sieges, nothing much was happening. Everything and everyone was waiting for Yale Meredith.

Below the castle, on the Charles Bridge, Charlie studied his tourist guidebook. At least with a big movie a writer got to see the world. It would be four in the morning in Los Angeles, but Yale would already be on the phone to Jake McKenzie; a little later Harvey would pluck up the courage to disturb Julie Wyatt; in the mean time everyone else was passing the time as best they could.

'There's nothing they can do. Nothing that will get them what they want, anyway,' Simone was saying at Charlie's side. Then, pointing to one of the stone statues which stood along the walls of the bridge, she asked: 'Is that the same Wenceslas as the other one?'

'I'm not sure. Everyone seems to be called Wenceslas in Prague,' Charlie answered. They walked on. 'But surely if you have a contract they can sue you if you don't honour it.'

For once Simone pulled her sunglasses over her eyes. The winter glare was bright. 'We're halfway through a movie. What are they going to do? In theory they can sue her. But it'll take years. There's a queue at a court in Delaware where they sort these things out that you wouldn't believe. And who's going to listen to Harvey and Bruno and Al Mutton rather than her. I mean, *look* at them. Brutes. Monsters. That's what they'll look like. Buffalo wouldn't have a hope.' She paused at the next statue. 'Who's that?'

'Er, let's see.' Charlie consulted his book again. 'Oh yes, St John Nepomuk. He was martyred here when Wenceslas IV had him thrown into the river because he refused to reveal the secrets of the queen's confessional. Wenceslas suspected her of being unfaithful.'

Simone leant over the parapet and looked down at the wide, dun river. 'Lousy death, drowning.'

362

'Yes,' Charlie agreed, but he was more interested in the movie. 'So, what's to be done?'

'Not much. If a girl doesn't want to take her pants off, in practical terms there's nothing much they can do about it with someone as big as Yale. Not at this stage. They'll have to accept it. Alice Bauccio has got to her. She won't change her mind. For her to budge now would be a loss of face.'

Charlie smiled. 'The Barnacle bites again.' This was one battle on which he had no opinion. He hadn't written nudity into the script. That wasn't his job. He didn't care how much of their bodies the actors showed. Yale was still ignoring him. He didn't care about that either. 'Maybe Bruno should pick on someone who can't argue next time he wants to film the sex scene of the century,' he reflected.

They walked on among the sightseers, passing other members of the crew enjoying the sunshine. A little way ahead two English hairdressers were taking snapshots of a juggler in a crowd. He knew before they reached them who the juggler would be. Here, among the Czech pedlars selling Russian dolls and alongside the man who played the theme from *A Man and a Woman* on bottle tops, Belinda was recharging herself.

He felt in his pocket and rubbed the lucky penny she had given him in Edinburgh. He always carried it. In the crowd Jack Dragoman was watching her intently, applauding her special tricks, catching her eye whenever he could. He even acted being an audience. Charlie moved on. She didn't see him watching.

(iv)

Sam Jordan put the phone down on Grubermann. Grubermann was his lawyer in New York. Jordan was pleased with himself. He would call it *Sam Jordan's Waterloo*, the game for armchair military strategists everywhere. He would get a percentage of every copy sold and the design would bear his face as Napoleon. For ever. His image would become part of folklore, like *Monopoly* money. The idea was simple. There were two primary players, Napoleon and Wellington, and any number of secondary ones, Ney, Gruchy, Blücher and the rest, generals who were in charge of various divisions. The board would show the area of land around Waterloo, with the crossroads at Quatre Bras, the farmhouse at La Hay Sainte and the hill protecting Wellington's forces. He would leave the details of the game for someone else to design. He didn't have to bother with detail, it was the genius of the idea that was important. If they got on to it now it could be on sale when the movie came out. *Sam Jordan's Waterloo*. Oh yes! What it would do for Christmas! Families all over the world refighting the Battle of Waterloo and for ever associating it with him. That was even better than being a movie star: better even than Paul Newman's salad dressing.

For a moment he wished he had someone to tell, to share his genius, other than his lawyer and the people who worked for Sam Jordan Enterprises: but only for a moment. Perhaps it might also be a Solitaire type of game, like computer chess, he thought, something he might enjoy himself during all the hours of waiting; something for people like him who didn't mix easily.

He went into his bathroom, swallowed a cocktail of vitamin pills with a glass of specially imported Irish Spring Water, and smiled into the mirror. His reflection smiled back and then faded. He hadn't enjoyed hearing Yale Meredith impugn the health and character of his penis. The story of what the bitch had said would have infected the entire unit by now. Alice Bauccio was the problem. She was poisoning Yale's mind. Without Alice he would have got into Yale's pants weeks ago.

His telephone rang. It was Delphine Claviers calling from Antibes. He guessed she had already heard about Yale's mockery. She had it in her head that as he was playing Napoleon and she Josephine a little adventure might be interesting. But she was too old. She was middle-aged, a voluptuous, married, lived-in forty-five, stinking of French cigarettes, her dark skin showing the stretch of two many lazy summers, her liver no doubt pickled in red wine. She disgusted him, as age disgusted him. She disgusted him almost as much as that pale fish Julie Wyatt at Buffalo who couldn't forget something he could hardly remember. Now Delphine Claviers was laughing down the phone inviting him to a weekend on the Riviera when they began shooting in France, a 'little, private weekend away from everything and everybody'. He told her he had to go out and hung up.

Vacantly now he began to go through a selection of publicity stills which needed his authorization before they could be released to the Press. There were fifty-nine in the latest batch. Quickly he narrowed them down to six, and then to two. Finally he selected just one. It showed him as Napoleon on his horse, Marengo. It was a good photograph; very good. With just a little retouching around the eyes, a softening of the nose, a tightening of the jaw and a smoothing of the lines at the corner of his mouth it would look just like him.

Chapter Forty-three

(i)

'Sorry, Sadie, the schedule's been changed,' Skip Zieff apologized.

It was just after seven. She wasn't properly awake.

'There'll be a car for you outside the hotel in thirty minutes. It's scene ninety-eight. Good luck.'

Ninety-eight! Oh God!

Gully Pepper explained the situation on the way across Prague. The impasse had lasted over a week, with agents and lawyers burning the phone lines between Los Angeles, New York and the Czech Republic. Nothing had changed. Yale was still refusing to undress. A decision had had to be made. It had. The studio had given in. Marie Walewska would no longer be seduced in the famous octagonal marble room. Camille de Malignon would instead.

At the castle art designer Hal Jobete beamed with relief as Sadie arrived. He had dressed the room for seduction, for flesh. Anything less would have been a waste. To an art designer it didn't matter much whose flesh.

Perhaps Sadie should have been more nervous, but she hardly had time. As they prepared her, first in the make-up trailer with body pancake to hide her faint bikini line, and then in wardrobe, it occurred to her that she was like a virgin bride being readied for her wedding night.

As she crossed the courtyard to enter the castle, her long skirts hoisted above her ankles, Charlie popped his head out of Harvey's silver car. 'Are you coming in, Charlie?' she asked, going to him.

He shook his head. 'Closed set, Sadie. I'll be thinking of you, though. You'll be terrific.' And taking her hand he pulled her towards him. She bent forward and he kissed her very lightly on the cheek.

Beverly, the make-up artist who had been following her, frowned slightly, as though afraid her handiwork might be ruined.

Jack Dragoman was already waiting in the octagonal room, staring intensely at a wall. He was always serious about his work, but this morning he looked crazed. 'I wouldn't want anyone in that state knocking on my door in the middle of the night,' Sadie murmured to the stand-by hairdresser, giving Dragoman a quick smile. In his trance Dragoman didn't respond. At least he wouldn't have much to say in scene ninety-eight, Sadie thought. It drove her potty when he kept looking over her shoulder the way all those boring method actors did, pretending to improvise, but actually just mucking about with the lines. In this scene she would be doing nearly all the talking.

She looked around the room. It was lit for night, black velvet having been taped to the outsides of the windows, while the light was warm and cosy from the log fire in the marble fireplace. The bed stood like a small altar in the centre of the room on top of the shimmering vinyl. They would be shooting from all angles, Giorgio Pescati explained.

For once Bruno was almost elaborate in his directions as they walked through the scene. 'You've got to remember,' he told them, 'you've both been repressed all your lives. Maybe Will Yorke never even got laid before. I don't know. But if he did he's sure as hell always been consumed by guilt about it. Then along comes this crazy assassin, this beautiful, aristocratic girl, and straight off he's knocked out. Right, Jack? Jesus, she's so out of your class you don't know what you're doing. You just know your guts are bursting for her. You come to her in the night. You know what she's planning. You know she wants to murder Napoleon. You've seen the dagger she carries. Right! You're not sure what you're going to do. You confront her. Will she attack you, too? Will you hand her over to the guards to face a firing-squad? You don't know.'

Dragoman's face was a mask of concentration.

'But you can't help yourself. You're alone. You're both on heat. Take it slowly at first, Sadie. Remember you've got all the time in the world. It's going to be a long night, you know what I mean?'

Sadie nodded earnestly, hoping her expression said that she was used to long nights of passion.

'You make all the early running, Sadie. There's a conflict in Will Yorke's mind between his duty and his body telling him what he wants to do. But in the end he can't resist you. And when you go, when you start to make it, both of you, I want everything you can give me. You're *that* desperate for each other. OK!'

Again Sadie nodded. What did he mean, *Everything you can give me?*

For a closed set it still seemed pretty busy. Inside the octagonal room there were, apart from Dragoman and herself, operator Stock Holden and his focus puller, the sound-boom operator, Continuity Jenny and Bruno himself, while immediately outside the door, a small legion of technicians was encamped around the video link: the sound mixer, stand-by hair and make-up, Bruno's assistant, Judy Goldberg, Al Mutton, assistant director Tony Delmonte, Markus the beanpole and Giorgio Pescati; and, ready to film all of these people watching the filming was Billy and his documentary crew.

'We're going to shoot the rehearsal, OK!' Bruno said as the last electricians left the room. 'First off we'll do the whole scene in one. Keep the energy going. Then we'll break it up later. OK!' He was tugging on his long hair. He always did that when he was excited.

From outside the door Sadie heard Tony Delmonte call for silence. She glanced at the boom microphone as it hovered over her. The operator nodded. The sound was recording.

'Ninety eight, take one,' she heard, and the clapper came down sharply on the board.

She had watched her for months, the dark-haired woman who lived in the mews house. Through her mirror in the eaves she had observed as the woman had greeted her lover, the first exchanges, nervous, the conversation, the first touches, awkward, the kisses: the bed. She had studied her intensely.

It was her only experience of sex. The passion of the first time had surprised her. Sadie had been a curious schoolgirl. She had missed nothing, memorized everything.

There had been no time for preparation, but she knew the lines. She was a schoolgirl about that, too. She was used to learning by heart. Every day she had rememorized the script as it had been changed. The dialogue for this scene had hardly altered: only the location was different. She had done part of it in her audition. Now she remembered the first performance in Edinburgh. That had been the moment she had realized she would become an actress: the red ribbon around Camille de Malignon's neck. Now it was around her neck.

Later she would wonder where the camera went. It came so naturally to her. Once she had begun she had no fear. It was, she thought, like an out-of-body experience, as though she were able to watch and control herself, not as herself, but as Camille de Malignon. And because she was controlling Camille de Malignon she found she could control Will Yorke, too. Jack Dragoman, the fanatical character actor, was responding at her pace. She had never felt such composure.

Bruno had suggested that after Sadie made the initial moves Dragoman should carry her to the bed: but that was not how it played. She led all the time. It was a confrontation. Will Yorke accused her of planning a murder. She did not deny it. *'Only one?'* she countered. *'Only one among so many? How many have died for this Emperor's ambition? How many died for your wonderful Revolution?'* Her voice had been rising, and he reached out to quieten her, to hold her. She struggled, refusing to be silent. They fought. Nothing could still her. She told him of the death of her parents. The details: the guillotine: the fountains of their blood. He listened in horror. She undid the scarlet lace around her neck. He watched. She drew him towards her: it was she who seduced him.

She had no idea where the scene would lead, or when they should stop. Between kisses and touches her dress tore. She felt his hands pulling it from her as she struggled with his shirt, his breeches. She felt his breath and kisses on her breasts, his hand between her thighs, and she remembered the mirror and the woman in the mews, and how she had pushed her face across her lover's stomach, kissing her way downwards. Dragoman's body was firm and white. She smelt his skin. She could feel his erection against her and wondered if it was normal for an actor to become excited when playing a love scene. When she had first met Dragoman and felt no attraction she had been afraid that she might not be convincing when she had to kiss him. But it wasn't him she was kissing. It was Will Yorke. And she was Camille de Malignon. And it *was* exciting.

She remembered the urgency of the lovers in her mirror, the way the woman had struggled on top of the man, how she had lowered herself on to him, holding him down, dictating the terms of passion. In the marble octagonal room Sadie's body was now entangled with Dragoman's, the two of them held by the lace drapes of the four-poster bed. She was naked. The woman in the mews had never known that she was being observed, and now her student had forgotten that she, too, was being watched, was being filmed. Her only thought was Camille de Malignon. She knew she was sobbing, unexpected tears running down her cheeks on to her body and on to his. She could feel him thrusting upwards against her. Her breath was coming in gasps, her body straining for release. She pushed down and down on him. Again and again. At that moment she was Camille de Malignon.

'And cut!'

(ii)

Charlie watched on the video monitor as Sadie sank back on the bed. Continuity Jenny tossed a gown over her. The screen went black. The sound operator alongside him lifted his headphones off to speak to the watchers.

'They ran out of film,' he said. 'They're just changing the mag.'

There was an awkward silence. At last someone spoke. 'Now we know why he shot the rehearsal.'

The door opened into the octagonal room and the clapper loader hurried in with a new magazine of film, followed by Beverly, the make-up artist, her face a question mark of astonishment.

Slowly, quietly, conversation rekindled. Charlie glanced at Billy. He looked upset. Billy was a father. He had always been protective towards Sadie.

'Well, well, Sexy Sadie,' said Tony Delmonte. 'Who'd have

guessed it? Not bad, eh!' He grinned lewdly at Charlie.

Charlie didn't answer. Sadie Corchoran was the most unself-conscious, unembarrassed actress he had ever seen. She was at ease with her emotions and with her body. She was extraordinary. But she was only seventeen. If Bruno had wanted to do this why hadn't he arranged for a body double? It wasn't fair.

He slipped from the room and went to find Agnieszka. He had never much liked peep shows.

(iii)

They had lunch brought in and ate it apart from the rest of the crew in a separate dining room in the castle. Bruno didn't want to spoil the mood with any outside distractions. Did Sadie imagine it or did she discern a new attitude towards her? It was a thoughtful time. Jack Dragoman looked awkward, embarrassed perhaps, and not quite sure what to say to her. Bruno said little from behind his mountain of fettuccini. When he did it was in a hushed tone to Al Mutton.

She was hungry. Making love, *simulating* making love, had given her an appetite. She wondered if the woman in the mews had gone back into the kitchen after her lover had left and made herself some scrambled eggs. She hadn't been able to see the kitchen through her mirror.

In the afternoon they got back to work: back to love-making. Now they shot the same scene from two other angles and then twice more using different lenses. After that Giorgio Pescati came in and they filmed it all over again with a hand-held camera, just the sex. This time it was mute and the sound of the camera was very loud. Pescati stood over them looking down, and knelt beneath them peering up. Dragoman never quite got his pants off. Sadie never kept hers on.

They broke at eight. By then she had lost count of the number of times she had pretended to be ravished.

She gazed comically at herself in the long mirror of her hotel bedroom. She was naked other than for one of Napoleon's three-cornered hats which she had tipped over one eye, and which the

371

girls in the costume department had given her as a souvenir of this day. In her hand she held a glass of champagne which she had taken from the mini-bar. Such extravagance. This was her second glass. Carefully she made an inventory. There was a bruise at her waist and two more on her thighs where Dragoman had gripped too tightly. But it was not the bruises that intrigued. It was her body. Neat and white and slim, she wasn't much more than flat chested. Twisting sideways she viewed her bottom. It was small and flat. Turning back she gazed at her triangle of black pubic hair; next her thighs, her stomach, her schoolgirl breasts, dark nipples against the blue-milk of her skin, and then back to the dark heart shape of her pudenda. Pudenda! She liked that word. It made her smile. Reaching for her glasses she looked again, all over, top to bottom. 'Pudenda, pudenda, pudendam, pudendae, pudendae, pudenda,' she intoned. It had been a joke of Latin homework when she was eleven. Finally, she shook her head. 'I dunno,' she muttered aloud to herself. 'Frankly, I can't see what all the fuss is about.'

(iv)

Belinda didn't know how she felt about it. Had they or hadn't they? It was the talk of the unit.

'Everything but,' Dragoman said. 'Sadie was extraordinary, as if she knew something about the scene nobody else did.'

Belinda puzzled about this over dinner in the hotel dining room. She knew that half the female members of the unit were making grumbling noises about exploitation, but one look at Sadie said that she didn't care. She was the same jolly schoolgirl, jollier tonight than ever it seemed.

It wasn't just the sex. Sadie enjoyed being on camera: something happened to her on the set. Belinda had noticed it on their very first day, and in every scene Sadie had appeared in since. The girl simply forgot herself.

Belinda couldn't forget. Every time she had to appear before the camera she was terrified. If she was good it was because fear made her good. She could disguise the fear from others, from her parents, her drama-school teachers, directors, even audiences, but never from herself. She had sometimes

372

tried to tell Charlie, but he wasn't an actor; he wouldn't have understood.

She felt increasingly like an impostor. She wasn't really a movie actress, not the way she had once imagined she might be. She was in the wrong place, doing the wrong thing. Little wonder that the part of Monika Wyszynska was the first to be cut every time a saving had to be made; in truth, she was always secretly grateful.

She tried to put her insecurities from her mind. It was a night of relaxation for everyone. One of the clouds which always hangs over a movie in production had been dispersed. A sex scene had been shot. The rumours were that Yale Meredith had not been best pleased to hear about the success of Sadie's day. Belinda liked that. Anything which aggravated Yale Meredith amused her.

'Can we share the joke?' Charlie was passing, carrying salads for himself and Agnieszka.

'Oh, it's nothing. How are things with you, anyway?' It was a polite enquiry.

'Same as ever. Bruno wants me to reshape the middle of the movie so that we can see more of Sadie undressing.'

'Will you do that?'

'I suppose so. If that's what it takes. If I don't someone else will. At least I'll have some control.' He looked unhappy for a moment but immediately cheered. 'I saw you juggling on the bridge again today? They say you're becoming such a tourist attraction Vaclav Havel wants to keep you here.'

She nodded. 'That's me. Still juggling after all these years.'

She phoned Philadelphia before she went to bed. She wanted to talk about those early days when she had first begun going to drama classes. She wanted to know what it was that had prompted her to follow her parents into the business. She couldn't remember any more.

Chapter Forty-four

(i)

T he pebble hit the windscreen of the Noblesse American and ricocheted away. The car heaved to a halt.

'Jesus!' Harvey exclaimed from the back seat. 'Did you see that? This is a new car.'

'And that's a vandal.' This was Sam Jordan.

Frank Bennetti, the driver, swore. Jordan's bodyguard, who was sitting in the front, climbed out of the car.

A man of about forty, wearing an imitation leather jerkin and work trousers, was standing on a mound of dry mud by a tangerine neon sign at the entrance to the hotel car-park. He was making no attempt to run away although two of the hotel porters were hurrying towards him.

'The cheek of the bastard! Look at that! Just standing there.' Harvey was flushed.

Charlie opened the door of the car and got out. Harvey followed. Sam Jordan looked faintly amused.

The man was shouting something in Czech, waving his arms and pointing at the Noblesse American.

Jordan buzzed down his window. 'Is he crazy or something?'

Charlie shrugged. 'Crazy? Who knows? He's mad, for sure.'

It was the unit's last day in Prague. They had been just leaving for the airport.

'Isn't it always the same when you've got a plane to catch! There's always some joker,' said Harvey, looking over the polished surface of his car for any abrasions. It wasn't uncommon for a film unit to be the subject of local hostility.

'Maybe I should take care who I ride with next time,' Sam Jordan called through his open window. His personal chauffeur had taken his car to Paris the previous day to be able to meet him there, and it amused him to accept the offer of a lift rather than take his replacement car and unfamiliar Czech driver.

Across the driveway the shouting was continuing.

'It sounds like he's saying something about Sam,' Harvey said, satisfied that the car was not damaged.

'Maybe he doesn't like the idea of Napoleon as a redhead with a cute backside,' Charlie muttered. He was irritated because Harvey had insisted they travel to the airport together so that they might talk privately, packing Agnieszka off on the unit bus, and had then killed any chance of conversation by inviting Sam Jordan along, too. When it came to sucking up to the above-the-title billing Harvey had few equals. 'What's he saying?' he called to one of the porters.

'It is a mistake,' came the reply. The porter looked embarrassed.

'Yes. But what's he saying?'

The porter didn't answer.

At that moment a bolus of spit landed on the side of the car as the man briefly broke free.

Jordan pulled a face in distaste. 'Well, come on, what is it?' he snapped imperiously, in a tone he had perfected for his Napoleon masquerade.

The porter shrugged. 'OK. I tell you. He is a madman. He says, "Sam Jordan, you are a criminal. You should be put in jail. You are a child molester." He says you slept with his daughter and she is only fifteen years old. And then you cheated her out of ninety dollars. "You are a bastard." He says he should kill you.'

There was an embarrassed silence. The bodyguard caught the driver's eye but said nothing.

Jordan hesitated, but his equilibrium remained. 'He said that! Fifteen years old? Well, what do you know!'

Harvey looked awkward. 'We'd better be going. We'll miss the plane.'

More spit hit the car as the three men climbed back in.

'Sorry about that, Sam,' Harvey apologized.

Sam Jordan sniffed. He was staring at the stone thrower who was still being held by the hotel porters. A police car was whining into the drive. For a second a shadow of doubt crossed his face, then, putting his hand into his pocket, he withdrew a wallet and pulled out several hundred-dollar bills. 'Tell him to buy something for his family,' he said, shoving the bills into one of the porter's hands as the car started. Then quickly he buzzed up the window and shut out reality.

'That's the trouble with fame,' Harvey tried to joke. 'Always some bastard trying to pin something on you. Isn't that right, Charlie?'

Charlie raised an eyebrow. 'Let them eat cake, eh?' he said.

Jordan didn't answer.

'Lucky we've got bullet-proof glass here,' Harvey babbled on, keen to change the subject. 'There's no way some hooligan throwing a stone is going to shatter these windows.'

Sam Jordan stretched back in the black kid seat, his handsome face a mirror of indifference.

There was no doubt about it, Charlie thought, as the Noblesse American drew rapidly away from the struggling man, there was no armour like fame.

On the plane Harvey insisted on sitting next to Charlie. He was fidgeting and nervous. 'He's despicable, right?' he said.

Charlie didn't answer.

'Fifteen years old! Jesus!'

There was a silence.

'Bruno, too. Only he's a megalomaniac. They're wrecking our lives, Charlie, you know that? I'm taking a couple of days off. Nathalie's in Paris. She still has her place there. She'll know what to do. She's a wonderful woman. Wonderful.'

'Yes.' Charlie said.

After some reflection Harvey spoke again. 'Things haven't been too good there recently. I think maybe sometimes I disappoint her.'

Charlie looked at the little man. Despite the location catering he had lost weight. He didn't look so ripe any more. 'We all disappoint sometimes, Harvey,' he said. 'It's the way life is. Things will be all right when the movie's finished. You'll see.'

Harvey stared at his hands. 'Will this movie ever be finished?'

Tim Westwood sat alone in his cutting room. It was lunchtime. His two assistant editors, and the four other editors brought in to cut the battle scenes, had gone off to the canteen still joking about the morning's rushes. He didn't see the joke. He would have thought they might have become used to it by now. The stuff had been coming through all week. He had heard the rumours before he had seen the material. 'Expect a surprise,' Continuity Jenny had warned. It had been more than a surprise.

Sitting in the darkness of the Pinewood viewing theatre he had felt the blows to his heart as he had watched. He had wanted to stop the film, to pick up the phone to the projectionist and tell him to bring up the house lights there and then so that nobody else would see. But he had just sat there, shocked into immobility. On the first day the footage had run all morning: over three hours of watching Sadie being undressed and degraded. Since then her naked body had appeared in rushes three more times. She had no embarrassment, no sense of modesty. That morning she had been touching herself in some of the later takes while watching Will Yorke from a bedroom window. Bruno Messenger had specifically asked for that, script supervisor Jenny had recorded on her continuity sheets. Jenny was one of those in the unit who thought Sadie was being exploited.

He didn't understand it. How could she? He had kissed her once in a lane in Poland and imagined making love to her, not in this violent, sexual way, but romantically, black and white, through a filter, Frank Capra style. Now he wanted to scream in outrage. There was no mystery left. Every part of her body had been examined in pornographic close-up. The freshness that had captivated him had been spoilt.

He didn't call her any more. He wouldn't have known what to say.

He pressed the forward lever on his Steenbeck viewing machine and found himself staring at a close-up of Sadie's thighs and body, Dragoman's face resting on her breasts, his hand between her legs.

The young editor ached with the pain of it. He was in love with this girl. He didn't want the world to see her in this way. How could she allow Bruno Messenger to abuse her like this?

Chapter Forty-five

(i)

They were talking about him, he was certain. The staff were looking his way and whispering. The other place at the table was empty. He had booked for two at a restaurant which had been their favourite before they were married. Nathalie was well known there and would chat with the waiters. He had liked men to admire her then, and in Paris Nathalie had always been admired in restaurants. Now Harvey sat alone. Was that what they were whispering about?

'I'm sorry, Harvey, but would you mind having dinner without me,' she had said. She had been lying in bed, her Walkman headphones on, speaking loudly as though she were deaf. She was over fifty (Harvey knew her real age so she couldn't deny it to him) and had suddenly developed an interest in rock music. It struck him as being slightly ridiculous in a woman of her age, but he never said that.

He had looked at her: she was a little slimmer these days, her bosom hidden beneath a black *Shadows on a Wall* unit T-shirt, and her hair had been lightened and restyled into a bob like one of those young girls out of *Vogue*. Vadim, the dog her mother looked after when she was not in Paris, had lain watching him on the bed, on *her* bed. At least Vadim had been welcome there. 'But we *planned* it, Nathalie. I was looking forward to it. Don't you remember? I called and asked you and . . .'

She had looked uncomfortable, bored. But then a phrase of the music on her headset had distracted her and she had looked away to the photograph of Penn Stadtler in the CD cover lying on her pillow, and her fingers had tapped out a rhythm to the music.

'I'd really appreciate it if you could spend some time with me . . .' Harvey had begun again, but then stopped as those famous, fleshy lips had edged that sad downward millimetre from pout to bored sulk. At that point he had had to leave the room.

Now he looked at the empty place at the table and toyed with his food. He shouldn't have come. Eating alone was a habit he thought he had left behind. The waiters were still looking at him. One of them guffawed and tried to hide it. People did still laugh at him. These days they had more reason than ever. He was failing, *Shadows on a Wall* was failing: and he was losing Nathalie.

He found a note in the hall requesting that he did not disturb her when he got home. Very gently he tried her door. It was locked. She must already be sleeping, he decided. He was undressing in the spare room when the telephone rang.

It was Gully Pepper. She was still in Prague. 'Sorry to disturb you, Harvey, but I thought you ought to know we have a problem with the Gellini marble floor.'

'I'm sorry?'

'The one in the octagonal room in the castle where Bruno shot all the screwing.'

'What about it?'

'We're getting complaints from the Czech Ministry of Culture that our art department covered the marble with some kind of fake marble vinyl linoleum . . .'

'That's right.'

'Using some kind of *super*-glue.'

'What?'

'Yes. Right! Apparently the stuff won't come off. The way they're calling it here is that we've ruined a perfect late-Renaissance marble floor. It's supposed to be one of the best preserved in northern Europe.'

Harvey shook his head in frustration. Bruno had wanted *shimmer*. That had been the word. And Giorgio Pescati and Hal Jobete had got it for him with vinyl linoleum and super-glue. Directors were the last dictators: they asked and they got. 'What about the insurance . . . ?'

'We're not sure. We've been on to legal, but Ted Sheh thinks it might not cover it. Besides I don't think that's exactly the point. All the insurance in the world isn't going to bring back Alberto Gellini to do them another floor.'

'I guess not,' Harvey said bleakly. He was watching a mental replay of himself pressing his foot on a bubble in the vinyl during the stand-off with Yale.

'I've had the Czech papers on this afternoon, and a couple of the agencies. I thought I'd better warn you. It could be a public-relations disaster.'

'Yes, I can see that,' Harvey said. A public-relations disaster. Why not? They'd had every other kind.

Thanking her, he put the phone down. It rang again immediately. This time it was Simone to tell him that some of the movie's equipment had been impounded at Prague Airport on the orders of the Ministry of Culture. 'They're very upset about the marble floor and want some kind of commitment from Buffalo before they'll release the stuff,' she said.

'What kind of equipment are they holding?'

'All kinds. Lenses, wardrobe, wigs. A real cross-section. Al Mutton says there's certain to be quite a delay before we can start shooting in France.'

'It's the albatross again,' said Harvey.

He was in bed, worrying, when he heard her. For a moment he thought she might be calling to him, but then he recognized her laugh: it was the laugh Nathalie used when she was flirting. Getting up he noticed that the light on the telephone was on, indicating that the line in her room was being used. He hadn't heard the phone ring, so she must have telephoned out. Only for him was she asleep. Stepping into the hall he stood by her door listening to her murmuring. The words were too low for him to catch much of what she was saying. Perhaps she couldn't sleep and was calling one of her girlfriends, he thought. But another low, dirty laugh told him that she was not.

Returning to the spare room he sat on the edge of his bed. It was so undignified, a woman like Nathalie screwing a rock star.

March, 1993

Chapter Forty-six

(i)

Somewhere above the Arctic Circle, Julie Wyatt put on her reading lamp. There was no sleep in her. The plot of the movie she had watched after dinner still irritated: she had had the script in development at Paramount and been happy to leave it behind when she left. That it was showing as inflight entertainment so soon after its release reassured her that at least she knew a stiff when she read one. She sighed miserably. Who was she fooling? She wasn't paid to spot stiffs. Any idiot could do that. She was paid to pick winners.

On the seat alongside her a copy of *Time* magazine lay open on the movies page. She had read the article several times already. Now, glancing across the aisle at the sleeping figure of Ted Sheh from the legal department, she began it again. In an interview about the troubles at Buffalo, Harry Weitzman had managed to mention her name four times with reference to *Shadows on a Wall*. It was, the reader was left in no doubt, *her* project. And that, in Hollywood-speak, meant her *fault*.

Fumbling in her purse she pulled out a packet of cigarettes. It had already begun: the company was distancing itself from the movie. She was the one who was going to have to carry the can. Even Harry was slipping out of the side-door, finding more pressing things to do trying to calm Reuben Wiener and corporate nerves in New York. It wasn't fair, but it was the way these things were done. The real bite had been in the last line: '*With shooting nowhere near complete and the two stars almost out of contract,*

383

movie insiders are saying some smart footwork will be needed soon to prevent Shadows on the Wall *from being Buffalo's last kick.'*

It was true; 21 March had been circled in everyone's diaries since Christmas. That was the day the extensions on the Sam Jordan and Yale Meredith deals ran out. After that Jake McKenzie could ask for a moon each for them and get them. Today was March 18. Weeks of talking had achieved nothing.

But he won't ask for the moon. He has points in the movie, a small voice inside Julie's head argued.

Common sense mocked her. Points in a seventy-five-million-dollar, out-of-control nightmare! *Net* points! Jake would forget his points. They all would. This movie was never going to recoup. There would never be any net.

The plane roared on. She thought about Sam Jordan. He had avoided her in Canada, but he had been under a lot of pressure. Maybe this time . . .

She pulled up her window blind and tried to look down. Somewhere below in the darkness lay Greenland. She hugged her blanket closer around her shoulders. It was getting cold everywhere.

'Look, er, I wonder . . . maybe you should try to get Bruno to show you a little more of the cut material,' Tim Westwood said awkwardly, fidgeting nervously with a splicer.

Julie frowned. She had come directly from the airport to Pinewood, more of a whistle-stop courtesy call to cheer along the editing team than anything. It was nine in the morning and the editor looked as though he hadn't slept, deep purple bags hanging under his eyes, his brown hair curling out seemingly uncut for months, unbrushed for days. The gossip was that sometimes he had even been sleeping in his cutting room.

'I think that might be tricky, Tim,' she said. He was leaning against a two-screen Steenbeck editing machine on which she could see separate close-ups of Sadie Corchoran and Jack Dragoman. What she actually meant was that if Bruno found out that she had been viewing assembled material without his permission there was no telling what kind of row would follow. 'We'd better wait.'

Westwood grimaced, his loyalty stretched by worry. 'Sometimes rushes can be misleading,' he said after a moment.

From the next cutting room Julie could hear the scream of film being run at very high speed through a viewing machine with the sound turned up. This was by no means the first time Tim had tried to get her to see the movie. There had been all kinds of hints. But could they take the risk of upsetting Bruno at this moment? She would have to talk to Harry. 'I tell you what. Let me come back to you on this,' she said. 'Maybe you could be running the material some time and I could just happen to come around, sort of by accident.'

Tim Westwood smiled a slight relief.

(ii)

When she had gone Tim returned to his editing. He hated it, but it was the fate of editors in movies to be inevitably at the centre of conspiracy. The director conspired against the studio, the studio against the producer and the producer against everyone. They all told the editor secrets and bad-mouthed everyone else, and the editor had to pretend to know nothing.

He felt guilty about making his worries so obvious. He was betraying Bruno Messenger who had hired him. But he was in a difficult position and he *was* worried. This movie had real problems.

The door opened from the next cutting room. Basil, one of the older editors he had brought in to cut the retreat from Moscow, peered at him. 'Ah, Tim, I thought I'd better wait until she left . . .'

'What? I'm sorry?'

'You haven't seen it, have you?' Basil looked sheepish. He was a rather polite, slightly bookish kind of man, with a long, untidy beard.

'Well, I guess not, whatever it is.'

Basil stepped further into the room and held up a tabloid newspaper. 'I don't think you're going to like this very much, old boy . . .'

Charlie considered the high walls of the bathroom, the wide washbasin, webbed with tiny cracks in its enamel, the polished, shining, bare pipes. He liked France. There was a robust feel about these old châteaux. In the Hotel Château de l'Abondance, near the town of Arras in Artois, he could smell dinner cooking two floors below. He didn't eat much but he liked the ritual of a French dinner.

Stretching forward he used both hands to turn on the large hot tap. A heavy torrent of water thundered into the bath sending a cloud of steam into the air. He had once read that Napoleon had lain in his bath for at least an hour every morning, having it topped up with hot water by his valet while the newspapers were read to him. A hot bath, Napoleon had reckoned, was worth four hours' sleep: in Charlie's equation a hot bath could, on a good day, produce enough ideas for two pages of script.

Napoleon. He had been daydreaming again, just for a moment back in his bath in London starting out on his play and waiting for Belinda to come home. The pictures in the steam had been different in those days. He had lost sight of the real Napoleon since the movie began; had been unable to imagine him as anyone other than Sam Jordan for months now. Lolling back in the water he struggled to recapture the images he had first dreamt. From nowhere Belinda appeared, bright and optimistic as she had been in those days. He didn't catch that dazzling smile so much any more. He couldn't blame her. No-one ever had a duller part in a movie. He hadn't been able to do anything with Monika Wyszynska. Belinda's great chance had ended up in soft-focus background while Yale Meredith looked beautiful and Sadie got on with acting everybody else off the screen.

'Jesus, what is she up to now?' Yale had whined the previous day as Sadie had carefully counted chestnuts in a corner of the frame while Marie Walewska had been looking at the rubies Napoleon had given her. A few weeks ago those big eyes would have welled with tears, but now Sadie just shrugged. Yale had sulked all day.

'You know she calls me a little English slut,' Sadie had confided one lunch-break.

'I don't think she really means it,' Charlie had consoled.

'Oh, I do,' Sadie had laughed. 'She's completely crazy. I've never known anyone so consumed by envy. She resented her first stand-in because the crew liked her and now she hates Agnieszka for the same reason. It doesn't seem to matter how beautiful or talented or good she is herself, she wants what everyone else has, too. She's a greedy girl.'

A greedy girl. It was true, but they were all greedy. *He* was greedy. Movies made you greedy. Dollars greedy. Sex greedy. Prestige greedy? He hesitated. He wasn't sure about that, any more. He was now a skilled secretary, writing as he was instructed, manoeuvring around the obstacles as they presented themselves, doing his best to find a way to satisfy Bruno's whims while keeping Buffalo as happy as was possible under the circumstances. He wasn't complaining. He was good at rewriting to order. Perhaps one day he might become a rich Hollywood script doctor, thinking up cute exit lines for stars to say so that they could steal the scene, rearranging other writers' work at the asking and the paying. Or would he rather swing on a star and be a Beverly Hills gynaecologist like the chap in *Animal House*? He smiled to himself, but the stray joke brought him back to Yale and the game she had played with him. In her mirrored world of self-absorption she would have no idea of what she had done. He had been a moment's fancy: a tiny victory, quickly forgotten. He remembered without desire their love-making. Then he thought of the gurgle of amusement as she had passed the phone to him. He pictured Belinda's expression as it must have been. A face in the dew on the bathroom wall; a face on the stage in James' Court Hall. *'Lie to me, Charlie, tell me I was brilliant.'* There had been no need for lies then. She had been good, but so frightened. She had never got over the fear, although he had pretended not to notice. She had always been terrified. Perhaps it would have been easier if he had never encouraged her.

The sound of the bedroom door opening told him Agnieszka was back. She came straight into the bathroom, her wide, pretty face breaking into a smile as she saw him. She was so easy to be with. How could a man be unhappy when he had Agnieszka.

'I've brought you a present, Charlie,' she said, kneeling at the side of the bath and passing him a paper bag. 'Something to help you write.'

It was a small plastic Napoleon. Unscrewing the famous hat he found three small biros, blue, green and red.

'A different colour for every rewrite,' she said. She was learning quickly.

'We'd need a rainbow,' he joked, thanking her as she leant over to kiss him. He was touched. She liked to give presents. Her mouth was wet. She smelt of lavender.

Making herself comfortable on the floor she began to gossip. There had been another tantrum from Yale, this time directed at Alice who had made the mistake of interfering while Yale was talking to a reporter from *Paris Match*. In the end Yale had bawled, 'For Christ's sake, Alice, who's he interviewing here, you or me?', and Alice had retreated in tears. Agnieszka chuckled as she repeated the story. Alice had regularly demonstrated her disdain for anyone as lowly as a stand-in.

Charlie listened fondly. It might be miserable for everybody else but Agnieszka was having such a good time with this movie. The hairdressers had cut her hair and Ruth Blumberg, the costume designer, had been out with her to buy some new clothes. The stern commissar of that first day in Poland had disappeared. It had been a false image. This girl loved shopping, loved France. Just the idea of America stunned her. 'When we finish the movie we will go to Hollywood, Charlie, yes?' she would say sometimes. 'I must learn good English, then I can act in English. Maybe good French, too.' He admired her enthusiasm. She had slipped so easily into his life; perhaps too easily, he thought as he listened to her now, because sometimes he felt she was reshaping her personality around his. And he wondered how she would have been if she had met somebody else in the park that day.

He didn't delude himself. They were only together because of the movie. It was a location affair.

They made love in the hour before dinner. That was what people did when they had affairs on location.

There was much excitement in the hotel dining room. Sadie was staring through her large glasses at an English newspaper, surrounded by a group of hairdressers and make-up assistants, her expression a contortion of surprise. A few yards away Billy and Freddie were filming her.

'Have you seen this, Charlie?' It was Belinda.

Sadie turned the newspaper around to show him. 'SCHOOL-GIRL STAR "LOSES VIRGINITY" IN FILM SEX SCENE', read a large headline on an inside page. Alongside was a photograph of Sadie in her Queen's Yard uniform and another of her sitting naked on top of Jack Dragoman.

Charlie looked at the piece. There was always gossip. He was actually surprised it had taken nearly four weeks for it to reach the newspapers.

'God,' Sadie was muttering. 'My mother will knit her knickers!'

Gully Pepper ran a hand angrily through her red hair. 'The story didn't come from here, and it isn't true,' she snapped to anyone who would listen.

Charlie swallowed a smile. Like all propagandists Gully could be very jealous of anybody else's lies.

(iv)

She did the easy bit first.

'*Dear Claire, Just in case you believed them, rumours of my deflowering are, as I told you, grossly exaggerated. Naked as an apple I may have been, but, word of honour, infacto I'm still intacto, although I'm beginning to understand why it's all the rage. Write soon, love Sadie.*'

Slipping the postcard into an envelope she wrote the address and propped it up on her bedside table. She looked at her watch. It was just after eleven French time. Ten in London. They would probably be home by now. There was no way out of it. Picking up the phone she dialled her parents. The phone was answered immediately.

'Mummy . . .'

'Sadie, darling, how are you?'

'Oh, you know . . .'

'We've just got in actually, just been talking about you.'

'Well, I was going to explain when I got home . . .'

'Yes. Some woman who lives in the house at the back wanted to know what it was like for us to have a star in the family.' Her mother was laughing, unnaturally friendly. 'We didn't know what to say.'

'In the *mews* behind our house?'

'That's right. A rather striking, dark-haired woman. She was at a drinks party at number thirty-five. You may possibly have seen her through the window. She used to be some kind of actress, I think, but doesn't seem to work very much now. Did she say she was Italian? I think she said she was Italian. After she went Wendy was saying that she's the girlfriend, well mistress, I suppose, of some European bigwig in banking who's set her up in that little house . . .'

In the background Sadie heard her father make a weak joke.

Her mother laughed. 'Daddy just said, "Not in banking, in bonking"! He's very vulgar these days. I think he was a bit taken with her—'

Again an interruption. 'Nonsense,' her father was saying. 'What would I want with a kept woman? I've got my own to keep.'

'Well, anyway, she seems to have seen every film ever made and knows everybody in the film business. I don't suppose she has much else to do if she's waiting about all day for her bonker to call around.' She giggled foolishly. 'But she'd heard all about you. She said the word is that you're going to be tremendous. What about that!' More laughs. 'Anyway, she said she'd love to meet you when you get back. We'll ask her round for dinner, p'raps, on her night off – if I can find a tin opener.' She laughed again. She was, Sadie decided, pretty drunk. It happened.

A dark-haired woman, thought Sadie, picturing the eager sex she had spied on. Could she really have been taking lessons from a 'kept woman'? *Kept woman*. She liked the sound of that. It sounded old-fashioned, decadent. She drew her mind back to the reason for her phone call. 'Look . . .' she began again, 'that article in the paper today . . .'

There was another laugh. 'Oh yes. Very exciting. The things they write. We were very amused.'

'Amused?'

'Well, yes, darling, the very idea that anyone is a virgin at your age these days . . . it's just too preposterous for words.'

Sadie closed her eyes in silent despair. They didn't know anything at all about her.

Her phone rang just before twelve. She was lying holding her script. It was Tim Westwood. He said he hoped he wasn't waking her, although he knew he probably was. One of the assistant editors had a friend who worked in a news agency. He'd had a frame of the film copied and sold it to the Press. He was gabbling even more quickly than usual.

'You haven't phoned recently,' Sadie said, cutting into his apologies.

He sounded surprised. 'Do you want me to?'

'Yes, please.'

(v)

Julie Wyatt's pale skin turned almost bright with pleasure. The biggest array of roses she had ever seen was sitting on the table in her hotel suite.

'They arrived earlier,' the porter explained as he put her bags down. 'Perhaps from the movie?'

'I don't know,' she beamed. Was it possible? Sam? She was so pleased she gave the man a hundred-franc note. He looked at it with astonishment before accepting.

When she was alone she walked slowly around the flowers. Who else but Sam? They *had* to be from Sam? Certainly not Jake, or Harvey. Only Sam. She had been thinking of him all day in London, and then Paris, and in the car on the way up the autoroute to Arras. She was always thinking of him. Roses. He must still care.

Perhaps he had instructed Jake to go gently on the renegotiations. What a coup that would be for her.

There was a small blue envelope with the name of a local florist tucked among the leaves. Reaching for it she caught her thumb on a thorn. A bubble of blood spread from the wound. She sucked it as she opened the envelope.

The writing was in a thin, young French hand. She was still smiling when she read the message. *'With best wishes, Carlos Gallego.'*

Her face crumpled in disappointment.

Chapter Forty-seven

(i)

G ully Pepper might have chosen a better moment to entertain the Press, Billy thought, as he filmed the five journalists picking their way between the corpses towards the location catering van. It was a tense time. Julie Wyatt was skulking about somewhere, there were Buffalo lawyers and accountants all over the battlefield, and Jake McKenzie was locked in a trailer with Sam Jordan.

The sound of a loud hailer cut through the air. *'More blood, more blood!'* Bruno Messenger was bellowing at the art department who had been pumping blood and mud on to fallen extras all morning. *'I want more blood.'* He always did.

They were preparing the Battle of Borodino. It should have been filmed three months earlier in Poland; now it was taking place on a rolling meadow in northern France. As Charlie had commented: 'Napoleon should have been so lucky.'

Spotting Harvey leaning against his Noblesse American eating boeuf bourgignon off a cardboard plate, Billy indicated to Freddie to pan around. Three of the journalists were approaching the producer. The documentary team stepped forward to eavesdrop.

'It looks as though we came on a big day,' a writer from the arts section of *The New York Times* was saying in the fake friendly way of journalists.

Harvey carried on eating, his eyes flashing nervously towards Sam Jordan's trailer.

The reporter tried again. '*Time* was saying that Buffalo may be running out of money to finish the movie . . .'

This time Harvey snorted, but continued to eat.

A third attempt: 'But it is a fact, isn't it, that Reuben Weiner and Candy Corn are losing patience with movies?'

Harvey put his plate down on a prop box and wiped his mouth on a paper napkin. 'I'm sorry, I can't comment on unsubstantiated reports,' he said.

A second journalist stepped forward. She was young and Irish. 'So why don't you substantiate the reports first and then comment.'

Harvey glared at her cheek. 'Will you excuse me? There's someone I have to talk to,' he said, beginning to leave.

'What about the marble floor in Prague. Can it be repaired? Will the insurance cover the damage?' called another reporter. They were hunting in packs today.

Harvey heard but didn't stop, darting away between the trailers, a pink man in a green jacket, escaping from his tormentors.

Billy drew a finger across his throat. 'Cut.'

(ii)

Harvey cursed as he hurried on across the battlefield. He would crucify Gully Pepper when the reporters left. The movie had paid for their flights, was picking up their accommodation tabs and arranging exclusive interviews for all of them with Sam and Yale. And all the bastards wanted was to poke their noses into what didn't concern them. What kind of journalists were these?

He floundered on through the mud. The legend was building. In movies everyone loved a success: but better than a success they loved a runaway heading out of control. *Schadenfreude*. That was what they called it in the smart newspapers. How they would love to read this in the Polo Lounge. Just so long as it wasn't *their* runaway, their career on the line, their marriage falling apart. He tripped over the outstretched leg of a fake corpse and then kicked at it viciously. No, not a runaway; only the budget and Bruno Messenger's ego were running away. And perhaps Nathalie.

393

He stopped and looked around, suddenly aware of where he was. There was mangled, bloody death everywhere. A boy of about eighteen with golden, shoulder-length hair and wearing a Russian infantry uniform was sitting watching him, a sword sticking out of his ribs, a wide stain of blood on his bodice. He smiled when he saw Harvey staring. *'Bonjour,'* he said coquettishly.

'Jesus Christ!' Harvey spat.

(iii)

Julie Wyatt saw Jake as he left Sam Jordan's trailer. He waved to her from the step. For a moment she looked for Sam, too, hoping that he might appear, but there was no sign of him. Harvey was in the middle of the battlefield, looking like a lost, surviving soldier seeking a fallen comrade. But, as everyone knew, Harvey Bamberg didn't have any comrades.

She had been awoken at seven with a call from Harry Weitzman in New York. 'Did you hear from Gallego?' Weitzman had asked.

'Should I?'

'Who knows? I can't figure the guy out. He's here, there and everywhere. He's up to something. He's been in London and Paris talking to bankers. He's there now. I think he likes you.'

She had let it pass without comment. The previous night she had put the roses out on the balcony. The thought of Carlos Gallego liking her had made her shiver. She imagined she could hear the rattle of his asthma, smell his scent, sweet, like a woman's.

Her breakfast had been served with a copy of *The Financial Times*. She had checked the Buffalo stock. It was down again, now at seventeen dollars, twenty-one. Galvanized by this she had arrived at the location early. Jake McKenzie, staying with the unit at the Château de L'Abondance, had got there earlier.

'Let's walk,' Jake said as she reached him, leading the way out towards where Harvey was waiting by an upturned cannon. Harvey was so quiet these days, more withdrawn every time she saw him. Silently he fell into step alongside them.

When he was sure he was out of earshot of any crew, extras or reporters Jake began to talk. His voice was casual. 'Well now, we've looked at this from all kinds of angles and I might as well say right off that the best we can do is an extra half-million dollars a week for any overage for Sam.'

Julie Wyatt's jaw froze.

Harvey coughed. 'You're kidding.'

'That's a joke? Right?' This was Julie.

Jake shook his head, his blue eyes flicking from Julie to Harvey and back.

'Half a mill . . .' She swallowed, and tried again. 'Half a million. You'd *better* be joking.' She looked around nervously. One of the assistants from the props department was helping a man from an abattoir disembowel a dead horse which had just been lowered from a truck. She looked quickly away, hoping no Press photographers were watching.

'No joke,' Jake said.

'You told us you'd be trying to help us out! That you *understood*! Christ, Jake!' Harvey's head and pointed ears had gone very red.

'I'm sorry, but the movie is way behind schedule and it looks as though it will run on for some time. I have to protect my client. God knows how many more weeks Sam could be tied up here.' He, too, had seen the dead horse and was looking slightly nauseous.

'*Your client? What is this?*' Julie Wyatt was almost spitting with rage. '*Bruno Messenger* is your client, and it's because of *him* that we're so far behind; *his* extravagance, his slowness, *his* perfectionism, *his* . . . vandalism . . . his . . .' she gasped: '. . . *masterpiece* . . .'

Jake McKenzie frowned his concerned agent's frown. He had stopped walking. 'Hey now, one thing at a time, Julie. We're talking *Sam Jordan* here, right! Not Bruno Messenger. For the purposes of this meeting Sam is my client, and with the movie overrunning like this he's having to turn down—'

'I know the words,' she snapped.

'You realize you could be adding an extra three million dollars, maybe more, to the budget for Sam alone,' said Harvey. 'This is what you call helping us—?'

Julie interrupted. 'Harry is going to blow. I know it. How are we going to tell Gallego? Supposing he won't pay. What then?'

Jake McKenzie looked saddened. 'Julie, I don't want to tell Buffalo how to run their business.'

'You'll drive us *out* of business.' She fidgeted in the pocket of her coat, pulled out a packet of cigarettes and lit one. 'Jesus, Jake, you could have told us this back in LA. What the hell am I doing walking around a goddamn field in the middle of France?'

The agent sighed. 'Julie, I didn't ask you to come out here. I *had* to come to talk with my clients. *You* came because I assumed you wanted to. And believe me, I've been trying for you. We've tried very hard to help you.'

'What about Yale?' Harvey asked abruptly.

Jake began to walk towards a row of cannons where members of the art department were fixing bayonets to muskets. A young woman in dungarees was pushing a lance into the heart of a fake artillery officer. 'For Yale we would accept two hundred thousand a week for any overage.'

A small cloud of menthol smoke and vapour exploded across the battlefield from Julie Wyatt's bloodless lips. 'You're out of your mind.'

'Is that two hundred with or without her clothes?' Harvey needled, his mouth stretched back across his teeth like some kind of bald rodent.

Jake McKenzie looked irritated, as though Harvey had broken the rules of the meeting and should have known better. A stray sword lay in the mud at his feet. Delicately he stepped over it. 'Come on, Harvey, you know that's a separate discussion, and it's been resolved.'

Julie could feel herself beginning to panic. This was raw agent-power. Jake had a stranglehold on the picture. He'd helped put the package together. Bruno Messenger, Sam Jordan and Yale Meredith were all his clients. Now he was dictating terms like a conqueror.

They were crossing through a line of cannon. Without warning a smoke canister exploded a few yards away. 'Sorry,' shouted Hal Jobete, 'we just wanted to see what it would look like.' The trio walked into the smoke.

'I'm not sure Bruno can finish this movie,' Harvey said suddenly as they headed back towards the cars.

'What did you say?' Jake looked genuinely surprised, as though he hadn't heard properly.

'I'm saying the guy's incapable of working to a budget, to a schedule. I'm not sure he has it in him to finish the movie. Maybe he was always too young. I think we made a mistake.'

'Harvey!' Julie was alarmed.

'Let him finish,' Jake said.

Harvey walked on, defiant now. 'If we're going to have to pay a ransom in overage I think we've reached the moment when Bruno should be replaced,' he said.

'Oh Jesus!' This was Julie.

'You mean you want to fire the director,' Jake replied.

'If that's what it takes.'

They were almost back to the trailers. Lunch had been called and waves of recently dead and dying soldiers were noisily surrounding the catering vans. In a queue Simone was chatting with the Italian costume assistant. She waved when she saw Jake. He ignored her. He was staring hard at Harvey. Slowly he began to speak. 'I think if you look closely at their contracts, Harvey, you'll find that Sam Jordan and Yale Meredith agreed to appear in *Bruno Messenger's SHADOWS ON A WALL*,' he said, his voice as dead as stone, 'not Harvey Bamberg's or Buffalo's or anybody else's. You try to change the director, to fire Bruno Messenger, and you risk losing either of them, or both of them, and having a seventy-five-million-dollar unreleasable white elephant on your hands. I'd think carefully about that if I were you.' He turned to Julie. 'Tell Harry I'll be waiting for his call.' And with that he made his way back towards Sam Jordan's trailer.

'Jesus, Harvey,' gasped Julie, 'don't you think you should consult Harry before you try to replace the director? Bruno will be worse than impossible when he hears about this.'

Harvey stared into the mud and scratched the pale stubble on the side of his head. Across the field the massive, and now seemingly immovable frame of Bruno Messenger stood surrounded by camera technicians and riggers, lining up the first shot of the day, a forty-yard track through the carnage. 'You don't know Nathalie, do you, Julie?' he said.

'He's demanding *what?*' Harry Weitzman erupted down the phone from New York. 'Jesus Christ Almighty!'

'Right!' The executive in charge of production was standing in the middle of a flat, green pasture, a quarter of a mile from the rest of the unit, a cellular telephone to her ear. Some yards from her Harvey waited, his hands in the pockets of his jacket. On a film set a wide open space was the only place they could be sure to be alone.

'Reuben will kill over this. Does Jake have any idea—'

'Jake knows,' Julie interrupted. Behind her on the hill, a scattering of burning carts and wheels was throwing a tar black smoke into the afternoon sky. The Battle of Borodino had begun.

In New York Harry was blustering and blowing. 'Well, that's it. We can't pay it. We *won't* pay this . . . this *blackmail* . . . ! We'll call the whole thing off. Shut down production. I'll show that bastard. Jesus Christ! What a mess! Is Harvey Bamberg there with you?'

'He's here, Harry.' Julie held out the phone. Harvey took it from her. As she walked away she noticed that the three-hundred-dollar shoes she had bought on Rodeo Drive were caked in cow dung. For the first time she realized what a pathetic sight she must make in her black tights and over-short black skirt. On the hill there was a loud explosion, followed by a second and a third. Flames belched into the air. The cloud of smoke was spreading across the sun.

'Yeah, that's right, Harry, a real mess,' Harvey was intoning into the phone, 'a real lousy mess.'

She walked on. At the edge of the field she passed Billy gazing down the lens of the Arriflex at Harvey, his team around him. She looked back: Harvey looked so small. 'Don't you guys ever give anyone a break?' she asked bitterly.

No-one answered.

She nodded. 'Sure, I know. That wasn't the deal.' It would make great television. Disasters always did.

She was in the next field when she saw it, a shining black sedan sliding silently across the grass towards the trailers, its tyres leaving a trail of mud all the way back to the lane. She didn't need to be told who would be sitting in the back seat.

'So, what you're saying is there's nothing I can do to stop this man from going on spending Familia Gallego money to make his masterpiece of a movie. Is that it?' Carlos Gallego tapped his knee with his forefinger.

She nodded, uneasy in this dark tomb of a car.

Running his hand inside his shirt Gallego gently scratched his skin. 'That's very neat,' he lisped.

'There has to be a way out.'

He raised an eyebrow. 'Maybe, maybe not. This Jake McKenzie, he's smart, right? The kind of guy we should have on our side.'

'We thought he was on our side.'

Gallego looked at her. 'He's an agent.'

'The legal department think things may not be so watertight for them . . .' she began.

He cut her off. 'We've all got lawyers. They've got lawyers, too, telling them they are watertight. Isn't that a fact?'

'Possibly,' she conceded.

'And Buffalo want to shut down and gamble on them backing down.'

'Harry's very angry.'

'What did he expect?'

Julie didn't answer. She could hear the air rasping in Gallego's lungs. His eyes looked slightly sunken, but he was, as always, neatly, expensively dressed, in a dark blue suit. He sat very still, his head cocked on one side, staring at her. She folded her arms across her chest.

'What are you thinking?' he asked, glancing at the dirt on her shoes.

'I was thinking . . . I'm surprised to see you. I was wondering why you came. It's a long way from London, from Paris even.'

'Don't you think I have the right to keep an eye on my investment?'

'Well yes, of course . . .'

'I move around a lot,' Gallego said after a moment. He rubbed one soft hand on top of the other. 'You received the flowers?'

She was embarrassed. His eyes wouldn't leave hers. 'Yes. Thank you.'

The car was empty other than for the two of them. Suddenly he smiled at her, the smile of the man who can afford anything in the world and knows no shame in asking the price.

She turned away. Outside in the field she could see three of his colleagues, or were they brothers, cousins, or minders, standing, in their suits, watching the make-up girls sunning themselves. It was the afternoon break and one of the location caterers had taken them a tray of tea and cakes. No-one came near the car, although everyone who passed gave sidelong glances as they hurried on. It was, she thought, as though there was an invisible exclusion zone, keeping back even the most curious.

'I like you, Julie,' Gallego said quietly. 'Maybe you could teach me about movies. Would you like to do that?'

She didn't answer. She was thinking about the roses delivered to her room, about how she had thought they might have come from Sam Jordan. She was thinking how plain, pale girls with top jobs would, for some men, never be anything more than stepping-stones.

Gallego sighed so that his breath moaned in his chest. 'Anyway, I promised not to interfere in the shooting,' he said after a few moments. 'I'll leave that to the people who know. Maybe one day I will know. In the mean time you can tell Harry he has my support in whatever action he takes. Familia Gallego will support him.'

It was the end of the tea-break. Crew and extras were drifting back to the battle. Gallego buzzed the window down and nodded towards his colleagues. 'I have to go,' he said quietly. 'I have things to do.' He had driven a hundred miles from Paris and not set one foot outside his car.

Across the field Julie could see Harvey watching. Gallego saw him, too.

'Tell me, what do you think of Harvey Bamberg?' he asked, as she began to open her door.

'He's in out of his depth,' she said. 'I guess, in a personal sense, I feel sorry for him.' She hesitated. 'And I think he's frightened of you.'

Gallego considered that. 'Some people are.'

'Yes.'

The three young men were back at the car, waiting for her to get out. For the brush of a moment Gallego took her hand and then lowered it. 'Take care,' he said.

It was only as the car slid away across the field that she realized she was trembling. Julie Wyatt knew about scripts. Gallego was from a different movie.

400

Chapter Forty-eight

(i)

Charlie sipped his coffee and read the item a second time. Things always looked different in print. This article in the *International Herald Tribune*, for instance. Anecdotally true, it scarcely began to scratch the surface of the power struggle that had been going on: *'Hailed as the new Treaty of Arras it should all have ended in peace and harmony but last night Napoleon, as played by Sam Jordan, was in exile in Cannes awaiting instructions from his Hollywood agent, while his screen mistress, Marie Walewska, in the shape of Yale Meredith, was lying low in Paris, after they both walked off the set of Bruno Messenger's* Shadows on a Wall *in a dispute over money. So far this troubled production is believed to have cost nearly eighty million dollars.'*

At his side in the bar Billy Yeo was leafing through the *Guardian*. 'NOT TONIGHT, BUFFALO, AS SAM AND YALE EXIT IN MONEY ROW,' ran a headline. 'The trouble with stars,' Billy reflected after a moment, 'is that no-one ever expects them to get up in the middle of the night to nurse the baby. A person can learn a lot of humility at four in the morning with a feverish child.' They had been shooting a long time and he was missing his family.

Charlie put his newspaper aside. There had been such a row when the stars had walked out, but what else had Buffalo expected?

Belinda could hear him from the bottom of the Rue de Callas. He had been at it for two days, shouting and bullying. Normally directors left the bawling to their first assistants, but Bruno Messenger was angry. He was also, she suspected, afraid for his movie. Naturally the Press had made the most of the walk-out, paparazzi mobbing and trailing the stars' cars, reporters mingling with the extras. Now, without the stars to film, the last days in Arras were being devoted to Camille de Malignon's flashback sequences. Not required for filming Belinda and Jack Dragoman were spending the day sightseeing in the rain. Belinda loved the history of it all.

'Did you know that Robespierre was born here in Arras?' she said as they turned a corner and headed back towards the set in the main square. 'Apparently he never ate more than a bowl of gruel a day and died a virgin.'

'Who was that?' Dragoman asked.

'Robespierre.'

'Oh yes.' Dragoman looked uneasy.

She didn't press the conversation. Dragoman was a sweet man, but he was a Hollywood actor; his research only extended as far as his own part. Now he was watching the performance of a butcher in a shop window, concentrating on the muscular arms, the rhythm of the chopping movements, the fat fingers digging into the liver and the smooth, high-blood-pressure complexion. He had, she knew, received an offer that morning to appear in an American remake of a Claude Chabrol thriller about a small-town butcher who murders people, and so far that day they must have stared in half the butchers' windows in Arras. His preparation had already started.

She walked on along the street. Through the open doorway of a corner bar she noticed Charlie and Billy sitting together, Billy's fingers lost in his unruly straw hair as he demonstrated something, Charlie bent over the table laughing. It was good to see them friends again. At the back of the bar, under a faded photograph of Jean Paul Belmondo and Jean Seberg, Agnieszka was sitting at a table listening to Simone, probably hearing more tales of Hollywood. For a moment Belinda wondered if she had the nerve to join them. She hadn't.

'Here you go,' Dragoman said, leaving a fruit stall and offering her a choice from two bags. 'What do you want, an apple or an orange?'

She took three of each.

(iii)

Sadie wanted to scratch her nose, but, because her arms were tied down at her sides, she couldn't. She wrinkled it instead. It was only a death rehearsal, anyway. When the real moment came she hoped she would meet it with appropriate dignity.

She was lying face downwards, strapped to the plank. High above her neck the blade was poised, still shrouded in black. In front of her a basket waited in the straw for her head. To one side a mule and cart stood ready to transport her remains to the lime pit. She peered short-sightedly across the wet cobbles. There had been cobbles in Edinburgh, she remembered, and she thought about Claire and her noisy packet of Polos. Mentally she began to compose the letter she would write that evening: *'Well, here I am again, back behind the arras. Sorry, I couldn't resist that. Actually, not so much behind the arras as up to my neck in it. Arras, France, I mean. Have you been here? I can't remember. If you haven't, let me tell you, it's all cobbles, and apparently looks very much the way the Place de la République looked in Paris in 1793. At the moment I'm waiting to be guillotined. No kidding. I'm lying here with my collar ripped off my dress and my neck out like a goose at Christmas, while everyone dashes about demanding more blood, more straw, more lights. Ah, well, I suppose being guillotined on the cobbles in Arras has to be marginally more entertaining than double history on a wet Thursday afternoon with Skull Tomlinson . . .'*

For a moment she was distracted as across the square she saw a sequence of apples and oranges rising and falling behind a tumbril, and watched as Belinda appeared, cool and beautiful, followed a moment later by Jack Dragoman.

A movement on the scaffold alerted her, and, screwing her head around and rolling her eyes upward, she saw the shroud being pulled away from the blade. Quickly she looked away.

'So, where were we? Ah, yes! My brush with the Reaper. Actually it's only a dream sequence, which poor Charlie has been desperately

trying to turn into sense for weeks. It seems that not only must Camille de Malignon always think about the Reign of Terror when she's having it off, but the audience must see her nightmares, first as a child watching her parents catch it in the neck, and then as an adult dreaming her own execution. I suppose it'll work . . .'

A bellow from across the square interrupted her thoughts. Alongside her on the scaffold Skip Zieff winced and pulled his walkie-talkie away from his ear.

'OK, Sadie, we're going for one,' he shouted, signalling to the make-up artist to add the final touches to the grime and tears.

Sadie lifted her face. The camera was on a platform on the other side of the square, and would apparently be performing a dolly-zoom manoeuvre as the blade fell, which, according to Charlie, was an old, and now abandoned, trick of Steven Spielberg's. She wished Charlie or Billy were with her, but it couldn't be much fun watching a close-up of someone pretending to be guillotined, when the blade was safely locked up there out of harm's way twenty feet above. *'Heaven knows what I'm supposed to do. I suppose Bruno will shout at the right moment and I'll grimace horribly or something,'* she added to herself.

At that moment an executioner in a black coat and a white powdered wig moved to the side of the guillotine. Something seemed to be amusing both Tony Delmonte and Skip Zieff, but Sadie couldn't see what it was. She wasn't happy. It was too quiet; a more or less empty square and only a tiny crew. That morning when Camille de Malignon's parents had been executed the place had been full of people, women knitting, tricolours, soldiers, spikes, drummers.

'Sadie, if you look up you'll see Bruno. When his hand comes down that's the signal for action. Don't do anything until then. It's quite safe. The blade can't fall.'

'I should jolly well hope not,' Sadie said. The swish of the blade that morning, chopping into turnips in the place of aristocrats' necks had been frighteningly realistic, as had the blood which had jetted from the supposed victims. It had been pig's blood, Hal Jobete had told her, and she fancied she could now smell it on the plank below her chin.

She wished they would get on with it. The waiting was making her nervous. She didn't like the way the boom operator was on his knees in front of her pushing the microphone in her direction. Did she have to scream, too? She supposed she must. Why couldn't Bruno tell her what to do?

'OK, quiet everyone. Quiet!' Skip was holding his hand up for attention.

All activity on the scaffold stopped; silence fell around the twin horns of the guillotine. Sadie gazed towards the camera. It had begun to rain quite heavily now and she could feel drops of water running down her face. Across the square Bruno was standing beside the camera. She waited for his signal. And waited.

She was frightened. She wanted it to be over. It was too real. She swallowed. The rain was running into her eyes. Her breath was beginning to come in gasps. She felt unable to breathe properly. For God's sake, hurry. Please!

Suddenly she realized she was trying to wriggle her legs free, to pull her arms out of the straps binding her. She was in panic. She couldn't control herself. *Please!* she was screaming inside. She tried to look around for Skip Zieff, to beg him to release her for a moment while she regained her composure, but she was unable to get her head round. She couldn't act like this. She was going to faint. She stared desperately across the square at Bruno. He met her gaze: he did not move.

'Please,' she gasped. 'Please, someone help me.'

There was no help.

'Please . . . I can't . . .'

The words froze on her lips. Something was happening to one side of her. It was the executioner. She could hear the heavy sound of metal chains on wood as the guillotine was primed. This was wrong. She had heard the same sound that morning, but only when the guillotine had dropped, when it had sliced the turnips. There must be some mistake. The guillotine wasn't supposed to be released. Oh God!

'No!' she shouted. 'No! Please!'

But it was already too late, because even as she screamed she heard the sound of the release of the blade and the heavy hiss of the falling metal as it raced down the frame of the guillotine at her neck.

As it hit, blood exploded. Her screams filled the square.

'My God! What was that?' Belinda stopped at the entrance to the cathedral and looked back across the cobbles.

'Pretty realistic, eh?' Dragoman said. 'Didn't I tell you she was good?'

The screaming was hysterical, wave upon wave.

'Not that good.' Belinda was already running back across the square.

They came from everywhere, from make-up and costume, from the props van, the bus stop, from behind market stalls, out of the cathedral and the bars and the shops, dashing across the cobbles, Charlie, Billy, Harvey, the unit photographer, dressers, location caterers who had been washing the pans after lunch, shop assistants, tourists, bystanders, sparks . . . And still the screaming didn't stop.

'And cut,' Simone heard Bruno Messenger shout as Charlie and Billy raced ahead of her. 'Terrific! You can get her out of there now.'

Simone ran on. Still strapped down across the plank Sadie was sobbing and retching, her face, hair and shoulders covered in blood. Above her neck the light, blunt, plastic replacement blade rested safely across a secure bridge of steel.

Leaning over her, struggling with the wooden collar which held her head in place, was Skip Zieff. 'OK, Sadie . . . OK. Nothing to worry about. You were quite safe. There was never any danger. No danger at all. There you go now, you can move your head. See. It's still there.' He chuckled. 'Pretty as ever.'

'Get out of the way.' Charlie pushed Zieff aside, his fingers already undoing the straps which held Sadie's wrists; Belinda joined him, releasing her feet.

From in front of the guillotine Simone watched as Sadie was lifted gently to her knees, her nose running, her body shaking, an arm up wiping the blood from her eyes with her sleeve. A police car was crossing the cobbles, its siren blaring. The crowd around the guillotine was growing bigger all the time.

'Did they do that on purpose?' She heard Jack Dragoman ask. 'I don't believe this movie.'

Harvey Bamberg was rushing towards Bruno. He had been detained by Al Mutton in one of the trailers while the shot was being lined up. 'Do you know what you just did?' he screamed at the director.

Towering nearly a foot over him Bruno Messenger began to make a leisurely way towards Sadie, accompanied by a swell of assistants. 'Wait till you see it on the screen. It was so realistic, you won't believe. We over-cranked it so that we can show it in slow motion. It was wonderful.'

'For Christ's sake, you could have killed the girl. She could have had a heart attack . . . a nervous breakdown.'

'It's going to be an *incredible* movie moment. *Incredible*. The best moment in the film.'

'And what about Sadie?'

Bruno shrugged. 'Sometimes you have to do these things. It was necessary for the movie.'

Harvey was shaking his head. 'You vicious, mean, mad bastard. You're out of your mind.'

The director wasn't listening. The crush of assistants and extras was carrying him forward to the foot of the scaffold.

Feeling a hand on her shoulder, moving her to one side, Simone looked around. Billy's documentary operator was focusing his camera on Sadie as she was helped down the steps. Billy stood behind him.

'Never trust a man who doesn't know the limits,' Billy said quietly.

They sat Sadie down at the foot of the scaffold. She was pale, wet and shivering. One of the caterers brought her a cup of tea; photographers were taking pictures, a tourist was getting snapshots; and a couple of gendarmes were asking questions.

'No,' Al Mutton said through an interpreter, shaking his head and smiling at them. 'No trouble at all. It was only a movie scream. There's nothing real about movies.'

A few feet away Bruno offered his profile as the tourist took his picture.

Harvey stood watching, his face wretched with worry, his green leather collar turned up against the rain.

Simone wished there was some comfort she could offer. She had never seen a man look so lost.

Chapter Forty-nine

(i)

He was sitting in his car when she approached, a little man in the back seat of a silver Noblesse American, not a car usually seen by the railway bridge in Arras. He had been weeping silently for some time. That was why he had sent his driver back on the unit bus, parked on this slab of waste-land and climbed into the back of his beautiful car. He needed somewhere quiet to mourn, and a cocktail cabinet to raid.

In his mind he was talking to Nathalie, not as he ever talked to her in real life, but in the way he always wished he could. What are you supposed to do, he was asking her, when you reach the bottom? She didn't reply in his imagination either. Whatever happened now *Shadows on a Wall* was doomed to spectacular failure, and him with it. After the obscenity of Sadie's mock execution did any of them deserve better? Not him: not Buffalo. Buffalo had called Jake McKenzie's bluff and it hadn't worked. They had no alternative now but to pay Yale and Sam Jordan what they were demanding. Only God and Bruno Messenger knew when the masterpiece would be finished. It hardly mattered any more: not to Harvey. Nathalie would leave him, perhaps for Penn Stadtler this year, or someone else next. Maybe one of Carlos Gallego's boys would put him out of his misery when Familia Gallego realized how much money they had lost. Harvey shivered at that thought. It was possible, the rumours insisted it was just possible. Jesus, help me, he pleaded, sinking his head into his hands, dropping his glass on to the soft black seat.

A tapping on a side-window roused him. It was already dark and the figure was lit by the yellow of a street lamp. The face looked somehow familiar. He buzzed the window down.

(ii)

Sadie sipped her brandy and continued to write. *'PS Luckily for me the day was sodden with rain and so was my dress because, the fact is, when the blade hit I'm afraid I wet my knickers. Absolutely feeble, I agree, but a rotten trick to play, wouldn't you say? Write soon, or wrong sooner, if you get the chance. Love as ever, Sadie.'*

She put down her pen. She could joke again, just about, see the almost funny side of it: but it didn't mean she wasn't afraid to go to sleep. She picked up the phone to call Tim Westwood.

(iii)

For Charlie there was no even remotely funny side. He was angry: mainly with himself. People only became bullies because other people let them. He knew that. Yet for months he and everybody else had been obliging Bruno's every whim. No wonder the blindfolded rhinoceros was out of control.

Unable to sleep he watched Agniezska's peaceful face bathed in the glow from the car-park which lay in front of the château. He considered turning on his bedside light and doing some work, or perhaps watching television: there was a movie showing on Canal Plus he wanted to see again. But Agnieszka was a light sleeper. It would be unfair. He thought about Belinda. Would she be sleeping; or doing what? And he remembered all the late-night movies on television they had watched in bed together.

The sound of a diesel engine and a growing argument in the car-park drew him to the window. A girl, her hair gelled up like a brush, was helping Harvey from the back of a cab, yelling at the driver in French that it was Harvey's job to pay. Harvey looked confused.

He should have left him to it, let Harvey sort out his own life.

But the little man looked so broken, leaning against the car, his head down, as the girl and driver shouted at each other. Charlie had never seen Harvey drunk before. It didn't look right.

By the time Charlie reached the lobby the row had moved inside. For a moment it occurred to him that the girl, in her over-tight jeans and swelling sweater, looked like Nathalie. She had the same pout, husky voice and uplift to her bosom. But then many French girls of that age, and this girl was hardly a girl, had once looked like Nathalie, and she like them. That had been part of Nathalie's appeal.

Feeling in his pocket Charlie found two five-hundred-franc notes and, thanking the woman for bringing Harvey home, pressed them into her hand. For a moment he thought she might be about to demand more, so he pulled out another two hundred francs for the taxi.

Grudgingly satisfied, the woman told them where to find the Noblesse American ('He wanted to drive . . . I said, "you can't even stand" '), winked insolently at the night porter and slipped out of the hotel lobby back to the waiting cab.

'Jesus, thanks, Charlie. I didn't know how to get rid of her.' Harvey's eyes were red and his breath smelt of brandy.

'Let's get some coffee, shall we?' Charlie said.

'We should have known after the incident with the albatross.'

'What?'

'The old guy . . . the one with the nose who died on us in Poland. He was the *Shadows on a Wall* albatross . . .'

Charlie refilled Harvey's coffee cup.

'We've been doomed ever since . . .' Harvey closed his eyes. 'The guy put a spell on us.'

Charlie glanced at the television. He had turned the volume low to enable Harvey to talk. He enjoyed watching these old, deep-focus, black-and-white movies with or without the sound. 'If he did put a spell on us we probably asked for it,' he said.

'Yes,' Harvey agreed, and went quiet for a few moments before saying: 'D'you know what really bothers me, what really hurts?'

Charlie did know. Harvey had told him many times. Nathalie bothered him.

'Do you realize she's never been out to see what it's like, to take a single look at what's going on. I thought that when we started shooting she wouldn't be able to keep away, that she might even become a nuisance. But there's been nothing. Only the music seems to interest her.'

'Perhaps she doesn't like to be around movie sets now that she isn't in them herself any more.'

Harvey disregarded the reply. 'She hardly even asks how we're getting along, although the whole movie was her idea. I mean, how far is Arras from Paris? A hundred miles? Two hours in a car. Less. I offered to go and bring her up here for a weekend, but you know what she said?'

Charlie nodded patiently. He did know.

'She said she was "too busy". Busy! The woman has nothing in the world to do. Nothing. Yet she was too busy.'

Charlie chose his words carefully. 'Well, let's face it, she isn't missing much in the way of fun, is she? And she never hit it off with Bruno.'

As if grateful for the offer of an excuse Harvey's mood changed from despair to indignation. 'And can you blame her? He's a beast. You were right about him from the start. The man's a . . . *selfish, crazy, ignorant, dishonest, brutal, tyrannical bastard.* Jesus Christ, what he did to Sadie today! What kind of guy would do a thing like that?'

Charlie didn't answer.

Harvey was lying on one side on a deep green sofa, his once-confident, plump body now wasted with worry. Being the producer he had almost the best accommodation in the château, the Bourbon suite, a *fin de siècle* place of much mahogany, Persian rugs, sweeping ceiling-to-floor curtains, dried palms, peacock feathers and green and red velvet upholstery. It didn't suit him: not any more. Charlie remembered how Harvey had once imagined himself as the next high-rolling Hollywood player, the sort of producer *Premiere* magazine would profile, with his fancy cars and fancier foreign wife. Now he looked like nothing so much as a small time hustler aware that what luck he had been dealt had finally run out.

Stretching forward Charlie helped himself from the bottle of whisky left as a gift to the producer by the hotel management. If Harvey wanted company until he sobered up, he might at least meet him halfway. Charlie wasn't a big drinker. He wouldn't have far to go.

He turned back to the television. Barbara Stanwyck was coming on to Fred MacMurray through a heavy gauze. They would be murdering the husband soon and leaving the body

411

on the railway track. This was the movie for which Raymond Chandler had provided the dialogue, which had made Billy Wilder's name. Together they watched in silence for some time. Charlie hoped Harvey might fall asleep, but, when eventually he glanced across, he realized the producer was staring intently at the screen.

Suddenly Harvey sat up on the sofa, easing his weight from one side to the other. 'You know, maybe our mistake was in trying to make the wrong movie,' he said.

'Maybe.'

'I mean, maybe this is the kind of thing we should have done. You didn't need all those extras in those days. What did they have? Two or three stars, half a dozen sets . . .'

'And a brilliant script.'

'Naturally. You can't make any halfway kind of decent movie without a brilliant script. The script comes first, middle and last.' Harvey was flattering Charlie's professional status. It was his way of being friendly. 'No Alice Bauccios on this movie, right!' He was coming back to life.

Charlie didn't answer. The thought of Alice Bauccio rewriting his dialogue still rankled. He watched the movie.

'It's an insurance scam, isn't it?' Harvey said a few moments later.

'Yes.'

Harvey nodded, pleased with himself. 'I think maybe I've seen it before. What is it?'

Charlie sighed. '*Double Indemnity*. And you must have seen it before.'

'I thought so. They bump off the husband and try to claim a hundred thousand dollars.'

'That's the one.'

'Good movie.'

'I think so.'

'The perfect crime.'

'*Almost* perfect.'

'Right! It goes wrong. He kills her, and then confesses into a dictaphone. They always get caught. Even in those days.'

'Particularly in those days,' said Charlie.

Harvey went quiet again as they watched the scene on the train in which Fred MacMurray impersonates the husband. 'Maybe it shouldn't go wrong,' he said at last.

'It has to. If it doesn't the movie would be condoning adultery, murder and embezzlement . . . all kinds of stuff. It's a rule of movies. Bad guys always have to get caught. Only in real life can they get away with it.'

Together they watched Barbara Stanwyck's car stalled by the railway track. Then Harvey said: 'That was then. Maybe an audience would cheer in a modern movie if the killers got away with it. Especially if the guy they bump off is a real pig.'

'Maybe.' Charlie wished Harvey would shut up. He was sobering up and becoming more tedious than when he was drunk. He poured himself more whisky.

'Maybe when this is over that's what we should do.'

'What?' Charlie had turned up the sound and been trying to translate Fred MacMurray from French back into English.

'Make a murder movie where the killer gets away with it.'

'Mmm.'

There was a pause, and then: 'Or couldn't you write that?'

'Ah, come on, Harvey, I'm trying to concentrate.'

'Sorry.'

It was all right for Harvey, Charlie thought. He had lived for years in Paris. He spoke excellent French. Charlie had to work at his translations. Somehow Raymond Chandler's dialogue didn't seem so slick when it ceased to be American.

They watched the rest of the movie in silence, Charlie being surprised, as always, at how quickly the end came. 'Did you know that they filmed an additional scene in the gas chamber with Fred MacMurray being strapped in and Edward G. Robinson as one of the witnesses, but decided it was too gory for the audience to take,' he said as he switched off the television. 'It must have been a little like what happened to Sadie today.'

'Is that a fact!' Harvey was quite bright now. 'Hey, why don't I make us some more coffee? You look like you could use it.'

'I should go to bed . . .'

'Just one cup. It'll help you sleep.'

Charlie didn't argue. He watched as Harvey went through into the tiny kitchen area and plugged in the kettle. At the Château de l'Abondance room service finished at midnight even for Hollywood producers. After a few moments Charlie heard water running in the bathroom, and then, strangely, at two in the morning, the sound of an electric razor. When Harvey returned he was smoothing the sides of his head with his hands.

413

His cheeks were less pallid. A reversal had taken place. Harvey was almost sober. Charlie was drunk.

'I suppose it takes a certain kind of writer, anyway . . .' Harvey began as he poured the coffee.

Charlie didn't follow. 'What takes a certain kind of writer?'

'You know, to write the perfect crime, the perfect murder, where no-one gets caught . . .'

'Oh, that . . .'

'Yes. It would need a certain type, I guess. A thriller writer, not a historical one like you.'

Charlie pondered this, stung slightly to be described as a historical writer. He was a writer. Period. He should be able to write anything. 'I could write a thriller,' he said.

'A perfect murder? I don't think so.'

'I do. I know I could.' He was insistent now. 'You learn these things writing for television, except in television you always have to plot it that they leave some clue so that the police can catch them. Often it's harder to think of the clue to get them caught than it is to dream up the way they do the crime.'

'Really!' Harvey passed him a mug. 'Here, you'd better drink some of this. You're slurring your words, do you know that?'

'It was good whisky,' Charlie said, although he doubted if he would have known good from bad.

For a moment Harvey was thoughtful, then he said: 'So, is that a deal then?'

'What?'

'Twenty thousand dollars for you to write me a treatment for a perfect murder.'

'You're kidding.'

'Never more serious. No more big movies for Harvey Bamberg. Something small and neat like *Double Indemnity*. But where the killers get away with it. The perfect crime. Can you do it?'

'Well . . . yes. But twenty thousand dollars for a treatment . . . ?'

'You want more? Let's make it thirty.'

'I didn't mean that. Look, you'd better talk to Larry. I don't think . . .'

'Oh God, no, not Larry again. Not you, too, Charlie. Can't we just do it between ourselves, as friends, for now? You have my word, if I want to go to a full screenplay I'll talk to Larry. Let's just see how it works out. OK? A ten-page treatment.

Thirty thousand dollars. Who knows what will happen? Maybe you won't have a story. Maybe you won't be able to think of a perfect murder. In that case we'll just forget the whole thing and I'll ask somebody else.'

'I'll come up with something,' said Charlie.

'Great!' Harvey smiled. He actually smiled. 'And by the way, can we keep this between ourselves for now? I wouldn't like Buffalo to think you were moonlighting on a treatment for me before we'd finished *Shadows on a Wall*.'

'OK. Give me a few days, a few baths. Something usually turns up. But I'll do it for nothing. Pay me if you like it.'

'I'll love it, and I'm paying you whether or not. I'm a producer. That's what I'm good at. Paying.'

Charlie swallowed a smile. He might be drowsy with drink, but he still knew a lie when he heard one.

There was a moment's reflection. Harvey shifted in his seat, and winced. Then, confidentially, he lowered his voice. 'Can I tell you a secret, Charlie?'

'After that girl tonight are you sure you want to?'

'Just between you and me . . .'

'Go on.'

'I've got piles.'

'Piles?'

'Haemorrhoids.'

'I know what piles are, Harvey.'

'Yeah, right, well, I got 'em.'

'I'm very sorry to hear it.'

'Thank you.' He eased himself another way in his chair.

Charlie suddenly grinned. 'Although I suppose, in a way, you could say it's almost appropriate on this movie.'

Harvey scowled. 'What the hell's appropriate about piles?'

'Didn't you know? Napoleon had them, too. During the Italian campaign. His doctors put leeches on them, two or three at a time to draw the blood.'

'No kidding!'

'No kidding. It must have hurt like buggery.'

Harvey grimaced. 'I wouldn't know,' he said. 'I don't know what buggery hurts like.'

It wasn't intentional, but it was the nearest Harvey had come to a joke in months.

Chapter Fifty

(i)

They were a couple of defaults, no doubt about it. Default One looked like Roadrunner, tall and stooped, with a large nose and a cropped, fundamentalist haircut. He was about twenty-two. Default Two was younger, small and pussy-cat ginger, with ears which stuck out like wing mirrors and Buddy Holly glasses. They were sitting out on the Carlton Terrace in Cannes, overlooking the Croisette, and Sam Jordan would have been enjoying the first blast of a Mediterranean spring, had it not been for the company. Where did Grubermann find these people?

'So, what do you think, Sam?' Grubermann was asking in his level New York lawyer's voice.

Jordan didn't think anything. He was actually wondering if Grubermann had brought these guys over first-class, and whether it had been necessary to book them in somewhere as expensive as the Eden Roc. They looked as though they usually slept on a bench in the bus station, the YMCA at best. He was also debating whether he should move seats to give the two paparazzi across the road a better angle. 'What was that?' he asked.

'Gary here was suggesting that the greatest skill of the military strategist is in out-thinking and then surprising his enemy.' Grubermann said, nodding towards Default One as he spoke.

'Well, obviously, yes,' Jordan agreed. 'That's always how the little guy gets the big guy. David and Goliath, the Vietcong. Surprise and kill.'

416

'Well, *surprise*, yes . . .' Default One hesitated, and then giggled nervously, a high-pitched laugh. 'We're not sure about the kill bit.'

Jordan didn't follow. 'What do you mean? *Waterloo* is a battle game, a war game. That's what my idea is, refighting Waterloo, two opposing commanders-in-chief, Napoleon and Wellington.'

'That's right, but . . .' Default Two brought up the reinforcements, 'to make this a family game we think it should be as bloodless a battle as possible.' He spoke in a whisper.

That's terrific, one giggler, one whisperer, thought the star. 'The Battle of Waterloo was hardly bloodless,' he said drily.

'True,' the giggler agreed. 'But we think the emphasis in the *game* of *Waterloo* should be on *teamsmanship*, not on body counts.'

'The most successful battle plan is the one where you lose the fewest of your own men in beating the other side.' This was Default Two. According to Grubermann, the guy had been some kind of New York City chess champion at fourteen.

'Right.'

'Well, we want to refine and extend that,' Default One said.

Now Grubermann joined the fray. 'Gary and Bryan don't think the educated families we perceive to be the *Waterloo* market will be too keen on encouraging massacres, not even hypothetical massacres.'

Jordan frowned. 'So, what are you saying? It's a lousy idea or something? You came all this way to tell me that?' He was irritated. He wasn't used to people disagreeing with him.

'It's a *terrific* idea,' Grubermann soothed.

The whisperer took off his glasses and breathed on them. Without them he had an unfocused, almost vacant expression. 'We think the object of the game should be some kind of equation where the winner is the general who loses the fewest of his men while taking the most prisoners of war. A prisoner of war, for instance, will be worth two dead enemies, and can, if certain conditions are met, be reprogrammed to change sides.'

Default One nodded vigorously. 'In this way we encourage the players to try to fight a war where no-one dies.'

Sam Jordan put a hand through the old gold waves of his hair, aware that a group of people had stopped in their stroll along the Croisette and were pointing at him. Affecting indifference he ignored them. He had dressed for this meeting in a navy-blue shirt and Levi's and was wearing a pair of dark glasses. He thought it made him look like the sort of movie star who was at home in Cannes, although none of his movies had ever been shown in competition here. Perhaps if they ever got *Shadows on a Wall* finished the French would take to him as they had taken to Robert De Niro or one of those other ugly guys. A cloud hovered: on the other hand, how would they feel about an American playing Napoleon? He turned back to the Defaults. 'The Pentagon may want to know how we have a war where no-one dies,' he said.

'By making *Waterloo* a game of feint and counter feint,' whispered Default Two.

Grubermann took over. 'What the boys have come up with is a game of bluff. Napoleon never goes for his goal outright; neither does Wellington. They both use their generals to confuse the opposition. That way the really brilliant guy can manoeuvre his opponent into a corner where he is forced to give in without fighting. The bloodless Waterloo.'

'We've been talking to some military historians and the classic way was always feint and counter-feint,' Default One explained.

'Games People Play are very interested in the non-violent approach,' said Grubermann. '*Sam Jordan's Waterloo*. They think it has a ring to it.'

'Definitely,' said Default Two.

'Kind of like team chess,' responded Default One.

A dead silence followed. Sam Jordan felt his back arching. *Chess?* Who were these little bastards?

Default Two glared hard at his partner. 'It's nothing like chess, Gary,' he hissed. 'It's better. Better than chess. Better than poker. It's a truly brilliant idea. The game for all the family. Not so élitist as chess. More player friendly. A game for groups. Feint and counter-feint, feint and counter-feint.' He repeated it like a mantra.

Jordan relaxed. 'That's right.' He smiled. 'Feint and counter-feint. I like that.' Maybe this default at least wasn't so dumb, after all.

'Can I ask a favour of you, Sam?' Default One said as Grubermann signed the bill. 'Would you autograph this for me, please?' Reaching into a bag he pulled out a magazine showing a photograph of Jordan on the cover.

Taking the waiter's pen Jordan duly signed.

Default One giggled.

His partner explained. 'We have a bet. Gary says that it'll help him with a girl we know. She's crazy for you.'

Sam Jordan looked at them. His autograph as a love potion? It might just work for some; but for these guys . . . ?

He jogged a little at first with a small dog yapping at his feet until he told it to shut up, whereupon it trotted obediently behind as if it knew it was in the presence of a movie star. Jordan liked that. The paparazzi had followed him on to the beach, watched as he had taken off his shoes and socks and would now be photographing him at the edge of the sea. He loved the image they would be getting. It was a Kennedy kind of image, Sam Jordan wandering barefoot through the shallow water with his jeans rolled up a couple of inches. He had chosen to go west along the pebbles because that would ensure that the sea was on his left, just like it had been in the picture of Bobby that last day in California. He had always liked the Kennedys as politicians. They had such great hair. It occurred to him as his trot turned into a stroll that it was unlikely he would ever see his shoes again, that one of the girls who had followed him across the Croisette would take them home to turn into a shrine. It didn't matter. A small loss. He always photographed well by the sea, and the mist which hung over the bay would soften the sharpening middle-aged edges of his features. There was nothing like a walk alone along a beach for getting coverage in magazines.

Even without the company of the photographers he would probably have chosen to go for a walk. He had some serious thinking to do. Firstly there was the percentage which Grubermann was suggesting he give the defaults. Twenty per cent. For doing what? For thinking up a few rules to a game *he* had made up, which would sell because it had *his* face and *his* name on the packaging. He would go no higher than five. They didn't even have their own lawyer. Grubermann had always been too generous with other people's money. Five per cent. They could take it or leave it. How many copies of *Waterloo* would they sell with Default One's goofy Roadrunner face on the cover?

Then there was Yale Meredith. There could be no movie without Napoleon and Marie Waleska, and so, inevitably, that morning Buffalo had capitulated to all of Jake McKenzie's demands. The next day they would both be rejoining the movie. And now, for the sake of his reputation, Yale's capitulation to *him* could not be delayed much longer. Earlier in the shoot the gossip columns had slyly wondered how long it would be before the great on-screen romance moved off-screen. Now some of them were beginning to make fun of his failure to begin it. To a man with as many conquests as Sam Jordan a gentle teasing in *People* magazine should not have mattered. But it did.

Yale Meredith obsessed him. He had tried everything he knew, but she had remained impervious. As the charm had flowed she had gazed uncomprehendingly, as if to say, 'Why are you looking at me like that?'; and, when he had tried ignoring her, she had simply ignored him, too, busying herself with the terrible Alice Bauccio.

The little dog which had been jogging with him suddenly barked for attention and, checking that the photographers were still following, Jordan bent down, picked up a stick and, after at first feinting to throw it one way, then another, suddenly sent it spinning across the lip of the sea. Yelping happily the dog splashed to retrieve it. There you go, a good example of feinting and counter-feinting, Jordan thought as he strolled on. *Feinting and counter-feinting.*

His thoughts returned to Yale. What was it he'd heard Sadie Corchoran saying about her? Something about being a greedy girl? '*A greedy girl . . . always wants what somebody else has . . .*'

He stopped. Feinting and counter-feinting. *Feinting and counter-feinting . . . Always wants what somebody else has . . .* That was it. He wanted to laugh.

He turned to the photographers: then, when he was sure they were all ready, he panned his profile slowly along the entire length of the Croisette, giving them lots of time to get everything right. Suddenly he knew exactly what to do about Yale Meredith.

April, 1993

Chapter Fifty-one

(i)

This time the pictures were in the clouds, but so confused they were of no use to him. He was sitting with Agnieszka at the rear of the chartered Fokker which was taking the unit back to Poland, staring down across the forests of Germany, wondering why he had ever agreed to become involved with Harvey Bamberg again. What did he know about writing perfect murder plots? Drunk, he'd scoffed away the difficulties; sober, he couldn't see anything but difficulties. Naturally, he had tried to wriggle out of the agreement the very next morning, reasoning that he had enough to do sorting out *Shadows on a Wall*. But Harvey had been insistent.

'Charlie, you *promised* me,' he had said quietly, pushing a cheque for thirty thousand dollars into Charlie's hand. That had been the real shock: it was from Harvey's personal account. 'And remember not a word, or everyone else will want paying.'

He could, of course, have simply not cashed the cheque. He didn't need the money any more. But his intellect had been engaged. There was a matter of pride.

But what to write? The daily problem. Vacantly he gazed down the cabin of the aeroplane. Billy and Simone were sitting together a few rows ahead. Simone's hair intrigued him, with its black stripe running the length of her parting where she was growing out a lifetime's bleaching. With the roots growing darker all the time she didn't look so much like a Shelley

Winters dumb blonde any more. Idly his mind wandered to their walk together across the river in Prague. What was the name of the saint who had been thrown off the bridge there? St John somebody or other. For a moment he imagined the terror of the fall, the cold splash of the water. Had the man been weighted down? Were his hands and feet tied together? If you sink you're innocent, if you float you're guilty. That had been the catch-22 of justice which women accused of being witches had faced in the Middle Ages. One way or another those judges made sure there were no winners but them. They would have made good film critics.

Feeling in his pocket he took out the small notebook he always carried with him. For a few moments he stared out at the clouds again, as if searching for something, then, quite slowly, he began to write; at first just a word; then a sentence; then he couldn't stop.

At his side Agnieszka read a movie magazine.

(ii)

Harvey chose to drive to Poland alone, a two-day vacation through the rain in his Noblesse American, sending his driver by air with the rest of the unit. As a very young man, he had once delivered cars, swanky Lincolns and Buicks, driving them down to Florida for those who were too busy to drive themselves. That was when he had developed his liking for big cars and learnt to love the sensation of driving. But he had never been given a car like this to drive. This car was perfection.

He broke his journey in Dresden, staying in a cheap, jerry-built, Eastern-bloc Sixties hotel where he ate alone and then watched *Raiders of the Lost Ark* on the only television with some off-duty Russian soldiers and a group of farm machinery salesmen. He spoke to no-one. He was hardly aware of anyone.

In his tiny, bleak room he tried to call Nathalie. There was never any reply.

★   ★   ★

The next morning, as the spring rains grew heavier, he slid across the border into Poland. It was the Sunday before Easter. He felt as though he had come home.

(iii)

It had to be a secret screening, which meant a Sunday, the only day none of the other editors would be present. Julie Wyatt had stayed on in Europe to complete the renegotiations with Sam Jordan and Yale Meredith, and now she settled into her seat in the Pinewood viewing theatre. Alongside her was Tim Westwood. He had worked through the night preparing the reels. It was ten in the morning. She was excited, if nervous. For months the rushes had told her how good the material looked, shot by shot. Today she would discover how good a movie they were getting for their eighty million dollars.

She left at seven: in shock. She had never seen anything like it. It was overpowering. For nine hours she had stared at stunning, beautiful film, vast armies on the march, magnificent panoramic views, skimming helicopter shots, soaring balloon vistas, intricacies of costume and colour all faithfully reproduced, elegant balls, spellbinding Prague, stately gardens, Polish palaces and French châteaux, meadows of canvas officers' tents, night hills lit by hundreds of camp-fires, horses by the thousand, bawdy baggage trains, Cossacks, wolves, assassinations, burning villages, dream sequences, raped and bleeding women, screaming children, guillotinings, disembowellings, a full forty-five minutes of Sadie Corchoran undressing and making love, Sam Jordan, never more handsome, Yale Meredith, hauntingly beautiful. She had never seen so much colour. She was dazed by the scale, mesmerized by the elegance of the photography, her senses made punch-drunk by this gigantic commercial for the Napoleonic Wars. This man, Bruno Messenger, could sell history like no-one else.

But how much of it had anything to do with Napoleon's affair with Marie Walewska? Bruno Messenger had filmed a pageant through which the original story only occasionally peeped. Despite everything on the grand scale he had still not shot at least half the major dialogue scenes between the two stars. Where was the human interest? Why would anyone, other than a military historian, want to see this movie?

She stepped from the viewing theatre into the cold English evening. This *wasn't* a movie. It was manic indulgence, splendour for splendour's sake, each frame a monument to the director's ambition, each scene lovingly, painstakingly photographed, but unconnected to any other.

Tim Westwood was at her side. As the hours had passed he had been silent. Now he read her expression. 'I've tried to tell him,' he said. 'I've been trying for months. He just won't listen.'

Julie walked to the car. The driver was asleep behind the wheel. She slipped into the back. He woke and started the engine. She asked for Heathrow Airport. She would take the flight to New York. Harry was there with Reuben Wiener. Perhaps she would throw herself on Reuben's mercy. Perhaps she would throw herself off the Brooklyn Bridge. The car raced through the Buckinghamshire countryside. She was numb. Even with the maximum co-operation from the stars, and even if the director trebled his normal speed of working, the latest projections would still be miles out. There was so much left to do, so much wasted material which could never be included in any finished film. This movie could not now be completed for eighty million dollars. But how much was it going to cost?

Chapter Fifty-two

(i)

Billy watched as dawn emerged through the rain. This would be the last day of shooting before the Easter break; thank God! All night he had been moving between tents looking for something interesting to film. Now he was wet and bored. Spending the night with five thousand members of the Polish army camped in the mountains which lay between southern Poland and Slovakia had, in anticipation, suggested the eve of Agincourt. In reality it had been surly and dull. Even the conscripts, who by day doubled as Hanoverian hussars, French cavalry officers and Saxon grenadiers, were fed up with *Bruno Messenger's SHADOWS ON A WALL.* Nearby 350 cows, finally transported from the Kapolska Palace, waited to make their movie débuts.

For days Billy had been wondering if he was, in fact, in the wrong place altogether, as rumours had spread telling of growing panic at Buffalo and yet another attempt at a revised estimate. Harry Weitzman and Julie Wyatt, it was said, were now permanently in conference with budget experts, Reuben Wiener had cancelled all other business, and Carlos Gallego was virtually camping in Familia Gallego's New York bank. The action was in the States. Here in Poland all Billy could see was mud.

Clambering from under a canopy he pulled his hood over his head. It had rained almost without break for four days. The ground was a quagmire and the rivers heavily swollen. It was the Thursday before Easter. He had his ticket booked for

London for the following afternoon, and was looking forward to a family Easter, chocolate eggs and a date with a rabbit in a pet shop in Primrose Hill on Saturday morning. But first the Polish army were pulling on their early nineteenth-century uniforms, and the Kapolska cattle were stumbling to their feet for the drive eastwards and Napoleon's march on Moscow.

It was as they filmed the army breakfasts frying that he heard the music. At first he thought it was coming from a transistor radio. But it was too loud and getting louder, whiplash drumming and soaring synthesizers exploding around the valley. The young soldiers, emerging from their tents with their tin plates, looked around in astonishment: even the cows turned to listen.

Then they saw it, a red sports car shooting out of a copse of oaks, a wedge-shaped thunderbolt of sound heading directly for them. The boy soldiers scattered, but with an extra roar the car dropped down a couple of gears and braked to a halt, its wheels digging deep into the wet earth by the open-air cookhouse. As the car's engine died the music stopped, too.

Cautiously the young men surrounded the car. It was a Ferrari.

A door opened. A famous face grinned. 'Sorry if I woke you.' Penn Stadtler smiled around, his golden hair unfolding in a tail from out of his tennis cap.

The conscripts gaped. 'Penn Stadtler . . . Penn Stadtler . . .' ran an excited ripple of welcome.

Stadtler's eyes found Billy. 'I thought I'd drop in to see how the video's coming along for my new album,' he laughed, looking across the valley at the thousands of soldiers, costumes and cannons. 'That was what I was just playing. It's called the *Theme from Shadows on a Wall*. Sounds like a hit to me. What do you think?'

(ii)

In the end it had come easily, certainly the easiest thirty thousand dollars Charlie had ever earned. His father would have taught for a year to earn that much money. No wonder they were losing touch.

As usual when he was working well he had got up early. The

plan was simple, but effective: the perfect murder, provided everything went right. Perhaps Harvey was on to something after all: perhaps the public were ready for a movie where the killers got away with it.

'More rewrites?' Agnieszka was lying with her head raised above her pillow watching him. He hadn't known she was awake. 'I thought you'd finished rewriting.'

She looked wonderful. Charlie hesitated. Then, pressing the exit key on his word processor he clambered across the bed towards her and burrowed under the covers. 'So did I,' he said. And putting murder from his mind, he kissed her.

'When we go to Hollywood, Charlie,' she said afterwards as they lay listening to the morning sounds of the palace, 'you will be able to take it easier, stay at home, enjoy yourself by your swimming-pool, or play tennis with your friends, while I go to the studio and make movies.'

Charlie smiled to himself. This was the Hollywood she read about in movie magazines, where every script was filmed and there was work for every girl if she were beautiful enough. It reminded him of another morning conversation he had had a long time ago in Edinburgh, and, as with Belinda, he never liked to extinguish Agnieszka's dreams completely. Why spoil it for her? Perhaps she was the one girl in a million. She was certainly pretty enough, more than pretty: she was unusual. People looked twice at her, and while they were looking they were also warming to her, actors, sparks, cameramen, flirting with her, offering to fetch her lunch. Even Jack Dragoman, in or out of his Puritan Will Yorke character, was friendly with her. In the company of stars Agnieszka, the stand-in, was never outshone.

He waited until she had gone off to the location before returning to his word processor. Rereading his work he was pleased with his efforts. It came to just fifteen pages. Two thousand dollars a page. Not bad! Very carefully he corrected, numbered and printed the pages, then putting them inside a red plastic folder he went downstairs to Harvey's room and slipped it under his door. He had worked out a perfect murder. He hoped Harvey would be happy now and leave him to concentrate on *Shadows on a Wall*. With panic in Los Angeles there was much to concentrate on.

Her lips were cracked and dry and she pushed them at him like bumpers on a dodgem car. He tightened his arms around her, and felt the outline of a staunch brassière through her heavy-duty sweatshirt. Cautiously he pushed his tongue into her mouth, then quickly withdrew it. He was fussy about where he put his tongue and he did not want this masquerade to get out of hand.

She gripped him tightly, barnacled fingers kneading his velvet Napoleonic breeches, nuzzled her body closer against his and made a little sighing sound.

There was a movement at the door. Right on cue. Over her shoulder he saw a head appear. It was Beverly, the make-up artist. He closed his eyes and kissed Alice Bauccio. This time her tongue made little serpent, darting movements against the barrier of his lips. They remained locked. Sam Jordan was even more particular about what entered his mouth.

Pretending Beverly's arrival had surprised him he disengaged and affected to look embarrassed. Alice turned in astonishment at what had just happened, her tortoise-shell glasses cock-eyed on her nose, her shining face in a silly grin.

Beverly had stopped in surprise, her bottom lip becoming visibly detached from the rest of her mouth. Inwardly Jordan congratulated himself. Beverly had found him several times before in his trailer in mid-embrace with various members of the unit, but she had never looked as astonished as now. Yale would hear the news for sure before the morning was out.

It had been a tricky manoeuvre. At first Alice had met his overtures with suspicion, but day by day he had flattered her, chosen discreet moments to approach her on the set, agreed with her theory that Marie Walewska and Camille de Malignon should have been written as early feminists, and even once rested an arm around her in the comradely way people did on location. Occasionally he had thought how much more fun it would have been to have feinted towards Sadie Corchoran or Belinda Johnson, or possibly the Polish stand-in who was sleeping with the writer; but his instincts told him it was Alice Bauccio who would have the biggest leverage on Yale. He could return and mop up the others when the main campaign was won. Inwardly he congratulated himself. No wonder

he had been cast to play the world's greatest military tacti-
cian. He was a brilliant strategist.

'I guess I'd better go and find Yale then,' Alice said as she
made her way to the trailer door and Beverly set about restoring
Jordan's make-up. 'Maybe I'll work on that line for you, too.'

'You will? That would be terrific, Alice,' the star smiled with
his just-for-you twinkle. 'I'll see you later. Maybe tonight!
Yes?'

Alice's glossy, damp complexion coloured. She hurried from
the trailer.

Jordan stared at himself in his mirror. Above him Beverly
worked at his make-up saying nothing. On another occasion
he might have been tempted to run his hand up between those
skin-tight denims to examine the part where the reinforced
stitching met. He often liked to do that, and Beverly never
complained. But not today. Beverly had an important mission
to carry out. He couldn't risk distracting her.

He closed his eyes and thought about how Yale had been
photographed by *Knave* at the beginning of her career. There
had been no problem with nudity then. That was how he would
soon be seeing her. And he ran the back of his hand along his
top lip, wiping away the taste of Alice Bauccio. It wouldn't be
long now.

(iv)

The new officer in the *Grande Armée* was enjoying himself.
'What do you think?' he asked as he strutted about the set in
his buckskin breeches and bottle-green jacket, his hair pinned
up beneath his hat. 'A colonel in the Chasseurs. Appropriate,
I think. Perhaps I'll use this uniform on stage when we tour
the *Shadows on a Wall* album.'

'It suits you,' Sadie said with mock seriousness as she passed.

Unsure of whether she was teasing Stadtler turned back to
Billy and his documentary. 'The fact is,' he said, half to camera
and half to Billy, although no-one had asked him to speak, 'I
finished recording in Paris two nights ago, and, as I've just
split with my girlfriend, I thought, well, why don't I just
take off for Kiev. Some of my family on my grandmother's

side still live there, and Poland's on the way. So, here I am, and already I have a part in the movie. What about that!' He smiled rock-star zanily into the camera.

Noticing the activity around him Bruno Messenger lumbered over. 'Hey, you look terrific. Doesn't Penn look terrific?' he bawled, laughing and bear hugging the composer in the way of celebrities. 'Do you want a couple of lines to say? Sure you do.' He turned to Continuity Jenny. 'When you see Charlie tell him to give Penn something to say, will you?' Playfully he punched the composer in the arm. 'Just so long as your name isn't bigger than mine in the credits . . .'

It was all on-set *bonhomie* for the documentary. They were both image builders. But Billy had his own thoughts. He was wondering from which girl the new colonel in the Chasseurs had so recently become detached.

(v)

'*How much?*' Charlie felt his voice catching.

'A hundred million dollars.' Simone was speaking quietly. Her skin matched the colour of the bleached parts of her hair.

'I don't believe it.' Charlie was standing just inside Harvey's turret office. He closed the door.

Simone held a fax out towards him. 'Seeing's believing,' she said. 'A hundred million dollars, give or take a couple of million. That's the estimate.' She tried to smile, but it didn't work.

Charlie stared at the fax. The movie had gone mad. 'How's Harvey taking it?' he asked at last.

'Quietly. Unbelievably quietly. He went off some place, maybe to call Nathalie. He hardly said a word.'

Charlie nodded.

Simone tried to change the subject. 'Did you want to see him about anything in particular?'

'Well . . .' Charlie hesitated. He had actually wanted to know what Harvey thought of his treatment, but now was hardly the moment. 'No, not really. Nothing special. Perhaps I'll go and look for him . . .' He began to leave, but then stopped by the door. 'The play only cost fifteen thousand pounds to put on in Edinburgh, you know.'

432

Simone did know. 'Fifteen thousand pounds to a hundred million dollars in less than two years. That's some inflation, even in Poland.'

Charlie found Harvey in the driveway. He was carrying a large, yellow bucket of hot water, a tin of polish and some new pink dusters. 'Simone told me,' Charlie said.

Harvey shrugged. 'It's stopped raining.'

'No movie can cost a hundred million dollars . . .'

Harvey looked at the sky. 'Probably it's just a break in the clouds.' He sniffed. 'Jesus! I never saw so much rain. Did you ever see so much rain?'

Charlie didn't know what to say. He looked at the producer. His skin, once smooth, was crêped and yellow. His jacket hung on his body. 'I'm really sorry, Harvey,' he said.

Harvey nodded. 'Sure. Sure.' He began to move off again. 'Anyway, I got things to do.'

He had gone a few paces down the drive before Charlie dared ask. 'I was actually wondering what you thought of the treatment?'

Harvey's face was expressionless. 'Very nice,' he said. 'Thank you.' And he continued on his way, the bucket banging against his right leg as he walked.

(vi)

He loved to see the shine come up like this: a real silver space-ship shine. Those kids never polished it properly, not in Finland, Prague, France or any damned place they'd shot, not the way a car like this deserved to be polished, *had* to be polished. Now he could see his face in the bonnet as clear as in any mirror. That was him, pink and bald and ugly, the hundred-million-dollar loser. He dabbed more polish on to the cloth and rubbed it on to the smooth, steel surface, smearing it across his own reflection, then pressed harder, as though trying to polish his image away. That was what he would do, he would polish himself away, polish the car until it shone like a mirror and consumed him. A Polish polish, he thought. He

433

liked the sound of that, and rhythmically, as his arm worked, he repeated the phrase in his head. 'A Polish polish, a Polish polish, a Polish polish . . .' Today he would make the Noblesse gleam like never before. Today was important like never before. 'A Polish polish, a Polish polish . . .' his mind ran on as he worked. Occasionally he fancied he saw the pincer nose and upturning jaw of the old albatross in the gleaming metalwork. But when he did he polished harder and polished him away, too.

'Are you all right, Harvey?' It was Belinda. He hadn't seen her approach.

He didn't look up. He had no time. He had to work. 'Sure, I'm all right. I'm just terrific. I've got to get the mud out. See the mud. There's too much mud on location. East European mud and salt and grit. Can't let it become ingrained in the bodywork or it'll begin to corrode it.'

'Couldn't somebody else do this?'

He could see the reflection of Belinda in the windscreen. She looked concerned. That amused him. Why shouldn't a guy clean his own car? 'Sure they could. But I'm doing it,' he said. 'I'll do a better job.' Lavishly he applied more wax, and put on more pressure.

'Maybe I can give you a hand?' She picked up a duster.

'No. Please, no. It's all right.' He took the duster from her. Such a sweet girl. 'Thank you for the offer, but I'm fine. Shouldn't you be out at the location?'

'I have a late call.' Still she hung around. 'Will you be coming out?'

'Of course. A little later. I'll see you there, OK!'

In the end she left, although it took a little time. He knew she was watching him as she backed away. When he was alone again he stopped work and stared at his reflection in the panelling. Such an ugly little guy, and such a beautiful car.

Inside the car he could see Charlie's treatment in its red folder: the perfect murder treatment. There was now no alternative. They had wrecked the movie. They had spoiled everything for everyone, for Nathalie who would never now be able to meet her cineast friends on equal terms, for Charlie and his play, for Belinda and for Billy Yeo. They were crippling Buffalo Pictures; they were making a fool out of Carlos Gallego. That Carlos Gallego would have his revenge on the man who had led him into this disaster he did not doubt. The thin, lisping voice frightened him; the wheezing of asthma, the struggle for breath, the sounds of strangulation. Strangulation: was that how it would come? Everything was ruined. There was no chance of salvation. At a hundred million dollars the only answer was in his own hands. He had checked the insurance. It would be the biggest claim in movie history, but it would work. There could be no movie about Napoleon and Marie Walewska if they were dead: no *Bruno Messenger's SHADOWS ON A WALL* if Bruno Messenger were dead, too. *Shadows on a Wall* would be remembered as the film that never was; perhaps as a tragically unfinished masterpiece. People would sympathize with him, wish him better luck next time. Nathalie might even stay.

He began to polish again, around and around. It was so simple: such a perfect answer to their problems. He wondered why no-one had ever thought of it before. All the producer had to do was to kill his director and his two stars.

Charlie had shown him how. He would do it that day.

Chapter Fifty-three

(i)

'What the hell does Alice think she's doing over there?' Yale Meredith stabbed a cigarette out in a slice of angel cake.

Sadie looked across the valley to where Napoleon and his generals were assembled. It had been going on all week, Sam and Alice, but usually in semi-private. Now it was public. Napoleon was ignoring his fellow officers to talk to the Barnacle.

At Sadie's side, Belinda, in a deep blue coat and matching bonnet, was sitting in a fold-up canvas chair reading a biography of Catherine the Great.

Yale's new hair-stylist, a puck of a boy she had had flown out from California when her old one had become temperamental, glanced towards Beverly, the make-up artist.

'I think he fancies her,' Beverly said, trying to conceal a smile with a powder puff.

'What?' Yale looked incredulous.

'He likes her. They were together in his trailer this morning.'

Loudly Belinda turned over a page of her book.

'Alice was in Sam's trailer?'

Beverly grinned, doll-like. 'Just a kiss.'

'Sam was kissing Alice? I don't believe it.'

It was, Sadie had to agree, surprising. Alice Bauccio had never struck her as exactly Sam Jordan's type. But then what was his type, the Italian from wardrobe, the journalist from *Premiere*, the French extra, the teenagers in Prague, Beverly?

436

'You know what Sam's like,' Beverly said. She did.

The hair-stylist smirked.

Sadie watched Yale. Her expression, at first one of disbelief, was gathering into a taut frown.

At that moment Belinda put away her book on Catherine the Great and stood up, allowing herself to become aware of the distraction across the valley. 'You know,' she said pointedly to Sadie, 'the really dumb thing about women tyrants is the way they always play up to the men.'

Yale overheard. 'Are you talking about me?'

'I don't know. Are you a tyrant, Yale?'

'*OK, everybody, we're going for one . . .*' The sound of a loud hailer interrupted, quickly followed by a translation in Polish.

'Right, ladies, when you're ready, first positions, please!' Skip Zieff darted forward nervously.

Yale ignored his request. 'You shouldn't have taken it so personally. Everyone cheats in this game,' she said.

'It isn't a game for everyone,' Belinda replied.

'You're just a lousy loser.'

'I hadn't realized I was playing.'

'For Christ's sake, the guy isn't worth it!'

'But he was.'

Yale shrugged. Across the valley Sam Jordan was mounting Napoleon's black horse, Marengo. She watched him.

(ii)

Taking her position Belinda could see Jack Dragoman alongside Napoleon arguing about something with Tony Delmonte, worrying away, throwing his arms about. The other actors would be sighing to each other and shaking their heads as they always did when Dragoman complained. He got on everyone's nerves, although he wasn't always wrong with his questions. Frequently he got things changed for the better. He had helped her to change. She asked questions herself now: not least of herself.

'Come back to Los Angeles with me?' he would implore when they were alone. 'Live with me. Start your career again in a town where they make movies.'

She had promised she would think about it.

Further up the hill Charlie was standing behind the camera waiting for the shooting to begin. Poor Charlie: still hoping for a miracle. It wouldn't have been a game for him either.

(iii)

It must have been seventy foot down to where the river swept past in full flood, khaki with mud washed from the surrounding hills and forests. The Noblesse American stood on a patch of sodden grass, its parking brake on, its nose pointing at a low, broken fence, the only thing preventing careless drivers from rolling off the side of the mountain and down the cliff.

Harvey had been to this corner before. The previous autumn he had asked his driver to stop here while he urinated against the side of the road, the result of too much location tea. It was the only place on this mountain where a car could stop. He had been out looking at a fort with the art director and Al Mutton. In the end Bruno had chosen to shoot somewhere else.

Stepping forward he took hold of the rail at the edge of the drop. The wood was rotten. A spar crumbled away in his hand. He tossed it over the cliff and counted until it hit the water, to be immediately dragged away downstream between the dripping pines.

How wide, how deep? he asked himself. 'Deep enough,' he heard himself answer. 'Deep enough . . . deep enough . . . deep enough. A Polish polish, a Polish polish . . .' The rhythm of the words chased each other senselessly. He squeezed his hands together. He had to keep control.

He kicked at the fence: more broke away. This time he heaved a heavy upright post and watched it fall. It submerged, surfaced and was carried away, too.

Nathalie had been crying when she had picked up the phone. She hadn't explained why. She had sounded disappointed that it was only him calling. *A hundred million dollars.* He had had to tell her, but she had hardly responded.

He walked back to the car, and ran a hand across its surface. Raindrops lay on the polished mirror of silver: a shimmering rash dappled his reflection. He climbed inside and his hands found Charlie's red folder. It seemed so easy on paper.

He called in at the location during the afternoon. 'We'll be working an extended day,' Al Mutton told him as he arrived. 'Maybe until ten, maybe later.'

Harvey didn't answer. On other days he would have tried to argue, but he was distracted. There were still holes in his plot.

'Where have you been? I was going to send out a search-party for you,' Simone said, jumping down from the catering bus.

'I had some things to do.'

Sheltering under an umbrella, she looked closely at him. 'Are you all right, Harvey?'

'I'm fine,' he said, striding on into the valley. She fell into step, spreading the umbrella over him, too.

It was when they reached the set that he understood Nathalie's tears. Penn Stadtler was sheltering under a tarpaulin. At his side was a pretty Polish girl, cast to play a prostitute. She was coming on to him and being encouraged. Some music was playing on a cassette-player. It was Penn Stadtler's *Shadows on a Wall* theme music, Simone explained, and for a moment Harvey pictured Nathalie lying in her bed listening to her tapes.

Seeing Harvey watching, Stadtler returned his gaze. It was contempt, Harvey thought. Stadtler had certainly laughed at him behind his back. He had been cuckolding him for months; now he was flirting with another girl while Nathalie, twenty-five years too old, wept in Paris.

He turned away. Nathalie had never talked about him, so he had never acknowledged Stadtler as her lover. If he didn't see him, didn't think about him, the affair would never have happened. A Polish polish, a Polish polish, a Polish polish . . .

He didn't notice Charlie approaching. 'The only difficult bit is in making sure we have a plausible reason for getting the victim to the murder site,' Charlie said quietly.

'What?' Harvey tried to move away.

'Your perfect murder plot.'

'Oh yes!' Jesus! Why did writers always want to talk about their goddamn scripts?

'The trick is to play up to greed and vanity.'

Harvey stopped. 'Greed and vanity?'

Charlie nodded. 'I think so.'

Another piece of the puzzle was dropping into place. Harvey

looked at Charlie. He was amazing. Despite the everyday pounding he had taken he could still tap new reserves of enthusiasm. Harvey admired him. It hurt that they would never be able to be friends again. He patted his arm. 'Thanks, Charlie,' he said. 'You've been a pal.'

'I still am, but don't ask why,' Charlie laughed and wandered off into the rain.

Harvey didn't stay long. Frank, his driver, asked if he should take over driving the Noblesse American again, but Harvey shook his head. He was enjoying driving himself, he said.

With almost the entire unit out at the location the Kapolska Palace was virtually deserted. Carefully parking the car out of view of the production-office window, Harvey slipped in through a side-door. At reception he asked for a duplicate key to Charlie's room. 'I'm sorry. I've locked myself out,' he said, taking the key, although he doubted that the porter understood. Then, going to his room, he telephoned Nathalie again.

Her voice was low. She sounded as though she had been disturbed from sleep. She had told him that morning that she had not slept the previous two nights.

'I just wanted to say that I'm sorry for letting you down.'

'Yes,' she murmured. She sounded old.

'Honest to God, Nathalie. You've got to believe me. I'll make it right for you.'

She didn't answer.

He tried to ask her what she had been doing, but she was in no mood to talk. He suspected she had taken a sleeping-pill. In the end he said: 'We'll speak tomorrow.'

'Yes.'

'I love you,' he added suddenly. 'I've always loved you.'

'Yes, Harvey. I know.' Her voice was weary.

After he had hung up he went into the bathroom, undressed and took a shower. Then he shaved his face and the sides of his head. He was very thorough. When he had finished he opened Charlie's red folder, took out the pages and very carefully set fire to them, one by one, over the bath, holding the pages out as they burnt and curled into blackened wafers. When they had all been destroyed he washed out the bath, polishing the enamel with pieces of toilet tissue. He was meticulous.

Charlie's room was a floor above his own. The duplicate

key was stiff in the lock but it worked. Closing the door, he crossed to the word processor and called up the index. He knew that Charlie worked in Wordperfect. It was one of the two systems he knew. A file named 'Harvey' caught his eye. It was a letter to him which had never been sent, listing all Charlie's complaints about the production. Running to several pages, it warned of impending disaster. He read it and then returned to the index, eventually finding what he was looking for under 'Double', as in *Double Indemnity*. Reading the treatment a final time he then erased it.

In reception the porter was watching *I Love Lucy* in Polish on television. He took the key back without comment.

It had begun, Harvey thought as he swept the Noblesse American down the gravel drive and into the evening. He was setting out to kill. He did not question whether the scheme would work. He would make it work. 'Play up to greed and vanity,' Charlie had urged. That was how it was done in movies.

He wondered at what point murder had become inevitable. Had it been in France when he had commissioned Charlie to write the murder synopsis? No. That had been no more than a germ of an idea, daring himself to see how far he would go. Only now, at the hundred-million-dollar point, had he made up his mind.

The car slid along the road: such a beautiful car to drive, it would be his only regret.

(iv)

The whores cackled and threw pieces of bread from their carts. One lifted her skirts to her waist: she was naked underneath. Another, smiling lewdly, looked up from servicing a young officer. Accompanied by a troupe of the Imperial Guard, Marie Walewska, Camille de Malignon and Monika Wyszynska hurried past the taunts to their carriage. Around them cattle steamed and camp-fires struggled to burn through the incessant rain.

The scene should have been filmed during daylight but they had run out of day. In the end a virtue had been made of necessity and cinematographer Giorgio Pescati had relit the farewell for night. Now, as worry stretched the beautiful face of the Emperor's mistress, and the horses drawing her carriage fought to get a hold on the wet earth, a presentiment of disaster fell. Camille de Malignon wept.

'And cut,' called the director.

The coach stopped. Climbing down, the actresses made their way under umbrellas towards the shelter of the trailers.

'Terrific, really terrific,' enthused Sam Jordan as Yale approached. He had been watching the shot on the video link. He was still in costume. The last shot of the night was scheduled to be their goodbye kiss.

Yale Meredith's actress eyes opened wide to him. 'You really think so, Sam?' she murmured.

'Wonderful, Yale. I promise you. Wonderful.' He, too, was holding an umbrella. Almost imperceptibly Yale moved a half-pace forward, from the shelter of Skip Zieff's umbrella to that of the leading man.

Standing in the rain Simone rolled her eyes to heaven. Billy laughed.

A voice cut through the babble which followed every shot. It was that of Alice Bauccio. She was approaching through the rain, holding a copy of *Variety* over her head as a roof, a dippy smile on her face. 'Sam,' she called into the swirl of umbrellas. 'Sam!'

Jordan pointedly looked the other way towards Yale.

Failing to realize Alice stepped closer to him. 'Sam . . . that line I was telling you about . . . I've thought of a much better one for you.' She was holding a copy of the script and pointing to some dialogue she had rewritten.

Jordan ignored her.

'Er, Sam!'

'Not now, Alice,' he snapped.

'It won't take a minute, Sam.'

At that moment the crowd broke and Yale emerged from its midst, one hand resting proprietorially on Jordan's tunic. 'You heard him, Alice. Not *now*,' she rasped. 'Don't you know Sam and I have an important scene to do tonight? What are you trying to do, ruin our concentration completely?'

The Barnacle blinked, her big face closing and opening in confusion.

'*OK?*' repeated Yale, and, sliding her arm through that of

442

her co-star, she led him into the director's trailer to join Penn Stadtler and Bruno Messenger.

Alice, her face collapsed in hurt, stared in after them, embarrassed by her exclusion. 'Sure, Yale,' she murmured. Whatever she had been encouraged to think earlier she was back to being the plain, shell-shaped woman with the pudding-basin haircut. Then, suddenly aware that she was the centre of attention, she elbowed aside a couple of electricians and scuttled away.

Simone and Billy watched her go. In the trailer the famous four were joking together like best and oldest friends.

'That's the trouble with fame,' Simone said, as she joined Billy in the documentary tent, 'it chooses your friends for you.'

Billy smiled. 'And whenever you behave like a rat there's always someone like us watching.'

(v)

It was all in the body language: the way she stood, facing him, open to him, one firm thigh brushing against his; the little touches, the warm breath on his hair as she passed, closer than at any time during the entire movie; then there were the looks, the way he caught her watching him, followed by the quick, shy smiles and the widening of her eyes, as though everything he said was fascinating; and, of course, the laugh, the famous, sudden Yale Meredith laugh, whenever he said anything remotely funny. Oh yes, if Yale Meredith hadn't been an actress Sam Jordan would have sworn she had become infatuated with him, instead of simply wanting what she thought Alice might be about to get. He didn't mind. Her motives were immaterial. All *he* wanted was to have this lovely, mad, selfish woman in his bed. Maybe then she might become a little bit infatuated, after all. Who could tell?

Watching her now in Bruno's trailer, her eyes that bit cocaine brighter, he knew he had won. It would happen tonight. He congratulated himself. He would take an extra couple of vitamin shots to be sure he was on top form. It was going to be some night.

Harvey was surprised at how calm he felt. He was a salesman. He was making a pitch. This was what he was good at. He was back to truffling. 'Do you have a minute, Bruno?' he called.

'Tomorrow.'

The director was heading back towards the set. All around actors and crew were preparing for the last set-up before Easter. Harvey had delayed his return to the location until the last moment. Now he delayed again until no-one could overhear. 'Reuben Wiener's here,' he said at last.

'What?' Bruno looked puzzled. 'Here?' He looked around.

Harvey lowered his voice. 'In Poland. In Cracow. He wants a meeting.'

Bruno stopped walking. 'With *me*?'

Harvey nodded. 'Tonight.'

'Come on, what is this?'

'No kidding.'

'Tonight? Tonight's impossible. You know that.'

Harvey waved his head. 'It's essential. That hundred–million–dollar estimate . . .'

'. . . is *crazy*. Buffalo are way out on that. Someone's trying to destroy my movie . . .'

Harvey was not deflected. 'The Buffalo board are for pulling the plug immediately. Candy Corn want out. Carlos Gallego, too. He can't take any more. Reuben's wavering.'

'Not this again. How many times do we have to go through it? They can't close us down now. They'd have to be mad. If it's money, why doesn't Reuben talk to you or Al? You handle the financing. It's nothing to do with me.'

Harvey swallowed that. It was everything to do with him. 'I think Reuben feels it's gone beyond money,' he said. 'He wants to talk to you as the director. Sam and Yale, too. Only the top creative people. He's a fan, you know, a Napoleon fan. That's why he's gone along with it for so long. He *wants* to keep going. But if he's to fight the board on our behalf he needs to be persuaded.' Sadie and Belinda were passing and Harvey lowered his voice still further.

Bruno shook his massive head. 'I can't see anyone tonight. Doesn't he know we're making a movie here?'

'You've *got* to see him. It doesn't matter what time. He'll be waiting. He's flown in especially from Moscow. Candy Corn are setting up there. But he leaves for New York first thing tomorrow. If he doesn't get to talk things over with you, well . . .'

'I don't get it.'

'Nor me. What can I say? He's an old man and a billionaire. And in his way he's a movie-lover. I think maybe he sees *Shadows on a Wall* as his contribution to the cinema. Popcorn sure as hell ain't much of a legacy. But he's eccentric. Hell, all those guys are. Look at Howard Hughes . . . Armand Hammer. All crazy.'

'What about Sam and Yale? What do they say?'

Harvey leant forward. 'I came to you first. You know they'll go along with whatever you decide.' Play on the victim's vanity, Charlie had said, and Harvey watched as the worm of flattery went to work.

They had reached the circle of marquees which made up Napoleon's quarters. Huge arc lights lit the area. Just inside a marquee Yale and Sam Jordan were standing close together, virtually canoodling.

Bruno tugged on his wet hair. 'OK,' he said at last. 'I'll talk to the man. How far is Cracow?'

'Forty, fifty miles. An hour's drive.'

'You'd better tell the drivers where we're going—'

'No!' Harvey cut in almost too sharply.

'What?'

Harvey looked around, shaking his head. 'No drivers. Reuben wants absolute secrecy. If word gets out that he's been dealing behind the back of the board it'll weaken his negotiating position. No-one must know. Drivers talk. We'll go in my car. I'll drive.'

'And they say actresses are difficult.'

Harvey beamed. He had him. 'It's a terrific car. You'll enjoy the drive.'

'Just so long as the bastard doesn't try to tell me how to make movies.'

'I don't think he'll be doing that,' said Harvey.

It was like kissing a different woman. How many times had they had to kiss during the movie? Dozens. Whole days had been spent in kissing scenes, and it had never been any fun. Now Yale was putting her whole body into it, and, despite all his years of practise, all his women, and all the feinting which had gone into attracting Yale, Sam Jordan could feel himself becoming excited beneath his breeches. They had worn them tight in those days. He hoped nobody noticed, although Yale certainly had.

'You know, I was thinking, maybe we should talk to Bruno about doing the nude scenes,' she whispered between takes.

'The ones you didn't want to do in Prague?'

'I'm sorry about that, Sam. I didn't know you so well then. Now would be different. What do you think? It would be a shame if the audience got off on Sadie Corchoran and Dragoman instead of us. It might unbalance the movie.'

'Sounds fine to me. Maybe we can talk about it tonight after we've got the all-clear from Reuben Wiener.'

She pouted. 'I don't like all that. Some little guy summoning us in the middle of the night; who does he think he is?'

'He's a popcorn manufacturer who became one of the richest men in America.'

'But tonight? Do we have to see him *tonight*?'

Jordan didn't want to see Reuben Wiener any more than she did, but he had been flattered when Harvey had told him that Wiener had seen all his movies. He had somehow never imagined old Reuben going for pictures like *Terminal Case* or *Replay Mode*. Under cover of his Napoleon's cloak he allowed his hand to run down the bodice of Yale's dress. 'We'll have plenty of time after we've seen him,' he said. 'Maybe we could get away somewhere together for Easter. Just you and me.'

Yale Meredith pressed the lower part of her body into his. 'I'd like that, Sam,' she whispered.

The voice of Tony Delmonte broke into their plans. 'OK, just once more, please, and that'll be a wrap!'

Happy in their new friendship the beautiful sixteen-million-dollar-pair turned to face the camera for the final shot of the day.

Standing in the gloom behind the camera crew, with rain running off his shiny head on to his green leather jacket, Harvey Bamberg waited patiently for them.

Chapter Fifty-four

(i)

It was a minor stampede. The unit had just wrapped, and props and equipment were being gathered, when the first of the Kapolska cows trotted nervously on to the set. Someone must have accidentally left the gate on the cattle-pen open, because suddenly seemingly half the herd was lowing nervously in the dazzling arc lights, jogging uncertainly between the marquees and lurching on between cast, crew and soldiers. To the conscripts it was a joke, and they threw empty beer cans at the interlopers; to the producer, watching from the sanctuary of his car as hussars and hairdressers joined in rapid escape, and Marshall Ney ran hand in hand with Beverly from make-up, it was symbolic. How had Charlie described this movie? 'Like some lumbering, primeval, runaway, blindfolded rhinoceros?' On nights such as this even cows could seem pretty primeval.

'Jesus Christ!' Bruno Messenger swore loudly, stumping through the rain to the door of the Noblesse American and throwing his fat backside into the front passenger seat. 'I want the bastard responsible for this off the picture. Right?'

Harvey nodded. He was looking anxiously towards Yale's trailer. Sam Jordan had been easy to convince, but Yale had sulked, wanting to talk to Wiener before setting off for Cracow. 'At this time of night? Let me call him. I'm sure I can talk him into waiting until tomorrow.'

'Sam and Bruno are going tonight, Yale,' Harvey had said firmly. 'Reuben won't wait.'

448

'Sam's going?'

'Sam's going.' Play on the victim's greed, Charlie had said.

Yale had shrugged her thin shoulders, without enthusiasm. 'OK.'

At least there was no Barnacle tonight to help her change her mind, Harvey thought. Alice Bauccio had been driven back to the Kapolska in tears earlier in the evening.

All around now as the cattle and extras still roamed and Billy's team filmed the confusion, cars and buses were pulling out of the field, Bruno's Mercedes and then Sam's BMW leaving empty as instructed. At last Yale's Cadillac began to edge away.

In the Noblesse Bruno was drying his long hair with a towel. 'You know maybe I shouldn't be talking to Reuben Wiener without Jake being with me,' he fretted. 'At least I should call him.'

Harvey felt his hands beginning to shake. Keep calm, keep calm, he told himself. 'If you do, and word gets out, Reuben will close the picture. Believe me. I know this man.'

The director shook his head. 'It just doesn't seem right.'

He was about to argue further but was distracted by the arrival of Sam Jordan, still in full Napoleon costume, and in great spirits. 'I figured if Reuben Wiener's a Napoleon freak maybe he'd like a preview of what he's paying for,' he joked as he climbed into the back seat.

Bruno guffawed obediently.

One to go. Harvey's stomach was cramping with nerves. The cows had now passed on down the valley.

Distracted, watching Agnieszka waving as she passed in one of the props vans, he didn't see Yale approach. Suddenly she was at his window, Penn Stadtler at her side. 'I told Penn,' she said abruptly. 'He's coming, too.'

'What?' Harvey swung around in his seat. Stadtler was already following Yale into the back of the car. 'No. He can't come . . .' Harvey was shouting.

Stadtler grinned confidently. Nobody ever said 'no' to a rock star. 'Oh, come on, Harvey. Don't be a spoil-sport. Reuben Wiener wants to meet the creative people, right? Well, I'm creative. I promise you. And I want to meet him. He's an American legend.' He slammed the door. He had spent most of the day sitting around drinking wine and was quite drunk.

Harvey struggled to control his voice. 'I really don't think so. Reuben made it clear—'

'Hey, Harvey, what the hell is this? Of course Penn should come,' bullied Bruno.

'That's right,' agreed Sam Jordan.

Harvey could feel himself sinking. He had avoided Stadtler all day, never even looked into the man's eyes. And now this.

'I'll make it right with that old Reuben,' Yale murmured in the pussy-cat voice she had once used in an advertisement for men's cologne. She was snuggling up to Jordan now.

'Look, if there's a problem I'll sit outside, and make sure no-one steals the car while you guys go in and charm the old fella,' Stadtler offered.

'I thought they said you had to be in Kiev or some place?' It was Harvey's last throw.

'I can't go to Kiev tonight. It's hundreds of miles. I'll go tomorrow, or the next day. There's no rush.'

Harvey sat silently. His body was wet with sweat. It wasn't going to work. Penn Stadtler had not been in his calculation. He had no reason to kill Penn Stadtler: no *real* reason.

'Well, are we going or aren't we, Harvey?' Bruno was complaining.

'Yes, come on, Harvey. Let's go,' laughed Stadtler.

Harvey put the car into drive.

He couldn't go through with it. He couldn't murder Penn Stadtler, and, with Stadtler present, he couldn't kill the others. A mixture of emotions rushed at him: frustration, relief, fear, despair. He was hopeless. They would soon discover that there had been no summons to meet Reuben Wiener, that Wiener was in New York and actually despised all of them for losing him so much money. He had no idea how he would explain.

He pulled the car off the track which led out of the valley and turned left on to the road up into the hills, the way he had planned to go. The Kapolska lay to the north and to the right. In his headlights the tarmac unravelled like a shining ribbon, a wash of yellow on black. He thought of it as a strip of film, and he wondered what the last frames of the journey would show.

He felt like an adult taking a group of teenagers on a drive. His four passengers were rich, attractive, famous, successful and young – even Sam Jordan was a lot younger than Harvey, although not so young as he liked to imagine – and at first they were boisterous and silly, talking about the day's filming, excluding him from their conversation. He knew now how limousine drivers must feel, hearing everything, yet being somehow invisible to their passengers. Little wonder drivers always had the best stories.

'Play us your music, Penn,' Yale said after a few minutes. 'Your *Shadows on a Wall* music.'

'You really want to hear it again?' Stadtler asked, affecting modest surprise, although already searching in the pocket of his coat for the cassette. 'It's only a rough mix, you know. Just to give you an idea.'

Apart from Harvey, everyone wanted to hear the music again. Harvey didn't complain, not even when Bruno turned the volume up high. He was only the driver. He drove on, wondering what to do. No-one noticed that they were heading directly away from Cracow, up into the High Tatra Mountains.

(ii)

He had pulled his cloak over the two of them like a rug. They were in the back seat. Yale was sitting in the middle between him and Penn, but was leaning into him, her leg pressed hard against his. There was no moon and it was dark up here in the mountains, quite black, in fact. He could feel her breath on his cheek. He leant forward in the darkness and kissed her long neck. A spasm seemed to run down her body and she shivered. Perhaps a little actressy, he thought, but he was sure she enjoyed it, because she immediately came back for more. Under the cover of the cloak he put his hand against her breast. She had changed out of her costume into a blouse, cardigan and skirt and a pair of bright blue running shoes. Her breasts were wide apart and he touched them through her blouse as a sixteen year old might on a first date. She was, he noted, not wearing a bra. For some adolescent reason this still excited him. At his side Penn Stadtler was leaning forward, talking to Bruno, something about using parts of the film for the video to promote the album, unaware of what was happening under the cloak. It made it more fun.

He kissed the side of her face and she turned her wide mouth into his, sliding her hand under the cloak and along his white, velvet-clad thigh at the same time. He wondered whether Marie Walewska had ever done this to Napoleon while travelling in the back of his carriage. He was sure she had.

With his right arm he pulled her closer while his left hand continued its exploration, one button freeing the way to her bosom. Her hand, meanwhile, had reached his groin. She was ahead of him. Diligently she set to work on his buttons. He was glad now that Harvey was taking them on this drive. It would prolong the moment. First times should always be delayed.

Satisfied that he had been polite enough to her breasts he slipped his hand down to her knee and under her skirt. Her legs parted accommodatingly. He ran his fingers up the inside of her thigh. She bit the corner of his lip. That was one of her party tricks. He had watched her do it in half a dozen movies. He stroked the warm cotton V of her pants, then, easing them aside, he put his hand between her legs. Adjusting her position she raised herself off the seat. With the back of his hand he edged her pants a little way down her thighs. Now that he was touching her she hurried at his buttons; one, two, three, four. Napoleon had been well buttoned. He was thrilled. He was victorious. It was working: the feint, as devised for *Sam Jordan's Waterloo*, was working.

At that moment she pushed a cool hand inside the Emperor's riding breeches. He gasped.

(iii)

It was too late. There was no way of turning back on this road now, not until the Slovakian border. It was too narrow, winding high along the mountain. He drove slowly around the bends, taking care not to skid in the rain. In his mind, Nathalie drove with him, sitting at his side, her presence a silent comfort. He remembered how she had been when he had first seen her that night in the Montparnasse cinema; he thought of how happy she had made his life. He thought of how, if things had gone right, if Penn Stadtler hadn't joined them, Charlie's plan would have been perfect.

Stadtler was still talking to Bruno, half-shouting against the music, sitting forward to Bruno's ear. He wondered why

Nathalie had never spoken about him. No. He didn't wonder. He knew. For once it had been more than sex. She had been infatuated. This conceited, arrogant, handsome young man had made her feel young again.

The car ploughed through a pool of rain water lying on the road, the reflection from the headlights momentarily lighting up the interior. Harvey glanced into his rear-view mirror. Sam and Yale were up to something under the cloak. They thought he couldn't see them. Probably they didn't care. He was invisible. But he wasn't deaf. The volume of the music had dropped. He could hear snatches of conversation.

'Looks like Sam and Yale finally made friends,' Bruno was saying.

Stadtler laughed.

'Maybe we should have brought a couple of the baggage-train whores for company. Looked like you were doing pretty good there.'

Stadtler laughed again, and yawned. 'Whores yes, just so long as they're *young* whores,' he said lazily. The wine was making him speak more loudly than he realized.

Bruno dropped his voice under the music to make a comment, but Harvey, his face expressionless as he drove, caught the gist of it. It was something about Penn Stadtler and an older woman: an old whore?

Stadtler's reply, whatever it was, made Bruno guffaw.

'No kidding!'

'No kidding! But never again,' he heard Stadtler say. And then, 'Jesus ... .' followed by a low whistle.

He couldn't hear all the words but he heard enough. Stadtler was talking dirty about Nathalie, betraying intimacies. Harvey's heart ripped with pain. He loved Nathalie and hated them so much. He hated their confidence in themselves, and in their youth, and he hated their contempt for him. They were spoilt and selfish. Their arrogance was numbing. Penn Stadtler had not needed to come with them on this drive. It was he who had insisted. So be it.

They had almost reached the corner of the mountain where the cliff fell sharply away down to the river. The rain was scudding into the windscreen. Very carefully Harvey pulled the Noblesse off the road on to the waste ground, its nose facing downhill a few feet from the broken barrier.

'Hey, what are you doing?' Stadtler asked.

453

Harvey put the car into neutral and pushed his foot on the parking-brake. 'I got to take a leak,' he murmured.

'Some driver!' Bruno whined.

Harvey climbed out of the car, and, leaving his door open, walked a few paces away. Behind him in the car he could hear Bruno and Stadtler complaining, and Sam Jordan asking why they had stopped. There was a peel of laughter from Yale when she was told. Someone turned the music up higher, Penn Stadtler's *Theme from Shadows on a Wall*.

There was a call from the car for him to hurry, and a joke about the trouble having a driver with a prostate problem.

'Just coming,' he shouted. He was a moment away from murder.

He turned back to the car. The parking-brake was located by the steering-wheel. He opened the door. It was so easy. Leaning inside he quite casually released the brake, and, slamming the door again, hurriedly stepped back as the heavy, silver car slid forward. Whether there was any shout of alarm he couldn't tell. The music was too loud.

It was only fifteen yards to the edge of the cliff, two seconds perhaps, as the car bowled past him and downhill into the broken fence. With a cracking of wood the nose of the car tipped over the precipice. It seemed to hesitate, to balance as though considering the drop below, the rear end rising up. 'Go, you bastard,' he screamed, throwing himself at the car, his hands underneath, heaving at it. For a second he saw Yale Meredith suddenly turn her head and look at him through the rear window. But in that moment, with a creak, the Noblesse American rolled forward and over the cliff.

(iv)

She had teased it out of his breeches and now Yale Meredith was holding his penis. Her pants were loose at her thighs: his hand was there. Yale Meredith and Sam Jordan, America's most beautiful couple, under a cover like a couple of kids in the back of a car, with the love theme from *Shadows on a Wall* playing loud on the speakers.

Then suddenly she was screaming. His hand gripped her flesh.

Harvey knew he was falling. He couldn't understand why. He felt that his arm was being torn off. Then he realized. The epaulette on the cuff of his green leather jacket was caught on something protruding from underneath the car. It was taking him with it. An epaulette? Now he remembered: Buzz going over the cliff in *Rebel Without A Cause*, his sleeve caught on the door handle. You see, Charlie, he was thinking, triumphant at last, I do know something about movies. He shouted for Nathalie. He saw her smiling. But all he could hear was the water rushing in the river below.

PART SIX

Easter manoeuvres, 1993

Chapter Fifty-five

(i)

Julie Wyatt watched the television news in a vacuum of shock. She should have been packing, rushing to meet Harry Weitzman at the airport where the Buffalo Falcon jet was waiting to take them to Europe, but she was unable to drag her eyes from the events unfolding in front of her. Every channel was covering the story, every radio station was playing Penn Stadtler records. Outside in the street television news-teams were setting up their cameras on the lawn to catch her dash to the car; inside her apartment her telephones were off the hook.

Kneeling over a half-filled bag, still wearing the shirt in which she slept, she watched mesmerized as the images of the Slovakian valley were run again: the silver car leaking on the bank, the sheet over the body of Yale Meredith, the small boy describing what he had found.

No longer able to get through to the Kapolska Palace and with the studio closed for the Easter holiday, television was her only source of information. 'Not Sam, please God, not Sam,' she had begged when the news had first been flashed. But she had heard his death confirmed, seen his picture on the screen.

When she had been first out of college she had worked in television news: she knew what would be happening behind the scenes; extra staff being called in everywhere, evening flights to Poland from Western European capitals booked solidly. There would be a blitz on seats out of Los Angeles and New York, the network television companies would be chartering their own planes, and on the autobahns of Germany camera-crews, reporters and photographers would be racing eastwards.

No-one could remember a story quite like this one, a television anchorman was droning portentously, drawing vague parallels with the deaths of James Dean and Buddy Holly. *'But they only emerged as very big stories after the event, perhaps with some hindsight. Only the deaths of Elvis Presley, Marilyn Monroe and Rudolph Valentino came near to having the impact of what happened in that little wooded valley in Slovakia earlier today, and what is happening all over the world at this very moment.'*

But what had happened? Julie zipped through the channels. A 'mystery,' one was reporting, 'a bizarre accident,' said the next. Suddenly everyone in the world knew about *Shadows on a Wall*. A rare glimpse of Reuben Wiener, looking fifteen years older than the shining presidential photograph in the Buffalo lobby, and wearing what looked like a toupee for a man with a bigger head, caught her attention. Reporters had spotted him in a Manhattan street returning from a Good Friday morning walk in the park. He had set out before he heard the news, he said; now he was shocked. He actually looked *shattered*, and, avoiding further questions, scurried into the sanctuary of his apartment building.

Julie sat on her bedroom floor. Next door, in her study, the messages on her fax machine unrolled. *'Please call, Debbie Goldstone, KABC'*, *'TRYING TO GET TO YOU, Monty Calendar, LA Times'*, *'Julie, where are you? Can you call me, please? Jim Freedman, Variety'*.

It was the second best Good Friday news story of all time.

The first copy-cat suicide was reported on the radio as the car taking her to the airport turned left off Santa Monica Boulevard on to the San Diego Freeway. A teenage girl in Corpus Christi, Texas, had borrowed her father's Oldsmobile and driven it into the bay. Bystanders reported hearing music playing loudly on the cassette-player as the car toppled into the water. When divers recovered the body the victim was discovered to be wearing a Penn Stadtler monogrammed baseball cap, a pair of long tennis-shorts, a T-shirt bearing the slogan of a dove enclosed in a condom, and an ear-ring which resembled a toothpick.

It is in the first moments of chaos that the biggest fortunes are made. When it comes to news, speed is money: exclusivity is riches.

Tomas Lendak stared at the picture as it came off the printer. It was better than he had dared hope. Yale Meredith was propped against the side of the car, her legs splayed wide, her skirt up above her knees, showing her pants pulled down across her thighs and a dark, narrow diamond of pubic hair. He leant over and stared hard at the still beautiful face, the wide mouth contorted almost into an accidental smile as though death had come as a joke in a last vague attempt to draw breath. Had it not been for the blind, glazed, open eyes, she might almost have been sleeping, resting perhaps, enjoying a picnic by a river bank. It was the perfect picture: for magazine covers, tabloid newspapers, posters. Tomas Lendak knew he was staring at a fortune.

But there was much more. He had shot everything, roll after roll, wide shots of the crumpled car with the sweating, harnessed horses in the background, the boy, the river, the anxious police: and, of course, the bodies. Other photographers and local television news-teams had followed him to the scene, and their pictures were already being transmitted to an astonished world, but the victims they had photographed had been covered in sheets. Only he had the death masks, taken in first one ambulance and then another as the corpses had been transported out of the valley. He thought about the picture of Robert Kennedy dying in the hotel kitchen in Los Angeles, of the bullet-ridden corpse of Che Guevara and of the dead Elvis in his coffin in Memphis, and his heart beat faster.

At his side now an old schoolfriend, Ivan Brovotny, was working carefully at the prints. Ivan was a good, painstaking technician, and, with a family to support, had leapt at the promise of two hundred American dollars to give up his Good Friday evening and go downstairs to his photography shop. 'Have something to eat with the children while I do the developing,' Ivan had offered kindly. But Lendak had declined politely. Insisting Brovotny use new chemicals, he had stood over him all the time. Even with someone as honest and careful as Ivan he would not risk losing sight of these negatives for one second.

As they worked they could hear a television showing a Sam

461

Jordan movie in the flat upstairs; the radio in the dark-room had just finished playing a Penn Stadtler album track and was repeating the news. It was the same all around the dial, Czech, Polish, Hungarian, Ukranian and German stations swamping the airwaves with astonished accounts of celebrity death. Lendak had rarely known news catch light so quickly. The macabre, noisy funeral procession down the mountain, with cars, motor bikes and even bicycles following the ambulances and police cars, had become a tumult reverberating around the world.

He had his plans ready. Even before they had begun the processing he had made a call to a French girl who had once worked for the Magnum picture agency. Her name was Bulle. He had something special to sell, he had said. He needed her book of contacts and her expertise in the international market. He had then asked her to book them into a suite at the nearest hotel to Charles de Gaulle airport in Paris for the following day and to wait for him there.

By ten the pictures were ready. Paying and thanking Ivan he made his way back to his car, the negatives and several copies of the prints under his shirt. Only by feeling them against his skin did he feel secure. There was an Air France flight to Paris from Prague at eight the following morning. He would drive through the night to be on it.

At the beginning of this Good Friday all he had wanted had been a Mercedes and enough money to get by. He was going to get much more than that.

(iii)

The basement bar was packed. Almost the entire unit had been drinking for hours, at first quietly, now more emotionally, as conflicting rumours duelled around the palace, explanations were suggested and sightings of Harvey Bamberg reported. Suspended in one corner of the room was a television on which CNN were running a Yale Meredith obituary, while all around local television crews were badgering for news, jealous already of the arrival of the first international journalists.

It was after twelve and Belinda was drinking coffee with Sadie and Billy. Billy had been filming for most of the day and had just finished negotiating to have a fresh supply of film shipped down from Warsaw.

Earlier they had watched together as Charlie had returned from the river. He had been muddy and trembling, two Polish policemen accompanying him. Inside the Kapolska he had sunk into a sofa. Instinctively Belinda had put out a hand in comfort. Dragoman and Agnieszka had watched.

'What about Harvey?' Sadie had wanted to know, her black eyes wet behind her glasses.

Charlie had shaken his head.

Belinda looked around the bar: at Gully Pepper, refusing to make a comment to a German reporter because the Buffalo head of publicity had not yet told her what to say; at Simone, anxious, but cool under pressure, drawing the attention away from the unit; at Jack Dragoman, monopolizing the bar phone, speaking to his agent in California; at Tony Delmonte, a kind of hero raconteur now, as he told again, in ever more colourful language, his surprise at seeing 'Sam Jordan's dead penis dangling out of his trousers like a worm from a blackbird's beak'; and at Sadie, quietly tearful at the rupturing of her family of film-makers.

It was late and everyone was tired. But, for once on location, no-one wanted to go to bed.

(iv)

He was frightened. He was in Poland and he was an accessory to murder. Did they still have the death penalty in Poland? It wasn't just any murder. Three of the victims were obscenely famous. The prosecution would make a mountain out of that. It would be the trial of the century, live on satellite around the world. He could imagine people stopping in shopping malls, standing in crowds outside television shops, gazing at him in the dock, shaking their heads that any normal mind could plan such a crime.

And he *had* planned it. He had devised a blueprint for an insurance-led murder and it had happened almost exactly as written, although in his version death had been in a car in a harbour. When the police read the treatment they would never believe it had been coincidence. They would look for motives and find him riddled with them; they would seek out resentments and he would be stooped under them. Then he thought about Harvey. Everyone was worrying about the disappearance of Harvey, but he knew Harvey was a murderer.

He lay in his bath, all but his mouth and nose submerged beneath the water. He had tried to lock the thin balsa-wood door, but it was warped and the bolt would no longer slide. He didn't know why he wanted to lock himself in: he might have to spend the rest of his life locked inside a small room. Unsure of what to do, he was acting like a guilty man.

'What are you doing here?' he had snapped earlier when Billy had found him in Harvey's office, kneeling in front of an in-tray.

'I saw the light. I thought perhaps Harvey had turned up.' Billy had looked puzzled. 'Are you all right, Charlie?'

Charlie had shaken his head. 'I'm sorry.' He had stood up. The red folder had not been in the office; nor had it been in Harvey's bedroom: he had been present when the police had searched there earlier. Had it been in the Noblesse American when it fell into the river? Were the Slovakian police studying a written translation at that very moment trying to decide whether to arrest him that night or to wait until the morning.

'Let's get a drink,' Billy had said, putting an arm out.

Charlie had shrunk from it. 'Thanks, but, if you don't mind, I think I'd be better in bed. I'm still shaken, I think.'

Billy had nodded understandingly.

Lifting his head from the water Charlie looked at his watch. It was nearly one in the morning. It would be early afternoon in California. He wondered whether Harry Weitzman and Julie Wyatt were airborne yet. They would be bringing a squadron of Buffalo lawyers with them. Would they bring one for him? And what about Carlos Gallego? Would he come? Would he bring his boys and his lawyers? Everyone would have lawyers except him. Even Harvey would have Mo Rosenbaum. He would need him. He wondered whether he ought to call Larry; agents lurked in the same dark corners as lawyers. He would need one, too.

'What are you saying, Charlie?' an imaginary Belinda sympathized. 'Why should you need a lawyer when it had nothing to do with you? It's just a terrible, terrible accident.'

An accident. That was what everyone was saying now, but for how long? And where was Harvey? Hiding somewhere in the forest? Would they go up into the hills, track him down with dogs and drag him out of the woods protesting his innocence?

Charlie took a sip from the glass of whisky which stood on the plastic tiles next to his bath. He tried to remember what he had written, the exact phrasings. Could it possibly be a coincidence?

A few minutes later, his bath towel stretched around him, he stared at the index on his word processor. It had been no coincidence.

(v)

Tim Westwood got through to Sadie's room just before one. She was still awake. He had been trying to reach her all evening, he told her, but all the lines had been busy. He had just wanted to reassure himself that she was safe, to know how she was feeling.

'I don't understand how I feel,' she said. 'Yes, I do. I feel older. So old you wouldn't believe. And lonely. I've been crying a lot, I don't know why. Shock, I suppose. I'm glad you rang. I can't help thinking that if there'd been four angels waiting to get their wings, like Clarence in *It's a Wonderful Life*, this would never have happened.'

There was a pause from the English end of the call. 'I don't know about that, Sadie. In *It's a Wonderful Life* Clarence threw himself into the river so that James Stewart would risk his life saving him and therefore not commit suicide. I'm not sure that Sam or Bruno or the others would have been prepared to risk their lives for anybody else. Movie stars only do that sort of thing in movies.'

465

Chapter Fifty-six

(i)

They had appeared overnight like a crop of mushrooms: now they covered the lawn in front of the palace, the satellite transmission dishes of world television. Standing at the window of her room Simone blinked as she tried to make sense of the new arrangement; the line of cars and station-wagons which stretched through the meadows, and the newcomers armed with their video cameras and microphones who were now staring up at the palace. The latest army of occupation had arrived at the Kapolska.

It was eight-thirty in the morning. It was not raining. She opened the window to let in some air, then, stepping across to her desk, dialled the number of the production office. Before going to bed she had organized a rota among the office staff so that someone would always be manning the phones. This morning she had only one question: was there any news of Harvey? There was not, she was told, although Nathalie Seillans and Edward Lampton had arrived by car from Warsaw during the night. She put the telephone down. She would be relieved to see Lampton.

A rolling sound on the gravel outside drew her back to the window. A black Lincoln Continental was drawing up. It carried diplomatic plates. Behind it came another black American car. As the limousine stopped Harry Weitzman, Julie Wyatt and Jake McKenzie stepped out; two familiar, wan-looking Buffalo executives and a couple of embassy types climbed from the

466

second car. Immediately a mob of television and radio reporters engulfed them. Pushing their way through, the party reached the palace doors. For one of the few moments in his life Jake McKenzie was left behind.

'No, I have no news . . . I'm sorry,' Simone could hear Jake saying. 'Please, may I go through . . . please, gentlemen . . . I'm very tired. Please . . .' The confidence had gone: he looked small down there, bewildered, encircled by the cameras and microphones. For a second, spotting a gap, he tried to break free, but reinforcements immediately moved to cut off his line of escape.

She watched, curiously detached, as the tormentors snapped at their victim. Jake's demeanour was unrecognizable from the super-agent of the Polo Lounge, the deal-maker who, only a couple of weeks earlier, had held the studio to ransom. He looked frightened. Sam Jordan, Yale Meredith and Bruno Messenger had been his top clients. The deals he had negotiated on their behalves had given him status. Without them he was just another player.

Leaving the window Simone went into her small bathroom. As the weak shaft of shower water fell on her she thought of Harvey, a sort of prayer unfolding. 'OK, I know, he's weak, indecisive, double crossing, manipulating, you name it. As a human being he may not be up to much, nor is he the smartest guy in the world. But as producers go he's a saint. Please let Harvey be all right.'

(ii)

Charlie watched her from the doorway. The Grave Digger had told him to go straight in, but he hesitated all the same. She was sitting on the edge of the bed, her wide hands resting on her thighs, her eyes staring into the pattern of the carpet. Her face was puffy and heavy bruises of exhaustion weighed under her eyes; even her famous bosom seemed reduced, slung lower across her chest. She was wearing a dark coat and skirt. There was no jewellery evident: little make-up. On a low table in front of her lay a breakfast tray. It was untouched. A cloud of cigarette smoke surrounded her. It was difficult to believe that this was the woman of *La Chambre* who had once enthralled him at the school film society.

'Nathalie . . .'

She didn't look up, but her hand went out to indicate that he should enter.

Cautiously he stepped into the twilight of the still-curtained room. He waited, hoping she might begin the conversation. She did not. At last he said: 'The police asked me to tell you they're searching the forest on both sides of the border . . .'

She nodded slowly.

'They will want to speak to you later . . . just a few questions, I imagine.'

This time there was no response.

'I'm sure that when Harvey turns up—'

'He was so young,' she interrupted.

'I'm sorry?' Charlie couldn't imagine that Harvey had ever been young.

'Penn. He was so very young. Such a beautiful young man. I was too old for him. But I think I made him happy . . . for a little while. He made me very happy.'

Charlie sat in silence, heavy with the weight of disappointment. Harvey deserved better than this, whatever he might have done. Charlie tried again. 'One theory is that he may be in shock, or perhaps he's lost his memory,' he said.

She breathed heavily, moving her shoulders in a backward circular motion, more an easing of tension than a shrug, but he knew it meant the same.

He didn't have much more to say, and, after a few minutes, he left her. He was depressed. With the morning, his fears of the previous night had abated only slightly. Wouldn't an innocent man notify the police of his suspicions? he asked himself. Didn't every hour he delayed increase suspicion of him, should the treatment be found? But then he thought about Harvey, torn apart with worry these last weeks. Perhaps there was some explanation. The least he could do was to give him the benefit of the doubt.

It was very quiet in the palace. While outside the besieging media army was growing with every flight into Warsaw, inside, members of the unit were shuffling through the apartments as though in the aftermath of some incomprehensible defeat. In Harvey's office he found Edward Lampton and a Czech interpreter. The interpreter was speaking on the phone, the Grave

Digger watching him. On the other side of the room Simone sat worrying. Returning down the marble staircase he came across Al Mutton in the props department. Mutton had heard the news on *The Voice of America* the previous night while driving back from a meeting in Potsdam. Now he was subdued. He had hitched his career to that of Bruno Messenger: now he was abandoned.

Charlie wandered on, the sound of the activity outside growing all the time. In one room Harry Weitzman was bent over a word processor with Gully Pepper picking out a Press statement; in another Buffalo lawyers were briefing the unit accountants. Looking into the dining room he saw Agnieszka and Jack Dragoman sitting in a corner together. He withdrew before he was noticed. Charlie felt guilty about Agnieszka. He could no longer think of anything to say to her. Their relationship had been built on mutual need. She could offer him no comfort now: and he would be a handicap to her.

In the corridor he passed Beverly from make-up flirting with two policemen.

(iii)

Tomas Lendak had bought the Czech and Slovak papers in Prague, and, when he arrived at Charles de Gaulle Airport, as many foreign daily newspapers as he could carry – French, German, British, Dutch, Italian, Spanish. There was only one story: 'SAM, YALE, PENN SIND TOT,' mourned *Bild*, 'ÉTOILES TROUVÉE NOYÉES,' read *Paris Soir*, 'STELLE DI HOLLYWOOD TROVATE MORTE,' repeated *Corriere Della Sera*, 'THE DAY THE MOVIES DIED,' wept the *Sun*. All carried photographs of the Noblesse American and portraits of the victims. There were no pictures of corpses.

In the taxi on the way to the hotel, his friend Bulle at his side, Lendak allowed himself a grim nod of satisfaction. He was still ahead of the pack.

The photographs were spread across a table when *Paris Match* phoned from reception to say they were on their way up. At

469

first there had been scepticism, but, if the magazine didn't believe Lendak, they had listened to Bulle. The agreement had been that Bulle would get the photographer to the right people: after that it was up to him to do the bargaining. Bulle was a rounded thirty-five year old, with a pretty face, a daughter of ten and an independent, hard-working life. Although they had slept together when she had visited Prague, Bulle and Lendak were friends more than lovers. Now, for a promise of 5 per cent of whatever the pictures brought, Bulle was more than happy to loan out her address book and, when necessary, act as interpreter. Lendak spoke some German and a little English; Bulle was fluent in French, Spanish, German and English. Lendak knew that if he had offered her a flat five thousand francs she would have been grateful, but with 5 per cent this was certain to be the best paying job of her life. That pleased him. He was fond of Bulle. It was good to be able to help her. And a regular agency would have wanted 50 per cent.

In the end he settled for two and a half million francs from *Paris Match* for all French rights, the prints to be handed over that afternoon when the cheque was delivered. While he had been negotiating Bulle had been on the telephone in the bedroom, talking to *Stern* in Hamburg and *The Sunday Times* in London. Both were flying representatives to Paris immediately. Next she would call *Oggi* in Milan, and, later in the day, *People* magazine in New York. Then there were the Dutch, Spanish, Scandinavians, Australians, Japanese, all kinds of smaller countries, and television rights everywhere. The word was spreading and the offers were coming in.

At this point, as Bulle outlined her day's work, Lendak telephoned the hotel manager and asked if his suite could be extended by another couple of rooms and at least four more phones. That agreed, he telephoned his brother-in-law in the Slovakian police. It was a lucky day for him, too.

It was like a storm which was endlessly building, Billy thought: at first over in Slovakia, where barricades had failed to prevent a pilgrimage of sightseers from reaching the river, then at the curve on the Polish side of the border where it was believed the car had left the road, and where already a drift of floral bouquets was beginning to form; now it was back to the Kapolska Palace for an official Buffalo Press briefing.

At the top of the main dining hall Harry Weitzman stood nervously at a long trestle-table, Julie Wyatt, Gully Pepper and Jake McKenzie on one side, and on the other, the remaining *Shadows on a Wall* producers, Nathalie Seillans, Edward Lampton, Al Mutton and Charlie. Perhaps four hundred reporters, cameramen and members of the unit faced them, pushing in through doors, mobbing outside around open windows.

A Polish government official spoke first, promising a full investigation, but adding that, as the bodies had been found on the other side of the border, a second briefing, with the results of preliminary autopsies, would be held in Trencin in Slovakia the following day.

After a short delay for various translations, Weitzman stood up to speak. He was trembling. 'On behalf of the Buffalo Pictures Corporation and every member of the production team of *Shadows on a Wall*,' he began, reading from a sheet of paper, 'I would like to say that it was with the deepest sadness and shock that we heard yesterday of the loss of four brilliant artists, marvellous, loving friends and wonderful, caring human beings.'

For a moment a fusillade of rapid-fire snapping shutters distracted him, but he quickly looked back at the script written for him by Gully Pepper.

'All of us at Buffalo Pictures, and every one of the family of cast and crew of *Shadows on a Wall* felt it a personal privilege to have the opportunity to work with such talented people. And I know I speak for everyone when I say we will miss them very, very much, as will the entire motion-picture and musical communities.'

Operating a second camera Billy found Sadie in his lens. She was sitting on a window-sill, scratching her head, looking slightly astonished.

'As you all know, our producer, Harvey Bamberg, is, I'm

afraid, still missing, which is very worrying for his wife, Nathalie, and for us, his friends and colleagues. We are all praying that he is found speedily and safely.'

Now Billy went close on Nathalie. Her head was bowed as she played her part.

'In the mean time, while the Polish and Slovakian police are conducting their investigations into the tragedy, and until an assessment can be made as to the best course of action which we at Buffalo Pictures might take, production on *Shadows on a Wall* is suspended. Thank you.'

Even before he had sat down, the questions had started. Who was the last person to see the victims alive? Did they always travel together? Where had they been going on the night of the accident? Had they been lost? Had they been drinking? Had they been taking drugs?

'Is it true that the final budget for *Shadows on a Wall* is likely to be in the region of a hundred million dollars?' came a question from the side of the hall.

Weitzman shook his head. 'We are over-budget, but I can't say for sure by how much at this moment,' he blocked.

More financial probings and dead ends followed before: 'Can you confirm that Yale Meredith and Sam Jordan were having sex at the time of the accident?' The question came piping, sharp and Scottish, from the midst of a throng of newspaper reporters.

Harry Weitzman's back straightened. 'I'm sorry, I don't think this is either the time or the place for questions like that.'

'But Sam Jordan's trousers were undone, were they not?'

'I'm sorry, that is a most unpleasant smear on a very great star.'

An American television girl's voice was next. 'We understand Yale Meredith was not wearing any underwear.'

'That is absolutely untrue. Now, if you'll excuse me, we all have a lot to be getting on with . . .' Weitzman was on his way, leaving it to Gully Pepper to do what she did best.

'There is no truth in any of the malicious rumours that anything unseemly may have been happening in the car at the time of the accident. All the victims were fully clothed when found,' Gully lied vigorously, but it fell on deaf ears. The Press conference was already breaking up. That wasn't what they wanted to hear.

It was all too soon, anyway, thought Billy. There was an order to these things. Yesterday the shock of the deaths had been the

472

main story; today it was the reason for the accident; tomorrow would bring the repercussions to the movie and Buffalo Pictures; only lastly, like leakage from their coffins, and when all other aspects had been exhausted, should the dirt come out.

He turned off his camera. He had had a miserable six months and he wished he was at home in London buying the rabbit from the pet shop in Primrose Hill; but he knew now that, barring interference, he had an extraordinary television series.

(v)

'Sadie! Could I have a word?' A plump young man in a navy-blue corduroy suit and a hand-painted tie was pushing through the cameras.

Sadie didn't recognize him.

'You promised me an interview.' He had the easy familiarity of show-business reporters everywhere.

'I'm sorry. I'm not doing any interviews until the film is finished, and certainly not now. I haven't promised anyone anything.' Sadie looked for another way out of the hall.

The young man followed. 'Oh, but you did. You telephoned me last summer and I gave you the address of the auditions. You promised me an interview when you became a star.'

Sadie stopped. It seemed so long ago, something that had happened to a schoolgirl she used to know. She hesitated. She wasn't a star, not in any sense, but she had been very grateful. 'Well, perhaps a very short interview.'

She wanted to say that they had all been horrible monsters really, the three she knew, anyway, and that Harry Weitzman had been talking through his ears because most of the cast and crew loathed them. But she didn't. They were dead. No-one in movies ever spoke ill of the dead, not the recently dead, anyway. I'm becoming such an old show-biz hypocrite, she thought, just part of the hype machine which will create more movie myths. But knowing didn't stop her. She told the lies the world wanted to hear. Millions of people were abject with grief: who was she to upset them further?

473

She did the interview sitting on a camera case belonging to one of the television crews. Around her the Kapolska lawn had turned into an electronic news-gathering bazaar. The threatened new downpour had not occurred, and everywhere interviews and negotiations were taking place. Jack Dragoman, as the movie's biggest star, now that those bigger than him were dead, was doing a live link with *Good Morning, America*; Tony Delmonte and Sam Jordan's bodyguard were talking money with the *News Of The World* and the *National Enquirer* respectively; and Delphine Claviers, who had hurried from Antibes as soon as she heard the news, was sobbing silently into an RTL camera. The part of the Empress Josephine had always been tiny, and likely to be cut shorter, and Delphine had loathed Bruno and Yale, and, when he had persisted in resisting her, Sam Jordan, too; but, as Gully Pepper had pointed out, this was Delphine's best publicity shot in years, and one not to be squandered.

And what had all this got to do with the magic of movies? Sadie asked herself, as she continued to mouth her own lies.

Everything. She had learnt that much.

(vi)

Belinda discovered Charlie in the orangery at the rear of the Kapolska. Scattered on the ground around him were some English newspapers he must have borrowed from one of the reporters. He still wore the haunted look of the previous night. It made him look very young.

'I called my mother. She says there's nothing else on the news. Apparently it's like when John Lennon was shot, only three times as big. Everyone's talking about *Shadows on a Wall*.'

'The movie that never was.'

'I'm sorry, Charlie.'

He tried to smile. 'We're the lucky ones.'

'What do *you* think happened?'

He shook his head.

She picked up a newspaper. 'So much space, so many pictures, headlines, articles. D'you remember how grateful we were for just the smallest mention up in Edinburgh?'

He didn't answer.

Because of her senior position the Polish police made an exception for her. She arrived alone, sitting in the back of a limousine, dark glasses hiding her grief, more monochrome than ever now.

'Wait here,' she told the driver, and, with a nod to the police while simultaneously ignoring a mute crowd of sightseers behind barricades, Julie Wyatt entered the white lodge.

She could sense his presence immediately. In the small hall, a raincoat and overcoat hung neatly on pegs above two pairs of polished gum boots; Sam Jordan had liked his world kept tidy. In the kitchen she found a stack of fan mail posted mainly in Europe, addressed to him here at the Kapolska, some letters opened, other screwed up and tossed in a waste-paper basket. A photograph peeping from an envelope caught her eye: it showed a voluptuous young housewife reclining on a patterned sofa in what looked like a housing-project apartment. Behind the girl was the front of a pram. She was wearing a black, shortie night-dress which revealed most of her breasts and buttocks. One hand was between her legs which were open. On the back was a name, Olga, and a Katowice telephone number.

Julie stared at the photograph. There was no letter. Sam would have looked at this picture. Perhaps on the morning of his death he would have seen it and been amused by the crudeness of the offer. She wondered who might have taken the photograph. A husband? Then she turned again to the name. Olga couldn't have known that Sam Jordan received such offers every day of his life. How would this young woman be feeling now? She knew the answer to that.

She moved on through the lodge, past the cartons of vitamin pills. It was gloomy, the shades in each room drawn, every star's defence against the paparazzi. In a sitting room there was a television and guide to satellite listings, a small library of books about Napoleon and a slide projector. She switched it on and set the carousel in motion. A hum, a whirr and a picture on a wall. One hand inside a dark green overcoat, the familiar white tunic, buttoned high at the neck, the three-cornered hat: the most beautiful Napoleon in history. She gazed at the slightly quizzical expression, as though teasing an admission out of a nervous subordinate, the easy athleticism of the posture, the film-star confidence. The next transparency was almost exactly the same: another followed and another, all virtually identical. She took the last one and slipped it into her jacket pocket.

In the bathroom a pile of scripts lay by the lavatory. Some had pages torn out. She picked up a comb: two or three dark golden hairs were caught in its teeth. In a cabinet was a siege supply of contraceptives. She thought about the abortion Sam had insisted upon. He had never used contraceptives in those days, and she had been too astonished by his attentions to suggest precautions. She had wanted to keep the baby, but Sam had insisted. He had sent her flowers and a present of an open, first-class ticket to anywhere in the world the day after the termination, but had not returned her calls. They had not slept together again.

By his bed she found an address book and looked for her own name among the hundreds of girls. It wasn't there. She was listed only under Buffalo Pictures. Perhaps he had never received her change of address card, she told herself.

She had often imagined this room, pictured herself there with him. She lay on the bed, the sheets neatly folded by the Kapolska maids, her face hidden in the pillow. She could smell him there: the memory of his body.

Taking off her clothes she pulled back the sheets: his presence was almost tangible. She slipped into the cool envelope of the bed. Her face was wet. She came quickly.

The Polish police watched her as she left the white lodge, but said nothing.

(viii)

Carlos Gallego arrived just before midnight in a black Mercedes. Standing at his window, Charlie saw him first. He had left Agnieszka in the bar with some French reporters.

Charlie had been thinking about Harvey, wondering how the little man could have been so sure that he would not run immediately to the police and tell them of his suspicions. But he hadn't: Harvey had guessed right.

476

At first, in his paranoia, Charlie half-fancied the large black car arriving so silently might be coming for him. In movie-lore a black Mercedes always suggested menace.

When he saw that it contained Gallego, accompanied by two of his lieutenants, he didn't know if it was good or bad. Carlos Gallego had his own kind of menace.

Chapter Fifty-seven

(i)

The Noblesse American rose again on the morning of the third day, an Easter Sunday spectacular for a world-wide television audience. All night the fans had kept vigil in the valley. Leaving their motor cycles and cars on the mountain track, they had camped in the forests or sat at damp fires around the ox-bow curve of the river. They were the ultimate devotees, the Penn Stadtler clones and the Sam Jordan and Yale Meredith look-alikes, buying hastily printed commemorative posters and T-shirts from the quicksilver pedlars who now lurked on the paths through the woods.

The position of the Noblesse American had been a problem from the start. Lying halfway up the river-bank, it had proved difficult for the forensic scientists to look for the cause of the tragedy, or indeed for it to be protected from souvenir hunters. It had arrived by water, but, with sharp rapids downstream, it could not easily leave by water; nor was there any track wide enough to get it through the forest. In the end the lifting power of a giant, Russian-built helicopter made glorious television.

'Now I can see why it was Harvey's pride and joy,' Billy said to Edward Lampton, crushed alongside him in the mêlée of observers, and the only one wearing a black tie, as the Noblesse ascended gently into the sky.

The Grave Digger nodded, scratched his chin thoughtfully, and then moved off to talk to some Slovakian officials. Since his arrival at the Kapolska he had been very busy.

478

Billy glanced around for something else to film. Carlos Gallego was standing alone by the edge of the river. In his expensive clothes, and with his neat Italian shoes caked in mud, he should perhaps have looked uncomfortable in these surroundings. But his intelligent face betrayed no unease. He was watching the crowd, observing everything, the police, the pilgrims, the Press. At last, as though content that there was nothing more to be learnt, he began his return up the mountain. A silent Familia Gallego lieutenant fell into step behind him.

(ii)

The boy saw the car being flown out of the valley on the lunchtime news. Now it really did look like a spaceship. He had just returned from Easter Sunday Mass where all the congregation had looked at him because he was now so famous. The girl who lived in the apartment upstairs had sat in the pew across the aisle and spent much of the service casting him long looks, until her mother had nudged her and demanded that she pay attention to the Agnus Dei. When the boy looked at her he found himself thinking about the dead lady and the patch of dark hair between her thighs. He was ashamed to have such thoughts, especially in church, but he couldn't stop them. And he wondered if the girl would invite him in to play with her again when her mother was out at work.

(iii)

'. . . *as I was saying before the heavens fell in, or, should I say, before the car fell in . . .*' began Sadie with the slightest cringe, '*you can't say life on* Shadows on a Wall *hasn't had its moments. Unfortunately at this precise moment we're all waiting around wondering what's going to happen, a bit like the days after exams at school when the whole point has gone. Tim's terribly kind. He sent me a chocolate camel today. He's also not mad the way I first thought. Well, I mean he's mad all right, barking really, but in a nice way. He's spending the entire*

479

Easter running the film over and over in his cutting room. That makes him sound like something out of Sunset Boulevard, *doesn't it? Max, the bald one, perhaps, although he's got more hair than a Pre-Raphaelite's harlot. Apparently he's been making films in his parents' basement since he was ten, shooting, editing, adding the effects, everything; some sort of child prodigy of the cinema, I suppose.'*

She looked around. She was sitting on the lawn again. The Kapolska was quieter today, all the Press and producers having gone off to Trencin to hear the results of the autopsies. That reminded her of something.

'Oh yes, before I forget, there's some disgusting gossip going around about Marilyn Monroe and what one of the morticians is supposed to have done to her. I don't believe it for one minute, but I keep thinking about Yale Meredith on the slab over in Slovakia, and . . . well, I mean, I didn't like her, but . . .'

There was so much that Claire would want to know.

(iv)

Force majeure. That was the phrase the lawyers were using, the one the insurance companies would be facing. 'The way I see it we don't have any *alternative* but to claim *force majeure*,' Harry Weitzman had been saying all weekend. 'It's tragic, but without Sam and Yale the movie is dead. It seems to me we have a perfect claim.'

'A *perfect claim*.' The words reverberated in Charlie's head. Was Weitzman trying to convince himself or had the insurance investigators, who had flocked to the Kapolska just behind the Buffalo executives, let slip their own initial assessments? Was it just possible that Harvey's plan had worked? His tormentors were dead. The movie could not be completed. It was the ultimate, hundred-million-dollar movie insurance scam. But, if it was perfect, why hadn't Harvey turned up to help claim the insurance? Where *was* Harvey?

The tapping of microphones refocused his thoughts. He was with a group from the movie in a packed gymnasium in Trencin waiting for the Press briefing to begin. Until the last minute he had not intended to be there. What if the treatment had been found, if the Slovakian police had had it translated and were waiting to arrest him? The thought had kept him awake most of the previous night.

In the end he had been unable to prevent himself attending. He had to know what had happened.

On a low rostrum, almost completely hidden by cameras, microphones and lights, with photographers hanging from the gymnasium wall-bars, a young interpreter was beginning to speak from a prepared statement. Her pronunciation was precise: the specifics not long delayed. 'The injuries to Bruno Messenger's vertebrae were consistent with the neck striking the back of the car seat in a fall from a great height. The pathologists concluded therefore that Bruno Messenger died instantly from a broken neck.'

There was a murmur around the hall as 'broken neck' was translated to non-English-speaking reporters. The interpreter, a dark woman with a slit in her skirt and a turquoise silk shirt, on the world stage for probably the only time in her life, waited for calm, and then continued.

'In the case of the three other occupants of the car, the cause of death was found to be from drowning, when the vehicle filled with water. Marks on the windscreen and windows suggest that attempts were made to break the glass from within. But, as the windows were made of reinforced glass, this would not have been possible. Nor was it possible to open the windows as they were electrically operated and the electrical system appears to have failed when the car was submerged. Attempts also appear to have been made to kick open the doors, but that would also not have been possible because of the weight of water pressing against them.'

The interpreter paused again allowing the significance of this to sink in. 'It is, therefore, the investigators' belief that the three victims who had survived the fall were alive and aware of the fate awaiting them for some minutes as the car filled with water.'

There was a shocked moment in the gymnasium. Ranks of journalists and photographers grimaced. Charlie examined his hands and thought about St John Nepomuk. Harvey would not have wanted anyone to suffer, no matter how much he had hated them.

It was at this point that he became aware of a gasping sound coming from somewhere close by. Almost hidden between the camera operators, Alice Bauccio, hardly seen at the Kapolska all weekend, was struggling to control her sobs.

At the front of the gymnasium the interpreter was making her final announcement. There was no news about the whereabouts of Harvey Bamberg; no evidence of foul play. It was a mystery.

There was also no mention of any treatment outlining the perfect murder being found. Harvey had been very thorough.

(v)

Carlos Gallego was standing at the front of the large crowd of sightseers and cameramen as Julie Wyatt and the Buffalo party came out of the gymnasium. Most of the other *Shadows on a Wall* people had already left. She dropped her head when she saw him. Nathalie Seillans raised hers.

'I was hoping you would wait,' Nathalie murmured huskily, moving towards Gallego's Mercedes as the cameras followed.

Gallego stared at her.

'It's been so terrible.'

Still Gallego did not reply.

A tremor of uncertainty shook her voice. 'I'm so worried for Harvey . . .' Her eyes filled with tears, her lower lip quivered.

Julie stepped forward to meet the Buffalo limousine as it approached through the crowds.

'Julie!'

She turned. Nathalie Seillans was staring into an empty space. Gallego had side-stepped her.

'I thought maybe you could drive back with me,' he said quietly. 'Give us chance to talk.'

'I'm sorry, I . . .' Julie looked to Weitzman for an excuse.

'Good idea,' the head of the studio encouraged.

The rear door of the Mercedes was already open. Julie glanced at Nathalie. The trembling lip had developed a scowl: the skin was flushed. For semi-girls like Julie Wyatt rejection had been a lifetime's occurrence: she was almost immured against it. For Nathalie Seillans it was incomprehensible.

He wanted to know everything. So many questions: about the movie and the shape it was in, about Buffalo Pictures,

482

Weitzman and Reuben Wiener; about Nathalie, Penn Stadtler and Harvey. He also wanted to know about her and Sam Jordan. He had heard all the rumours: he wanted facts. He was leaving for London that evening. Julie talked, he listened. Carlos Gallego was a good listener.

(vi)

Jack Dragoman and Belinda had sex for the last time to the sound of a Spanish television cameraman singing *Unchained Melody* in the style of the Righteous Brothers. The singer was very good and very loud, his voice carrying through the palace. The sex was bad. Afterwards they lay in silence. They were in Dragoman's bed.

From outside in the drive came the sounds of journalists and television crews arriving and departing. The Kapolska's basement bar never closed.

At last Belinda said: 'I've been considering what you said . . . about going back to the States with you . . .' She was gazing at the light patterns on the wall, looking at the pictures they made.

Dragoman didn't speak. He was a different man again since the deaths. She could understand that. For months he had been obliged to comply with the whims of the bigger names. Now he was the centre of attention and relishing it. He had even flown a personal Press assistant from London to help schedule his publicity. When he was not doing interviews he was talking to his agent in Los Angeles. Belinda had always known he was a man of changing personalities, but this latest opportunist was unrecognizable from the diffident Will Yorke who had befriended her.

She pushed on. 'Well, thanks for inviting me. For a little while I was tempted. But I'm going to say no. I don't think it would work. Not you and me. Not me and Hollywood.'

'Are you sure?' he asked after a few moments.

'Certain. I'm sorry.' She wondered why she was apologizing.

He moved in the bed and put an arm out to her. 'I know. I've been thinking the same thing.'

'Really?' She didn't know whether to be relieved or insulted.

A short time later he put his hand back between her legs. She moved it away. Now that the words had been said it felt like a violation.

He sighed and turned away. 'Well, I guess I'd better get some sleep. I have a live link with the BBC tomorrow morning. I don't want to look as though I've been lying awake worrying all weekend.'

So what did you expect, she thought as she let herself out of the room: pleas to reconsider, promises of eternal friendship, synthesizers which sounded like violins . . . ?

Who was she trying to kid? The guy was an actor, for heaven's sake! He didn't play that kind of part.

(vii)

The discovery was made in the early hours of the Monday morning by forensic scientists working through the night to satisfy media demand for information.

Attached to one of the rear bolts holding the Noblesse American's twin exhausts in place were fragments of green leather.

Chapter Fifty-eight

(i)

'We'll be flying them home today,' said Edward Lampton, keeping his voice low. 'I thought you might like to be with us.'

For a moment Billy didn't follow. 'You'll be what?' It was just after ten on the Monday morning.

'Permission to remove the bodies from Trencin morgue has just come through. Lampton Funerals International will be taking the remains back to the States. We're very familiar with this kind of business.'

Billy's one eye blinked. The Grave Digger must have been lobbying for this since the moment he heard the news.

'Our London office will be making the official announcement,' Lampton was continuing, 'just as soon as the US Customs have given the all-clear. I thought it would be good for your documentary if you came with us. The President is sending a jet to collect the bodies.'

'The President?'

'The President of the United States. He's very keen on show-business. He plays the saxophone.'

'Yes, that's right.' He had a strange way with conversation, this Grave Digger.

'Penn Stadtler's body will, of course, be going to England. Virgin have offered to fly it to Gatwick. We'll take over there again.'

Billy was surprised. 'I'd no idea it would be so soon. I

imagined there would be all kinds of red tape . . .' At that very moment he knew detectives were driving up from Bratislava to interview members of the unit.

The Grave Digger nodded. 'To be honest, I think the Slovakians are embarrassed by all the attention. Obviously their enquiries are continuing, and the insurance investigation could go on for ever, but they feel it could reflect badly on them if that prevents the bodies from being decently buried. When we offered to help they jumped at the chance. And naturally the White House doesn't want to be left out.'

'Naturally,' Billy repeated. Who *would* want to be left out of the media-fest of the year?

'So, you'll be coming with us?'

'Absolutely.'

The Grave Digger smiled, a professional funeral director's smile, signifying satisfaction rather than pleasure. 'Good. Well, I'd better be getting along then.' And with that he hurried off to beg a favour of the art department: with Lampton Funerals International taking care of arrangements he wanted to be sure there was a Lampton's eternal-life olive-tree motif on every hearse. This was the best advertising opportunity they were ever going to get.

(ii)

'Attached to the *underneath* of his car?' Charlie repeated, as the strip of green leather was carefully withdrawn from the polythene bag. 'How could that be?'

The interpreter passed the question to the two detectives. They shrugged. One muttered something to the other. 'Perhaps he was run over,' came the translation.

'By his own car?' Charlie frowned. 'And if so, where is he?'

More translations and shrugs followed. Every day, as Charlie's paranoia about his unwitting involvement receded, his worries for Harvey increased. He stared at the remains of the epaulette. Many of the costumes for Napoleon's army had had epaulettes, but none like this.

'I'd have to say, yes, this looks as though it might belong to Harvey Bamberg's jacket,' he said. He actually had no doubts.

486

One of the detectives began to write a note in his book, but at that moment Jack Dragoman, accompanied by Agnieszka, entered the hall and began to make his way up the marble staircase. 'Harry Twomey,' the detective exclaimed.

His colleague flushed. They were both excited to find themselves in movie circles.

Waiting for the squall of international television fame to pass, Charlie watched Agnieszka and Dragoman. They seemed right together. With Dragoman, Agnieszka already looked the star she wanted to be.

'So, thank you very much . . .' The interpreter was saying as the two detectives prepared to leave, still glancing up the stairs as though half-expecting Gary Cooper or Jack Nicholson to materialize.

Charlie shook hands. The leather epaulette was back inside its polythene bag. But where was Harvey?

(iii)

In the late afternoon Simone watched through the production office window as the Buffalo general staff withdrew. For two days individual members of the crew had been deserting, cadging rides to the airport with reporters who were following the story out of Poland. Now the top brass were slipping away, too, leaving the field to the insurance investigators. Harry Weitzman looked strained again today. The latest rumours, in a place where there was nothing but rumour, were that the insurers would aggressively question the excessive cost of the movie: a hundred million dollars meant a lot of questions.

Jake McKenzie was the last into the limousine. As he was ducking his handsome head inside the car his eyes caught those of Simone at the window. He didn't smile: but he raised his hand; an apology of a sort. She nodded. Throughout the production he had been careful to avoid her. Things were different now.

She had been sorry when Edward Lampton had left to organize the shipping of the bodies from Trencin. He had been very supportive during these past three days. Her feelings towards him puzzled her. He was hardly her type; almost old enough to be her father.

487

She had asked him the previous night how he could have been naïve enough to let Harvey talk him into paying for the script. 'Naïvety had nothing to do with it,' he had replied. 'I knew the risks. It seemed like fun.'

'You mean Nathalie seemed like fun?' she had probed.

'Perhaps, at first,' he had conceded. 'But Harvey's enthusiasm was so infectious. You've no idea how exhilarating it was for me to become involved. It still is.'

As the limousines sped away Simone returned to typing the movement order for those taking the charter to London the following day. Weitzman's last instruction had been to get everybody home and off the payroll as quickly as possible. The suspension of production was now indefinite.

(iv)

It was a glossy display of celebrity death and Julie Wyatt was sickened. The international magazines must have reached the news-stand at Warsaw Airport just ahead of them, and Jake McKenzie was now staring in shock at the pictures of his dead clients. Scooping up a handful of magazines she fled to the Ladies room. Gully Pepper had warned that the photographs might be brutal, but nothing had prepared her for this. She did not want to look at the pictures of Sam Jordan, but knew she must. When she did, she was surprised. It was not a former lover lying there. It was a dead film star.

Weitzman was hurrying to board the Buffalo jet when she rejoined the party. He was grey with shock. 'I've just been on to New York,' he said. 'It's a melt-down situation. Buffalo stock opened nine dollars eighty down on Wall Street this morning. Reuben's screaming for blood. We're going through the floor. It's all over.'

It was like watching a snake devour its tail, she thought, as hour by hour the jet raced back across the Atlantic and the rush out of Buffalo and away from the Candy Corn Corporation continued.

No matter that Candy Corn could absorb its Buffalo losses while barely missing a beat. After an Easter weekend of headlines and speculation, the markets had seen the photographs, too; a one-hundred-million-dollar write-off movie, insurers looking difficult and a terrible death in Kodachrome had its own logic.

Sitting in a corner of the cabin she watched as Weitzman and the other Buffalo hierarchy monitored their own fall from grace amid the tumbling prices. Sometimes Weitzman would speak to Reuben Wiener or to the Buffalo bankers in New York, but equally often he would be on to his personal lawyer, his private banker, his stockbroker. She couldn't blame him. The studio was in free fall and so was he.

Perhaps it should have occurred to her that her own career was also at that very moment being kicked around the floors of the markets. But with the magazines on her lap she was processing other thoughts.

(v)

'This is a sad day for all Americans,' husked the President of the United States and bowed his head. Solemnly the coffins bearing the two most popular corpses on earth slid silently into two white Cadillac hearses. Across the tarmac Bruno Messenger's remains, as though impatient to be off, were already being driven away.

'Amen,' murmured a Wonderwoman reporter from *Entertainment Today*, and blew her nose.

Billy was exhausted. It had been the busiest day of his career. He glanced at Edward Lampton. It had been the *best* day of his career. The Lampton Funerals International stage management had been perfect.

Billy glanced around, not wanting to miss anything. The flag beside the Andrews Air Force Base control tower was at half-mast: the American media at full strength, their pictures already encircling the earth.

Having welcomed the dead heroes home just in time for a live link on the seven o'clock news, the President now returned quickly to his car.

'And cut,' Billy said quietly to Freddie as the hearses headed for the main gates and the President accelerated away to the White House. There was no point in wasting film.

It was too late to telephone home so, when he reached the hotel, Billy sent a series of faxes to Ilse and the children. They were in the form of a strip cartoon, showing himself with a large net on the end of a pole pursuing an Easter Bunny from Poland to America. In each frame one of the children's names was mentioned. He felt guilty about missing Easter, and the image seemed appropriate, anyway. What else did documentary makers do other than chase about trying to capture fleeting moments on film?

When he had finished he was so sleepy he could scarcely keep his eyes open, but he couldn't resist a quick look through the television movie guide. He still had his ambitions.

Chapter Fifty-nine

(i)

The evacuation of the Kapolska Palace was virtually complete. The last of the coaches had pulled away down the drive, the tears from the Polish girls, who had made the unit so welcome, had been shed, and the bar had been closed. It was up to the insurance companies now.

Stepping out of the strangely silent palace, Charlie walked on to the lawn. The daffodils were broken and trodden, the grass scattered with litter: cigarette packets, chewing-gum wrappers, film containers, beer cans, a used contraceptive; by the orangery the last of the portable satellite dishes was being dismantled and stowed in the back of a Swedish television estate-car.

He ought to leave Poland, he knew. But that would be disloyal to Harvey, wherever he was, whatever he had done. The man was disturbed. He would need a friend when they found him.

He walked on. It was finished for everyone but him. Agnieszka had flown to Paris the previous evening. It had been a friendly farewell: inevitable. Location was over. It had come as no surprise when he had discovered that Jack Dragoman was also going to Paris. Belinda and Sadie had left together earlier, Sadie close to tears, handing out little presents to members of the unit, Belinda talking about taking a trip home to Philadelphia. Charlie had been sorry to hear that.

'It's really time we discussed the flat,' she had said as her bags were being packed into the car. 'I hate to leave it all up to you. Maybe if you can find a buyer . . .'

491

'I'll call you when I get back to London,' Charlie had said. 'We can work something out then. It's difficult to think properly out here. Say hello to Stagger Lee and Hannah for me, will you?' And he had slammed the door before she could reply.

He had now reached the fenced pasture at the end of the lawn. The cows were back, grazing placidly. He watched them for some time, his hands in his pockets, his fingers playing with the lucky penny. It didn't seem to have brought anyone much luck.

Someone called. 'Have you got a minute?' It was Al Mutton. He was approaching along the side of the fence. It occurred to Charlie that he had probably been watching him for some moments.

'Of course.'

The Australian stopped, leant heavily on the fence and gazed across at the cows. 'Jesus, I don't know . . .' he began at last, rubbing a large hand through his stubble. His eyes were washed with red. He looked terrible. 'Seems like the only people still here are accountants and insurance people . . .'

Charlie nodded.

Mutton started again. 'To tell you the truth, Charlie, I've got a bit of a problem. You never know, you might be able to help. I'll make it worth your while if you can.'

'What sort of problem?'

Mutton stared at the cows. 'Well . . . the way Bruno figured it was, we buy cheap, fatten them up, and then sell for slaughter. A quiet, little deal. Then this happens. Jesus!'

'I'm not with you.'

'The cows. I'm talking about the cows.'

'I'm sorry?'

'*Our* cows.'

'The cows are *yours*?'

'Sort of. And Bruno's. We set up a little Polish cattle company. Nothing dishonest in that.'

Charlie shouldn't have been surprised. It was the oldest scam in movies. Usually it was cars: sometimes it was horses or a dog or land; now it was cows. After a moment he said: 'Let me guess. You've been renting the cows out to the movie, and the movie has been paying to feed and pasture them for six months? Something like that? Right? And all for that one scene.'

'Yeah, well, we didn't know when we'd need them, did we?'

'And now you think someone's going to notice before you can sell them.'

'I *can't* sell them.' Mutton spat. 'Those bastards in there are going over the books with microscopes. I had a deal all set on Friday in Potsdam. Then this happens. I need Bruno's signature to sell them. The buyer pulled out. There are too many people watching. And now some insurance bastard is saying I have to move the cattle to some other place. Jesus! Where the hell am I supposed to put three hundred and fifty bloody cows? Can you tell me that?' His bulbous face had turned mauve with indignation.

For the first time in days Charlie felt like smiling. 'How can I help?'

'Hell, I don't know. You're creative. Think about it. There must be some way. Maybe you can talk to someone. Everyone trusts you.'

'You mean you want to make me an accessory?'

'Jesus, it's hardly murder we're talking here. Just a few cows, for Christ's sake! You think of some way out of this, something I can give to the accountants and lawyers to get them off my back, and I'll see you all right? OK?'

Charlie thought about Harvey. He had been here before.

'Well . . . ? What do you say? Any brainwaves?' Mutton looked as though he was already regretting trying to enlist Charlie's help.

'Sorry,' Charlie said. 'I'm not much good at cows.' And turning away he began to make his way back to the palace.

From behind him he heard the sound of a globule of spit hitting the grass. A cow lowed.

(ii)

Sadie's parents were out when she arrived home. It was seven in the evening. They had not been told to expect her. Heaving the larger of her suitcases up the three flights of stairs to her room she flopped down on her bed.

In the taxi from the airport she and Belinda had read the worsening news from Wall Street, although she didn't understand much of it. The main *Shadows on a Wall* story was now

493

off the front page, but there were several articles inside, ranging from new speculation about the reasons for the accident to the snowballing after-effects. Penn Stadtler's most recent album had gone back to the top of the rock charts, three of Yale Meredith's movies were being repackaged for video release under a 'late, great' logo, and in America the last film Sam Jordan had made before starting *Shadows on a Wall* was being rushed into the cinemas. There were also reports of more copy-cat suicide attempts, as well as something about a board game which Sam Jordan was said to have devised called *Sam Jordan's Waterloo*. Sadie was puzzled about that. Wellington's Waterloo or Napoleon's Waterloo, perhaps. But *Sam Jordan's Waterloo*?

She lay on her bed and stared up at her mirror. There was no activity in the windows of the mews house behind, and she wondered if the kept woman was now unkept. Slowly her eyes travelled around her room, at the postcards, the certificates, the school photographs. It didn't seem much like home any more.

(iii)

There was a large heap of mail on the mat, and, while the coffee percolated, Belinda sorted it into three piles, Charlie's, hers and a joint one for bills. Then, taking her coffee, she went into the living room.

It was a fine, spring London evening, with the first pink blossoms showing in the street outside, and she was surprised at how light and spacious the flat looked. No wonder they had been excited when they found it, she thought. This was the room she had redecorated and she examined her handiwork with some pride. There were only a few streak marks, and no brush hairs left in the matt finish. When she and Charlie had lived there together they had taken their pleasant home for granted: now she thought of what could have been done to make it even better. They had never had any money to buy furniture, and when the movie had brought some, it had been too late.

Opening the door to Charlie's study she felt a sudden draught of loss. He had always been there when she had come home, always until Hollywood, anyway, scratching his head, drinking his tea and looking for the pictures in his word processor.

Whatever had happened subsequently he had, she knew, written *Shadows on a Wall* for her. Perhaps things would have been better if he hadn't. Dropping his mail on to his desk, she closed the door again.

She didn't have a study of her own, just a corner of the bedroom decorated with some posters of small productions she had appeared in, next to a couple of shelves bearing scripts she wished she hadn't done and plays she wished she had. On a fold-up card table lay a copy of *Contacts*, an envelope containing publicity photographs of her as Marie Walewska and a pasting book of her best reviews.

Reaching under the bed, she pulled out the suitcase she had brought with her when she first came to London. Opening it, she very deliberately began to unpin the posters from the wall, roll them up, and drop them inside. The cuttings followed, then the plays and the scripts. Lastly she rummaged among the things she had brought back from Poland until she found her screenplay for *Shadows on a Wall*. That, too, went into the suitcase. Then she locked it.

In the bathroom she ran the shower and made a note to herself. She was going over to see Ilse Yeo in Belsize Park, and had to remember to pack some playing-cards. The children would expect conjuring tricks even if she had retired from the business.

Chapter Sixty

(i)

I t was ironic, but welcome. Bill, the mechanically kicking buffalo over the studio's main gate, was having a new foreleg attached. For months the amputee had been shrouded in a yellow nylon sheet while efforts were made to apprehend the vandals. Finally, however, accepting that the limb wasn't coming back, a new leg and hoof had been commissioned, and now, just as the studio itself was tottering to its knees, Bill was almost up and pawing again.

Julie Wyatt watched from her window in the producers' block. It was Thursday afternoon, midway through a week of funerals. For two days she had been enclosed in her office, hidden behind ramparts of secretaries and assistants, as everywhere the future of Buffalo Pictures was discussed. 'Just keep holding the fort,' Harry Weitzman would call to say several times a day as he emerged torn from meetings with Reuben Wiener and Buffalo's New York bankers. But there was little in the fort to hold. No new projects could be discussed and none of those in development could proceed. Meanwhile, with Penn Stadtler already buried amid scenes of hysteria in England and Bruno Messenger quietly in New Jersey, Hollywood was mourning as only it could. No matter that Buffalo Pictures was sliding further under by the day, it was Klondike time for anyone else who had ever had dealings with Sam Jordan, Yale Meredith or Penn Stadtler. Already the supermarket tabloids were selling out as quickly as they could be printed; soon would come the memorial fan mags, the instant biographies, the television sob specials, and the cheapo-biopics. Everyone was making money except Buffalo Pictures. With *Shadows on a Wall* unfinished they had nothing to sell.

The latest business update on the television news distracted her from the window as another fall in the price of Buffalo stock was noted, down to under eight dollars, less than a third of its price when she had joined the company. Flicking off the television she took the top script from a new pile; and then put it down again. There was no point.

Her phone buzzed. 'Julie, it's Carlos Gallego.' Cathy, her secretary, had been blocking calls all week.

'Didn't you tell him I'm in a meeting?'

'He didn't believe me. He's insisting he speak to you.'

She hesitated. She didn't want to speak to him.

'He says he won't go away, Julie, not until you pick up the phone.'

Another pause. 'I suppose you'd better put him through.'

'Julie?' The familiar, light voice breathed down the phone.

'Yes. How are you?'

There was the slightest pause. 'Julie, can you tell if someone is listening in to us?'

'I can tell. There's no way of anyone listening without my knowing. What is it?'

Another moment passed, as though for once in his life this man was uncertain of himself. 'Well . . . I was thinking, how would you like to work for me?'

(ii)

The white coffin, decked in white lace and festooned with garlands of daisies and apple blossom, was just passing when Billy heard the news. At first he didn't believe it. A Chicago-based news producer, trying to push his way through the crowds to his reporter, had told him.

'Are you sure?' Billy asked.

The newsman nodded. 'It just came through in the van. Any idea who this Carlos Gallego guy is?'

'A two-eyed optimist, I'd say,' Billy replied, and turned back to the funeral. Yale Meredith was about to be confined to the ground and he was anxious not to miss the moment. Dust to dust, ashes to ashes, and all in shimmering white. Lampton Funerals International, aided by a local Grand Rapids florist and funeral parlour, had done a spectacular job.

'To us Yale was always pure at heart,' Yale's sister, a look-alike without the looks, had said dry-eyed into the lens of the Arriflex a few minutes earlier. 'So, we're having a simple ceremony, not a funeral, but a celebration of the passing of a spiritual virgin.'

Billy had nodded kindly. Maybe the whole family was nuts. Now, as Whitney Houston sang 'I Will Always Love You' over the tannoys, Alice Bauccio, along with several hundred other women, sobbed, and Freddie filmed Harry Weitzman, Jake McKenzie and a dozen or so Hollywood friends of the dead star, as they waited to toss a handful of soil into the grave, Billy tried to puzzle things out. How on earth could *Shadows on a Wall*, Charlie's little fifteen-thousand-pound play, have cost a hundred million dollars, killed four people and toppled an entire Hollywood studio? And what on earth did a Florida Cuban car-park operator of mysterious background like Carlos Gallego think he was doing buying the Buffalo Pictures Corporation of California?

(iii)

'Carlos Gallego has bought Buffalo Pictures? I don't believe it.'

'Strictly speaking, no. Familia Gallego has bought out the Candy Corn Corporation's controlling interest. But it means the same. Reuben Wiener is out, Carlos Gallego is in.'

'Who says?'

'CNN. It was announced during Yale Meredith's funeral.'

Charlie stared at Simone. She was his only friend left in the Kapolska. She was staying behind until she heard about Harvey, too. He had been reading in the orangery when she had come running to find him. 'I don't get it,' he said at last. 'Why?'

'Who knows? The magic of movies, maybe.'

'Gallego doesn't know anything about movies.'

'You think the other owners of studios do?'

Charlie closed his book. Getting up he walked several paces

498

down the orangery, shaking his head. 'What about that! A *coup d'état*. Maybe Gallego locked the doors and had all the Candy Corn directors jumping out of the windows.'

Simone looked puzzled. 'No-one jumps out of windows in New York. It's too far to fall.'

'That was what happened in the Eighteenth Brumaire *coup* which brought Napoleon to power,' he explained, looking around, remembering his history. 'They were in an orangery, too. Well, well! Now Buffalo have their own little Napoleon. Who would have believed it? It's just like my father used to tell me at the school film society all those years ago.'

'What was that?'

'Always make sure you put the end reel up last.'

(iv)

Julie Wyatt pulled through the gateway into the concourse between the two wings of the Beverly Wilshire Hotel and, turning up her car radio, sat listening for a few extra moments. *'According to insiders, yesterday's take-over was the culmination of five days' brilliant strategic play by Familia Gallego. Through their New York bankers, the Florida based company had watched all week as the Buffalo stock price had fallen, testing the water occasionally with small skirmishing acquisitions before withdrawing to wait for a better day. That day came yesterday. With an estimated hundred-million-dollar insurance claim which could take years to resolve following the* Shadows on a Wall *Easter tragedy, and the uncertain situation thought likely to deter other potential bidders, popcorn tycoon Reuben Wiener surrendered his large private shareholding and that of the Candy Corn Corporation to Familia Gallego without a struggle. The word is that at seventy-five the billionaire just wants out of movies . . .'*

Stubbing out her cigarette Julie took a ticket from the waiting car hop and made her way into the hotel. It was just before eight: Gallego had been flying in from New York with the dawn, virtually his first act at Buffalo having been to take command of the studio Falcon jet. In the lobby she headed for a house phone, wishing now that she had resigned when he called the previous day. She might need a new job, but not from Carlos

499

Gallego. She had seen the way he looked at her. She wasn't the type to be the cute assistant.

Stepping out of the elevator on the seventh floor a troupe of uniformed security guards scrutinized her. She gave her name. It was passed on. A door was opened by one of the Miami sentinels.

She could hear him before she saw him. He was asking questions, quietly lisping out enquiries for figures and facts, grosses and nets, domestic and overseas, from every domain of the Buffalo empire. Stepping into the room she found him standing at the window staring down at the traffic on Wilshire Boulevard as he spoke, looking shorter than usual against the high window, his skin sallow and smooth across his cheeks. For a man who could scarcely have slept in days he showed no sign of fatigue. Sober in a navy-blue suit he appeared at home in the Spanish-style furnishings of this old California hotel. Facing him in an uneasy semicircle were a group of executives from distribution. They were not used to meeting the owner of the studio. Reuben Wiener had kept them at arm's length.

She waited by the door. The boys from distribution nodded, failing to hide their surprise at her presence.

'Ah, Julie . . .' Gallego was suddenly smiling at her, breaking off from a question, seeming to momentarily forget the other people in the room. Then abruptly he said: 'So, thank you, gentlemen. We'll continue this afternoon at the studio. Five o'clock.' His hand moved outwards in a gesture of dismissal.

There was a rapid shuffling of chairs as the executives hurried out.

'Thank you for coming. We need to talk,' Gallego said when they were alone. 'Shall we go through?' And, opening double doors, he led the way into a private dining room where a table was set for breakfast.

'I must tell you,' she began as soon as the waiter had taken their order and they were alone, 'I've decided it's time I got out of movies.'

'Production. I want you to be in charge of all production at Buffalo,' he said.

She thought she hadn't heard properly. 'What?'

'I need someone I can trust, someone I know.'

She wondered if it was a joke. 'Production?'

'Head of production. You can choose your own title. I understand titles are important in the movie-business. Whatever the words, it will be absolutely your decision which movies we make. You'll answer only to me.'

She stared at him. 'I don't understand.'

'What is there to understand?' he said. 'Please start.' He indicated the melon in front of her. 'I'm a newcomer to movies. I need someone I respect. I respect you very much.'

'*Respect* me? You don't know what you're saying. You don't *know* me. My project, *Shadows on a Wall*, has cost us maybe a hundred million dollars. I'm emotional, unstable. I'm a joke. I was in love with Sam Jordan for years. He did everything he could to avoid me and I refused to see it. I couldn't get arrested in this town after what's happened.'

He savoured his melon. 'It's too early to say how much we'll have available for production this year, but while we're finding out I'd like you to start putting together some projects—'

She shook her head, interrupting. 'I'm sorry. You're making a terrible mistake. I'm the wrong person. You'll be a laughing-stock in the industry.'

'I don't think so. No-one laughs at Familia Gallego.'

'Oh no? Maybe not in Miami, but they will here. You'd better believe it.'

He stared sternly at her for a moment as though his pride had been hurt, and then relaxed into a smile. 'It's no use, Julie. Can't you see? My mind is made up. Now, please, eat.'

She ate. She didn't know what was going on. Until this moment she had known him as a man who asked questions. Now he talked, going off in all directions, about his son, about moving to Los Angeles, the need to find a family house, his plans for the studio, and how she must try to give up smoking. She couldn't concentrate. She began to think about Sam Jordan, about the pictures of his lifeless body, about the day she had met Harvey Bamberg, and the millions of feet of wasted film over in the cutting rooms in England. But mostly she wondered about Carlos Gallego. What kind of man was this? Was there any truth in the rumours about how Familia Gallego had got its start in America?

'I still don't understand,' she said as they finished their coffee. 'Why me?'

'Because I think we'll make a good team. I need someone who knows about movies, someone I admire, someone intelligent I can work with, but who won't be taking advantage of me. And you . . .'

'And me . . . ?'

'You . . . I think maybe you need someone to take care of you a little . . .' He looked at her grey skirt and jacket. 'And to perhaps bring a little colour into your life.'

(v)

Belinda told her parents during Sam Jordan's funeral. She had arrived home late the previous night. 'Actually there's something I should have said as soon as I got back . . .'

On the television in front of them a procession of the most celebrated mourners on earth was snaking through a Rocky Mountain glade towards a sheltered patch of grass. Uniquely among the four *Shadows on a Wall* victims Sam Jordan had had the foresight to leave instructions for his funeral. He was to be interred in his own Oregon valley. Even in death Sam Jordan would be keeping himself to himself.

'. . . you see, I've given up acting . . .'

On the far side of the river a small herd of buffalo, Sam Jordan's buffalo, was watching the cortège.

'To be honest, I think I've been putting it off all my life, because the fact is, I really can't remember why I became an actress in the first place, other than wanting to do what you did. I've always been terrified.'

Like millions of other Americans Bob and Cherry Johnson were watching Sam Jordan's funeral live. It was Saturday afternoon in Philadelphia, just after ten-thirty in the morning in Oregon. In the midst of preparing a salad for lunch, Bob tossing the lettuce, Cherry slicing the avocadoes, they were keeping a semi-professional eye on the unfolding handkerchiefs on the screen. Belinda was standing behind them, awkward in her admission.

'Is this serious?' her mother asked, a stolen slice of avocado frozen halfway to her lips. 'You're really thinking of giving up?'

'I've already given up.'

'Is it because of the disappointment? There's always disappointment in whatever you do.' This was her father.

'No. I know about disappointment. I can take that. It's just that . . . I'm not cut out for it.'

'But you're good, you know that, don't you?' her mother came back flatly; a statement of fact rather than one of encouragement.

'Well, so some people say. But I never felt good. And even if I am, that isn't enough. I just don't want to do it. When you were my age you'd have killed for a part, and you loved doing it. You still love doing it. The people I've been working with are the same . . . even the monsters. The need to act just devours them. And they all think they're brilliant, even when they aren't. I never felt that. I'm sorry if I'm disappointing you.'

Her father shook his head. 'Who's disappointed? Are you disappointed, Cherry?'

There was a hesitation. Her father's eyes stared fixedly at those of her mother. Her mother shook her head. 'No.'

'But I thought you wanted me to be an actress?'

'Only if *you* wanted it. You always seemed to. So we went along with it,' he replied.

Her mother pursed her lips.

Belinda looked back at the screen, it was awash with famous Hollywood acting faces now, people who had never had her doubts. She watched as the camera panned on, found Jack Dragoman, and then lingered on Agniezska. Would she become famous? That was what she wanted. Who could tell? Next to them, Delphine Claviers was weeping theatrically, her black French veil lifted off her face for the cameras. Even Oregon wasn't too far to go for a little publicity.

'I was trying to make you . . .' Belinda stopped. To say more would be to blame her parents. She *had* been pushed as a child, they couldn't deny that. Then suddenly she saw it. All her life she had lived in the crossfire, between talent and drive. Her mother had been all drive. She was a timid version of her father's talent with her mother's looks. But talent wasn't enough: there had to be a need which was bigger than the fear which everyone felt. She looked at her parents. From her letters and phone calls they must have anticipated this moment. Her mother had already surrendered. 'So, that's all right, then?' she asked.

'If it's what makes you happy, of course it's all right.' Her father was beaming, as though there was a weight off his mind, too. 'Do you know what you'll do instead?'

Belinda shook her head. 'I thought I might go to college.

Take some courses. I can afford to. I've been well paid for the movie.'

Her mother nodded. She wasn't smiling, but she was accepting.

Belinda thought about Charlie. Had he known? She knew he had.

'Hey, was that Warren Beatty?' Her mother interrupted her thoughts. She was peering hard at the television in some excitement. 'I think I saw Warren Beatty and that Annette what's-her-name. I didn't know he was losing his hair. Did you know he was losing his hair, Bob?'

At her side the man who had once been Stagger Lee shook his balding head. 'It can't have been him. Stars don't lose their hair. They dye it.'

Belinda watched the television, picking out the faces for them. There was Julie Wyatt standing next to Carlos Gallego as the coffin was lowered into the ground; further along Jake McKenzie was cosying up to Jack Dragoman. At the back of the picture Edward Lampton, the Grave Digger, as handsome as any star, presided over everything. If he had been twenty years younger he would have made a wonderful Duke of Wellington, tail or no tail.

(vi)

Charlie could feel his stomach bubbling as he stared at the round, polished head. It didn't look much like Harvey's head any more. It was no longer pink, and the ears, which had always seemed so big and elfin, looked smaller against the now bloated face. He turned away, putting a handkerchief to his mouth. Rodents had been at the bottom lip. He nodded, then hurried out of the police morgue.

Sitting in an office he was given a cup of milky tea and a chocolate biscuit. The body, he was told, had been spotted on a mudbank the previous afternoon by a couple of teenagers looking for somewhere to be alone. It had been several kilometres downstream from where the Noblesse American had come to rest. This year's floods had been exceptional.

'There was a preliminary autopsy last night,' a young man in rimless glasses explained in good English. 'The cause of death was drowning: the victim was, however, concussed at the moment of death, almost certainly from a fall. Most puzzling were burn marks on the victim's fingers. More analysis will be carried out in Bratislava, but it is believed the burns were a result of holding the exhaust of a car. There will be an inquiry, but . . .' He shrugged.

It was over, Charlie thought. There would be no arrest, no charges of being an accessory, no imprisonment. As Belinda had always said, he thought too much.

'It will probably always be impossible to say exactly what happened, but we feel that most probably the car stopped for some reason. Who knows? Perhaps Mr Bamberg wanted to relieve himself. Then something happened and the car began to run away. Perhaps he tried to stop it falling over the cliff . . .' He looked at Charlie. That was the best scenario he could offer.

Charlie wanted to tell him: it was the scenario he had himself devised.

The young man was standing up. The problem had now crossed the Atlantic and was for the insurers to sort out, he said. Copies of the police reports and autopsies would be sent to them.

Outside it was a windy, bright day. The rains had finally gone. A car was waiting to take him back to the Kapolska. Simone was sitting inside. She had not wanted to see the body. He would have to telephone Nathalie. Simone would tell Edward Lampton. When the time came Lampton Funerals International would fly the body home.

He had tears in his eyes as they drove back towards the border. Simone was crying. Harvey had been such a hopeless little fellow, good for truffling and not much else. But they'd been fond of him. Charlie would miss him. He was already forgetting that Harvey had also been a murderer.

May, 1993

Chapter Sixty-one

(i)

S adie walked slowly down the stairs, shrinking against the wall as a couple of Spanish boys hurried past, late for their class. The place smelt of old dust and dry books: the smell of school. She remembered the same smell from the school in Poland on her first day of filming. That was the day she had met Tim Westwood. She pictured his haphazard halo of curls and freckled nose, his tall, awkward intensity and gabbling enthusiasm. Mad could be nice, too, she thought, then frowned. She had been trying not to think about him.

It had obviously been a location crush. She hadn't seen him since she had been back in London, and when she had managed to reach him on the phone he had said he was too busy to talk. She found that hard to believe. The movie was dead. What could be busy about dead? Obviously he had become bored with her. That hurt, because he didn't bore her. He fascinated her. Everyone said that location romances rarely survived the return to normality, but their romance had hardly even got started.

She hadn't expected sympathy when she arrived home, and hadn't received any. The blush of *risqué* amusement her parents had experienced, when, for a moment, she had become a tabloid celebrity, had faded with the collapse of the film. For days her mother had been smug with contempt, as though she had always known it would end in disaster. To be here, enquiring about crammers, was Sadie's admission of defeat. The big adventure was over.

Reaching the street she walked on to her favourite Italian sandwich bar, and, ordering a cappuccino, took it to the stand-up ledge by the window. Miserably she examined her crammer brochures. The thought of going back to any kind of school filled her with despair. She had tried to talk about it to Claire, but, with exams looming, Claire had had no time to worry about any problems other than her own. Even the people in the agency who had made such a fuss when she joined them the previous autumn were now being discouraging. 'Don't expect to work again too soon,' they were saying in distant voices. It was as though everything associated with *Shadows on a Wall* was tainted with failure. What was it Charlie had told her Napoleon would ask of a young officer before promoting him? 'Does he have luck?' Once Sadie had thought she had all the luck in the world.

She was gazing unhappily, unfocused, out on to the afternoon when she caught sight of him, his hair billowing in waves, his face tilted forward urgently like that of a bloodhound on the scent. At first she thought he might be going into an auction at Christie's, but then, not finding what he wanted, he moved on to a pottery shop and then a supermarket, staring in through the windows before hurrying on. She waited. At last, he looked along the parade of shops across the street. He smiled when he saw her.

'Come on!' he beckoned. *'Come on!'*

Sadie took off her glasses. He looked as dotty as she had ever seen him, a boy version of Doc from *Back to the Future*.

'Come on,' he mouthed again, dodging the traffic as he hurried right up to the window.

'It's nothing to do with me, but I think the young man wants you to go some place with him pretty quick,' the fat Italian lady who cleared the empty cups said, staring warily through the window. 'Maybe you better see what he wants.'

Sadie was on her way.

'Hey! You forgot something.' The fat lady held up the crammer brochure.

But Sadie was already through the door and into the street. 'What is it?' she asked, giggling, as he grabbed her. 'You look as though you've just reinvented the flux capacitor.'

'Maybe better than that. Maybe better than anything. I've been

510

looking everywhere for you. I want to show you something.'
And, taking her hand, he began to run her down the street
towards his car.

At the sandwich-bar window the fat lady shook her head,
and dropped the brochure into the bin. This girl wouldn't be
coming back.

'*How* much film?' Sadie was gaping.

'Over two million feet,' he said, striding on down the studio
corridor.

Hurrying to keep up, Sadie peered into cutting rooms, left and
right, every one neatly tidied, swept and lined with aluminium
cans. Everything was there except the editing staff. With the
exception of Tim they had all been paid off. 'Two *million* feet.
Crikey! That's what . . . six-hundred and sixty six thousand
yards . . . That's, er . . . How many miles?'

'I don't know. Hundreds. Don't bother to calculate. Too many.'

'It's like the *Marie Celeste*,' she said. 'You know, nobody here,
and a feeling that something terrible has happened.'

Tim didn't answer. They had reached the last room in the
block. This one was different, as overflowing with signs of
industry as the others had been empty. This was his cutting
room and film was everywhere, spiralling and looping across
the workbench, trailing from the spools of the rewind handle,
snaking in parallel tracks through the pic-sync and hanging
like creepers into cloth trim bins. On a window-sill a line of
paper cups measured the days with dregs of stale coffee, while
Sellotaped across a wall was a vast, multicoloured, much revised
wall-chart of drawings, arrows, scribbles and notes.

As Sadie looked around Tim opened a can of film and began
to thread a reel into a Steenbeck viewing machine. All the way
down to Pinewood he had refused to explain the urgency. 'All
right, now will you tell me?' she asked again.

Pulling up two chairs he placed them in front of the Steenbeck.
'You'll see,' he said. 'Sit here.' And, crossing to the windows,
he drew the curtains.

She sat down and waited. He was soon ready. Sitting next
to her, he pushed a lever forward. The reels began to turn.

'Titles, titles, titles . . . music, music,' he began to say as
pictures of a vast battle appeared.

Sadie stared at the screen.

He took her for a walk around the studio-lot before he allowed her to say anything. She was bewildered, emotions charging in every direction. She had never seen herself on film before. Bruno hadn't allowed it. Now she had just sat through over three hours of watching herself as Camille de Malignon. That in itself was extraordinary, Sadie Corchoran in the middle of the Napoleonic Wars. Was she any good? She had no idea. Was that how she had imagined the part should be played when she had first seen the play in Edinburgh? She wasn't certain of that either.

But there was something else. Despite all the gaps and inconsistencies, there was no escaping the fact that in what she had just watched Camille de Malignon was no longer a secondary figure playing out her life behind Napoleon and Marie Walewska. Quite the opposite: Napoleon's story had become a historical backcloth in the love affair between Camille de Malignon and Will Yorke.

'So . . . ? What do you think?' They were walking past a giant, locked soundstage.

'I don't understand,' Sadie said. 'I mean, the balance is wrong. *Shadows on a Wall* is about Napoleon and Marie Walewska.'

He was smiling. 'It isn't wrong, Sadie. This is the only way to do it now.'

'Do what?'

'Finish the movie.'

'What?'

'Finish the movie,' he said again.

'But it can't be finished. Everybody's dead.'

'No. Of those who appear on screen only Sam and Yale are dead.'

'But Sam and Yale are the story.'

'So, we change the story.'

'I'm sorry, I . . .'

'If we can't have Napoleon and his mistress any more, we make the movie about Camille de Malignon and Will Yorke. What I just showed you was just a few ideas cut together. But I *know* I can make it work. All we need are a few new scenes.'

He really is mad, Sadie thought. She'd been right all along.

'I'm not crazy,' he suddenly smiled, reading her thoughts. 'This is the beauty of film. Every day in the cutting room we reshape scenes and sequences based on what we have, rather than what we wish we had. Nothing ever finishes up as the writer or the director envisage. Not exactly. Too many things change along the way. What I just showed you is one way of looking at what we have. We can't now have Napoleon going off to Elba, or Marie Walewska meeting him there. And we can't show him losing at Waterloo. But we *can* show you and Will Yorke . . .'

'. . . and turn Sam Jordan and Yale Meredith into supporting players . . .' She wanted to giggle.

'That's right. That's exactly right.'

She hesitated. 'But what about the story? Everything would have to change.'

'Not everything. Just the emphasis and the end. Camille de Malignon was always a brilliant part. I remember when I first read the script thinking how she and Will Yorke seemed too well written to be in the background. It can be done. Can't you see?'

She didn't answer. She realized now why he hadn't called, and the significance of the wall-chart in his cutting room.

'You have to remember that you can tell any story from whatever point of view you want. Like in *Rashomon*, you know,' he began to explain.

She shook her head. 'I'm sorry, I don't know.'

'It doesn't matter. It's just some Kurosawa movie they show you at film school to teach point of view.'

She brightened. 'Like *Rosencrantz and Guildenstern Are Dead*, you mean?'

It was his turn to look uneasy. 'Probably.'

Sadie smiled to herself. It was the first point she had ever scored off him.

They walked on, past the plaster shop and the fake, rejected balustrades and busts lying in the nettles, all the time Tim talking faster and faster, outlining his plans to make the impossible possible. Sadie didn't know anything about recutting and reshaping movies, but it was thrilling just being with him. She slipped her arm through his. He might be a madman, but he was her madman.

513

Charlie listened to the racing voice with growing astonishment. 'Salvage *Shadows on a Wall*? Crumbs, Tim!' He hadn't had much to do with Tim Westwood, but he had heard about his reputation for eccentric, obsessive brilliance.

'That's right. But it all depends on you, Charlie. We can't do it without you. When you see the material . . .'

Flattery. Always flattery. This was how Harvey had begun. For *anything* to be salvaged from *Shadows on a Wall* it would take more than him, more than a genius of an editor: it would take a miracle. He didn't believe in miracles. He didn't think the Buffalo Pictures Corporation did either. 'I really don't know, Tim. To be honest, quite apart from whether it's even remotely possible, or even a good idea to reshape a story which we all liked the way it was, or whether Buffalo would even be interested in committing more money to shoot the new scenes, which I very much doubt, you have to remember there's a police investigation still going on back in Slovakia and then there's the insurance . . .'

Tim Westwood wasn't listening. 'If I can just show you the reels I've worked on. All I'm asking is that you take a look at them. Then if you don't want to be involved . . . well, I can understand that, too . . .'

Charlie looked around his study. On the table which ran at right angles with his desk were all the various screenplays for *Shadows on a Wall*, burgundy, yellow, pink, blue, red. Reaching out he opened the top one. His eyes fell on Camille de Malignon's attempt at assassination. Sadie had been brilliant in that scene.

Tim was still talking. 'What I really want to do is work out some kind of plan, and then take it to Julie Wyatt. It was always her project. Now that she's head of production, I'm *sure* she'll listen.'

Charlie could have stopped him there, put an end to his crazy dream. But he didn't. He was a writer. He knew about dreams.

He refused to be easily convinced. All day they sat in the cutting room and looked at the material, first the reels Sadie had seen, then other sequences and alternate takes. They could have sat for a month, there was just so much film, each scene having been covered from a multitude of angles. He didn't want to agree, he was sure Buffalo would spit in their faces, but, every time he raised what he thought was the clinching, killing objection, Tim would grin, scratch his curly head, and come up with a solution. He had an extraordinary grasp of both movies, the one Bruno Messenger had been making, and the one he was now suggesting.

In the late afternoon Sadie joined them, sitting on a high stool at the back of the room, watching everything, or dashing off to bring coffees and snacks from the studio canteen. She reminded him of the little helper she had been when *Shadows on a Wall* had been playing at the Jupiter.

At around ten in the evening, with his eyes weary from staring at the viewing machine, Charlie sat back and took off his glasses. 'OK, so it's a million-to-one shot, but just supposing I *can* reshape the story and make the sub-plot work, and the studio and insurers are interested in trying to salvage something, and they *do* provide money to shoot a new ending, just who do you have in mind to direct?'

Tim Westwood looked him fully in the eyes. 'Well, me, actually.'

Chapter Sixty-two

(i)

'They're crazy!' Simone's thick eyelashes batted in astonishment. 'Even if it's the most brilliant restructuring job ever, who's going to trust the salvaging of a hundred-million-dollar catastrophe to a twenty-three-year-old boy who's never directed anything before?' And she plopped down into her deck-chair.

Tanned the colour of a chestnut, Edward Lampton looked up from his work. 'In a rational world, they wouldn't,' he replied. 'But this is the magic world. That's what they're hoping, anyway.'

'Magic, schmagic! I'm surprised at Charlie for letting Tim Westwood even contemplate that this could happen. Magic's out of style. There are no fairy stories, any more, not in Hollywood and especially not for *Shadows on a Wall*.'

'But you didn't exactly say that to him, did you?' Lampton chided gently.

'Well, no . . .' She stopped. God! She sounded so negative. Was this all she'd learnt from *Shadows on a Wall*?

Charlie had telephoned a few minutes earlier from a hotel in Los Angeles. He, Tim Westwood and Sadie Corchoran were going to see Julie Wyatt that afternoon, and he'd been hoping to meet and talk Simone through the revised shape of the movie beforehand. Her first reaction had been to think it was some kind of unfunny joke. 'The Camille de Malignon story?' she had gaped. Charlie had kept talking.

Perhaps it was better that she hadn't been at home in Encino,

516

she had reflected as he explained, that her answering service had directed him to this rented house up the coast, too far away for them to meet that day. It was easier to hide incredulity over the phone. She sympathized with him. She really did. She knew what writers were like when it came to clutching at straws. There wasn't much a movie writer wouldn't do to see his script on the screen. This one was even prepared to change the weight of his entire story.

She looked across at Lampton and wondered if she would have more nerve when it came to him. Working quietly here he had nearly finished the screenplay he had been writing for the past year. He had been very secretive about it, but later that day he would ask for her opinion. 'If it's hopeless you'll only have to tell me and I'll forget the whole thing,' he had said casually. That was what they all said, first-time writers: then they cut their wrists.

He had brought her to this small house above the Pacific when, still mourning Harvey, she had stepped off the plane from Poland a couple of weeks earlier. They had both needed time to recharge, he had insisted. That was what she liked about him. He was thoughtful, and he genuinely cared about her. Now he seemed to want to care *for* her. She would have to think about that. A few days earlier Nathalie Seillans had tracked him down, calling from Paris. Not being of star status the release of Harvey's body was being held up by the insurance companies and Slovakian authorities, and she had wondered if Edward might intercede on her behalf. She had played the lonely widow while simultaneously letting it be known that she was available. In the gentlest possible manner he had let her know that he was not.

Simone had only begun sleeping with him after that. All through location she had rejected overtures from members of the crew. But at last, peaceful together by the ocean, she had wondered how it would be with a man in his sixties: it had been friendly and comforting. Now she feared the possibility of hurting him. If the script were bad, and, let's face it, he *was* an undertaker, she wouldn't be able to hide it.

From her deck-chair she looked out at the ocean. At her side Lampton chuckled to himself as he re-read his screenplay.

He was laughing at his own jokes! My God! She closed her eyes. Given the choice she'd rather be in Charlie's place today. All he faced was ridicule.

'There you go, Sadie, that's Bill.' Tim Westwood pointed up-wards as Charlie's rented Toyota edged off Melrose and under the newly re-limbed, mechanically kicking buffalo at the en-trance to the studio.

Sadie smiled in recognition. Although she was seeing the mascot for the first time it was so familiar it was like being re-acquainted with an old friend. But then *everything* here was familiar, she had been thinking all the way from the hotel, as she had gazed out from the back seat of the car. Everyone in the world knew what Hollywood looked like.

They had arrived in Los Angeles the previous afternoon, but it had been almost ten before the hastily re-cut reels of film had been cleared through Customs. Refusing to leave the airport without them, nervous at even having them out of his sight, Tim had tried to send Sadie on to the hotel. She had preferred to stay with him.

Now as they waited for security clearance Tim and Charlie were once more nervously rehearsing the pitch they would soon be making, Tim's speech so fast it was virtually out of control.

'*Buffalo Pictures Inc, a division of the Familia Gallego Corporation,*' Charlie suddenly interrupted, noticing an engraved plate, newly attached to the old water tower. 'Carlos Gallego hasn't wasted much time, has he?'

The young editor stopped talking, a shadow crossing his face. Carlos Gallego was an unknown quantity, even less of a film man than Reuben Wiener.

The bar on the gate went up, and the car pulled on to the studio lot.

'Don't worry!' Sadie said, leaning forward between the two front seats. 'Never forget what Napoleon said.'

'What was that?' Charlie asked.

'He said, "Every French soldier carries in his cartridge pouch the baton of a marshal of France." In French.' And she kissed them both for luck.

'You do know there's a hundred-million-dollar insurance claim already filed, don't you?' Julie Wyatt said as they took their seats in the viewing theatre to watch the recut. 'I'm not sure that legally you should be tampering with this film at all, or that any of us should be even looking at it.'

'When you see this you won't need the insurance,' Tim replied, with all the chutzpah of twenty-three years.

In the twilight of the theatre Charlie noticed Julie pout wryly to herself as they waited for the projectionist. It was understandable. At least she had listened. In some of the other studios they would have been back on the street by now, the film locked in a safe.

Through the corner of his eye he watched her. She was almost unrecognizable from just a few weeks earlier. Perhaps it was the red suit which most surprised, as red as a bus, matching the lips, the jacket military-fitted; but it was the eyes he was picturing, lighter, more cheerful than he had ever seen. He had always felt slightly doomed in her old, monochrome office, but her new one had been altogether more colourful and friendly; and wider, of course, as befitting a Buffalo head of production. Not only was Julie Wyatt now in Technicolor, she was in Cinemascope, too.

What she had been thinking he didn't like to imagine. Her face had puckered with disbelief before dissolving into complete bewilderment when he had told her he wanted to rewrite his story.

'Are you trying to tell me that Sam Jordan, Napoleon, will become a support in this new scheme of things?' she had asked, reaching hurriedly for her cigarettes.

Charlie and Tim had nodded.

'And that Jack Dragoman will be the nearest thing to a star in a leading role?'

'And Sadie,' Tim had said. 'Sadie will be a star when the movie is released.'

Julie had gazed at him for a long moment, before turning to look at Sadie.

Sitting in a corner, stroking the dog Marsha under the chin, with her black hair falling around her shoulders, her saucer eyes and her bright, intelligent face quietly composed, Sadie had smiled, perfectly at ease. It was for these moments that they had brought her along. She was so still, so unselfconscious, completely comfortable in her surroundings; on film and in life.

Sadie had grown up a lot, but she was still very young. And now that the movie was about to be run she had suddenly decided to take the dog for a walk, rather than watch herself on film.

On the screen Tim's rough re-cut was about to begin.

(iv)

She had for ever to fill, but she was in no hurry, and she was very inquisitive. Marsha was well known around the studio, a real favourite, and Sadie was a very pretty girl, so they were both welcome wherever they went.

No-one knew who she was, this dog walker, and she talked to everybody she met: the gardeners, the woman pushing the snacks trolley, a security guard who asked for a date, a group of secretaries in their break, and a woman from wardrobe who wanted to know if she was an English nanny for the Gallego children. Some of them were worried about the future of Buffalo: they didn't know what to think of their new owners and they blamed *Shadows on a Wall*. She wanted to apologize to them.

For a while she played ball games with Marsha on the lawn in front of the executives' building, sending the big dog jogging first this way and then that. And then, when she tired of this, she borrowed some paper from a man in an office and settled down under a stately old palm tree to write a '*Good luck in the exams*' letter to Claire, Marsha panting at her feet. It was a day out for Marsha, too.

She didn't see them watching her, although later she would be told that they had stopped a meeting and stood at the board-room window for a full five minutes before deciding to go down and join the screening.

She slipped back into the viewing theatre for the last couple of reels. She was surprised. When she had left, only Julie Wyatt and a couple of story editors had been with Tim and Charlie. Now there were at least half a dozen more people.

There was no sound as the final reel ran out on the unfinished film, and when the lights came up, no reaction of any kind. The small audience looked, if anything, stunned. She glanced across at Tim and Charlie. Their faces were frozen in a private misery. Ah well, it had been worth a try.

At the front of the theatre Carlos Gallego slipped away through a side door. A couple of minutes later, still without commenting, Julie Wyatt followed.

(v)

'How much do they say they'll need to finish it?' Gallego asked finally, his head emerging from the mass of documents and figures.

'Five million dollars.'

'Another five million dollars. Do you think they're mad?'

Julie hesitated. 'Movie mad.'

He smiled. 'I have to learn about that, right? Have you made up your mind?'

'Yes.'

He didn't ask. 'I think you're right. The girl . . . even I can see that she's . . .' He searched for the word.

'Extraordinary?'

'I think so. On film, in person. Am I right?'

'Yes.'

'What about him, the boy who wants to be a director?'

'In his head he already is one. I think he might be slightly brilliant.'

Gallego stood up and walked across his office his hands behind his back. 'OK, so let's talk to the insurers. Let's see what kind of a salvage deal they'll give us. Maybe we'll be making them a little happier, too.'

Julie turned to go. A mountain of work loomed, more struggles about availabilities, more battles with agents. But a decision had been made. It was all so much simpler when you were working with a dictator.

521

Five million dollars. That was the figure Tim had blurted out, the first one to come into his head. They had never properly costed the work they wanted to do, but now five million was what it would be. It was an appropriate figure: it had been five million dollars Harvey had gone looking for in the beginning, five million he had never been able to find.

It was starting again. *Shadows on a Wall* would be completed, perhaps not as the film Charlie had first envisaged, but at least it would exist. It wouldn't all have been in vain.

At first, when Julie Wyatt had told them, they had been speechless. Now, sitting in a Mexican restaurant on La Cienaga, celebrating together in the silly way of people who hardly drank, Sadie and Tim were laughing together, showing their youth; Charlie was watching, happy for them.

He should have been happy for himself, too; happier, anyway. But he was thinking about Belinda, trying to picture her when she heard the news. Would she smile, would she dazzle again? He didn't think so. It wasn't good news for her. She had written to say she had given up acting. He had been glad. He wouldn't write her into any new scenes. They could finish the movie without Countess Monika Wyszynska. Her letter had asked him what was happening about the flat, and then gone on to tell him how she was enjoying being back in Philadelphia, seeing old friends again. He had wondered if that meant old boyfriends.

They had finished dinner and the wine was gone. He was tired. Across the table from him Tim was telling Sadie about the plot of *Mr Deeds Goes to Town*, her eyes seeming to grow wider the longer he spoke. They were good chums.

He felt as though he was drifting away from them, as though he had now passed *Shadows on a Wall* on to a new generation. He was trying to listen to Tim's story, but somehow the noise of the restaurant was scrambling his thoughts, feeding in snapshot flashbacks at random, of Billy down to his last pennies but buying the drinks in The Last Drop, of Harvey's manifest joy in showing off Nathalie, of Belinda juggling in the snow in Cracow. She had dazzled then all right.

'I was wondering . . . I mean, I thought perhaps you might invite me back to your place tonight,' Sadie said, looking at her hands. She was sitting in the passenger seat of Tim's old car, parked in the street outside the hotel. Charlie had said goodnight and gone to his room when they had got back from the restaurant, and she and Tim had been talking for nearly an hour before she'd finally plucked up the courage. Well, someone had to make the first move.

'Well, yes, sure . . .' Tim hesitated. 'What for?'

If Sadie hadn't known him better she would have sworn he was doing a James Stewart ingenuous Forties'-style impersonation. 'Well,' she said, trying again, 'not to put too fine a point on it, all good things come to an end, don't they?'

He looked wary. 'Good things?'

'You know, childhood, skipping, bicycle rides, virginity, stamp collecting, that sort of thing.'

He didn't answer.

A slight panic seized her. 'You don't mind, do you? I was terribly good at gym at school.'

At last, more bashful than any young man of twenty-three had any right to be, he smiled.

Crikey, that's a relief, she thought. I bet Camille de Malignon never had to beg.

Simone read Edward Lampton's script in one sitting while he sat outside on the verandah worrying. It was called *A Small Story About Death*, and was a ghoulish slapstick about the modern etiquette of dying and disposal. That was surprising: what was astonishing was that it was very funny, frequently hilarious, the story of a trade war between rival undertakers. Simone, who hadn't yet got over the death of Harvey, had never read so many bad-taste jokes about death, but she had been laughing for a solid hour.

She peeped outside. Lampton didn't see her watching. He

looked such a mournful man when he was thoughtful, an occupational expression, no doubt. She didn't understand it. He wasn't a particularly funny man: he actually said very little, and before he had become involved in movies he had rarely been to the cinema. Yet here he was, writing one of the most original comedies she had ever read. She smiled. This was why she liked writers. They could always surprise her.

She became practical. Could they get John Cleese? What about Bob Hoskins? She was already thinking like the producer she wanted to be. They'd find the money, no problem at all. If Charlie and Tim Westwood could get *Shadows on a Wall* going again, *anything* was possible.

Chapter Sixty-three

They met in New York in a bar on Lexington. He was on his way back to England to start writing the new scenes. She had come to do some shopping and look around for an apartment; maybe to enrol at college. She wanted to study history.

He had got there early. She was late and arrived with all kinds of bags, new shoes, clothes, books, her hair so cream and her smile so wide other shoppers turned to see who she was.

He didn't waste a moment. 'I'm sorry for everything. Everything. I love you, Belinda. I want you to come back with me,' he said, '. . . to come back *to* me.'

She shook her head.

He told her again, a little longer and a little louder. A woman at the next table turned around to look.

'I'm sorry, Charlie,' she said.

'I'm not giving in. I'm going to keep asking you until you agree.'

'I'm really pleased about the movie.'

'I mean it.'

'Give my love to Billy, will you? And Ilse and the children.'

'Why not?'

'And wish Sadie good luck . . .'

'I love you.'

'I can't stay long. I'm going back to Philadelphia tonight.'

'Come back to London with me instead.'

'No.'

*   *   *

He saw her off at the station. When she reached her carriage she stopped and looked back. Her arms were too full to wave, but she smiled. And then she was gone.

He didn't sleep on the flight back to London. His mind kept rerunning the clip of Belinda stepping on to the train. Just west of Shannon he pulled his script out of his bag. He had four weeks to get it right.

PART SEVEN

December, 1993

'What do you mean, does it have a happy ending?
Certainly it has a happy ending.
Don't movies always have happy endings?'

Harvey Bamberg, 1934–93

Chapter Sixty-four

(i)

The boy clutched the edge of his seat as the limousine slid through the falling snow. It was the first time he had been in a car like this. It was longer even than the one he had discovered in the river. Now he knew how those film stars had felt just before they died. He was glad this car didn't have to go near any rivers tonight; he had looked at a street map so he knew. On either side of him his parents sat stiffly, his father awkward in his hired suit, his mother more glamorous than he had ever seen her, gazing in embarrassment as the people stared in through the car windows.

No-one spoke. His mother damped his hair down with her hand. He didn't push her away. It was comforting, considering everything that had happened. Three days ago his father had smacked him hard and told him he had disgraced the family after the man in the photograph developing shop had telephoned the police. The boy had admitted his guilt: yes, he had borrowed his father's camera to take photographs of the girl in the apartment upstairs. Her mother had been out and he had wanted to make her look like Yale Meredith, the way he had seen her sitting by the American car. He hadn't known it was against the law to take such pictures of little girls, that his father might get into trouble. He had cried himself to sleep. He'd thought his father might go to jail.

The invitation for this night had come from the office of the Buffalo Pictures Corporation in London: a teacher had

529

translated it and, when the news had spread, a Bratislava news-paper had asked him to write a review when he got home. He was still slightly famous in Bratislava. Perhaps that was why his father had been so angry. People talked about you when you were famous.

Silently the limousine edged round a large tree-filled square lined with police, barricades and people, and drew to a halt. The door was opened, umbrellas held aloft, and the boy and his parents stepped out on to a red carpet. It seemed silly to put a carpet on a pavement in a snowstorm, the boy thought, as flashes exploded around him. He looked about, confused by all the excitement. Perhaps she was here already, he suggested to his father, the Princess his mother had been so looking forward to seeing.

His father didn't answer. He was leading the boy past the tele-vision cameras, one arm gently guiding his wife. She had been afraid she might trip in her new shoes and long dress. *Shadows on a Wall* was the first world première for all of them.

(ii)

Billy had got there early. Still cutting the last episode of *The Making of Shadows on a Wall* he was waiting for the coverage from this evening to complete the series. The BBC had begun transmission before anyone knew how the movie would turn out, and the viewers were now watching the last sad, squabbling weeks of Sam Jordan and Yale Meredith in fascinated millions. In America it was being networked every night this week.

Standing on the balcony of the cinema foyer he looked down at the guests. A few minutes earlier Freddie had shot Nathalie Seillans' arrival, her dress, slinky black, her bosom miraculously raised again as she pressed it against Larry Horner's arm. Oh yes, Larry Horner. Charlie had tried to warn him, but Larry was an agent: he never listened. Now Larry's wife was finally suing for divorce and his wide-bottomed secretary had found another job. The joke around town was that she had taken the rug with her.

The snow had come as a surprise and Billy wondered whether it was a good omen. Certainly it seemed to fit the love-in-a-cold-climate mood of *Shadows on a Wall*. He hoped Ilse was all right. She had arrived with him and was already in her seat. Unlike the women below, worrying about their expensive hair and clothes, Ilse had washed her own hair and come in a raincoat over the simple party dress she always wore to functions. She had also brought a book on the Masai to read until the film started. The glamour of movies impressed her even less these days, although she had sent Sadie a sweet letter. Her excitement would come when they took the children on holiday to Kenya after Christmas. They could afford to do these things now.

Along the balcony Freddie was focusing on two young boffins being interviewed by a punky girl television reporter. Billy knew who they were. They had made up the rules to a new boardgame called *Sam Jordan's Waterloo* which was being marketed around the world for Christmas. Sam Jordan had pulled a fast one over Buffalo there, but it was these gauche young boys who had really won first prize. The game would, apparently, make them both into millionaires. The magic of movies was quite random.

Drawing a finger across his throat Billy indicated his team move down to the front entrance. The bigger cars were now arriving, disgorging the best and the beautiful, footballers, cabinet ministers, fashion models, television personalities. He didn't want to miss the arrival of the world's newest movie emperor.

(iii)

'You've met my mother, haven't you, Charlie?'

Charlie had been standing by the main door, staring into the snow, and hadn't seen him approach. It was Neil Burgess, the first Napoleon from Edinburgh. On his arm was an elderly lady in a leopard-skin coat.

'Oh yes, how are you? Looking forward to seeing how Marshal Blücher gets on?' Charlie had to shout. He knew the old lady was deaf and the din of expectation was growing all the time.

She looked uncertain but smiled, anyway. It was a Royal charity première: everyone was smiling.

'And will he, do you think, be noticed?' asked Neil with a twinkle.

He would indeed. With the Battle of Waterloo reshaped and

virtually built in the cutting room from unused footage of the Battles of Borodino and Jena, the German star earmarked for the Blücher cameo had withdrawn. At a moment's notice Neil had stood in and been brilliant.

Smiling in expectation Neil daddied his mother away as another hand shook Charlie's, then another, and another. So many hands to shake, friends, cast, crew; naturally his parents were there, too, looking forward to the film.

Turning back towards the door, Charlie looked out at the storm: still no sign of her. A busker was entertaining the freezing, watching crowds penned behind the barriers in front of the cinema, juggling and playing a trumpet simultaneously. He wondered if Belinda could do that.

They had kept in touch all through the extra shooting and months of editing. She had always been cheerful, busy with her new life in New York. She had begun a history course at Columbia and had a small apartment on the Upper West Side. She was happy, she told him. He didn't ask about men and she didn't tell him. There was bound to be somebody. She was so wonderful. He hadn't dared go to see her. He might find out.

In their conversations she had been surprisingly lacking in curiosity about the movie. It had already become a past part of her life. He wondered if he had, too. The flat was now in his name only.

Two weeks earlier he had sent her an invitation to the première with an open-return airline ticket. He would understand if she couldn't make it, he had written. He had meant he would understand that hope was gone. When she hadn't responded he had telephoned her, but never got an answer. He had then called her parents in Philadelphia. Her mother had been vague, suggesting that she might have gone down to Atlanta as part of her American Civil War course. 'She could have saved herself the journey by taking a look at *Gone With The Wind* again, right, Charlie?' Cherry had joked, in the awkward way parents affected for their daughters' unwanted suitors.

Outside the cinema the snow had grown heavier, covering the roofs and windscreens of the cars as they brought still more guests. Even the busker had given up.

The handle turned and the door rattled impatiently, but remained locked. It was the fourth time that had happened in three minutes. Simone didn't care. She had been emotional all day. Now she was afraid she was about to break down. She was sitting in the Ladies, hiding from the mob. She had been thinking about Harvey. Tonight was the night he had dreamt about. That afternoon, before the snow had started, she had taken a taxi out to the cemetery at Roehampton to deliver some flowers to his grave. *'Congratulations,'* the card had read. *'We did it!'* She knew that wasn't strictly true, that Harvey hadn't done it at all. But that was a detail. Harvey had always overlooked details.

The door handle turned again.

Jesus, she thought. What was it with these glamorous women? Why couldn't they go before they came out like everybody else?

She blew her nose, picturing Harvey bright and hearty as he had been when they first met in Los Angeles. For a plain little guy he had had some very endearing ways. He had taught her so much, mainly about truffling. She was a producer herself now. She had put the package together and found the money. They would start shooting in February. The director had been a gift. With the success of *The Making of Shadows on a Wall* Billy Yeo was now turning down big movie offers. She'd got to him first, and he loved the script. That was important with Billy. *'A Small Story About Death,'* he had smiled. He'd always wanted to do a comedy, an Ealing comedy. Now Simone smiled, too. Maybe tonight Edward would ask Billy if he would like to be their best man.

She dried her eyes. 'God bless you, Harvey Bamberg,' she murmured and unlocked the door.

Tomas Lendak stared through his viewfinder as the Rolls-Royce processed around the square. At the edge of the red carpet security men stood with police staring into the crowd. Beaming confidently Carlos Gallego stepped from the car accompanied by his wife and children. Lendak's shutter opened and closed, again and again, a rapid-fire sniper, preserving for ever the arrival of this new tsar.

Lendak could have gone to the première; he could have been inside having a drink at the bar, rubbing shoulders, perhaps even being photographed himself. But that wasn't for him. The tickets he had manoeuvred he had given to Bulle and her daughter. They liked the glitz. He had photographed them going in.

For Lendak, with his new silver Mercedes 320 SL, eighty thousand dollars of sheer fantasy, parked safely out of the snow in the hotel car-park, the view from the crowd would always be truer.

(vi)

Small talk didn't suit him. He was on edge, pacing continually, firing questions right and left. They were in a crowded ante-room, being served champagne, trying to appear relaxed. Carlos Gallego never relaxed. He hated to be kept waiting.

Julie Wyatt glanced at her watch. Because of the weather everything had been put back a quarter of an hour: fifteen minutes more to worry. She was exhausted; everyone was. No race would ever be more closely run than this one. With no time for previews, no chance of reviews, this would be the first public showing, to be followed the next night and the next with openings in Warsaw, Paris, New York and Los Angeles.

It was all one magnificent gamble. Within the next few days two and a half thousand prints would be delivered to cinemas across America of a film only completed that week, a two-hour, forty-minute piece of history which centred on an unknown English girl, a movie cut together from hundreds of miles of overmatter, remoulded into an entirely new shape.

The additional shooting had been intense. It had lasted for just four weeks, every day Tim Westwood growing in authority. Off the set he was still nervous, talking too quickly: but, when shooting, he was quiet and controlled, editing each scene in his head before the camera began to roll. He had asked for five million dollars and spent four.

Gallego had not interfered. Occasionally he had enquired how Sadie Corchoran was getting along, but he had not asked to meet either the new star or the new director. He saw himself as a commander-in-chief. He liked to delegate. Tonight would be the first time he had seen any of the film in its finished state.

Julie watched him as he continued to pace, breaking off for a word to his wife, handshakes for Jack Dragoman and congratulations for Agnieszka Zlotow whose first American television commercial was now running, orders and questions everywhere else. Julie knew about the gossip. The movie world functioned on rumour: it was the hors-d'oeuvres in deal-making. The gossip said that Julie Wyatt was Carlos Gallego's mistress. She would only have quibbled with the modern understanding of the word. It wasn't just sex. Gallego could have sex with any number of beautiful women. Perhaps he did. He was a secretive man.

Tonight he would leave his wife and come to her. He would want to talk, to ask questions, to listen to her answers. Sometimes he would joke bitterly that she was his college education. She remembered she had once been frightened of him, that he had repulsed her. Now she wondered why. 'I *enjoy* you so much,' he would tell her as they talked. *Enjoy*. No-one had ever said that to her before. Once, early in their relationship, she had asked what his wife thought about her. 'Paula is compliant,' he had replied, translating from the Spanish.

It was a terrible, chauvinistic view, but it had not been meant condescendingly. Gallego separated the role of mistress from that of wife without difficulty. They inhabited different worlds; they had different expectations. Paula Gallego was a dark-eyed, attractive woman in her mid-thirties who took care of their home and childen and watched her husband with unquestioning awe. They had known each other since childhood. Their families had business connections. The world and Familia Gallego had moved on, but Carlos Gallego's attitudes had been fixed.

Close by the loud voice of a woman journalist trespassed into Julie's thoughts. She was talking to Jake McKenzie, telling him how she was looking forward to seeing Sam Jordan as Napoleon, how upset she had been when she heard of his death. Jake, summer tanned in December, was nodding patiently. He now represented Jack Dragoman and Sadie Corchoran.

Champagne in hand, Julie moved through the crowd. For a moment Gallego caught her eye, held it and then looked away.

She felt a blush of happiness. She had been infatuated with Sam Jordan, it was true; but Sam had only ever been acting the part.

(vii)

So here they were, she was Cinderella and Tim was the Prince, and they were going to the ball. No wonder it was snowing. It always snowed in fairy stories. They were nearly there. She hoped they weren't late. It was terribly bad form to arrive after Royalty.

Tim was calmer now. He was staying around the corner from her in a hotel, and, when the limousine had picked him up, had been panicking. The bow-tie he had bought with his new dinner jacket was a proper one, without the elastic and clip, and he'd had no idea how to tie it. Sadie had known. She'd had no trouble with her own outfit. She was wearing a Camille de Malignon gown they'd given her after the film.

She looked out at the traffic. Through the excitement a small sadness bled. This was an ending for her, her last tumbril ride as Sadie Corchoran, private person. Until tonight, although she had spent months being filmed and pampered, she had been a schoolgirl on the run, as anonymous as the snow. In three hours the public face of Sadie Corchoran would have been born. Whatever the fate of the film, it would inevitably change her.

Tim would change, too. She regretted that. He was the new young sensation among directors. As an editor he had hidden in the cutting room, getting what he wanted by persuasion: as the director he made demands. It had been his decision to cut most of the material of Sadie making love with Jack Dragoman from the finished film. Now much was suggested but little shown.

They had been lovers for more than six months, but not chained to each other. Sadie still lived at home, and after filming, had spent the summer Inter-railing around Europe with Claire, doing the things other girls of her age did. She didn't want to miss too much.

'OK, Sadie. Are you ready for them?' Tim said quietly. The car was pulling into Leicester Square.

Sadie cleared the evaporation from her window with the back of her hand. The cinema was waiting, the words *Shadows on a Wall* brilliant in neon, a giant cut-out of Camille de Malignon and Will Yorke embracing above the canopy. She gazed at the image of herself: how tall was she, she wondered. Twenty feet high? As tall as a guillotine?

'Sadie?' Tim asked again, anxiously.

She nodded. 'Ready.'

(viii)

He had been outside several times, standing in the snow, looking across the square. Now finally he made his way up into the circle to his seat. The one next to him lay empty.

A respectful hush fell over the cinema. The Royal party progressed to their places.

With much dignity Edward Lampton stepped on to the stage. 'Your Royal Highness, Lords, Ladies and Gentlemen,' he began.

Charlie looked at his programme.

'You will all be aware of the terrible accident which befell the making of our film, *Shadows on a Wall*, just a few months ago, when our producer, Harvey Bamberg, our director, Bruno Messenger, two of our stars, Yale Meredith and Sam Jordan, and our composer, Penn Stadtler, sadly lost their lives. They are all very much missed.'

There was a murmur of agreement from those who didn't know who they were missing.

'While we all mourned the deaths of those fine talents, my personal, greatest sadness lay in the loss of my friend, Harvey Bamberg.' He hesitated, looking around. 'Harvey Bamberg was not a very famous producer, he had not had a string of successes, his was not a household name. But, let me tell you, Harvey Bamberg was a good man. Harvey Bamberg cared about people . . .'

Charlie closed his eyes. The Grave Digger was talking about a multiple killer.

'He was a committed man, committed to the art of film.'

He was cinematically illiterate.

'So, tonight, in recognition of the quiet contribution Harvey Bamberg made to the cinema, and of his own bravery in losing his life while trying to save the lives of his colleagues, Buffalo Pictures and some of Harvey's friends in the film industry are proud to inaugurate an award in his honour. From tonight the Harvey Bamberg Award is to be given annually to the most deserving of independent producers: to the producer who has really made a difference.'

Charlie could feel a lump in his throat. Harvey had made a difference all right. No-one would ever know now that the Slovakian investigators had drawn the wrong conclusions. Harvey Bamberg would be remembered as a hero.

'And now, if I may, I'd like to invite Nathalie Seillans, to accept, on behalf of the Harvey Bamberg Foundation, the first cheque for a hundred and five thousand pounds, raised tonight by this Royal Charity Performance.'

Delicately Nathalie Seillans stepped on to the stage, her bosom tremulous inside her silk dress, her lips full and pouting. Carefully, between two fingers, she took the cheque. 'Thank you,' she husked emotionally into the microphone. 'And . . .' she looked vaguely heavenward, 'thank *you*, Harvey . . . darling.'

Charlie felt sick. There was a murmur of 'Hear, hear!' It grew louder. Applause swelled. And the Penn Stadtler overture for *Shadows on a Wall* began.

(ix)

It was just a little place, one of those old flea-pits that used to show sex films but which must have been taken over by some crazy cineast. Freshly painted, with enlarged reviews stuck in a glass frame by the entrance, it blinked with optimism: '*François Truffaut season. Late show.*' Belinda stared.

With a jolt the cab pulled forward and then stopped. All around engines were revving: the traffic jammed solidly.

She had changed into her party dress on the way from the airport. She had known the driver had been watching through his rear-view mirror, but she didn't care; just so long as he got her there on time. The plane had been late leaving New York, London was in the middle of a snowstorm and she was afraid she was going to miss the best moment of Charlie's life. She cursed herself for staying longer than necessary in Atlanta. She had been testing herself, cutting it as fine as fine, making absolutely sure.

The West End had been in chaos as they approached Piccadilly, but, with his concentration finally off her bra, the cab driver had made an inspired detour and was now approaching the cinema through the side-streets of Soho. That was when she had seen the little picture-house.

Anxiously Belinda looked out at the jammed street. 'Look, I'll walk,' she said, pulling some notes from her purse.

'Have you seen the weather out there?' the driver exclaimed, seemingly reluctant for her to leave.

'It's all right.' She pushed the notes into his hand. 'Thanks for trying. I hope you enjoyed the show.' Then, picking up her bag, she stepped into the snow.

(x)

Whether it would have sounded the same had Penn Stadtler still been alive no-one would ever know. His theme was already a world hit, but the *Theme from Shadows on a Wall*, as recorded for the overture by the Budapest Philharmonic Orchestra, was almost heroic. Stadtler had been a good choice for composer, Charlie thought. Bruno Messenger hadn't got everything wrong, not by a long way. Now applause erupted as the music ended. The lights in the cinema faded further. Soundlessly the red brocade curtains swept apart. Charlie thought of his parents and the school film society. But mostly he thought about Belinda.

'Excuse me, I'm sorry . . .' An American voice: urgent, apologetic. 'I'm sorry, Charlie.' She was sliding into the seat next to him, her coat and dress dripping snow, her hair shining wet.

'Sshh . . .' someone hissed behind them.

She pulled a funny face and slipped further into her seat.

He stared at the screen. He couldn't look at her. She took his hand. The front credits were emerging across a vast, mute shot of the Battle of Jena, a gigantic soundless battle stretching from horizon to horizon: one by one, they came, '*Sadie Corchoran,*

Jack Dragoman, Sam Jordan, Yale Meredith, SHADOWS ON A WALL, Directed by Bruno Messenger and Tim Westwood, Produced by Harvey Bamberg, Written by Charles Holyoake'.

At that point, despite the person behind, she leant across and kissed him.

It came in waves: a tumult of applause. He could feel hands beating his back. Along the row Sadie Corchoran was laughing, waving to a friend downstairs. A few moments ago she had been up there on the screen in the new ending he had written, Camille de Malignon in the early nineteenth century, sailing off to a new life in America, Will Yorke's arm at her waist.

People were trying to catch his eye. He couldn't see properly. He cried in movies, even when he'd written and written and rewritten the script. It wasn't the *Shadows on a Wall* he had planned, not the story of Marie Walewska. But it was the *Shadows on a Wall* the world would love, he had no doubt.

On it went, the roar of acclaim. He could see Tim Westwood being mobbed by well-wishers, reaching out for Sadie. He looked so young, embarrassed, one hand in his hair. This kind of reaction didn't often happen. Somehow they'd caught the moment.

Belinda was saying something but he couldn't hear. She pressed closer, her lips at his ear. They could see over the balcony. His parents were there, staring up at them, his mother waving, his father smiling, nodding.

They were in the lobby before she could tell him. She whispered it.

'Really? Where?' he answered.

'Just around the corner.'

Massed batteries of cameras and faces were waiting. It was a simple decision. 'Come on,' he said, pulling her towards a side-exit. 'Tell my parents we'll see them later, at the party,' he shouted to a smiling Billy and Ilse as they passed them. 'We've something to do.'

Whether Billy answered he didn't hear. They were already outside, pushing through the crowds, running through the snow, hand in hand into the side streets.

The cinema was virtually empty. The movie was just beginning. They felt for their seats in the dark.

The titles were blue on black, opening on to a Paris street-scene and a Metro station. Jean-Pierre Leaud was climbing the steps. The camera moved on, finding Jean Pierre Aumont. Then came the famous slap and Truffaut's voice. *'Coupez!'*

Belinda was finally seeing it, *La Nuit Américaine*, François Truffaut's *Day for Night*, on the big screen, the way movies should be seen.

They settled back, catching their breath, their première clothes splashed and wet. She kissed him in the darkness. He didn't have to tell her that he loved her, but he did, anyway. He felt her face crease into a smile. She was nodding. He knew what that meant. It was cosy in this little cinema. He could feel her warmth through his jacket.

He was watching *Day for Night*, but he was thinking about them. Camille de Malignon had gone to America to begin again. He had sent her there in his script. With Belinda now at college in New York she couldn't very well come back to live in London. But he could go there. They could reshoot their own ending. They could begin again, too.